RISE OF THE GREY

RISE OF THE GREY

CARL PERRON

Book cover by Tukoshimura (via 99designs by Vista)

Substantive and stylistic editing by Genevieve Clovis (cloviseditorial.com)

Line editing and proofreading by Ana Joldes (houseoffables.com)

First paperback edition October 2023 (ISBN 978-1-7390096-1-8)

First eBook edition October 2023 (ISBN 978-1-7390096-0-1)

To my two favourite differently animated people in the whole world—my wife and daughter.

PROLOGUE

YERSINIA PESTIS

The dead will be the death of us, Bartolo Alessi thought as he ate boiled oats and salted pork at his reserved table—being the owner of the Nuovo Mondo had its perks. It was early March 1348, and his merchant caravel rocked chaotically in the waves of the Atlantic, as it had done all week. Alessi's thoughts were on the dead sailors stacked in the bowels of his ship. The men who'd succumbed to a mysterious illness after leaving London. Countless more had passed before their last port during their journey from the Black Sea. He felt the constant presence of death stalking them.

The latest bodies were wrapped in cloth and stored at the farthest end of the ship's hold. The rotting cadavers, with their black noses, black fingertips and mould-like growths under their armpits, were separated from the crew by nothing more than a thick hanging wool sheet. Their stench carried throughout the vessel.

Alessi was resolute, though, and would not let death slow his trading caravel. They were heading to Norse Greenland. The Eastern Settlement was the largest village on the edge of the known world, established four hundred years ago by Icelandic Norsemen. Alessi was on this journey because rumours that it provided access to new and mysterious lands full of riches and resources had surfaced in Europe. Once there, the sole heir of the great Alessi house—a house as powerful as any in the merchant guild of Genoa—intended to seize land and set up a trading doorway into this new world.

Alessi thought of the future and wondered if this evil curse following his ship would allow him to see his dream fulfilled. He worried about his legacy, ironically unaware of the silent death his caravel was spreading from port to port, a legacy greater than what he was dreaming of, a gift which would decimate more than half the planet's population, close to three hundred million people. And, as terrible as this was, Master Bartolo Alessi's impact on the world would not end there. In the modern world, seven hundred years later, death would continue to be his legacy.

With his breakfast done, Alessi made his way back to the icy deck outside. He grabbed hold of anything he could find to steady himself and slowly made his way to the quarterdeck on top of the cabins and galley. There, he joined the captain, who was bundled up in his thick wool jacket, cold puffs of air escaping from his mouth. The gruff-looking seaman was holding on to the helm with his eyes glued to the towering glacier cliffs approaching the side of the ship.

The ice cliff accentuated the beauty of the Nuovo Mondo. It was the jewel of its time. The ship was made of cork oak and covered in knotless pine planks with mahogany interspersed regally throughout. Its three burgundy sails, striated with gold threads, loomed majestically over the ship and were framed by the ice-white backdrop of the glacier.

"We are still four days away from the settlement, but there is a small cove here with a beach at the foot of the glacier," the captain said in his broken Italian while stroking his thick grey beard. "There, we can get rest from these waves and bury the dead."

Alessi should have been happy to get rid of the bodies, but he wondered if the dying would ever stop. He answered softly, "I can't help but fear these bodies will be the death of us—I feel a growing blackness inside of me. A shadow stalking us." He wrapped his arms around himself and retreated to his musings of the new world that this darkness may never allow him to see.

The towering glacier loomed on the port side of the anchored Nuovo Mondo, barely a hundred feet away. The deckhands were busy preparing the bodies of their dead comrades for transport to shore. It was slow work, each movement painfully careful lest the wrappings be torn, exposing infected skin. Master Bartolo Alessi and his captain watched patiently.

"You see, Master Alessi, the bodies of these fine men, who were not sailors, will be put to rest as they should be, and in the end, they were not the death of us after all!" the grizzled captain boasted loudly—too loudly for Alessi's liking.

The words echoed across the cove, bouncing off the glacier wall and triggering a deep rumbling from inside the ice. Alessi looked up along with everyone else as a slim fissure slithered up the giant wall of compressed ice and snow. For a moment, Alessi thought that was the extent of it, but then it exploded into a crack the size of their ship before a deafening roar burst from its deep crevice. A thousand tonnes of ice broke away from the glacier and came crashing down on top of them.

It took three heartbeats for all light to disappear—like a candle snuffed out in a dark room. Master Alessi, the rich merchant from Genoa, had one last thought on the third beat, *The dead were, in fact, the death of us.*

LYSSAVIRUS

The phone chimes started quietly, but quickly escalated to an obnoxious level. Tom Virtanen reached over to the nightstand and jabbed at the phone's screen repeatedly until he hit the off button. He looked up from his crumpled pillow to see the hazy white number: *3:30 a.m.*

He rolled over and slowly sat up on the side of his bed. Groaning, he rested his head in his hands with his elbows on his thighs. *Thank God I'm single. No woman in her right mind would put up with these crazy trips out to sea for weeks at a time.* The truth was, he'd never had a chance to meet anyone since he moved to St. John's, Newfoundland, on his first Canadian Coast Guard assignment.

After shaking off the cobwebs in his mind, he got up and shuffled over to his dresser, where his poorly ironed Coast Guard uniform hung from one of the drawer knobs.

He slid on his pressed blue shirt and slacks, slipped his leather belt through his pant loops and laced up his spit-shined boots. Flattening down his short, messy hair, he made his way to the washroom and robotically brushed his teeth. *Will anyone notice I haven't showered or shaved?*

As he spat out his toothpaste, the honking of a car broke the pristine silence around his small bungalow.

Damn it! He couldn't believe the cab was here early. He looked at himself in the mirror once more and wiped a bit of toothpaste spittle from the corner of his mouth. Tom was grumpy about having to ship out right in the middle of his time off, but some sort of unexpected escort request for his ship was dragging them back in. He grabbed his duffle bag, flung it over his shoulder and picked up his smartphone: *Three forty-five! Stupid cab was supposed to be here at four.*

His nose wrinkled as he passed through his kitchen; the garbage was overflowing and already starting to smell. On his last trip out to sea, he'd left a full bag of trash stewing and had come home to a kitchen infested with maggots and fruit flies. It took him weeks to get the house aired out and all the crawlies exterminated.

He wasn't going to go through that again. He doubled back, pulled out the garbage bag from the bin and tied a knot in it. The cab honked again as Tom exited the house into the cool pre-morning air. He stomped to his half-opened, dented metal garbage can at the top of his driveway. The cab honked. Tom glared at the driver. The man was barely a shadow in the darkness, but he looked half-dead, leaning into the horn of his steering wheel. Tom, still staring at the cab driver, pushed the cover of his garbage can aside.

The attack was a blur. A rabid ball of brown fur and gnashing teeth sprung out and chomped down onto his left hand. The sharp little teeth pierced his skin and penetrated deep into muscle tissue. Tom tried to pull his arm back, but the weight of the animal surprised him. Then, just as quickly, it let go. The furry assailant scurried off into the darkness under some bushes before Tom fully realized what had happened.

"Damn it!" The razor-like pain shot all the way up to his brain.

The cab honked again, unaware of the ambush that had taken place.

"Stop honking, asshole!" Tom shouted.

The driver looked up and pulled his hand away from the steering wheel.

"I'm coming!" Tom was seething while he pulled out his Guard-issued pocket handkerchief and wrapped his bleeding hand.

PART I - HENRY DAWSON

THE ICEBREAKER

The massive plow of the Canadian Coast Guard ship Henry Dawson sliced through the calm waters of the Atlantic Ocean. Reaching sixteen knots, the T-1200 class icebreaker raced to meet the rising sun. It was heading northeast, away from the island of Newfoundland, Canada.

John Vanderfeld stood stiffly in front of the bridge walkway's wooden handrail. Perched four levels high in the superstructure, the floor-to-ceiling windows offered the seasoned captain an unimpeded view of the hulking red and white ship's bow. He looked at his watch: five twenty-one, then robotically took a sip of his steaming coffee.

The straight-postured captain rubbed his thick salt-and-pepper beard, which showcased over thirty years in the Coast Guard. The frowning wrinkles around his eyes hinted at how upset he was that they were behind schedule. One of their two huge diesel-electric engines had seized up like a mule right after leaving St. John's. Something had been missed in the engines' pre-start inspection, which caused the failure, and he abhorred when things got missed.

"Why did it take so long to fix?" he barked to everyone on the bridge. "I'll want a full report on what the hell happened in that engine room when we get back to port." He turned and looked at his Officer of the Watch. "We're two days behind!"

"Yes, Captain," Officer of the Watch Rebecca Fields responded crisply, avoiding his glare.

On the horizon, the sun peeked over the edge of the world. Maybe they could make up some of the time since it was the summer solstice, which meant they'd have the maximum amount of daylight to continue full throttle.

The grizzled captain thought about the thirty-one sailors and the thousand tonnes of steel under his command. The same weight as one thousand cars was how he had described it to an elementary school class once. He preferred rescuing ferries and cargo ships stuck in the dangerous frozen arctic waters in winter, not gallivanting in summer waters, escorting scientists on secret epidemiology missions to some nondescript fjord in Greenland. The warm months were for the ship to get cleaned up in port while its crew received training and much-needed rest.

He let a low groan escape from his throat. He was not happy to have recalled his sailors for this mid-summer mission, but the request to get scientists out to a hot zone site of a possible viral outbreak was not the kind of order you pushed back on. His crew was the only one trained in hazardous and viral material transport this far north in the Atlantic, and the Henry Dawson had the only ocean-going virology lab in the Canadian Atlantic fleet. Vanderfeld stood up straighter—if that was possible—and took another sip of his godawful coffee.

***

As the Henry Dawson tried to make up time, Abelone Jensen meandered her way through its tight passageways and hatches and went up and down steep staircases. *Ladders, not stairs*, she reminded herself. That was what stairs were called on a ship. The passageways and ladders all looked the same, and even after a few days on the ship, she still got turned around.

She'd been up since five in the morning, her body still on European Time since she'd flown to Newfoundland from Copenhagen. She was on a trek to find food in the bowels of the ship, a rat in a maze trying to get to the cheese. After adjusting for a few missed turns, she reached her prize, and the mouth-watering smell of bacon and eggs struck her as she entered the spacious mess deck. The room was nearly empty except for a cook going in and out of a massive freezer beside the galley kitchen and a couple of sailors sitting in a corner finishing either their breakfast or dinner, depending on which shift they were on.

As she made her way through the bolted-down tables and chairs, she could feel the two men's eyes tracking her. She was used to it. She had stood out all her life, whether it was at Cambridge getting two PhDs in epidemiology and virology or as the youngest person ever to hold the Danish government's head epidemiologist role at the Danish Institute of Rare Viral Diseases. Abelone let her work and her smarts disarm any preconceptions people had of blonde-haired, blue-eyed Scandinavians.

At the buffet counter full of chafing dishes piled with bacon, eggs, sausages and hash browns, she took in the smell and helped herself to generous portions of everything. She made her way to one of the round tables in the middle of the room and sat with her back to the crewmen who were still eyeing her.

As she settled in to conquer her mountain of food, two other men walked in, chatting away. *Right on time.* Alex Deangelo from the Bureau of Field Investigation of the Public Health Agency of Canada out of Winnipeg and Jonathan Brown, Centre for Disease Control and Prevention Special Envoy from the Office of Infectious Diseases, National Centre for Emerging and Zoonotic Infectious Diseases out of Atlanta. *I need to remind him to shorten his title lest patients die before he has time to fully introduce himself,* she thought and snorted at her joke.

"Abby!" Jon bellowed.

She smiled and waved at them awkwardly. She was not as outgoing as her American counterpart but knew Jon liked to make a statement that she was with him, even though it was only as colleagues.

"Think you got enough food there?" he asked as he walked by, not bothering to wait for an answer as he made a beeline for the warm food calling his name.

Alex, on the other hand, raked a hand through his almost completely grey hair, wished her good morning and went for the coffee. During the ten years she'd known the soft-spoken Canuck, Abelone had learned he was not a morning person. Alex was the oldest of them. Abelone guessed early sixties, but he would never admit it. He was like a father to her and, over the years, had played the role of mentor and coach as she made her way through the epidemiological community. As both men joined her, other people started shuffling in, a mindless horde with their arms stretched out toward the food.

"Hey, big-shot scientists!" Eric Martel, a balding, rotund man, plopped down on a chair beside Abelone.

Abelone smiled at the Montreal-raised Haitian, having taken a liking to him since she'd arrived. He was their unofficial host aboard the Henry Dawson.

"Doctor Martel!" Jon made the ship doctor jump in his seat, interrupting him and claiming property of him as he had of Abelone.

"Good morning, Jon," Martel greeted the American. "Two days away from Greenland, and you guys get to do your thing. You must be excited?"

"These sample-gathering missions are rarely exciting, Eric," Abelone responded. She pulled her plate closer when she noticed he was eyeing her double-sized serving.

Doc Martel noticed. "Don't worry, I'm fasting." He smiled. "I was on my way to see the captain and thought I would check in with you three."

Relieved, Abelone forgot about her food. "The exciting part is the story that led us to this fjord. Have you ever heard of the . . . Nuovo Mondo?" she whispered the name to make it even more mysterious.

"Hmmm . . . uhhh . . ."

Abelone was shocked; he was without an answer to something for the first time since they'd boarded the ship. The doctor opened his mouth once or twice, but no answer came out.

"Do we tell him, or do we let him go research it on Google?" Alex teased. If not for Doc Martel's dark skin, his face would be red.

"I never! Tell me already!" Martel huffed.

"All right, all right," Alex said, laughing. "It's a ship!"

Doc Martel's eyes grew big and round. "A ship?"

"An Italian Genovese merchant ship from the fourteenth century, to be exact," Abelone clarified. "The Danish government thinks it's been found in a small cove on the outskirts of a melting glacier a few hours south of Nuuk."

Doc Martel's eyes sparkled as he put the pieces together. ". . . and by 'the end of the fourteenth century', you mean the tail end of the Dark Ages, eh? The period in human history when the most devastating plague ever to curse the earth wiped out half of the planet's population in only a few years?" There was the encyclopedic robot she had gotten to know.

Doc Martel got excited. "And, if *you* are here and this ship . . . the *Nuevo Mondo*, is from that period, it must have been carrying . . . the plague!" He looked exhilarated that he had tied the pieces together.

"Quiet down, Eric. We don't want to frighten people for nothing." Abelone talked in a hushed voice, hoping Doc Martel would do the same.

"A month ago, an Icelandic fishing boat spotted wooden debris sticking out of a melting glacier on the Greenland coast," she continued while Jon shovelled food into his mouth and Alex slowly sipped his coffee. "They took a zodiac to shore and collected several artefacts—mostly gold pieces and religious relics—but they also found a ship nameplate with the name *Nuovo Mondo* on it."

"The mahogany wood plank was still intact in a block of ice," added John with a fork in his mouth.

"Pretty much confirms the ship, eh?" Doc Martel reasoned.

"Yes, but that is not the most interesting part. Less than a week later, when the fishermen came back to port in Reykjavik, they all got sick. It took doctors a few days to figure it out, but they'd contracted Yersinia pestis." Abelone let her comment sink in.

Doc Martel sat there unblinking. His brow furrowed as his mental wheels were turning.

Jon took this as his cue to pick up the story. "The Nuovo Mondo is referred to multiple times in mid-fourteenth-century port journals and historical records. The ship belonged to an Italian merchant named Bartolo Alessi. His family was famous for having been some of the first to trade extensively with the East via the Black Sea. This guy inherited his family's fortunes and continued the extensive trading with the East, but tried to go west as well."

Doc Martel listened intently.

Jon took a sip of his hot coffee, which allowed Alex to jump in. "But he never really made it. Kind of just disappeared. One journey, in particular, has always stood out to historians *and* scientists alike. Around 1350AD, the trading ship went on what historians believed was its last journey. It can be traced from the port of Kaffa on the Crimean Peninsula all the way to Reykjavik, Iceland, but then the historical records end. There is no indication anywhere of what happened to the small caravel after it set sail from the little Nordic port."

Doc Martel worded his next question slowly, "And I'm guessing the actual disappearance of the *Nuevo Mondo* is not what was interesting regarding this merchant ship's last voyage?"

"Indeed," said Abelone, back in the conversation, her plate of food almost all cleaned out. "The *Nuovo* Mondo," she enunciated the proper ship's name, hoping it would sink into Doc Martel's head, "is believed to have spread Yersinia pestis from port to port from the Black Sea, through Constantinople to London and everywhere in between. This small caravel is believed to be THE Trojan horse that brought the plague to Europe."

Doc Martel whistled softly.

"Doc, I'm not sure how informed you are concerning the history of the plague?" Jon asked.

Doc Martel frowned at the insinuation he didn't know something. "I know plenty. It's not because I didn't know the name of a ship that I don't know about the Black Death, eh." The doctor took a breath and started spewing his knowledge. "The world had never seen a disease as virulent and deadly as that one, even to this day: COVID, SARS, Ebola, they got nothing on this one, eh? Something like two hundred million people died—"

"More like two twenty-five," interrupted Jon.

Abelone gave him a smirk, knowing he'd done it on purpose.

"Yes, more like two hundred twenty-five million," Doc Martel corrected himself, piqued. "Anyway, more than half of the planet's population at that time, eh? This was a time when the plague was thought to have reached its apex in efficiency, wasn't it?" He wasn't asking anyone. "It was spreading from host to host and leaving maximum decimation in its wake. It ravaged Asia, Russia and Europe." Doc Martel was giddy, but had reached the end of his knowledge on the topic.

Abelone felt it was safe enough to add more without hurting his feelings. "It's a little-known fact that, in its most evolved state, Yersinia pestis mutated to more than the bubonic plague. It had evolved into the even deadlier septicemic version. People could get infected as easily by the bite of a tick or by coming in contact with an infected's saliva or blood. As you said, the world had never seen a more evolved disease. Its sole purpose was to spread from host to host to survive."

Alex added more, "The reason all of humankind was not wiped out is that the plague ran out of hosts. Back then—by today's standards—villages and cities were far apart, and it took forever to travel between places on foot or, at best, on horseback. Villages and cities were wiped out before it could spread to other locations. After cutting down half the planet's biped population, it became extremely difficult to spread."

Not to be outdone, Doc Martel added one last fact, "And it was also thought that when it reached Scandinavia, it stopped spreading. Something in the Viking blood that made them resilient to it."

"Yep," Jon muttered with a mouth full of food. "And we're heading right for that disease-carrying ship." He smiled.

"Don't worry," Abelone reassured. "We have vaccines against the plague. The whole crew is immunized to it."

Doc Martel caught on to another important fact. "And that's why the Henry Dawson was chosen as the escort for you three? We're the only fast-response biohazard and pandemic-trained ship in the Northern Atlantic. The crew gets the whole array of shots done yearly against pretty much everything out there, including Yersinia pestis."

Abelone nodded.

"What happened to the crew of the fishing vessel that found the *NuOvo* Mondo?" Doc Martel asked. Eric had finally grasped the pronunciation of the Italian vessel.

"Three of the ten sailors died," Abelone said solemnly. "The other seven are still under quarantine in a Reykjavik hospital, but they should recover."

"Fascinating," Doc Martel said as his watch beeped six o'clock. "I'm going to be late for my morning appointment with the captain. He likes his visits early. He's enough of an eh-hole on a regular day, but I hear he's been stomping around chewing everyone's ear off because of the two-day delay. I don't want to give him any more excuses for being mad at me, eh!"

Martel got up. "Your fascinating story made me forget; Abelone, you should stop by the medical bay when you are done here. I want your opinion on something. A young engineer was brought in this morning with a nasty fever and a ghastly bite on his hand. Looking like rabies, but could use the advice of someone with your credentials."

Abelone smiled. "I'll swing by and check it shortly."

"It's a date!" he called out, then scurried off through the mess-deck door into the rat maze.

From the corner of her eyes, Abelone saw Jon's chest puff up and his facial expression grow stern at Doc Martel's insinuation.

4

REACHING FOR EXISTENCE

Abelone knocked on the metal door with the large red cross on it. The thick door opened, and a short but stocky woman greeted her.

"Ms. Jensen, hello, I'm Medical Assistant Barns. Come on in." The young woman let Abelone in and shut the hatch behind her.

The medical bay was not big, but it was more spacious than most other rooms on the ship. Abelone stepped further into the brightly lit L-shaped room. Her gaze swept over the counters and medical equipment at the top of the letter and past the steel patient table in the middle before taking in the bunk bed at the lower part of the L. That was where she saw Tom Virtanen for the first time. The young engineer was lying under a wool blanket, unconscious. He looked the furthest thing from restful. His face was pale and drenched with sweat, and there was a hint of sickly sweet musk in the air, which she recognized right away as the smell of infection.

"Abelone, glad you came." Doc Martel waved her over to the opposite end of the room, where he was getting some things ready. "This is the young man I was telling you about. He was brought to us earlier, pretty much in a delirious state. Pretty sure it's from the bite on his hand, but no one could tell us where and when he got bitten."

Eric pulled some naproxen from a bottle and put two pills beside a syringe and a glass of water. "Trudy cleaned his wound, and now I'll give him something for his fever and his HRIG shot."

"You're following PEP to the letter. You sure it's rabies?" Abelone asked.

"Well, it's definitely a bite, so following protocol. We don't know anything concerning what and where. A couple of other engineers brought him in. They said he'd been working on reassembling the engines all night when we left port, and when the engine failed, they weren't able to pull him out of his cot because of his fever. He couldn't even stand. They left him there for another twelve hours while they finished repairs and saw he hadn't gotten any better."

Abelone followed Eric to the bunk bed. She tried to calculate how many hours it had been since they left port and then how much time this crewman had before his infection would potentially turn deadly.

"Tom. Can you hear me?" the doctor repeated the question a few times.

The young man winced and struggled to open his eyes. The way they fluttered was enough to tell Abelone he had a fever and probably one hell of a headache based on his wince. "Where am I?" Tom croaked.

"You're in the medical bay. I need you to take these. They'll help with the fever," Doc Martel said, bringing the naproxen and water toward Tom's mouth.

The closer the water got, the more Tom seized up. "Stop!" he coughed.

"You got to take these, Tom. I'm still trying to figure out what is driving your fever, but it's looking like it might be the injury to your hand. Is it a bite? Was it in the engine room?" Doc Martel brought the water closer to Tom's face.

Tom's fear turned to rage. The young man swatted at the glass and clawed at the doctor. Doc Martel pulled away and stepped back. He looked at Abelone.

"Fear of water. You are probably right, Eric." It was rare for her to deal with rabies cases, but she'd seen a few. Terror of water was a symptom of a rabies-infected patient. "It has to be from the bite." She wondered if the young man had been bitten on the ship and if others were at risk.

Trudy Barns gently tied Tom down with restraints. The burst of rage Tom had displayed had vanished, and he let himself be secured to the bed, now a rag doll with no energy.

Abelone and Martel stepped to the opposite side of the bay, as far from Tom as they could.

"I know, I know. If it's been more than seven days, there is nothing we can do for him . . . after that point, the disease is fatal," Doc Martel said.

"Don't say that. There is always a way to save a patient. There are new experimental drugs to cure rabies. He still has a chance." Abelone did not mention that this was only the case if the Nuuk hospital had the experimental drug.

"You're a real optimist, eh?" Martel stated more than enquired.

"If I don't believe people can be saved, why bother doing what I do?"

"What's going on?" Virtanen spoke up in a moment of lucidity.

Martel nodded at Abelone. "I'll feed off your optimism then," he whispered before making his way back to Virtanen's bedside.

He tried to explain to the young sailor that he had rabies. He tried to ask if he'd been bitten on the ship and how long since it had happened. Unfortunately, Virtanen was going in and out of consciousness and provided no clarity.

"Tom, try to stay with us," Martel urged. "We are a day away from our destination, at which point the ship's helicopter will be in range to transport you to the hospital in Nuuk. They have the medical support there to help you." Martel looked up at Abelone and shook his head lightly.

Abelone walked to Eric and put her hand on his shoulder. "We'll get him there in time. Everyone can be saved, Eric."

Virtanen moaned loudly, fighting off whatever nightmare was haunting him. To Abelone, it sounded like he was disagreeing with her.

***

Abelone stood on the outside deck of the Henry Dawson's command bridge. It overlooked the rear of the ship, and from this vantage point, she could see most of the massive white ship funnel (another term she'd been taught, this one for a chimney), the helicopter hangar and the large square helipad beyond it. Resting in the middle of the helipad was a small Bo 105 helicopter, which was completely red except for a large vertical white stripe near its tail. Three deckhands were scurrying around the helicopter. Two other men stood on the side, going over what she guessed were pre-flight checklists.

She shivered, even though she was bundled up in a thick black parka and it was late June. The air this far north in the Atlantic was still chilly in the morning. She had the hood pulled up tight around her head to protect her from the wind gusting around the Greenland coast. They had finally reached the Nuovo Mondo wreck. From where she stood, she could barely see the wooden skeleton of the ancient caravel partially buried in ice and sand on the fjord beach. The beach was rocky, small and only accessible from the water. The exposed wood was black from time and frost, and the mound it rested in could as well have been dirt and rock if seen from afar. Up this close, one could see the silhouette of the ship, the broken mast and the rectangular shape of the officer's cabin.

But the exhumation of the potentially deadly relic would have to wait. Tom Virtanen had to be evacuated. After he'd been brought to the medical bay, it had taken four days to get the ship in a position from which the Bo 105 could take him to the hospital in Nuuk.

Beside the helicopter, the pilot, Jerry White, distinguishable because of his bright yellow flight helmet, barked orders. They'd had lunch together, and he'd explained that taking off and landing on a platform like the one on the Henry Dawson took more skill than landing a Navy jet on an aircraft carrier. Something about whirling winds, the constantly moving helipad due to the back-and-forth side-stepping of the ship as if to the music of the ocean and the danger of the myriad radio antennas sticking out from the ship's superstructure. She couldn't help but focus on the wind howling around the Henry Dawson this morning.

The door to the command bridge opened, and Captain Vanderfeld stepped out, another audience member for the show below. He was followed by Rebecca Fields, who tended to always be with or near the captain. They were bundled up in their own parkas and lined up shoulder to shoulder beside her as a quartet of men carrying a stretcher emerged from the port side of the ship's main deck. The men straight-lined it for the Bo 105. Behind them was Doc Martel, who did not need a yellow pilot helmet to be recognized from afar; his short, round silhouette left no doubt it was him. Plus, even from up here, Abelone could tell he was talking non-stop, flailing his arms and yelling at the men carrying the patient.

"I'm still worried about this wind, John . . . Captain," Fields corrected herself. "The fjord and glacier are making it spin around the cove. Jerry's good, but still."

"I know. I know," said the captain, not acknowledging her name slip-up.

Fields pulled her parka tighter. "I know. We're out of options. We need to take the risk," she matched the captain's tone.

"People are never out of options. They simply don't like the ones that are left," Vanderfeld said. "Virtanen either dies here on the ship, or we take the risk of flying him to Nuuk. Once in the air, Jerry can bridge the five hundred kilometres to Nuuk in three hours."

The three audience members watched the show go on. The performers loaded the stretcher, followed by an intricate pattern of work as precise as ballet dancers doing *pliers* and *sauters* around the chopper until they all bowed away, leaving the Bo 105 as the star attraction. The final act was about to begin.

Abelone wrung her hands and willed the wind to die down. Jerry White entered the helicopter. Everyone on deck dispersed as the helicopter blades started to spin.

"If something happens, it will happen in the next minute," stated the captain loud enough for Abelone to hear. His voice was unwavering and revealed no hint of doubt.

As the helicopter's main rotor blade reached maximum velocity, the small aircraft's landing skids magically floated off the helipad. At that moment, a furious wind gust rushed around the superstructure. It collided with the fjord's ice wall, bouncing back toward the ship and making it rock violently from side to side. Abelone grabbed hold of the deck railing so as not to lose her footing.

"Crap!" Vanderfeld half-shouted.

Fields let out a breathless shriek.

Abelone's breath stuck in her throat. She could see the wind—filled with snow flurries—as it scooped up the small helicopter and swung it in a circle, then lifted it abruptly, ready to smash it back down onto the deck. Barely a metre from the deck, the wind disappeared and released the helicopter. The snow flurries slowly floated down like nothing had happened.

Time stood still, and the helicopter hovered over the deck almost level with the three observers for what seemed like an eternity. Then another gust of wind spilled over the top of the fjord glacier and poured down the icy wall, rushing toward them. Jerry White must have sensed the oncoming wind. Abelone saw him look up through the cockpit glass. The wind enveloped the Bo 105 again, this time spinning it into larger and larger arcs, its tail boom picking up speed.

"Inside now!" ordered Vanderfeld. He grabbed both Abelone and Fields by the arms and, in one swoop, shoved the two women inside the bridge, slamming the door behind the three of them.

Abelone stumbled to the bridge windows and saw the helicopter heading toward her. Everyone inside ducked for cover while she stood watching, unable to move. At the last second, the helicopter hit turbulence and jumped up a few metres, barely missing the large windows. Instead, its landing skids and tail boom razed all the radio and satellite antennas from one end of the superstructure roof to the other. The buzz-cut of snapping antennas, scraping metal and ripping roof slabs thundered in the bridge. Everything around Abelone shuddered, and one of the floor-to-ceiling bridge windows bulged outwards, as if holding its breath. The bulge grew, and Abelone couldn't help but stare until, in one big exhale, it shattered into a thousand pieces of candy glass. The cold air of the fjord came roaring in, mixed with the screeching noise of the helicopter.

The helicopter's skids caught on a mangled antenna base and held the flying wrecking ball in mid-air. It hovered, blade rotating angrily, anchored to the roof. The pause was enough to break it free from the turbulent wind. The wind gust moved on. For a few heartbeats, the helicopter looked serene, and Abelone thought it was over. Then the skid snapped off, and the helicopter made a beeline for the beachhead.

Everything slowed; Abelone thought of Jerry and Tom and wondered if a helicopter crash could be survived. Everyone around her froze like she did—staring at the impending crash. *It has to avoid the wreck! The bacteria are still virulent.* All her fear dropped deep into her stomach when the helicopter went straight for it—straight into the Nuovo Mondo. Its rotors pulverized the seven-hundred-year-old grave, sending debris everywhere. The blades obliterated the carcass of the oak, pine and mahogany ship. Ice, wood and metal erupted in all directions.

Abelone held her breath. A blanket of silence fell over everything.

Captain Vanderfeld was the first to move. He sprinted to the ship's intercom. "Deck crew! Jack, get the two zodiacs into the water now! I want two crews of four to accompany Doc Martel to the crash site. The mission is to rescue Jerry and the kid. I want them back onboard for medical treatment, stat!" The captain moved faster than Abelone could process. He faced his COO. "Fields, you have the bridge. Use Mac and Smith to figure out what damage the chopper did to the ship's communication capabilities. We need to know if we can communicate with the mainland. I want eyes on the topside of the structure to assess the damage." In a blink, he was at the back door. "I'm heading down to the deck. By the time I get back here, I want a full sit-rep." He looked at Abelone. "Ms. Jensen, come with me."

Abelone stared at him.

"Now!" the captain urged.

She snapped into motion and followed him to the outside stairs.

"How bad is it?" Vanderfeld asked as he moved down the stairs.

The captain's question didn't need an explanation. "If they survived the crash, they are almost certainly exposed." She thought for a second. "They should both have their vaccines against Yersinia pestis. That's why the Henry Dawson was chosen for this mission." She struggled to keep up with the older captain. "The way the rotor blade tore up the wreck, the biomaterial frozen or thawed will have been spread everywhere. But if we get them in quickly and administer a booster antigenic vaccine, we should be able to nullify the bacterium before it grabs hold inside their lymphatic system. But again . . . that's if they survived the crash."

"Ms. Jensen, I've seen crews survive all kinds of crashes, some worse than this." Vanderfeld puffed as they made their way down the super-structure stairs in the cold air. "If they are alive, I expect you to administer the booster as soon as they are onboard."

***

It took all of twenty minutes to get Jerry White and Tom Virtanen to the medical bay located on the weather-deck level of the ship's super-structure. White was wailing, and Doc Martel had to yell his orders to be heard over the fracas. The rescuers set up the pilot on the examination table and Virtanen on the lower mattress of the bunk bed. Once they were in place, the doctor barked at everyone to get out. With a quick and efficient flick of the hand, he ordered the captain and Abelone to stay. Trudy Barns was already cutting clothing off White.

Both men had survived the crash, as the captain had predicted. White had gotten the worst of it with a fractured forearm, a massive gash on his cheek, and a deep laceration on his left thigh. The rescue team had rudimentarily patched up the injuries, but blood was already seeping through the white bandages. Virtanen, on the other hand, was miraculously unscathed. Being tightly secured to the stretcher and wrapped in thick blankets had protected him. Other than a few cuts on his face, he was no worse for wear.

The blades of the Bo 105 had ground the Nuovo Mondo into confetti, which covered the two injured men—confetti of wet, decomposing wood and human remains. The smell of rot permeated the medical bay.

Doc Martel pulled Abelone and the captain together while Barns began the gruesome task of changing White's blood-soaked bandages.

"I need to clean up Jerry. His fracture needs to be reset and stinted, and those lacerations need to be cleaned and sutured. I'll need my space, but first, I need to give you my medical opinion. We need to get these men to a hospital. Jerry's going to need surgery on his arm, or he might lose it."

"What about the kid?" the captain asked, crinkling his nose at the smell of White's open wounds when the bandage came off.

"If what Ms. Jensen says is accurate concerning rabies, Tom might have twenty-four hours max, after which he'll be past the point of no return. He's unconscious because of his fever, but other than that, I don't think he got seriously hurt in the crash—bloody miracle. We won't know until we get him to a hospital, but it needs to be ASAP."

"We're working on finding another way to get them to a medical facility," said the captain. "The chopper took out all of our main means of communication, as well as our backups. The AM/FM VHF and HF Micom, the Rockwell radios, are all down. Even the Inmarsat and MSAT comms—total mess."

"Damn!" Doc Martel gasped. "What about the emergency LEO satphone? I know you keep one in your cabin."

Abelone recognized the acronym as she owned one herself; it stood for Low Earth Orbit satellite phone.

"Fields is getting it from my cabin. We should be able to reach the GMDSS and get them to fly out a Cormorant to pick up Jerry and Virtanen."

"GMDSS?" Abelone repeated. She knew the Cormorant was a rescue helicopter, but not what GMDSS stood for. Doc Martel jumped in eagerly.

"Global Maritime Distress and Safety System is the international maritime emergency system. It uses terrestrial and satellite technology and ship-board radio systems. It's typically used with normal ship communications; however, LEO satphones can connect to it if needed."

He paused and turned to the captain. "Can the Cormorant reach us, though? The base in Gander is what . . . two thousand kilometres away?"

Relief crossed the captain's stern face. "For once, luck is on our side. The Coast Guard's Cormorant was reassigned from Gander to Goose Bay last month. So that puts it significantly closer, around nine hundred kilometres away. With its five-hundred-kilometre reach, we should be able to meet up with it in fifteen hours and transfer Jerry and the kid over. It will be faster than taking the ship to Nuuk. After that, the boys should be in the Goose Bay military hospital by morning."

"It'll be close," said Doc Martel.

"Let's get to it."

On that note, Doc Martel joined Trudy Barns and helped her with the preparations to reset Jerry's fractured arm.

Captain Vanderfeld hurried out of the medical bay and up to the bridge to set up a meeting with a Canadian Armed Forces Cormorant in the middle of the Atlantic Ocean.

***

Doc Martel was helping his assistant tidy up around Jerry White when a junior bridge officer cautiously entered the medical bay. The young man stood in the doorway with his hand on the latch, his eyes round like saucers and white as a ghost as he looked around. *He's probably never seen a mess like this*, Martel thought.

"Barns, finish up here. I'll see what the kid wants." Doc Martel stepped out in the passageway lest the kid pass out in his medical bay.

"Sir, the captain sent me to let you know we are three hours away from meeting up with the Cormorant. He wanted to make sure Jerry . . . Commander White . . . I mean . . . the patient . . . is ready to go," stammered the young deck officer.

"Patient*s*," clarified Doc Martel, emphasizing the *s*, the same way an English teacher would correct a student by sounding out the forgotten letter.

"Huh?"

"Patient*s*. There are two of them," Doc Martel said sternly.

Barns interrupted the two men and stepped out into the passageway to join them. "Eric, I was wondering if we should change Jerry's headdress." She slowly closed the door behind her so as not to disturb the patients. The latch clicked and secured the door tight.

***

The click echoed through the quiet medical bay until it reached Tom Virtanen's ears. It resonated as loud as an unseen car's horn. He stirred on his bed, and his fingers slowly curled and uncurled. His heavy eyelids laboured open as if for the first time. He was unaware of how deep and fast Yersinia pestis had burrowed when it entered his body, unencumbered by immune-system defences which had been completely wiped away by the rabies virus that had preceded it and was now hijacking the bacteria itself.

He could not see his own eyes, but if he did, he would have seen grey eyeballs with dark blood vessels meandering across the vitreous body. His usually brown irises were completely black and almost fully dilated despite the light in the medical bay.

Tom turned toward the source of the noise that woke him. His mind, although not conscious, was trying to understand where he was. A soft moan from nearby drew his attention, and he briskly turned his head toward the sound. Tom could make out a body on the table, but no recognition broke through the smoky mist in his consciousness. All he knew was he had to get to it. An unconscious, famished inner drive flared within him. Getting to this body was a matter of survival. His legs slid awkwardly off the bed and found their footing on the floor. His arms pushed his upper body upright. For a few seconds, the room spun, and he paused to get his bearings before he heaved his body up to stand.

He shuffled one foot forward, testing out his balance, then his other foot moved and momentum built. His clear hunger for survival drove his every step. There were noises behind a door. Noises he did not recognize as voices, but again, something stirred in him, telling him those noises were a beacon to feed his inner drive. For a few seconds, he stood there, unsure of which calling to go to. Both were compelling; both offered survival.

A gargled cough from the body on the table decided things. Tom's head snapped toward the sound, and his whole body lunged at it, his arms outstretched, reaching for existence.

5

INFECTION

Doc Martel frowned. "Tell the captain both patients will be ready when we meet up with the Cormorant, eh . . . And please make sure the helicopter can accommodate two—"

A bang on the medical-bay door made Doc Martel jump. His first thought was for his patients. "What the hell!" Martel looked through the door's small window to make sure both patients were okay. "Virtanen?" *What the hell is he doing up?* Doc Martel was not easily surprised, but seeing the young engineer standing on the other side of the window went against any common medical sense he had.

"Why's he banging on the door?" asked Barns as she reached for the latch and pushed the door open. Tom threw his weight into the door again, slamming it shut.

"Move back from the door, Tom!" Barns yelled. She gave the door another push, which made Tom stumble back a few steps, giving her enough room to open it completely.

"What are you doing up? You've been unresponsive for so long," she said, stepping into the medical bay.

Doc Martel had seen it all in his long career—well, almost all—so when he saw something new, his caution elevated. He stopped Barns with a hand on her shoulder. Something didn't seem right. Tom's eyes didn't look right, and he had blood dripping from his chin.

"Hold on," he said.

Barns had already started into the room. Tom stretched out his arms and lunged at her, releasing a blood-curdling shriek. He clasped Barns' shoulders, the force of his lunge pushing her back into Martel, who fell into the junior officer. Martel fell to his side, hitting his head on the passageway bulkhead. Pain radiated through his skull, and his vision swam as warm blood trickled down the side of his face. The junior officer was luckier, if only for a few seconds, as he caught his balance and steadied himself.

Barns, however, fell to the deck with Tom on top of her. His hands were still locked on her shoulders, and he opened his mouth wide. Tom's tongue and gums had turned black as he leaned into Barns. Martel pulled back, aghast, as Tom slowly sank his teeth into her left cheek, piercing skin and pulling off a huge chunk of flesh as the medical assistant screamed.

Uncomprehending, Martel watched through the blood flowing over his eyes from his head injury. The junior deck officer stood frozen, a wet stain growing near his crotch, filling the passageway with the smell of urine.

"Pull him off her!" shouted Martel, trying to get up, but still too dizzy.

The junior bridge officer barely snapped out of his stupor and tentatively grabbed Tom's arm. He started pulling, like a child trying to get his mother's attention.

Tom nonchalantly reached over and gently took hold of the officer's right arm. For a second, Martel thought Tom was getting up, but instead, he lowered his mouth on the junior officer's hand and chomped down, severing two fingers off at the joint. Blood spurted all over Tom's face as well as Barns' still writhing beneath him. The junior officer jumped back, freeing his arm in the process, but he tripped and landed on his rear end. Both he and Martel stared at the hand with two missing fingers, blood spurting upwards to the beat of an imaginary drum.

This was madness. Martel tried to get up again, but the bulkheads spun, and he paused. Tom crawled off Barns and onto the junior officer's outstretched legs. He held down the limbs and sank his teeth into the junior officer's trousers, partially ripping through the fabric. The young man groaned as blood flowed through the material pooling on the floor beneath them. Tom bit down again and shook his head, trying to rip through the remaining fabric. Martel could tell the junior officer was in full shock as he simply looked down at his leg without making a sound. It took a few more bites for the pain to register, and then he screamed.

Tom abandoned the leg and dragged himself up the man's body.

Doc Martel, his head still spinning, managed to get up on one knee. He watched as Tom ripped off a quarter of the junior officer's face in one bite. The man stopped screaming.

Doc Martel had been in plenty of situations where life or death was determined by whether he froze at the sight of some horrific event, injury or blood. His experience stopped him from freezing, even if he did not understand what he was seeing.

Move, move, move! he thought. *If you stay down here, you're next!* He mustered his strength and slid himself up, holding onto the bulkhead. The passageway whirled around him.

His movement caught Tom's attention, and the engineer turned toward him. Blood dripped from Tom's jaw, and a large piece of skin was caught between his teeth. He pulled his legs underneath him and started to rise, keeping his eyes on Martel. Martel was in no state to run; he could barely stand.

Beyond the immediate threat of Tom, Martel caught a glimpse of movement in the medical bay. Jerry White was getting up off the table. He had patches of blood on his neck and arm. Martel noticed how grey the helicopter pilot's skin had turned and, looking back at Tom, realized the young engineer had the same tone to his skin.

"What the hell is going on?" Doc Martel muttered, trembling. His breathing was deep and not helping his dizziness.

Tom lunged for him, but Martel lifted his arms to intercept his assailant by the shoulders just in time. Tom's jaw snapped as he tried to bite him. They were at a standstill. Neither budging.

I need to move! Doc Martel thought as Jerry White came into his field of vision again, stepping through the medical-bay door.

Martel's adrenaline surged. He twisted his body and aimed Tom's momentum sideways into the oncoming White. Both blood-covered men tripped over Trudy Barns' body and fell to the ground in a messy heap.

The push made Martel stagger backwards. He tripped on the door-frame of the science lab opposite the medical bay and fell inside. As he fell, he reached out, and his fingertips grazed the edge of the compartment door, closing it violently. He landed on his back, a blast of pain shooting through his body all the way to his throbbing head. The ceiling spun even faster. *Get up! Get up!* he shouted in his mind. *Lock the door!*

He scrambled to pull himself up, barely able to hold his balance, and fell forward on the compartment door as it was opening. It slammed shut again. Martel pushed down on the door latch, locking it in place.

He could hear gargled shrieks and moans between the thuds of multiple arms hitting the door. Once he was sure the door was locked, Martel looked out the small round window, expecting to see Tom's bloody grey face with skin hanging from his denticulation. He gasped when his eyes met the now black, soulless eyes of Trudy Barns. Half her right cheek had been ripped off, revealing muscle, cartilage and teeth.

"What the hell!" he screamed. He stared into his medical assistant's transformed eyes. Confused and scared, the spinning in his head became worse. *What the hell is happening?* His vision blurred, and everything went black.

***

Rebecca Fields was used to the loud environment of the Henry Dawson. From cranks to pistons, the massive engines filled the ship with a constant purring and the occasional mechanical cough. Even shouts and screams from sailors were a frequent occurrence as people needed to be heard over the fracas. But the blood-curdling screams she heard now were different. These screams didn't have a place in the symphony of the icebreaker.

"What now?" the captain growled. "Fields, take Marshall and go check it out. They better have a good reason for screaming bloody murder down there."

"Aye, Captain. By the sounds of the echo, it's at least two floors down." She tapped deckhand Marshall on the arm, and they made their way to the open bridge door.

They descended the bridge ladder two-by-two and fast-paced it through the officer's quarters level. Fields slowed when a head popped up from the stairwell in front of them. She recognized Danny Rondo, the junior officer she'd sent to talk to Doc Martel earlier. He didn't look right. More precisely, he didn't walk right. He seemed . . . drunk.

"Rondo!" she called out. He couldn't be drunk; he was fine a few minutes ago. "What the hell is going on down there?"

Rondo didn't answer and kept walking toward her and Marshall. Something dark covered his uniform, and he accelerated to a wobbling half-sprint. With every step, he looked like he was going to fall over. Fields watched him, confused, as he barrelled down on her and Marshall. Only when he was a few feet away did she realize his face, usually young, fresh and nervously smiling, was missing its bottom half. A good chunk of his chin and cheek had been ripped off, and his left eye and nose were gone.

"What the fuck?" Marshall said as he stepped in front of Fields.

Rondo needed help and would collapse in Marshall's arms. He didn't. Instead, he bear-hugged Marshall, knocking him off balance. They were going to fall. She instinctively wrapped her arms around them, and for a few seconds, the three of them held each other up. Fields stared into Rondo's face, uncomprehending. One of his eyes had been scooped out, and all that remained in the cavity was loose strands of the optic nerve, which wiggled over an exposed sinus where the upper cheek normally would have been. A warm, minty breath wafted over Rondo's exposed jawbone and past the line of teeth standing at attention until those teeth sank into Marshall's neck.

Marshall screamed as skin and muscle were torn from his neck. Hot blood splattered Fields' face, causing her to let go of the two men. Rondo took another aggressive bite from Marshall's Adam's apple this time. The crunch could have been mistaken for being from an actual apple. Marshall's screams stopped dead.

Fields stepped back and stared at Rondo as he let go of Marshall's body. It crumpled to the floor, squirming in muted pain. *Run!* She spun and ran back down the passageway, heading for the bridge ladder. Her heart pounded, and she felt like a child in a nightmare. She passed all the cabins again, and when she reached the ladder, she jumped up the first three steps in one bound. Her feet got caught up together, and she crashed face-first. She lay on the ladder, lip bleeding and head spinning. Fields tried to get up, but Rondo grabbed her foot in a vise-like grip, and she couldn't pull free. She looked over her shoulder, and her body went cold as Rondo lifted her foot to his mouth. She felt the pressure of the bite, but no pain rushed through her leg. Her pounding heart and her tunnel vision slowed her thought process, but by the second bite attempt, she understood. *My boot!* Her leather combat boots were too thick to be pierced by human teeth. Rondo seemed puzzled as his one intact eye looked at the boot intently and tried to take a third bite. Fields twisted her body enough to get leverage and kicked with her other boot right in the middle of the junior officer's chest. He tumbled down the handful of steps and landed with a thud at the feet of deckhand Marshall, who now stood at the bottom.

"Run!" Fields shouted at Marshall. "He's crazy. He will bite you again!" She stood. *Why isn't he running? What is he doing?*

Marshall looked up at her and stepped up the ladder. Her breathing, already rapid and shallow, simply stopped, her brain unable to tell her lungs to inflate and deflate. Marshall's eyes had turned black, like Rondo's, with the same little dark veins meandering throughout his grey eyeballs.

Why and how he had changed, she did not know, but she knew she had to move. She turned and started back up the ladder on her arms and legs. She didn't look back and went as fast as she could. With every step, she expected a grey, bloody hand to clutch her foot. When she reached the top, she ran right into the large, hard chest of the six-foot-six Roger Powers.

"Fields, what the hell is going on?" the ship's first officer said.

She drew in a shaky, inefficient breath and wheezed out, "Something is wrong..."

"What are you talking about?"

Fields mustered the courage to look and point down the ladder at the two men behind her.

Abelone Jensen ran up to them, and the big man squeezed Fields' shoulders and eased her into Abelone's arms. He turned back to face Marshall, who was almost at their level.

"Deckhand Marshall. Stop where you are!"

Marshall can't answer. His throat has been ripped out. But Fields couldn't get the words out.

Marshall, with his chest and shoulders covered in blood, kept methodically lifting his feet from step to step, closing the gap between them. His black eyes were fixed on the people he was trying to reach.

"Marshall, I'm warning—" Powers cringed, obviously catching sight of Marshall's mangled neck.

Marshall kept coming.

Fields' breaths were short and shallow, and the lights were spinning. Abelone's grip was keeping her up. She barely saw Powers' massive leg kick forward and catch Marshall in the shoulder. The blow spun the deckhand around, and he crashed down the ladder, tumbling right past Rondo.

The large bridge officer was taking control of the situation, and Fields breathed again. Powers walked down the steps, speaking to Rondo, who was more than halfway up. "Rondo. Stop where you are! How did you get hurt like that?"

As the men got closer to each other, she wanted to shout to Powers not to get bitten. But it was such a stupid thing to say. He couldn't be biting others.

"Careful," was all she ended up saying.

Powers grabbed Rondo by the shoulders, swung him around and pinned him against the stairs' bulkhead. They were face to face. Only an arm's length from each other. Powers looked straight into the chewed-up face of the junior officer. Even from the top of the stairs, Fields heard him gag at the sight. The big man keeled over and vomited onto Rondo's shoes.

The moment Powers let go, Rondo bent forward and tried to bite him, but Powers took a step back and punched the young man's head. His fist connected right to the bitten-off part of the cheek, and Rondo slammed back against the bulkhead. Powers grabbed him by the throat and pinned him again. Fields could tell Powers did not know what to make of the gruesomeness he was seeing. She didn't either.

With Powers blocking the stairs and Abelone's firm grip steadying her, Fields was able to even out her breathing. Marshall was getting back up, so she shouted until Powers snapped out of his enthrallment with Rondo's face, or lack thereof, and finally turned to look at her. That wasn't what she wanted. She pointed frantically past him, unable to find the right words. It took Powers a few seconds to catch on and look the other way, just as Marshall's teeth sank into the massive forearm that was pinning Rondo to the bulkhead.

***

Abelone cringed and stepped back as Marshall sank his teeth, bone-deep, into Roger Powers' forearm. Pain gripped the big man's face as the deckhand bit off muscle and skin. His expression changed quickly from pain to outrage. Powers snatched Marshall with his free hand and lifted both him and Rondo by their necks. The two smaller men squirmed in his grip, their shrieks barely squeezing out of their throats. With a growl, Powers threw both infected down the stairs. They bumped mid-air, their limbs intertwining before they crashed at the bottom in a crunch.

Abelone watched, aghast, unable to move, unable to process what she was seeing. The two men untangled themselves, at first slowly but then faster, as they figured out whose limbs were whose. She urged herself to focus. A bone stuck out of Rondo's forearm, and Marshall's knee bent at an unnatural angle. They should not be able to move, yet both got up and navigated the stairs, albeit more clumsily this time.

Powers turned and ran back up the stairs. Abelone was swept up in one of his massive arms, Fields in the other, as he part-guided, part-lifted them down the passageway.

"Get the door! Get the door!" shouted Fields as they entered the bridge.

"What the hell is going on out there?" Vanderfeld shouted back. He and the comms officer were working on one of the radios.

Abelone directed Powers to a chair near the main navigation console in the middle of the room while addressing Jon Brown, "Jon, those sailors . . . they were acting crazy."

"Close the door!" shouted Fields again.

The communications officer acted on the order, jumping forward, slamming the door shut and locking the latch in place.

The captain repeated his question. "What the hell is going on? Ms. Jensen, what do you mean?"

"What I saw out there, how those men were acting, they were . . . they must be infected by something. They were fine fifteen minutes ago . . ." She shuddered. "We have something nasty on our hands."

Abelone expected more questions, but instead, the captain walked over to Fields and gently put his hands on her shoulders.

"I'm fine," she said.

Abelone's adrenaline was pumping, and her mind was in analyzing mode. What she had witnessed in the passageway did not fit into any pattern or infection she had ever seen. But it was dangerous.

"We need to contact the mainland!" Abelone blurted to no one in particular.

Vanderfeld turned away from Fields and looked at Abelone, then at his communications officer. "Laurier, get the satphone. We'll need to connect Ms. Jensen to . . . whomever she needs to talk to."

The wind was howling through the broken window, and Abelone could barely hear the captain.

"Ms. Jensen, all our communications equipment was damaged when the Bo 105 hit us. We're down to one satphone that can reach the mainland. We'll patch you into the maritime emergency station, and they can redirect your call where needed."

Abelone and Vanderfeld turned to the communications officer, Laurier, for the satphone. He stood still, his palms in a position of appeal as he stared at Jon Brown, who held the bridge's C8 close-quarter rifle. The stock of the rifle rested on his shoulder, and the barrel was aimed at Roger Powers' chest.

"Son, what are you doing?" Vanderfeld said. "You'd better have a damn good reason for breaking federal law. Handling the bridge rifle and pointing it at a Coast Guard officer is some pretty serious shit. Both could send you to jail for several years."

"My apologies, Captain, but if what Abelone is saying is accurate, this man is infected and needs to be quarantined. He is a threat to everyone on this bridge."

Abelone looked at Powers. Jon was right. How could she have overlooked that? Powers was wheezing in his chair and staring at the ground. His bite marks weren't bleeding and had already scabbed over with black puss. *That's not normal.*

"I don't care what you think, Mr. Brown. This is my bridge, and I won't have anyone handle that rifle other than a bridge officer. Listen to me very carefully—"

The captain stopped mid-sentence when Abelone put her hand on his arm. "Look at his arm."

Vanderfeld glanced at Powers' arms and frowned, but his gaze darted straight back to the rifle. "We'll get Mr. Powers the treatment he needs. But for now, the threat I see here is a non-commissioned man aiming *my* rifle at one of my officers. Stand down, Mr. Brown." The captain's voice was calm and steady and sliced through the wind coming in through the broken window.

"Jon, it's okay. We'll quarantine him in the storeroom," Abelone shouted, hoping her voice would carry the way Vanderfeld's had.

Jon nodded in agreement as a mad hammering started on the bridge door.

Abelone's attention abruptly shifted from the rifle to the onslaught on the door. Fields collected herself quickly and stretched her neck to look through the small round window. She cringed and pulled back, putting her hand on her mouth. Abelone stepped past her and looked through the window herself.

"It's Marshall and Rondo. How are they still even moving?" She was asking herself more than the others. Their black eyes and grey skin stunned her. In all her years of studying viruses, both in the lab and in some of the most remote areas on the planet, she had never seen anything like this.

Captain Vanderfeld, Jon Brown and the comms officer all stepped to the door but stopped as soon as they caught a glimpse of the disfigured faces.

"What the hell! This is insane!" blurted Laurier. He stepped away from the door with the satellite phone still clenched in his hand. "Are they zombies?"

"Don't be ridiculous, Mr. Laurier." Abelone was irritated by the absurd suggestion. "Zombies don't exist. There is no medical evidence of any kind supporting such a condition. Marshall and Rondo are alive. They seem to have been infected with some sort of septicemic rabies virus." She sounded confident, but she questioned her assessment. She worked up the nerve to inch her face closer to the window to get a better look. *They can't be, can they? It happens with bugs. Mould can hijack a bug's brain and make it attack its own kind.* She couldn't discount the idea.

"Septicemic?" quizzed the captain, still staring at his men in the passageway.

"Transferred via blood or saliva. It's how animals like raccoons or bats usually transfer rabies to other hosts. But I've never seen or heard of rabies affecting humans this way," Jon Brown answered.

Abelone switched her attention back to Roger Powers, worried he could be a danger to the group. "Captain, we need to move your first officer to the back room and lock him in there. You see how those men out there are acting"—she pointed at the bridge door—"the same thing seems to be happening to Mr. Powers."

"Because of the bite on his hand?"

"Yes. I'm hoping the infection needs an entry point to the blood via saliva or blood transfer. I sure as hell hope this thing isn't airborne," she said, her voice cracking with concern.

Vanderfeld stared at her for a few seconds. "Fine, Ms. Jensen. But the rifle goes to a bridge officer. We have one rifle on this ship, and it's going to one of my crew."

Abelone looked sternly at Brown, who was still holding the C8. He frowned, but complied and handed the rifle to the communications officer beside him. However, Abelone wondered if that was a better option. The communications officer looked more shaken up than anyone else on the bridge.

"Thank you, Jon," she said. "Help me with him."

"Right, I've never been able to resist that accent of yours," said Brown with a half-smile.

Abelone turned toward Powers—or where Powers was supposed to be. The chair was empty. Powers stood a few feet behind her. His skin had lost all signs of life and had already turned grey. His eyes were riddled with popped veins, which were turning his irises black. The big man's powerful arms reached for her head.

Abelone recoiled, and Brown jumped. He grabbed Powers by the shoulders, and they engaged in a struggle of strength that Brown was not equipped to win. Powers pulled the smaller man closer. What saved Brown from getting his face bitten off was his right hand holding Powers' throat, and consequently his jaw, at bay.

Laurier, still holding the satellite phone in one hand and the rifle in the other, aimed the C8 at the struggling pair.

"Get out of the way. I need a clean shot!" Laurier shouted, panic in his voice. He was shaking from head to boots, and it was a miracle he hadn't squeezed the trigger yet. If Laurier fired the rifle one-handed, who knew where the bullets would go?

Captain Vanderfeld had the same thought. "Laurier, don't!"

It was too late; Laurier squeezed the trigger. The room filled with the slightly sulfuric scent of gunpowder. The first bullet hit Brown in the left arm. The next couple of bullets hit Roger Powers in the chest and shoulder, making him take a half-step back and forcing him to let go of Brown. The recoil spun the gun and Laurier's arm in an arc, and the next twenty or so rounds sprayed across the compartment. Abelone dropped to the floor as the bullets showered the communications equipment along the back wall.

Powers was unfazed by the peppering of bullets that hit him. He was already stepping toward the communications officer. Laurier looked crazed. He screamed and aimed the rifle into the oncoming Powers' gut and squeezed the trigger again. Flesh, organs and bone erupted as the last few bullets traversed Powers' body. Yet the big man reached up, grabbed the communications officer by the head and lifted Laurier toward his giant maw. Laurier kicked his legs futilely as Powers bit down on his neck like it was a piece of fresh fruit. The bite almost severed Laurier's head from his body. The spine and a few neck muscles barely kept both parts together.

Captain Vanderfeld dashed forward and slammed into Laurier's back, which pushed the now lifeless body into Powers, who tumbled backwards to the edge of the broken windowpane. *Not far enough!* Abelone sprang to her feet and hurled her own body into the back of the hanging communications officer as Vanderfeld had done. Her feet left the ground, and the collision between her and the two men sent them plunging to the deck four floors below.

Abelone's momentum carried her over the edge. Her arms flailed, trying to find something to grab onto. *I'm going over!* Luckily, someone grabbed her by the belt and held her angled over the edge for a split second before adjusting to her weight and pulling her back in.

"I got you," Brown said.

In that split second, when Abelone balanced between falling and being pulled back, she saw the two men crash on the deck below. The satellite phone, too, hit the deck and shattered into pieces like fine china on a tiled floor. Bile filled her mouth.

"The satphone!" gasped Abelone as Brown pulled her back in.

Once she was safe, Brown fell to his knees, putting pressure on his bleeding arm.

"Jon!" Abelone knelt beside her friend. She pointed at Fields. "Get me the first-aid kit!"

Fields snatched the first-aid kit off the wall and brought it over. Abelone rummaged through it until she found medical scissors, hemorrhage-control dressing and gauze wrap. She cut Jon's sleeve off at the shoulder, revealing a torn triceps where the bullet had gone through. She quickly applied the dressing as Jon winced.

"Relax, you baby," she said. "It's not that bad. It went straight through and didn't damage any bone." It was worse than she let on, but she tried to smile reassuringly.

Jon smiled back. "That accent of yours can always make me feel better," he said painfully.

"Alright, calm down," Abelone said to a perpetually smitten Jon. He was a close friend, and she didn't like to see him play tough when he was hurt. It wouldn't change how she felt. "This isn't as bad as the rotavirus you got in Sierra Leone. I've never seen anyone have diarrhea that bad," she said, angling the conversation in another direction.

Brown smiled even more. His smile changed to a grimace when Abelone wrapped a bandage around the dressing to lock it in place.

Having finished with Brown, Abelone looked up at Vanderfeld and Fields standing by the broken windowpane looking down. Despite the wind, she heard yelling making its way up to the bridge. She propped Jon up, and they shuffled over to the window. From the top of the superstructure, they could see a deckhand with a yellow tuque standing over the bodies of Powers and Laurier. He shouted over his shoulder to people Abelone could not see and pointed up at the bridge.

"Ms. Jensen, what are the chances those bodies can infect my crew down there?" asked the captain.

"Unless they ingest blood or saliva . . . they should be fine . . . probably. Best they do not touch the bodies, though. Just in case."

The captain cupped his hands to funnel his shouted warnings downwards. But the sound of his voice was whisked away by the wind, and the man on the deck simply stared up at them.

Three other men came running and stopped when they saw the bodies tangled up on the deck. It took them a few seconds to muster the courage to step closer. Their body language suggested they were talking furiously, their arms waving and pointing at the bodies, the bridge and the rifle.

"Those idiots need to get to safety," said Jon.

"Why?" Fields asked. "There is no way those two survived that fall."

As if on cue, the crowd below got even more agitated. Limbs moved in the mangled pile of Powers and Laurier. An arm stretched out and pushed the smaller body aside. Powers' legs and arms folded and pushed the big body to all fours. Then he stood up.

The deckhands tried to help Powers. Even from four decks up, with the wind howling, Abelone heard the first scream. Three men were quickly bitten. The fourth deckhand, the one with the yellow tuque, moved back, staring at the grisly scene. He looked up at the people staring at him from the bridge and the captain frantically waving his arms to encourage the man to run. He took off running while Roger Powers feasted on the three other deckhands, who squirmed amidst a massive circle of blood on the deck.

"We need to call for help," said Abelone, her voice trembling. Her mouth was still saying things, and her body was still moving, but she was floating above herself, watching but not comprehending. Her field training took charge as if this was an Ebola outbreak. But her spirit knew this was not what she had been trained for.

She looked to see if anyone had heard her. Everyone on the bridge was in their own state of automation. Like Abelone, they were trained to take action, to solve problems, to save lives. But Abelone knew no one was ready for people eating people.

Vanderfeld and Fields stood in front of the communications equipment, nodding as if it was a normal captain problem to solve. But no solution was being uttered.

"Whatever communications system might have been salvaged is scrap," Fields said with a tremble in her voice.

"Was that your only satphone?" Abelone asked, slowly adjusting to reality.

"Yes, we have no way to communicate with the mainland anymore," Fields answered almost dreamily.

"We don't need to," said the captain, clarity in his voice. He walked over to the intercom panel at the back of the bridge and fiddled with it for a second before turning back to her.

"We don't need to communicate with the mainland or the Cormorant from here. As long as we are close enough, we can use our ICOMs."

Abelone wished Doc Martel was there to give a thorough description of what an ICOM was. She caught herself wondering where he was when Jon's voice snapped her back to the moment.

"What's an ICOM?" Jon croaked out while sliding his injured arm into the sling he had swung over his head.

"It's our expedition handheld VHF radios. We have six of them. They are tough as hell and have an eight-mile radius, so we should be able to call out to the Cormorant once it reaches us."

"Perfect," said Abelone. "Get them out."

"It's not that easy, Ms. Jensen," Vanderfeld said flatly. His stare drifted to the bridge door where Rondo and Marshall were still hammering away.

"Captain?" She moved between him and the door to cut off the view of the monsters going bump in the night.

The captain snapped out of his stupor. "They're in the ship's supply storage below deck, and the only way there . . . is through them."

***

"I'm going with you," Abelone said to Vanderfeld after hearing his plan to descend via the exterior stairs to the main deck, then circle to the superstructure doors.

Vanderfeld looked at her, clenching his jaw.

"You need Fields up here as she is the only other ship officer, and Brown is as useful as a chocolate teapot," Abelone added.

"Hey!" Brown protested. "First off, that's a weird expression, and second, I'm not useless." He tried to get up from his seat, but the effort made him wince, and he sat back down. "Okay, you might be on to something," he admitted.

The captain stared at Abelone; she stared back and didn't blink. "Fine," the grizzled captain conceded.

"The parkas," she said and walked over to a series of thick black parkas hanging by the door. "Put this on," she said, handing one to the captain.

"The cold is the least of our worries. Once we are inside, we won't need them. We are wasting time."

"This isn't to protect us from the cold. It's to protect us from them—the bites. The virus seems to transmit via saliva or blood, but it has to get into the host's system first." Abelone pulled at the outer layer of the parka, which was thick and rigid. The captain understood and slipped a parka on. She did the same.

Abelone stepped to the broken windowpane and ignored the frigid wind that blew past her face. "There are five infected down there," she pointed out grimly. The three crewmen Roger Powers had attacked were stumbling around with Powers and Laurier like drunken sailors leaving the local pub.

"It doesn't matter," said the captain. "It's time to go. We need those ICOMs if we're to stop this—whatever it is—from spreading."

He and Abelone exited the bridge deck to its balcony. The ocean was calm, and the Greenland coast was well out of sight. The air was warmer than when she'd stood out on the same deck in the early morning. She still couldn't comprehend what was happening, but this was an outbreak, and they had to communicate with the outside world.

With no signs of movement on the deck, she followed Vanderfeld down the three flights of stairs. Once at the bottom, they crouched behind the square frame of the empty helicopter hangar, its customary resident lying in pieces on a beach at the foot of a glacier back in Greenland.

With a look and a wave, Vanderfeld pointed around the corner of the superstructure, where the deck narrowed and led to a door. She nodded.

"Stay close to me and move quickly."

They made it into the superstructure without incident, but the captain hesitated.

"What's wrong?"

"My cabin is right up this ladder. I have a sidearm in my locker."

"Let's go get it. What are you worried about?" Abelone inquired.

"These are the same stairs leading to the bridge three decks up. We'll be a floor away from Marshall and Rondo. If they hear us . . ."

"Are there any other guns on the ship we can get a hold of?" Abelone whispered.

"No, the bridge C8 and the captain's pistol are it. Guard ships are not allowed to carry weapons beyond those two." It felt like a stupid rule to Abelone, but she was not knowledgeable concerning Canadian law on arming ocean-going vessels, so she didn't debate the topic.

She nodded approval, and the captain went up instead of down.

As they reached the officer's quarters deck, Vanderfeld grabbed Abelone by the arm, stopping her in her tracks. "The banging's stopped," he whispered.

She cocked her head to the side. *He's right.* They stood unmoving, listening.

"Well, if they are still there, they've gone awfully quiet. My cabin is right around the corner as soon as we go through the hatch." He moved forward, and Abelone followed. To her relief, neither Rondo nor Marshall came running down the passageway. They entered the captain's cabin, and Abelone quietly closed the door behind her. Vanderfeld opened his locker and pulled out his gun box. He opened it to reveal his SIG Sauer pistol. He slid the two extra bullet clips into his pockets and hooked his pistol holster with the pistol to his belt. After he put the box back in his locker, he pulled out a bottle of rum, uncorked it and took a long swig. He offered the bottle to Abelone.

"Isn't that a bit cliché?" she said, amused despite the circumstances.

"What's that?" the captain asked, confused.

"A sea captain drinking rum."

"Ms. Jensen, what's cliché is a bunch of fucking zombies running around my ship, eating my fucking crew. We've seen this movie a thousand times already. Yet here we are."

She conceded the point and took a large gulp from the bottle, all the while thinking, *They're not zombies; those don't exist.* She knew better than to correct the captain at this point. She gave the bottle back and turned to the cabin door. "Ready?"

They quietly made it back down a deck with no unwelcome encounters. Then they traversed the width of the superstructure to reach the ladder that would take them to the level housing the supply-storage quarters.

They hugged the bulkheads as they crept. Even from far off, Abelone could see a mess in front of the medical-bay door near the ladder they were heading for. It looked like dark paint had been splattered everywhere. As they crept closer, Abelone realized it wasn't paint; it was blood. A hell of a lot of blood.

Vanderfeld stopped. Abelone did the same. A barely audible noise was coming from around the corner of a smaller passageway. It sounded like someone slurping soup from a bowl. The hair on Abelone's neck stood on end, and her muscles tensed. Vanderfeld crept to the junction and pulled his sidearm from its holster. He leaned his head over the corner slowly to peer down the passageway. He pulled back just as slowly, revealing that the blood had drained from his face.

Abelone stepped up behind him and leaned one eye over the edge of the corner. Rondo and Marshall were bent over the body of the deckhand with the yellow tuque. Even though they were a good ten metres away, she could see their grey skin and the large bald spots where clumps of hair had fallen off. The parts of their bodies that had been bitten had stopped bleeding and were covered in dark, dry scabs.

Abelone pulled back and leaned into Vanderfeld. "Their backs are to us; we need to move."

Vanderfeld nodded, and they crept carefully into the passageway junction. They were barely a few steps out when Rondo and Marshall stopped devouring the sailor. Both stood up.

Did they hear us? Abelone thought, panicking.

The sailor with the yellow tuque stirred. His arms moved and pushed his torso around. His legs bent and lifted his body. The captain grabbed Abelone by the sleeve, pulling her to the safety of the other corner. A step away from being out of sight, something crunched loudly under her foot. It might as well have been a dinner bell as it resonated down the passageway, and the three infected turned. She lifted her boot to see a handful of crushed teeth.

"Run!" Vanderfeld shouted as he shoved her ahead of him.

Abelone sprang to life and darted ahead of the captain for the ladder hatch. She almost lost her footing as she stepped into the massive pool of blood covering the floor in front of the medical bay. At the hatch, she turned and saw the captain still at the passageway junction with his pistol raised. In the confined space, the crack of the 9mm was painfully amplified. Three consecutive shots echoed off the walls and pounded in her ears. A pause, deafening in comparison, was followed by three more shots.

Vanderfeld spun and ran. His feet slipped on the blood-slicked floor, and he sprawled to the ground. Abelone was quick to help him up.

"The shots didn't do anything. They didn't even go down!" Vanderfeld said as the three infected shambled around the corner.

"Hurry!" she yelled.

He jumped forward, but as he landed, his blood-covered boots slipped from under him again, and he tumbled head-first into her.

"Ah, fuck!" he muttered as he slammed into her midsection, and they crashed down the ladder in an avalanche of bodies and limbs before landing at the bottom in a heap.

Abelone's ears rang, and blood trickled from a split lip. She got up quickly, holding different parts of her bruised body. She could hear the gurgling shrieks of the infected coming from the top of the stairs.

"We need to find a place to hide," she said, looking around. The nearest door, which led to the crew quarters, was covered in blood, worse than the passage in front of the medical bay. *Not in there.*

She pulled the captain the opposite way toward the supply-storage quarters and the mess deck. As they reached a four-passageway intersection beside the mess-deck door, they stopped in their tracks. A head popped up from the ladder in front of them. She saw the clumped hair with missing patches first, then what looked like a permanent shadow over the person's face, which she quickly realized was not a shadow at all but grey skin. She recognized the face—it was Tom Virtanen.

The young engineer, whom she had last seen in the medical bay, was in the passageway ahead of them, grey-skinned and ambulating. He was followed by a couple of other infected covered in bite marks and with various pieces of their faces ripped off. It struck Abelone that Tom seemed to have fewer bites than the others. His chin and chest were covered in blood, and he was more sure-footed, but if he had bites, she couldn't see them.

Being an epidemiologist, Abelone's mind always worked in a cause-and-effect manner. A virus infects the first person, that person infects a couple of other people, then they infect multiple others and so on. Part of her training was to identify the original host, the source of the infection. That was the key to fighting whatever virus she had been sent to fight. That was how viruses were defeated, and the obvious was staring her in the face.

There was a crash behind her, and she spun around. One of the infected chasing them tumbled down the stairs with the two others in tow.

"The ICOMs are in the supply storage down that passageway!" Vanderfeld pointed to a small dark passageway to their right just as another grey-skinned monstrosity with bite marks on its face and hands materialized from its shadows. It shrieked in delirium.

Vanderfeld fiddled with his holster, then looked up in disbelief. "The gun, it's gone. It must have fallen out."

Infected were coming at them from three directions. To her surprise, Abelone did not freeze. Instead, she crouched down, ready to fight. Then the mess-deck door opened, and four arms reached out to grab her and Vanderfeld. They were yanked backwards and went sprawling onto their backs as the door slammed shut, cutting them off from the onrushing infected.

6

GIVE OR TAKE

Abelone had to shake her head to make sure she recognized the face staring down at her.

"Alex!" Abelone muttered as she lay on her back, stunned to see her friend.

"Got you just in time," Alex Deangelo said.

He was surprised, too, by the look in his eyes. He stretched out a shaky hand, made even more nervous by the onslaught of infected on the mess-deck door.

"Abelone, what the hell is going on out there? We've been holed up in here for an hour."

"We?" the captain asked, getting up from the floor on his own.

"Yes sir," a young man in a cook's uniform stepped forward. "I've been with Mr. Deangelo the whole time. I was in the galley when those things—I mean, those guys—attacked each other." He paused to compose himself, on the verge of tears.

Alex continued, not much more composed himself, "I was getting coffee, when—hell, I don't even know how to describe it." He rubbed his chin. "Shouting began down the passageway, so the kid and I stepped out to see what was—" He took a deep breath. "A couple of guys were disfiguring another sailor—" Alex shook his head as if trying to shake away the image. "We were barely able to lock ourselves in here."

"It's some sort of infection. Alex, I've never seen anything like it," Abelone said.

"We wanted to help—it was too late; they were . . . There was blood. We didn't know what to do . . ." the young cook stuttered.

"It's okay, son. There's nothing you could have done," the captain comforted the cook.

"Whatever it is, it seems to be septicemic." Abelone peered out the little round window.

"We're not going through those guys anytime soon," Vanderfeld said as he walked to the door at the other end of the compartment. "We could exit through the back," he said, looking through the window of the rear door. "But that won't get us to where we need to go."

"And where is that?" Alex said cautiously.

"We need our ICOMs. We need to get to the supply-storage area on the other side of that passageway." Vanderfeld pointed at the door with the infected slamming on it.

Alex looked between Abelone and Vanderfeld. She could tell he was not thrilled. She took a minute to recap everything that had happened on the bridge. When she was done, Alex and the young cook both sat at a table, flabbergasted.

"We need those ICOMs to communicate with the Coast Guard helicopter, which is on its way to meet us," the captain said stiffly. He was as sturdy as Abelone had seen him since this all started.

"Alex, we need to make sure the outside world knows to quarantine this ship at all costs. It is some kind of virus—it has to be a virus—which transforms . . . err . . . causes aggressive behaviour in the host. It spreads quickly from a simple bite, and believe me, they do everything to bite," Abelone added, suspecting she was voicing what Alex already knew.

"Whatever this virus is, it must be shutting down the host's pain receptors because the injuries these people have should cripple them," Alex said. "I've never seen anything like this either."

Abelone was relieved her friend, her mentor, understood.

"I've seen viruses that rewire the brain and pain receptors, but those are rare and nothing like this," she added.

"It doesn't need to shut down the pain receptors. Pain is an output of the brain, not an input from the body. All a virus has to do is shut down the hypothalamus, and you can walk around with a fractured leg, a burnt arm or, in this case, a ripped-off face—"

The captain interrupted impatiently, "Whatever the science is, it can wait. We need to get those ICOMs. That chopper is meeting us soon, and we're going to need to talk to them. With all our comms down, we haven't even been able to communicate with the other people on this ship."

"With the bridge, you mean," Alex said matter-of-factly.

Both Abelone and Vanderfeld stared at him.

"What do you mean?" the captain asked.

"Well . . . we've been communicating with the other people on the ship. The intercom still works. The bridge and the medical bay are the only main compartments we haven't been able to contact," Alex said, shrugging.

Vanderfeld grabbed Alex by the shoulders. "How many? How many are still alive and safe?"

"Alex, the intercom on the bridge was down. The captain could not talk to the rest of the crew," Abelone explained.

Alex described how four engineers were barricaded in the engine room on the bottom deck, two more were in the battery room next to it but planned to join the others in the engine room, and the quartermaster was in the storage room. Everyone was in a similar situation, locked in their compartment, while a handful of infected roamed the passageways, looking for dinner.

"Let's get a hold of the QM!" Vanderfeld said, moving swiftly to the intercom.

"Well, that one stopped responding ten minutes ago—sorry."

This was confirmed quickly by Vanderfeld, with a few unsuccessful tries to reach the QM.

Abelone counted out loud. "So that's four, two, possibly one—plus the two on the bridge—and us four, for a total of thirteen. Captain, how many people are on the Henry Dawson?"

"Thirty-two." Vanderfeld did not hesitate.

"That means there are potentially nineteen infected roaming the ship," Alex barely managed to get the words out above a whisper.

Can that many be infected? Abelone wondered.

Vanderfeld did his own math. "The seven outside our door here, the three still on the outside deck . . ." He wasn't as fast as Alex on the math. "That leaves . . . nine that we don't know the status of, if they are infected or hiding."

Abelone wondered if this virus could spread that fast. That would make it more virulent than anything she'd ever seen. She could tell Vanderfeld was distraught by the way his shoulders drooped, the stiffness momentarily leaving him. This was his ship, and the idea that this virus had infected all those people was crushing him. His crow's feet deepened, and he stared at the ground as he ruminated over the numbers.

***

Alex was used to seeing death up close in his line of work and had developed a thick skin. But this was something altogether different. He looked to Abelone for behavioural cues, knowing her optimism would be a balm in an otherwise chaotic scenario. She was one of the few people in their profession who had managed to keep this belief they could save everyone whenever they were dispatched to viral hot zones. She had always been passionate and caring and felt all life was precious. He knew she always held out hope her patients would recover or that she would find a cure to save them. Even now, he could tell by the way she looked at the infected hammering at the door that she was thinking about how they could be saved. That reassured him.

Alex knew if someone could find a cure, it was Abelone. At the very least, a vaccine so some could be saved, but his optimism was nothing compared to Abelone's.

"How do we distract the infected in the hallway?" Abelone was all business.

"Hmm . . . I can exit by the back door of the mess deck." Vanderfeld pointed to the smaller door near the galley. "The smaller passageway connects to the main corridor. I can attract them down that way far enough to allow the rest of you to cross to the supply storeroom undetected."

"It can't be you, Captain. We need you to guide us to the ICOMs, then we need you back on the bridge," said Abelone.

"It's my ship, Ms. Jensen. If someone's to put their life at risk, it will be me."

"Captain, we need you to find these ICOMs."

"She's right," said Alex. He'd accepted they had to leave the safety of the mess deck, so he might as well be helpful. "I'll go. I'm tired of being cooped up in here, anyway."

The young assistant cook spoke up, "No offence, Mr. Deangelo, but you'd get lost the second you turn the first corner." The young man turned to his captain. "Sir, I know this deck by heart—I'll go. Let me do this for my shipmates, who are gone."

The captain's face contorted with the decision, and his eyes welled up.

"Son, you are very brave." Vanderfeld stood tall. "I'm proud to have you on my ship. You get their attention, and you run like hell to the forward-galley storage compartments . . . Do you know the ones near the front of the bow? You lock yourself in there, and you don't come out until we come and get you with help. You got that?"

The young galley cook swelled with pride. He stood as straight as his captain. "Aye, sir. I won't let you down." The young man strode to the door at the back of the compartment and stood ready.

Alex followed him and put his hands on the door latch.

"So you know, kid, I have a great sense of direction. I wouldn't have gotten lost . . ." Alex told the young man, smiling. " . . . probably."

With a nod from Vanderfeld, he unlatched the door and swung it open. The cook sprang into the hallway, yelling all kinds of obscenities as only a young man could.

It got the infected's attention. They stopped assaulting the main door as soon as the yelling started. They listened for a few seconds, then whether angered by the foul-mouthed insults or attracted to fresh prey, they took off running after the cook. The young man was already sprinting the other way.

Alex watched all seven infected run by his little window. "It's clear," he whispered.

Vanderfeld slowly opened the main mess-deck door. He looked both ways to make sure there were indeed no infected lurking, then stepped out and headed straight for the supply-storage compartment passageway. Abelone was behind him, and Alex, after taking one last look at the safe and comforting mess deck, followed them quietly.

At the junction, the captain stopped and pointed at a sign: *Quartermaster Storage*. With a sharp chopping hand signal, he pointed down the smaller, darkened passageway, barely illuminated by a flickering emergency light.

Alex's heart dropped. "We're going down that?" He tried to keep his voice as quiet as his panic allowed.

"That's where the ICOMs are."

"But . . . we can't see a thing!"

Vanderfeld ignored his complaint. "They should be in the last storage cage twenty metres down. Something must have happened to the lights down here, but yes, this is where we have to go," Vanderfeld whispered harshly, indicating he was not happy with the unnecessary noise. Vanderfeld's authoritative demeanour had returned. "A few metres past the flickering light at the far end is the outer lower-deck door to the ship's stern. We head aft, and if any infected show up, we run for that door. Understood?"

Alex nodded, but was not thrilled by any means.

He followed Vanderfeld and Abelone as they crept along fenced storage compartments filled with crates, bags and boxes.

They approached a cage that looked different from the others. It had a counter behind the fencing with a square opening in the mesh to pass things back and forth.

"That's the quartermaster's desk," Vanderfeld whispered.

If only he was there to pass us what we need, Alex thought as he quietly walked by the cage.

Out of the shadows behind the mesh, a silhouette sprang and hit the fencing with a loud rattle. Alex jumped back. A small-statured infected bounced back and forth against the rattling fencing. It shrieked and tried to grab Alex through the open slot above the counter. The infected, presumably the former quartermaster, was dressed in grey coveralls. Its hair was half ripped out, and its eyes were piercing black and hardly distinguishable from the shadows. It hissed saliva all over the counter and tried to slide its head and arms through the fencing hole. Fortunately, the slot was too small. The infected threw itself against the fencing again.

"Jesus!" Alex yelped.

"Shit. That's Mac. Mac Osborn," said the captain solemnly. "He's our quartermaster. We now know why he wasn't answering your calls anymore."

The infected's hand, Mac Osborn's hand, was ripped off above the wrist. Chewed off was a better description.

Must have been through the slit in the cage fence, Alex thought as he noticed the counter was covered in blood.

The captain gave the cage a concerned look. Alex was just as concerned.

"Mr. Deangelo, watch him and watch our backs. The ICOMs are a few cages down. Ms. Jensen, you're with me." The captain's orders were confident and unwavering. Abelone nodded. For a second, Alex considered arguing, but instead, he sighed and nodded as well.

Vanderfeld and Abelone walked further down the passageway until they disappeared in the shadows of a cage. Alex stood still in the shadows, gazing at the dark corridor leading back to where they had come from. The light from that passageway gave the entrance to their smaller passage a near-death experience glow to it. *Don't walk toward the light,* he thought, trying to distract himself.

Mac Osborn kept rattling his cage, resolute that he had to get to Alex as if his survival depended on it.

A noise far off down the hallway stopped his train of thought. Not a noise, a voice. At least, he thought it was a voice. He was *sure* it was a voice. Not seeing anything, he looked back to the cage where Abelone and Vanderfeld had disappeared. Nothing. *Ah damn, I can't believe I'm going to do this.* He crept toward the junction, ready to run back yelling at any sign of trouble.

As he approached the junction, he held his breath and peeked around the corner. *Nothing.* He let himself exhale. Another sound, this time from the crew quarters at the bottom of the stairs down the main passageway. Even from this far away, he could see the deck and bulkheads covered in dried blood. *Hell, no. I am not going down there. Back down my own spooky tunnel I go.*

Alex turned quickly to head back, but he knocked over a metal bin. It hit the floor, clattering on the metal deck and echoing throughout the main passageway. *Fuck! Of course, life-and-death situation, and I knock something over. So fucking cliché.* He stood still. His breath held. He listened. *Nothing... No, what was that?*

Rapid footsteps pattered toward him, followed by a high-pitched shriek. The infected in the yellow tuque came running around the corner near the mess deck. Part of his right cheek was scratched half an inch deep, and a chunk of his neck was missing. His left ear was partially detached and hung by a strand of skin. The man's shoulders and torso were covered in blood.

Alex froze.

The infected hissed and jumped on him. Alex barely had time to put his arms up and catch it by the throat. He held his mouth at bay, stopping it from sinking its teeth into his face, and fell to the floor. No dexterity would stop that fall. Alex and the infected wrestled. They rolled to a stop, with Alex at the bottom. He stared into the infected man's eyes and saw the black veins that meandered away from his pitch-black irises. Its sclerae were grey, and puss oozed from its tear ducts. If it wasn't for the adrenaline pumping through his body, Alex would have curled up in a ball out of fear. The infected gnashed at him, and Alex glimpsed bloodied teeth and a blackened tongue. Blood drained from Alex's upraised arms as he held the attacking maw at bay. His arms started to shake. *I have to get free. I can't hold on much longer.* The infected kept pushing and pushing.

SHIT! Alex panicked as his arms gave. A gun-metal grey barrel appeared in his line of sight, placed itself on the temple of the infected, and an ear-splitting deflagration cracked loudly, making him blink hard. The smell of burnt gunpowder overpowered Alex as the opposite side of the infected's head splattered on the wall beside him. The infected's limp body slumped onto Alex, and without thinking, he rolled it to the side and let his tired arms fall to the deck as he heaved for air.

The round, bloody face of Doc Martel popped up over him.

"Mr. Deangelo, are you okay? Were you bitten?"

Adrenaline still pumping, the questions didn't register right away. Doc Martel helped him sit up and asked again.

"Were you bitten?"

"What? Bitten? No, I don't think so," Alex said, staring back at Martel.

"Alex, Eric!" Abelone ran out of the small shadowy supply compartment passage into the main passageway, followed by Captain Vanderfeld.

"What happened? Eric, we thought you were dead!" Abelone gasped.

"The gun? The head? How did you know to shoot the head?" Captain Vanderfeld asked, eyeing his pistol.

Doc Martel, true to his loquacious nature, explained in detail how he had been knocked out in the science lab and how, when he came to, he'd made his way out to the cleared passageway. To his surprise, he'd found the captain's pistol in front of the medical bay, and when he heard yelling one deck below, he had followed the noise to see if he could help. In the crew quarters, he'd seen one body despite the blood bath everywhere. That body had a crowbar firmly planted in its head. That was when it dawned on him that going for the head would be the smart thing to do.

Vanderfeld finally interrupted. "All right, we get it, Doc." He turned to Alex. "Mr. Deangelo, are you bitten?"

Alex was out of breath, but looked over his hands and arms this time. "No. Will everyone stop asking me that?" he snapped while pulling himself up off the ground. Abelone, Doc Martel and Vanderfeld all took a step back as he got up.

"What? What is it?" By their reaction, he knew something wasn't right. They were looking at him as if he'd coughed in public in the heyday of COVID. "I'm not bitten, I swear," he said, more hesitantly this time.

"Your face, Alex," Abelone said.

He wiped his face from cheek to chin. His hand came back covered in blood. He wiped the back of his sleeve across his mouth, and it came back red.

"Oh crap," he muttered as he furiously wiped his mouth with his other sleeve. He had to get it off his lips. *Did I swallow some?* He couldn't tell. He rubbed furiously at his mouth.

He stuck his fingers down his throat and made himself gag a few times—finally, he threw up. He tried as hard as he could to regurgitate any blood he might have swallowed.

"It might not have made it into your system," Abelone said.

He knew better. Abelone's eyes welled up, and she put her arms around him, not saying anything else. There was nothing to say.

Alex knew it, too. He'd been in this line of work for long enough. He'd helped thousands of people over the years who had been infected with Ebola, SARS and Marburg. He gently pushed Abelone to arm's length and, in his usual self-deprecating way, smiled and said, "Well, I was always afraid I would die alone, an old man in my old worn-out chair. At least this way, I get to serve a purpose." He brought up his watch and started the timer. "We'll know exactly how long this virus takes to infect a host when infected blood is ingested."

Abelone smiled at his courage. She went in for another hug and squeezed him harder this time.

"Okay. Okay. We need to move. Wouldn't want those other infected to ruin our moment," Alex said, pushing her gently away again. He saw no reason to dwell on the possibility. He was either infected or he wasn't. God, he hoped he wasn't.

He changed the subject. "Captain, when we were in the mess deck, we talked with your chief engineer via the intercom. He's locked in the engine room with a few guys. He said one was banged up pretty bad with a concussion or something and needs the doctor's help."

The captain again asserted himself and took command of the situation, which Alex was grateful for.

"We need to get them one of these ICOMs so they can communicate with the bridge," Vanderfeld said. "The guys down there will need to make sure the engines stay on so we can navigate." The captain spoke specifically to Abelone. "Ms. Jensen, you need to bring these to Fields up on the bridge." He waved the radios and handed her two of the yellow ICOMs. The little radios were sturdy, with a small digital screen on the front and six rubber buttons below it.

"I'll set the engineering room on channel seven so we can communicate. Fields will know how to reach the Cormorant when it is in sight."

The captain's tone softened, and he spoke to Alex next. "Mr. Deangelo, I am sorry for what is happening to you. But we need to get these radios to the bridge if we want a chance at warning the outside world."

Alex pressed his lips together in a tight line and nodded. He understood the situation.

Doc Martel extended the 9mm pistol to Abelone. "Here, take this . . . just in case."

She hesitated, but took the handgun and slipped it into her belt. Surprisingly, relief flooded through Alex. He pretended not to know why Martel gave her the gun, but he felt lighter, knowing Abelone could take care of him if he started to change.

***

Abelone watched the captain and the doctor disappear down the ladder toward the engine room. Alex was staring at his watch. *He's counting down his time.* "We can find a cure," she told him. "I know who Patient Zero is!" she said excitedly, but she knew, as well as Alex, that this was not enough. Even if they had the original carrier's blood, they'd need to transport it to a vaccine-making laboratory.

"Abby, it's unlikely I will make it that long. If everything you've told me concerning the incubation period is accurate, then, at best, I can help you get back to the bridge. At worst . . ."

"We'll make it to the bridge," Abelone asserted. She had to believe this. He meant too much to her. "There's a storage room where we can lock you in. We'll keep you in there, so you are safe until we reach the mainland and find a way to help you." She didn't say it was also so she and the others would be safe.

Alex put his hands on her shoulders. "That's always been your strength, Abby. You've always felt every infected person in the world could be saved."

Abelone teared up, and all she could do was stare into her mentor's eyes. What she saw made her breath seize. A speck of black the size of a pixel burst in Alex's left iris, then another and another. His capillaries were bursting one after the other.

"It's starting. I can see it," she gasped.

Alex reached for his eyes gently. "I can feel it. It's the weirdest feeling. It's almost like . . . I can sense my cells dividing."

Barely had he finished those words when a spasm hit him. His head twisted sideways, and his jaw clenched. He keeled over, letting go of Abelone's shoulders. Placing his hands on his knees, he breathed out heavily.

"So that's what a contraction is like," he joked painfully.

It took all of Abelone's willpower to lift the 9mm pistol to her friend's head. Her hands shook, and she could barely see through the tears pooling in her eyes.

"It's okay, Abby. Do it, please. Don't let me become one of those things." Though his eyes were rapidly turning black, Alex was still in there. His kind face beseeching her to do something awful.

"They're not things. You're not a thing. You're a person . . . who can be saved." She believed this unequivocally, but her friend's pleas were revealing a crack in her armour.

Alex looked past the barrel of the gun. Abelone tightened her grip on the butt of the pistol and put an unsure finger on the trigger. Her breathing sped up, and she squeezed her lips together. Alex closed his eyes, and Abelone held her breath. Three seconds went by, then three more. Unable to pull the trigger, she gasped for air and dropped her arms. Tears flowed down her cheeks.

"I can't. Alex, I just can't," she said. "We'll get you a cure. We'll lock you in the bridge storeroom, and we will get you a cure."

Alex opened his eyes, no relief in them.

"All right, kiddo. Whatever you say."

Gurgling and groaning floated around the corner of the junction. The galley cook shuffled around the corner in an unsteady gait, his head tilted to one side and one leg dragged when he walked. His stare landed on them, and a loud shriek rose from deep in his throat, a signal for others to come. He sprang forward, and an uproar of other shrieks and hisses echoed as the rest of the nearby infected came running around the bend.

"Run!" Alex shouted. He shoved her down the dark supply-room passageway.

They ran, supply-storage cages whizzing by. At this speed, they crossed the quartermaster's office in seconds. The infected, who was formerly Mac Osborn, threw himself against the cage, shrieking and spitting as they sprinted by. The pack of infected kept pace with Alex and Abelone but did not gain on them.

Abelone kept her eyes on the exit light above the growing door in front of her. Her lungs burned from the exertion, and her temples pounded with pumping blood. Little by little, Alex fell behind.

Abelone got to the door and opened it. The shrieks and hisses were close behind her. She turned to look back just as Alex reached over her shoulder, grabbed the side of the door with one hand, and shoved her through the opening with the other.

She fell and turned to see him still inside, holding the door ajar. His body blocked the way, and three infected latched onto his back. His eyes were already completely black, and his skin was a tint of grey. The infected sank their teeth deep into his neck and arms.

"Three minutes, thirty-seven seconds," Alex muttered, "give or take." Then, with one last smile, he slammed the door shut. The latch engaged with a definitive click. Barely a foot away, on the other side of the hatch, Alex screamed.

Abelone sank to her knees, the palms of her hands on the door. She barely registered the cold air on her sweaty face. The wind jostled her hair, covering part of her face. But all she knew was her friend's screams. It lasted for thirty seconds, then it stopped. She knelt there listening, barely breathing. In one swoop, she was overcome with emotion. She sobbed angrily and hit the door with the underside of her fists.

"Why! How is this happening?" she screamed. Her anger matched her pain. The furious banging of multiple hands on the other side of the door answered her. She hit her side even harder, her bleeding fists shooting pain up her arms.

How are you still alive? That was her one question. There was no logic behind what was happening. After some time, she stopped her assault on the door. She rested her bleeding hands on her lap and her forehead on the metal door. Abelone focused on the drumming from the other side. The rhythm lulled her into a trance as she sobbed quietly with her eyes closed. She stayed there, unaware of the time. Focused only on the rhythm.

7

MAYBE HE WASN'T BITTEN

More than a few moments passed before Abelone realized the banging had changed to a thumping. She opened her eyes and looked up while resting her right palm on the door. *They've stopped.* No banging came from the other side, but the rhythmic thumping kept going. *What is that noise?*

She got up and noticed her surroundings for the first time. She was on the outside rear under-deck of the Henry Dawson, a couple of levels up from the water and a ladder away from the main weather deck. The thumping was coming from above, out of sight. She cautiously made her way up.

A few stairs from the top, she stopped and peeked over the edge. The air trembled around her every time there was a thump. Above her, floating twenty metres over the Henry Dawson, was a massive four-blade bright yellow helicopter. It had a red and white Canadian flag emblazoned on the tail.

The Cormorant!

Abelone watched from her hiding spot while the massive helicopter circled the Henry Dawson. She noticed the ship had slowed to allow the Cormorant to match its speed. *Fields must be adjusting the ship's speed,* she thought.

She considered running into the open to wave at the helicopter, but she was afraid there might be infected on the main deck. The noise and visual stimulus of the huge yellow helicopter would surely act as a beacon for them. So she waited patiently. Her attention shifted back and forth between the deck and the helicopter. A few minutes went by, and nothing happened.

She was crouching near the top of the ladder, below the eyeline of anyone who might be on the main deck, when the large side door of the Cormorant slid open. Two men in orange jumpsuits appeared and started attaching something to the winch outside the opening.

Her peripheral vision caught movement on the deck. Squinting to see clearer in the bright sunlight, Abelone made out a man crouching between the empty helicopter hangar and a stack of crates. Like her, he was watching for any sign of the infected. *He's afraid of going out in the open, too.* She wondered who he was. From this far away, she couldn't recognize the person, but she could tell he had engineer coveralls on.

The men in the helicopter had attached a rescue basket to their winch and slid it out into the open with another orange jumpsuit-clad man in it. *They are sending someone down!* She choked out a *no* and waved her arms frantically. As much as she wanted help, her innate drive to control any virus outbreak was steadfast. The ship needed to be quarantined. But from her hiding spot, the helicopter crew could not see her. She had to do something and looked for the engineer by the hangar. He was nowhere to be seen.

The rescue basket of the Cormorant descended toward the deck. *I need to warn them!* She contemplated running out in the open to wave them off. *Why are they doing this? They can't have communicated with Fields on the bridge; she doesn't have the ICOMs yet*—she swore at herself for not thinking of it sooner. She dug through her large parka pockets and pulled out one of the yellow ICOMs the captain had given her to bring to the bridge. Holding her unit with two slightly shaking hands, she switched the radio on and held the transmit button down.

"Cormorant. Cormorant. Hello. Can you hear me?" Letting go of the transmit button, she waited. Silence. She pressed down on the channel button and tried the next channel. "Cormorant. Hello? Hello?" Nothing. She cycled through two more channels when, finally, the ICOM crackled back.

"This is the Cormorant 904 of the Royal Canadian Air Force. Henry Dawson, do you copy?"

Abelone almost screamed when she heard the voice. "Do not come on the ship. I repeat, do not come on the ship!"

The rescue basket, with the man in the orange jumpsuit, was halfway to the deck.

"Who is this? Are you an officer of the ship?"

"Listen to me! Do not board this ship. There is a viral outbreak. Anyone who comes onto this ship is putting their lives in danger. My name is Abelone Jensen; I am the assigned epidemiologist from the WHO for a viral outbreak mission to Nuuk. We found . . . there was . . ." She was not sure how to describe what was happening, so she kept it simple. "If you board this ship, your lives will be in danger."

Abelone felt like screaming, but her years of dealing with viral outbreaks took over and kept her under control. After an unusually long pause, the voice came back on.

"Ms. Jensen, we have you listed as the Head of the Danish Institute of Rare Viral Diseases. Please confirm."

"Yes! That's me!" Her shout into the ICOM led to another long pause.

The basket jarred to a halt four feet from the deck.

"Ms. Jensen, we've been trying to make radio contact with the Henry Dawson for hours. We're glad to finally get through. We will retract our rescue basket and personnel. However, I need to talk to the captain."

The winch reversed its pull, and the rescue basket moved up slowly.

A scream came from the deck. "No! Take us off this ship!" The engineer jumped out from behind a stack of crates and sprinted to the rescue basket.

The trap was sprung. As soon as the man ran into the open, three infected appeared from behind the helicopter hangar. They swooped in on him as he jumped up and grabbed the railing of the rescue basket, his weight pulling it down a couple of feet.

"Take me up, please!" the crewman begged.

The rescuer instinctively reached over the edge and grabbed the man under his armpits to stop him from sliding off. The basket's momentum recovered from the added weight and resumed its upward journey, but the infected had latched on to the engineer's waist.

The additional weight reversed the direction of the basket again and pulled the whole thing toward the deck. The engineer screamed as the infected bit him at his waist above his belt. Blood dripped from the crewman's legs onto the large white H of the helipad.

The winch squealed in effort, and the whole contraption sounded like it was going to snap. But it didn't. Despite three infected latched to the crewman, who in turn was latched to the basket, the rescue basket reversed direction once more and headed upwards—slower this time.

The rescuer in the orange jumpsuit leaned over the basket's side, reached one arm over the crewman's head and grabbed him by the belt to heave him up. That was when one of the infected grabbed his hand and tried to bite it. *Did he get bitten?* Abelone couldn't tell, but she needed to warn him. *If he got bitten . . .* The man pulled his arm free from his attacker and punched two of them off. Both fell four feet to the deck and landed on their backs.

The rescuer leaned over the edge again and pulled the engineer further up. The last infected lost his grip and fell six feet down, landing on top of the other infected who'd started getting up—they all shrieked in frustration. In one final heave, the rescuer pulled the engineer over the basket railing.

Abelone watched anxiously as the rescue basket made its way up to the Cormorant when the yellow ICOM, still in her hand, buzzed to life and startled her.

"Ms. Jensen, what the hell is going on? What was wrong with those men?" The voice from the helicopter asked, confused and angry. "Where is Captain Vanderfeld?"

Abelone ignored the questions.

"Please listen to me. You must not bring that engineer into your helicopter. He is infected," she whispered into the radio. She tracked both the basket, which was rising, and the three infected on the helipad, who were limping in circles, staring up at the giant yellow form in the sky.

"Please say that again, Ms. Jensen. We can barely hear you. Speak up; the engines make it hard to hear."

"Don't bring those men up," she said a bit louder as the basket got closer to the Cormorant sliding door. *He has to hear me. They are our hope of rescue.*

"Don't bring those men up!" she repeated louder.

One of the infected on the helipad turned her way.

Too loud! The horrible realization made her bladder void urine down her leg.

The infected's black eyes and twitching head sized her up, and he released a loud gargle from deep in his chest. He cocked his head and sprinted at her. The two other infected also looked her way, then followed the first in a dash.

Abelone spun around as she dropped the ICOM into her parka pocket. She stopped. At the bottom of the stairs stood a mountain of a man looking up at her. *Powers!* His skin was rotten grey, most of his hair had fallen out, and there was dry, caked blood all over his jaw.

Abelone barely missed a beat and changed her direction. She headed for three large piles of crates on the port side of the helipad. Each pile was tied down with cargo nets over six feet high. She quickly climbed the cargo net of the nearest pile as the three infected reached her.

With their arms outstretched, they could almost grab her feet. She focused on keeping her balance in the middle of the crates, barely out of reach of the grasping hands. She looked for an escape route. Powers was at the top of the stairs. With his long reach, she wouldn't stand a chance. She eyed the next stack of crates four feet away, then took a deep breath and with a two-step start, she lunged over the gap and landed on the neighbouring pile of crates.

She wobbled for a second but found her balance. Abelone looked back. Two of the infected had crawled up the nets and reached the top of her previous pile. They seemed confused to find her gone.

What now? She needed to move again. Powers and the other infected on the deck rushed to the bottom of her new perch and grasped at her feet. The two infected who had climbed her previous crate spotted her and took off toward her.

Oh God, they're going to jump!

When the infected hit the gap between the piles of crates, to Abelone's surprise, they didn't take flight. Instead, both their legs gave way under them. Their momentum sent them forward but downwards, and they crashed into the side of Abelone's new pile of crates, making the whole thing shake.

They can't jump! she thought as she looked on in relief. *They can climb, but the bastards can't jump!* Her scientific mind assessed this new fact. She figured either proprioception or gravity must be too complex for their infected brain.

Roger Powers' huge hand came up the side of her tower of crates and snagged her by the ankle, making her fall. Abelone barely managed to wrap her arm around the cargo net in time to stop from falling to the deck. She kicked, frenzied, at Powers' hand with her other leg, and when she broke free from the giant's grip, she did not hesitate. Abelone darted to a third pile of crates, jumping over the gap again. This time, however, Powers' long waving arms smacked her feet in mid-air as she sailed over his head. It tipped Abelone forward, and she tumbled onto the top of the next set of crates and spilled over the furthest edge.

Abelone grasped for the cargo net and managed to slow her fall, but she still landed hard on the metal deck. Her ears rang from the impact, and she considered not getting up. Her heart was fighting to explode out of her chest. The smell of urine wafted up to her nostrils, reminding her she had peed on herself. The day flashed through her mind and finally rested on one image that motivated her—Alex.

She sprang up. Spotting the open garage door of the Bo 105 hangar, she made a dash for it as the smaller, faster infected came around the corner of the crates. Reaching it, she jumped and grabbed the long manual chain of the hangar door and put all her weight into pulling it down. The large metal contraption crashed down as the infected reached it, trapping an arm between it and the deck. The arm got crushed, but it acted like a wedge, stopping the door from fully closing. Within seconds, several hands slipped into the small gap, and the door started to rise inch by inch.

Abelone looked around frantically, trying not to fixate on the seemingly disembodied fingers reaching for her. Her gaze caught on a fire axe. She pulled the cold metal tool from its hook and hefted it, adjusting to its weight as she strode back to the arm beneath the heavy door. With a quiver in her chest, she set her legs and aimed the axe at the elbow of the trapped arm.

She stood with the axe over the arm and stared at it. If this was Alex's arm, would she chop it off? What will happen to this person after he loses his arm? Will he bleed out and die? After what felt like an eternity, and slowly bringing the axe up and down countless times while the door crept higher, she held her breath, the axe at its apex. Seconds went by. Abelone made a decision. The axe came down, striking the metal deck beside the arm. She couldn't bring herself to sever it. She took one hand off the axe, and the heaviness of it swung to her side, with her other hand holding the handle. Abelone bowed her head and shook it. She could save these people.

The door of the hangar nudged up more as half a dozen hands lifted in an uncoordinated fashion. When the gap below the door was big enough, the head and upper torso attached to the crushed arm slowly squirmed through. Abelone moved to the back of the hangar. She positioned herself behind a large orange zodiac, the axe held in front of her. The infected's scalp was partially hairless, and his shoulders were covered in dried black blood. A massive chunk of his nape had been ripped off, and a loose muscle was hanging from the wound. As the infected gained his feet, she caught a glimpse of bone sticking out of the crushed forearm. The infected's arm stretched out with his useless hand hanging limp.

The infected moved forward, never taking his dark-black eyes off her. Behind him, the other infected were still clumsily lifting the wide hangar door when suddenly, it slipped from their hands and slammed down on the deck. The noise startled the infected with the broken arm, and he turned to the source.

Move! The distraction was all Abelone needed. She sprinted to the ladder, which went up to the hangar's ceiling. She reached it before the infected reacted and scaled to the top. Out of breath, she turned and saw the infected had clumsily wrapped his arms on the ladder and placed his feet on the rungs, pulling himself up laboriously.

Abelone pulled herself outside through the hangar trapdoor. The wind chilled her warmed-up cheeks. She slammed the trapdoor shut and slid the axe between the handle and the U-shaped hold to secure it.

From where she stood, she couldn't see the infected, but she could hear their hisses and shrieks. She did, however, have a close-up view of the Cormorant barely twenty metres above the ship and still matching the Henry Dawson's speed. From her perch, she could see the pilot of the massive helicopter. She brought her hand to her mouth to stymie a scream when she saw the pilot in a fight with another man in an orange jumpsuit.

Despite the rush of the wind, the thumping of the helicopter blades, and the shrieks of the infected, Abelone heard a soft popping. Something flashed inside the Cormorant, followed by a splattering of blood across the inside of the cockpit glass.

He shot him! Maybe he wasn't bitten. That hope dissipated quickly when Abelone saw two more silhouettes spill into the cockpit, and the pilot had to fight for his life again. She heard two more gunshots, but saw no blood splatters this time.

The Cormorant swayed side to side, followed by a few hard dips. Abelone's eyes widened, and she held her breath as the massive yellow helicopter took one more turbulent dip straight toward the hangar she was standing on.

She ran for the back edge of the hangar. As she reached it, the Cormorant hit the front of the structure. The thin sheet metal walls and roof of the hangar crumpled like paper. The collision of the helicopter into the hangar shook the Henry Dawson from aft to stern. The ship moaned a painful metal song as every rivet strained against the torquing force of the impact.

Abelone launched herself off the end of the hangar and, fifteen feet above the ground, grabbed a snapped wire that normally stabilized the hangar against the wind. She swung away from the crumpling hangar and slammed into the wall of the superstructure a few metres away, knocking the wind out of her lungs. Hanging there, trying to breathe, she half let go and half slid down the wire, falling the remaining distance to the deck.

The Cormorant plowed through the small hangar. Its nose tore deep into the deck. The massive yellow helicopter ground to a halt barely metres from Abelone.

The smell of gasoline filled the air, and the heat of the crashed helicopter engine warmed her face. The infected, who hadn't been ripped to pieces by the Cormorant, ran in frenzied circles, stirred up by the crash. More infected emerged from the carcass of the burning yellow behemoth, like spiderlings from a killed spider. An infected saw her and shrieked as it navigated its way over the smoking debris to get to her.

Abelone painfully picked herself up from the deck—still dazed by the impact with the wall—and hobbled toward the port side walkway lining the superstructure. She limped as fast as she could and slammed the superstructure door closed as soon as she was through. Abelone didn't stop until she reached the medical bay. Dried blood covered the deck and bulkheads. Her senses were becoming attuned to which noises signalled a threat, so she heard them before she saw them. The inconsistent running footsteps were coming from the small passageway ahead of her.

I can't catch a break!

She turned back and ran to the stairs, heading away from the bridge. She sprinted down as three infected came rampaging around the corner of the side passageway beyond the medical bay.

When she reached the level below, she darted to the open door of the mess deck, where she had been safe earlier. She could hear the shrieks of the infected on the stairs behind her as she jumped through the door Alex had pulled her and the captain through. Holding her breath, she quietly closed it behind her as the three pursuing infected reached the bottom of the stairs. She stood motionless and peeked through the round window as they ran by hunting for her. When they disappeared down another set of stairs, she breathed out in relief.

Her breath was too loud. She needed to calm herself. Abelone took slower, deeper breaths. Still too loud. Her brow furrowed, and her breathing stopped.

It's not me, she thought as a gargle mixed with the heavy breathing. She spun around. The blood in her veins turned ice cold. An infected stood at the opposite side of the mess deck, in front of the galley freezer. Their eyes locked, and Abelone recognized him—*Tom Virtanen.*

He was standing hunched over, looking straight at her. Most of his hair had fallen out; his dark-grey skin was lumpy and putrescent. His Coast Guard uniform was almost completely covered in dried blood, but the blood was not his own. She got a better look at him this time and didn't see any bites. *Maybe he wasn't bitten?*

Abelone and Tom stared at each other. Seconds ticked by. Sweat trickled down Abelone's back, making her shiver, and she realized she was still wearing the heavy parka.

Tom hissed and lurched forward, meandering around the bolted tables to get to her. She countered, moving sideways behind the other tables. Virtanen kept coming at her, but Abelone kept moving, keeping tables between them. They played cat-and-mouse until Virtanen climbed onto a table and paused.

Abelone didn't move, unsure what he was doing. He lurched forward again, this time scrambling over tables and chairs. Abelone was more surprised by how he had adapted to the situation than scared. She stumbled back into the galley. Her thick parka caught on the serving counter railing. She pulled at it once but couldn't pry it loose. She unzipped it in one swoop and spun out of it like a clumsy ballerina, knocking over pots and pans from the counter in the process. Everything crashed to the ground with a clatter.

Within seconds, Tom was on her. She blindly grabbed something and swung it. It caught him on the head as he dove for her with his arms outstretched. The impact redirected his momentum, and he crashed to the ground beside her. As he groaned and squirmed, she glanced at the dented steel frying pan in her hands.

From this close, she could see his fully black irises and dozens of black veins meandering around his sclerae. The smell of his breath made her gag.

Abelone bounced up to a crouch and moved back toward the freezer, glancing at the mess-deck door and wondering if she had the time to reach it. She hesitated too long. Tom rolled over and lunged at her from the ground. She swung the frying pan again, hitting him on the shoulder this time. It changed his trajectory enough that he continued straight past her into the freezer and collided head-first into metal shelving, which collapsed on top of him. He shrieked, in what Abelone assumed was anger, and quickly pushed the shelving aside, then recoiled to pounce back through the freezer door. Abelone kicked the door shut with a slam, and the metal popped out where Tom's head collided with it.

Abelone got up quickly. *There!* She grabbed the large freezer padlock from the galley counter, jammed it into the door handle and snapped it shut. She stood stunned for a few seconds. She had Patient Zero. Her satisfaction disappeared when Tom hammered wildly at the door from the inside. The ferocity of his attacks made her hesitate, but she slowly moved to the door and peered through the thick square window. It took a few seconds for her eyes to adapt to the darkness inside, and his face materialized a few inches from hers. Black drool spilled from his mouth.

The door shook from Tom's hammering. The lock rattled in place, and Abelone noticed the keys jiggling in it. She pulled them out, nervous the lock might open, and tossed them in the sink.

"You're the answer to this riddle, Tom, and you're not going any-where."

8

BELLY OF THE BEAST

C aptain Vanderfeld and Doc Martel sneaked their way from the mess-deck passageway, where they'd split up from Abelone and Alex, all the way to the engine room on the lowest deck of the ship. The massive diesel engines rumbled along, propelling the Henry Dawson through the Atlantic toward the coast of Labrador.

The lower deck, so far, was eerily empty. Vanderfeld looked up and down the passageway nervously. *Will they be alive?* he wondered as he placed both hands alongside the door's round window to look inside. Doc Martel stood back to back with him, keeping an eye on the passageway.

All the lights in the engine room were off, and it was too dark to see. The captain slowly turned the door latch, but it jammed after a few inches, blocked by something on the inside. He considered knocking on the window, but Doc Martel tapped him on the shoulder and tensely pointed down the passageway where the corridor bifurcated. A dozen or so infected shuffled around the corner. The group of defiled sailors had not spotted them yet. Vanderfeld and Martel leaned tightly against the bulkhead, partially hidden by pipes that stretched from deck to overhead. He'd never felt so trapped in his own ship. They were hidden but would be visible shortly as the group of infected ambulated slowly in their direction.

A young, grease-covered face with big, round eyes appeared in the little window of the engine-room door. Startled, Vanderfeld took a step backwards, bumping into Doc Martel, which sent the doctor stumbling into the middle of the passage.

The pack of infected stopped in their tracks, more surprised than startled by the appearance of the man in front of them. After a very long and tense few seconds, the lead infected shrieked and ran at them. The rest followed suit, hissing and gurgling in excitement.

Vanderfeld banged on the engine-room door frantically.

"Let us in! They're coming!"

"Are you bitten?" the young man yelled from the other side of the door.

"What! Let us in. That's an order!" screamed Vanderfeld.

"Captain, we need to go!" Doc Martel joined the yelling.

The young engineer on the other side of the door was paralyzed in fear. Vanderfeld realized he would not open the door, but as he was turning away, JD Percival—the ship's chief engineer—shoved the young man aside. The sound of metal sliding against metal resonated through the door, and it swung open. Both the captain and the doctor jumped inside as the chief engineer slammed the door behind them.

The infected started hammering at the metal door. This door was built to resist thousands of pounds of ocean pressure if the ship were to sink, so the door would not budge.

"Captain, you're alive!" Percival bellowed while sliding a two-foot-long metal wrench into the door latch. He hugged both men energetically.

The chief dove right into his recounting of how he and his engineers had barricaded themselves in the engine room after they saw a half-dozen infected attack some of the gear heads.

When his story was finished, he asked, "Captain, what is going on?"

"We don't know, but it's ugly. Some sort of virus. It gets passed through bites or blood. That's the best guess those scientists had." Vanderfeld paused, counting the men in the room to confirm how many there were. "With us, in this room, it means there are at least eleven non-infected I know of."

"That leaves potentially over twenty infected if we assume everyone else is compromised," added Doc Martel.

"Twenty? Eleven left?" Percival looked at them.

"Fields and Mr. Brown from the CDC are locked in the bridge. Ms. Jensen and Mr. Deangelo were heading back to the bridge with an ICOM last we saw them, and—" Vanderfeld realized what he had said. He fished through his jacket pocket and pulled his ICOM out.

Everyone in the engine room went quiet and clustered around him. He turned the ICOM on, switched the digital channel to seven, and held his breath. Static.

He pressed down on the talk button. "Fields, can you hear me?"

Pause.

Static.

"Fields, are you there?"

More static.

"Maybe they haven't reached the bridge yet," offered Doc Martel, stepping closer to Vanderfeld.

"Maybe . . ." the captain muttered. What if there was no one left out there? Most of his crew was gone, and he had no contact with his bridge, but worst of all, he did not know how to offer hope to his men.

The hammering on the door was non-stop, so the captain and the group moved away and sat together between the two purring diesel engines. Doc Martel tended to an engineer who had banged his head and lay unconscious on a makeshift bed of jackets and blankets. The captain recounted to Percival and his engineers everything that had happened to them. None of it offered hope, but it distracted them with new information. The engineers listened as best they could amidst the relentless onslaught on the engine-room door.

Doc Martel looked at the door, concerned.

"Doc, don't worry. Those doors are made to withstand pressure from a flooded lower deck. It's gonna hold," the chief engineer said when he caught Doc Martel's gaze.

"Yeah, but for how long?"

It was a rhetorical question, but Percival answered it, anyway. "It would take an act of God to weaken those doors—"

Almost on cue, the room shook violently, and the screeching of metal tearing overhead reverberated through the engine room.

What is happening to my ship? Vanderfeld and everyone else were slammed downwards, then up, some almost as high as the ceiling. He was suspended in mid-air before he crashed back to the floor. Bolts popped out of metal bulkheads; lights fell from the ceiling, their bulbs exploding on the ground; pipes burst, spewing steam, and the ship contorted and moaned as if it would snap. Finally, it stopped.

"What the hell was that?" yelled the chief engineer as he picked himself up.

"Something hit us. Something big," replied Vanderfeld as he helped a few crewmen get up.

"An iceberg, maybe?" one engineer said.

"It's not an iceberg. The impact was from above. Something fell out of the sky and crashed into us . . ." Although implausible, the captain realized it could only be one thing. "It has to be the Cormorant."

To his surprise and relief, the ICOM was still in his hand. He called the bridge again. He tried Abelone. He flicked through all the ICOM channels. No answer.

Percival barked orders for his men to check the engines for damage and turned to the captain. "How could they crash into us? What could have happened to them?"

Someone let out a yell. "The door!"

The top hinge of the door had snapped straight off, and the lower hinge, partially broken itself, barely held the door in place. Captain Vanderfeld was the first to look out the window and see the infected slowly getting up from the floor. He inspected the lower hinge and then looked around the engine room.

"Barricade the door!" he shouted.

Everyone who could move at the order stacked things against the barely hanging hinge on the compartment door. The infected started their assault on it again. With each blow, the door rattled and looked like it would buckle. Vanderfeld shouted at his men to keep piling things against it. It took a few minutes, but when everything not bolted down had been moved, the group stood in a semi-circle and watched.

The captain looked at the men and women around him. He saw fear and confusion in their eyes. He opened his mouth to speak but was interrupted by the ICOM coming to life.

"Captain Vanderfeld, are you there?" a voice crackled through.

"Captain Vanderfeld? Can you hear us? Please answer." The voice was clearer this time.

The captain fumbled in his pocket and pulled the survival radio out, almost dropping it. He recognized the voice. "Ms. Jensen? Is that you? We're here!"

"Captain, you're alive, thank God!"

"What hit us? Was it the Cormorant?"

Abelone quickly detailed what befell the rescue helicopter and how she got back to the bridge.

"Ms. Jensen, I need to speak to Fields." Vanderfeld's heart thumped in anticipation. He needed to know she was safe.

"I'll get her, sir. But I need to tell you; she hasn't been totally there since I got back to the bridge. When I told her we had split up and I wasn't sure what had happened to you, she seemed to lose hope and grew more and more distant."

"Let me talk to her."

There was a long pause on the other end of the ICOM, and Vanderfeld grew more restless as the seconds passed. The incessant banging on the engine-room door made the wait worse. Fields' tentative voice came through.

"John, is that you?"

His face softened. "Hey, yes, it's me. I'm alright," he said, relieved.

Fields sobbed loudly on the ICOM. After a few breaths, she stuttered, "I thought you were dead. Abelone didn't know where you were. I thought you'd left me."

"I'm here. I'm still alive. I'm with Doc Martel, the chief and a bunch of his guys. We don't have much time, though. You must listen to me." He wanted to hold and keep her safe, but there was something more important to tend to right now.

"What do you mean you don't have much time? What's wrong?"

"Listen to me," Vanderfeld said more sternly than he'd wanted. "You need to set a course for Peaks Bay. It's thirty hours away, but it's the only hope we have to get help. They have a deep enough harbour for the ship and a Canadian Forces military hospital that will be able to take point on the quarantine. We'll keep the engines running down here. All you have to do is steer the ship."

Fields didn't respond to the order.

"Fields . . . Becky . . . tell me you understand."

"Yes . . . I got it . . . set a course for Peaks Bay. I'll do it right now," Fields answered, followed by a determined sniff. "John, the Cormorant . . ."

"Yes, I know."

"The damage, it doesn't seem to have hindered the ship too much," Fields said, a tinge of hope in her voice. Vanderfeld didn't tell her the infected were close to breaking in. She didn't need to hear that. Not yet.

"Be careful down there. I love you," she said.

He turned his back instinctively to his men but did not respond in kind to her declaration of love. To his relief, Abelone came back onto the radio.

"Captain, Peaks Bay? Are you sure?"

"It's the best place to go, based on what you told me about how infectious this virus is. Peaks Bay is as isolated as it gets. It barely has a couple thousand inhabitants, but more importantly, the town has a harbour deep enough to accommodate the Henry Dawson. And a small military hospital meant to serve northern Labrador and northern Quebec. It's run by a handful of civilian medical personnel and some military Field Ambulance officers." He paused, waiting for her reaction, but it was the first thing he'd been sure about since realizing how bad this virus was.

"You're right, Captain," Abelone said, with no hesitation in her voice.

"Make sure Fields gets us there okay," he said, almost calling her Becky instead of Fields. "Let's save the ICOM batteries and touch point every fifteen minutes." He put the ICOM away and joined Chief Percival, who sat on a stool in the middle of the large room, staring at the engine-room door. The door rattled every time an infected smashed against it. And every time, Vanderfeld thought the remaining hinge would break.

***

Vanderfeld looked at his watch. Twenty hours had passed since the Henry Dawson's course had been adjusted for Peaks Bay. Neither he nor his sailors had been able to get any sleep. Like the ceaseless bass from an inconsiderate neighbour, the constant drumming of arms against the door, bone against metal, and the ear-splitting shrieks kept everyone in the engine room up. They were all jittery, and Vanderfeld did not know how much longer they could stay sane. He prayed they would last until they reached Peaks Bay.

Vanderfeld got up and walked to Doc Martel, who sat beside the still unconscious engineer with the head injury. "How's he doing?"

"He's in and out of consciousness. If we get him to a hospital, he might recover. Looks like a pretty bad concussion."

The unconscious man looked serene and clean, while Doc Martel was a frazzled mess with his blood-covered uniform shirt. The dried blood made the light blue shirt match his dark navy pants. The ICOM in Vanderfeld's pocket buzzed.

"John, are you there?" the soft voice of Rebecca Fields crackled from the yellow radio.

"Yeah, I'm still here, Becky. They haven't made chow food of us yet."

The pause on the other end made him realize Fields did not find his humour funny. "Sorry. Bad joke, I know."

"You have to come back to me. It can't end like this," she answered.

"I will, I promise." His heart ached. He wanted to be there for her. He wanted to be there for his crew and his ship.

"I've made the final course adjustment for Peaks Bay," Fields said, more composed. "At this speed, we should be at Huntingdon Island in eight hours. Once we get there, we can adjust speed to ease through the shallower waters between the island and the mainland, and I can navigate us into a safe position in the harbour—"

"—and from there, we should be able to contact the mainland with the ICOM. It'll be imperative they not board us until they've set up proper quarantine protocols," Vanderfeld finished her train of thought. Maybe there was hope after all. He breathed a sigh of relief, innumerable hours of stress flowing out. His peace was short-lived. From behind the captain came a shout.

"They're coming through!"

Vanderfeld spun in time to see the final hinge twist as the door slowly bent inward.

"What? What's going on, John?" Rebeca yelled through the ICOM.

"Get the ship to safety in that harbour. And remember . . . I love you."

The captain calmly switched off the ICOM and slid it back into his pocket. He walked to the semi-circle of men facing the barricaded door and picked up a large red wrench from the floor. The metal felt cold and heavy in his hands. He took up position in front of his men without saying a word. He nodded toward Doc Martel, and the good doctor pulled the unconscious sailor behind one of the engines.

Vanderfeld stood as tall as he could amidst his crew. That led to his men standing taller around him. They were armed with whatever they could find: crowbars, wrenches and anything else swingable. They stood patiently, waiting for the inevitable. Finally, the door fell inward onto the makeshift barricade. This reinvigorated the infected. They slammed against it, pushing and pulling at whatever they could grab. When the barricade was ajar enough for them to slip in, they started cramming into the engine room, hissing and shrieking, angry at having been kept at bay for so long.

"These might have been our friends, but they aren't anymore. It's time to stand up for our ship! It's time to stand up for our fallen comrades!" Captain Vanderfeld shouted at his men and charged straight for the first infected. He swung his wrench in a wide arc and hit the infected square on the temple. The makeshift weapon cracked through the skull and penetrated the former sailor's brain. The infected crumpled to the floor; the wrench held deep inside the head by the suction of the cranium's soft matter.

The engineers watched their captain's display of bravery and grotesque slaughter, frozen in fear and awe.

The second infected to wedge through the door went straight for Vanderfeld. With difficulty, the captain pulled the wrench out of the first infected's head with a slurp, in time to cock his arm back and swing it again in a similar arc. This time, the wrench caught the infected on the forehead and bounced off, peeling away skin and revealing bone and dark, gooey blood. The blow barely slowed the infected. It leapt onto him and grabbed him by the chest.

Two other infected squeezed through the barricade and swarmed him; the first's teeth sank into his neck, which triggered a scream of orgasmic pain. His howl was cut off by a second bite into his jaw, right through his thick grey beard. Blood spurted upward from a punctured artery. A fourth infected joined the fray and grabbed the captain's legs, sinking its teeth into one of his thighs and ripping through the grey Coast Guard-issued pants. Captain Vanderfeld went down slowly, with four infected latched on to him. The grey bodies of former sailors who once admired and followed him dragged him to the floor, and he was lost under a pile of frenzied grey bodies. The last thing that went through his mind was his hope that the Henry Dawson would make it to Peaks Bay and Becky would be okay.

***

Martel watched, frozen in place. His captain had fallen, his friend John, the leader of everyone in the engineering room. A guttural scream burst from Martel's lungs, followed by screams from every other sailor in the room. They all stormed the incoming infected. They smashed and stabbed at their former shipmates—yelling at the top of their lungs as much in anger as in fear. The group of survivors got the upper hand early, knocking three infected down quickly. Martel's fear subsided momentarily. Until those infected started to get back up.

More infected kept streaming in via the breached door. Even though the sailors kept knocking them down, the infected would get back up, and slowly, one after the other, the survivors were dragged down, and the tide shifted. Bodies on the ground were ripped apart by gnashing teeth and tearing fingernails. The pool of blood around Captain Vanderfeld expanded with the blood of his sailors. Pretty soon, half of the engine-room deck was painted red.

Doc Martel backed up and looked at the unconscious engineer. He had to defend that man. He ran around the engine corner, but slammed right into a walking wall—Roger Powers. The man was almost as tall as the engines. His rolled-up sleeves exposed large black veins popping out of his arms. As Doc Martel bounced off Powers, the behemoth emitted a gurgling from deep inside his soot-coloured throat.

Martel looked for a weapon, anything he could swing. He picked up a screwdriver and hesitantly stepped between the unconscious sailor and the infected mastodon. His heart raced, and sweat trickled down his forehead as he held the screwdriver in front of him. When Powers reached out, shrieking in glee, Martel sidestepped away from the arms and stabbed him in the belly. The makeshift weapon penetrated the skin easily, and thick black blood trickled out like molasses.

Martel stared at the ineffective wound. The giant infected grabbed the shorter doctor by the head like a basketball. Despite his corpulent size, Martel felt himself lifted and felt the pressure mount in his suddenly brittle skull between the two giant grey paws. Black gums and a black tongue waited for him between stained teeth, with snippets of skin stuck between them.

Doc Martel noticed something else too: Powers' submandibular glands, the ones below the jawline, were swollen and black, standing out from the sickly grey skin. Not the same black as the infected's eyes or even the blood oozing out of the screwdriver wound. He recognized what he was seeing. He'd seen glands like that in medical books and online.

It's a variant of the plague! A bacterium turned into a virus? How can that be... but it's the plague! I have the blood samples of the original virus in the sickbay. We can make a vaccine. Abelone is right!

Powers' vile, acidic breath made him gag, and with his vision blurring, Martel swung his right arm at the big man's face. The screwdriver caught Roger Powers square in the temple, puncturing cleanly through the softer tissue between the temporal and parietal bone plates and sinking deep into the brain behind the eyeball.

Powers swayed on his feet, still holding Martel. He teetered, fell forward and landed face down on top of the doctor, who cracked his head on the metal deck. Martel's already blurred vision began to spin—again. The weight on top of him expelled the air from his lungs. Blackness crept in. The last thing Doc Martel saw as he lay under the limp body of Roger Powers was two other infected ripping into the unconscious sailor he was protecting. Then, for the second time that day, Doc Martel passed out.

9

THE LAST BITE

T he early afternoon sun glimmered on the calm ocean water, and the blue sky was cloudless. A band of greyish haze on the horizon separated the sky and ocean. For a few seconds, Abelone forgot about the infection, forgot about the infected, and simply admired the view out of the bridge's large windows. It had been over an hour since their last communication with Captain Vanderfeld. They had all heard the captain's goodbye to Fields when the engineering door was breached, and then nothing.

Fields sat at the command island, her hands on her knees, simply staring at the yellow ICOM. Every five minutes, she would pick it up and call out to see if someone answered. When no answer came forth, she would put the ICOM back down and stare at it some more.

Abelone had made it back to the bridge after her encounter with Tom Virtanen in the mess deck, barely encountering any infected. She deduced most had been attracted to the engine room, somehow summoned there by the other infected. The lone infected she had crossed paths with had looked disoriented and more scared of her than she was of him. He had lost his mind; he grabbed a lifebuoy and hurled himself overboard, screaming. It was odd behaviour for an infected, who was already prone to the odd behaviour of trying to bite people.

All the infected were back now; more than a half-dozen had found their way to the outside deck door, while some were at the passageway door. Former sailors, covered in blood with grey putrescent skin, black eyes and gnashing teeth. Their arms were deformed by bruises and broken bones from their incessant use as battering rams, and all had bite marks on their exposed skin. The hammering on the doors was non-stop, but more and more, Abelone was confident they would make it to Peaks Bay alive. They would make land. They would get help. They would create a vaccine. People could be saved.

Abelone squeezed her arms around herself to stay warm due to the cool air flowing in through the broken bridge window. She longed for her discarded parka.

When a dark line appeared through the band of greyish haze on the horizon, it took her a few seconds to realize what it was.

Land!

She grabbed the binoculars from the command island. Squinting through the field glasses, the coast of Labrador materialized.

"Land!"

"Rebecca, land!" she said again, her half-cheer attracting Jon to her side.

Fields didn't look up, still transfixed on the yellow ICOM. Abelone looked at the Officer of the Watch. She walked over and shook her gently to stir her from her stupor. Fields looked up.

"Land," Abelone said and handed Fields the binoculars.

Fields brought the binoculars to her eyes. "Peaks Bay is behind the island we can see on the right. I'll adjust our course for their harbour," she said dispassionately.

"Damn, we're going to make it after all. I was sure we were going to be in this tin can forever," Jon said, half-smiling at Abelone.

Fields spent the next ten minutes adjusting the course and speed of the Henry Dawson. On her own, it was a slow process, but finally, she looked up. "Done. When we are closer to the harbour, I can adjust the speed down so we can cruise in and set anchor a few miles out. That way, no one will be able to board us right away."

The lack of emotion in her voice was disconcerting, but Abelone pushed it from her mind. "Jon, once we are within range, we'll need to radio the harbour and issue a quarantine warning so no one approaches the ship. They will need to contact the WHO and the CDC immediately to get some teams flown up here."

"How close do we have to be for the ICOM to reach the mainland?" asked Jon.

Shrugging, Abelone asked Fields. "Rebecca, what is the range on these things? How far out will we be able to make contact?"

When Fields did not answer, Abelone and Jon turned to where she had been sitting. Finding the chair empty, Abelone's gaze darted around the bridge and found Fields standing across the room in front of the passageway door. She was staring through the round window into a familiar face—the bearded face of Captain John Vanderfeld. Abelone's eyes squeezed once, and her throat constricted when she noticed Fields had one hand flat against the window . . . and the other on the door latch.

Despite the noise from the onslaught of arms against metal and the wind rushing in from the broken window, Abelone heard Fields say, "You've come back to me, my love."

Every muscle in Abelone's body tensed when Fields lifted the latch and swung the door open.

Captain Vanderfeld stood in the doorframe, straight and tall as always. But he wasn't the same man. Not anymore. Even from across the bridge, Abelone could see his black eyes and the missing chunks of skin and muscle in his neck and face. His shoulders and captain's epaulettes were dark with blood. Vanderfeld stretched out his arms toward Fields, his—former—lover. He seemed to want to embrace her. Fields, mesmerized, responded likewise and reached out for him. She walked straight into his comforting arms, and they wrapped around her. She looked up and drew in closer to kiss him. As their faces met, for a split second, Abelone thought they were kissing, until blood dripped from Fields' chin. The captain's grey beard turned red as blood soaked into it, and his teeth dug deep into Rebecca Fields' lips.

Abelone stared until, from behind the two lovers, infected after infected spilled in, all tripping over each other, shrieking, and sprinting toward her and Jon.

"Storage closet!" Jon shoved Abelone toward it.

Everything happened so fast. When Abelone grabbed the storage-closet handle, a cold grey hand with encrusted fingernails grabbed her forearm. She pulled the door open, but with the infected pulling her forearm at the same time, the door flew open and hit the infected in the face, staggering it back. Another pair of hands grabbed her by the right shoulder.

"Abby!" Jon was beside her. With one hand, he grabbed the infected holding her and ripped it off. As she turned her head, she was shocked to see Jon holding on to two more infected on top of the one he had pulled off her. He had slipped his left arm out of his sling, and blood seeped through his bandage. The three infected he was holding back were creating a logjam in front of the rest, who were still coming in through the open door of the bridge. It looked like the entirety of the Henry Dawson crew was flooding in.

"Get in the closet!" Jon's voice boomed over the shrieks and howling wind. But instead, she reached out to grab him by the collar to help him break free. That was when one infected partially got by Jon. Despite its grey skin and the bite marks all over its face, Abelone recognized Alex Deangelo. For a split second, Abelone and Alex's eyes met. A flicker of hesitation crossed Alex's face, and then he sank his teeth deep into Abelone's left forearm.

Abelone screamed.

"No!" Jon yelled. He kicked Abelone backwards into the storage closet. This made him unstable, and he was overcome by the rest of the pushing infected. The whole pile of bodies fell forward, knocking the storage-closet door shut.

Abelone crashed sideways, and her face smashed into the back wall. Blood poured from her nose and covered her chin and chest. As she rolled back up to her knees, she reached for the door and tried to push it open.

"Jon!" She pushed and pushed, but the door would not budge.

She couldn't leave him out there. Jon screamed, and excited shrieks grew louder in response.

Blood oozed under the door, puddling around Abelone's knees. For the second time that day, she listened to a friend dying a few inches away. She was reliving the nightmare she'd gone through with Alex. When the screams ended, she knew what would come next: the banging on the door would start—it did. She quickly slipped a broom behind the door handle to stop it from moving. The impact of each blow rattled the door and the closet.

Abelone sat against the closet's back wall. The thumping lulled her once more. Jon's blood fully covered the closet floor, and she traced one finger through it mindlessly.

It took Abelone a while to even bother to look at her forearm. The bite was deep, but she could still move her hand. Blood dripped slowly from it. She wrapped a cleaning rag around the wound, then tilted her head back to stop her nosebleed. As she did, her head spun, and her vision blurred. She passed out with one thought flashing in her head—*I've been infected*.

PART II - PEAKS BAY

10

INVISIBLE SCENT OF DEATH

B enjamin Keefer stood by his old Jeep Wrangler, admiring the meandering coastline. The little peninsula below Lookout Point cropped out for five kilometres into the ocean. As the sun rose, the usual morning fog slowly lifted, revealing the small town of Peaks Bay, Labrador.

This never gets old, he thought. Whenever he missed the bright lights and skyscrapers of Montreal, he would drive up to the highest hill behind the little town, and the view would make him feel better.

Enjoy it while I can. He was halfway done with his four-year contract at the Peaks Bay Canadian Army Reserve regiment. It wasn't a regiment in the true sense of the word but a rag-tag group of local part-time government employees and rescue volunteers who maintained the basic military hospital facilities in case they were ever needed for emergencies. He'd been sent here from the 51st Field Ambulance in Montreal to spruce up the military medical facilities with the new local hospital, which had opened due to the town's growth following an eco-tourism boom.

Peaks Bay had exploded from a cozy hamlet of five hundred people to a booming town of over two thousand. Ever since the Trans-Labrador Highway had been built, linking Peaks Bay to Quebec City and Montreal, tourists and tourist companies had flocked to the little settlement. It helped that it was the one coastal settlement in Labrador that boasted a natural harbour deep enough to welcome the giant cruise ships that were migrating to northern landscapes. The cruise industry was expanding and in search of new tourist attractions: whale and sea bird watching; tours of Iceberg Alley; sub-arctic tundra walkabouts; and northern ocean sea kayaking expeditions. These were all the rage in a booming northern vacation industry, and Peaks Bay was at the centre of it.

I can see why people want to come here, he thought as he stepped into his open-top Jeep. The engine rumbled to life, and he let out a piercing whistle that sent a handful of birds flying from the nearby meadows. "Tigger, let's go! Time to get back to town!"

He pulled himself up by the rollover bar and stood in the Jeep to look for his four-legged partner. He took in the calm, sprawling landscape again before it came fully alive for the day. Cars milled around the harbour and massive wooden dock as shop owners made their way to work. The town was coming alive. The semi-circle of heritage storefronts around the newly built stone harbour plaza gave way to a maze of streets and alleys leading to small grocery stores, camping outlets and numerous little mom-and-pop tourist traps.

A sparkle on the horizon caught his eye. Keefer reached down and pulled out an old pair of binoculars from the glove compartment. *There isn't any cruise ship scheduled this week*. He adjusted the focus, and a red and white ship crystalized into view. *Coast Guard?*

As he scrutinized the ship, his smartphone vibrated, and he picked it up.

"Hey, Moe."

"Keefer, Sergeant Reilly asked me to find you. He needs ya in the harbour," said the gruff voice with a thick, sea-faring accent.

"Well, hello to you too, Moe. It's always good to hear from you. Oh, I'm good too. Thanks for asking." Keefer had befriended the grumpy old harbour master when he first moved to Peaks Bay. Most town folks avoided the bitter old man when they could, but Keefer had taken a liking to him.

"Argh, ya city slickers, always going on about feelings," growled Moe. "How many times do I have to tell ya? I don't care how you're feeling. Now get your arse down here."

"That hurts me deeply, Moe." Keefer feigned insult. He knew his friend didn't mean it, even though he would never admit it. "What does Reilly want? Is it concerning that ship coming in?"

"You're brighter than you look. Just get moving. The sergeant is gathering everyone in the plaza."

Moe hung up. No details. No goodbye.

Keefer smiled and tossed his smartphone back on the passenger seat. He whistled once more and, this time, got a series of barks as an answer. A furry brown and black head bobbed up and down in the high grass nearby as the dog ran to the Jeep. The German Shepherd leapt into the back seat and, with one bark, indicated he was ready to go.

***

Keefer navigated the dirt roads back to town and dropped Tigger at his bungalow in a small residential neighbourhood outside the harbour area. A Coast Guard ship visit was not the kind of thing that happened without a heads-up. It had to be some sort of emergency. He understood why Sergeant Reilly asked him to come down to the harbour, as there weren't many medical personnel who called this little seaside town home. There were two doctors and five nurses in the civilian hospital up the hill behind the town, along with one ambulance driver.

By the time he parked by the harbour plaza, he could see Sergeant Reilly's Stetson hat bobbing up and down in a group of people. Keefer settled into the circle of people and said a quick hello to everyone: Mayor Ryerson, Moe, a medic and a nurse from the hospital, a couple of RCMP constables, and Dirk Danerson, the town's ambulance driver.

Great, Dirk is here, Keefer thought, irritated.

"Pretty boy finally decides to join us," Dirk chided, his long, messy blond hair partially hiding the smug look on his face.

Moe cleared his phlegmy throat to interrupt the uncomfortable exchange. As he rubbed his leathery, sunbaked chin, he said, "Sarge, I made sure no fishing boats get in the way of our unannounced guests." He spat on the ground. "If they'd manners, they'd have called ahead."

Sergeant Reilly nodded and explained, "Three hours ago, the mayor and I got a call from the Coast Guard brass in Halifax. One of their ships, the icebreaker out there called the Henry Dawson, is on its way here." He paused to let that sink in and looked at everyone in the circle.

Satisfied everyone was paying attention, he continued, "It was on some sort of a mission out to Greenland when Halifax lost all communications with it. They then—"

"All communications? How does that even happen? Those ships are completely tooled up through and through—" interrupted Dirk.

"—they said something about a helicopter crash that ripped out all their communications capabilities," answered Reilly, visibly annoyed by the interruption. From his towering height, he stared at Dirk with steely eyes for a few extra seconds and crossed his spindly arms across his chest. He watched Dirk the way he would someone drunk and disorderly. Dirk stood his ground, looking insolent.

"Whatever the reason is, it's coming our way now," said Reilly.

"Sorry to interrupt, Sarge, but how did you get a call three hours ago that it was coming our way if they had no communications capabilities at that point?" Keefer asked, hoping to break the tension between the sergeant and Dirk.

"Good, productive question, Keefer," said Reilly, smirking at Dirk. "That's the even crazier part. Before the Henry Dawson lost their SAT communication, they set up a rendezvous point with a Coast Guard Cormorant that was stationed in Goose Bay. Some of you might have seen it fly over our heads a day or so ago. They were going to do some emergency evac of an injured crewmember or something. Halifax was dodgy on that part."

"Not injured—sick," interjected the mayor. "Whoever they were evacuating was not injured. They said *sick* on the phone." Mayor Ryerson did not like being left out of a conversation for very long.

"That's right. In any case, it sounded like they didn't know what was ailing one of their engineers or something. That's not the important point, though. They lost contact with the chopper shortly after it met up with the Henry Dawson. No communications since."

"What do you mean, nothing?" quizzed Dirk, not learning his lesson or simply not caring. "A ship and a chopper don't just lose all ability to communicate with the outside world. That makes no sense."

"We know that," snapped Reilly. "Whatever the reason, Halifax is still receiving the ship's transponder signal."

"And it's coming here?" Keefer asked the obvious aloud.

"Correct. So, since we aren't clear on what is going on, and if people are injured or sick, we need to be ready. Keefer, that's why I called you down here. I'd like you to lead the triage operations on the ship when it gets here."

"Hold on, Sarge. I should be the one leading that. I'm with the hospital. I'm the rightful authority here," protested Dirk. "Keefer's a temp and isn't even part of the hospital staff."

Looking down on Dirk from his six-foot-four-inches of height, Reilly cleared his throat again. "I'm the authority here, Dirk. I run safety operations in a crisis, not the hospital. Keefer's been in Afghanistan, and he's dealt with some serious casualty-type situations. He'll handle the triage operations on the ship." It was a clear rebuke, and Reilly did not look like he would take any pushback. Dirk shook his head but did not protest further. Reilly offered him an olive branch. "Dirk, I need you here with the ambulance. If anyone needs to be rushed to the hospital, that's your job. Your first-responder skills will be better used here."

Dirk subtly rolled his eyes.

"All right, let's get ourselves ready. Moe was telling me the ship would be in the harbour in thirty minutes. We'll have the tugboat meet it at the entrance channel."

Everyone broke off to attend to their assigned tasks. Dirk walked to his ambulance in a huff and bumped shoulders with Keefer as he went by him. Keefer smiled, knowing that calling Dirk out would simply make matters worse.

Sergeant Reilly approached Keefer. "Don't worry about him. He'll get over it. I need your experience on that ship."

Keefer nodded his understanding.

For the next ten minutes, Keefer conferred with the field medic and Elsie, the hospital nurse. The three of them, with the help of the two police officers, pulled out the first-aid equipment, including two stretchers, from Dirk's ambulance. Dirk ignored them and went about preparing on his own.

When they were ready, Keefer left the others at the ambulance and walked down the long pier to join Moe at the far end overlooking the ocean. The old harbour master was waving out his tugboat as Keefer walked up to him. Both men watched the small tugboat chug its way to the mouth of the harbour, where it would meet the icebreaker.

Keefer turned and admired the massive wooden pier that the locals called the Pride of Labrador. The nickname was a bit over the top, and Moe grumbled all the time, that it should be called the *Money Pit of Labrador* instead, as it had cost the town almost as much as their two-floor hospital. The pier was over three hundred and fifty metres long and fifteen metres wide, with a wooden frame completely built from Labrador timber. The pier's structure looked like a giant game of Kerplunk with all its crisscrossing timber.

"Ya know why he hates ya, don't ya?" Moe said more than asked.

Keefer didn't need to ask who. "I assumed it was my good looks."

"That right there, that smart-ass routine of yours, could have something to do with it. But no. There's always been something off with that guy, ever since he came to town. If ever there was a self-centred shit-disturber gene, he got it for sure."

Keefer couldn't agree more. The guy just wasn't right. He reminded Keefer of the whackos who joined the army for the sheer fact they could kill people legally. But Dirk was smarter than them, snake-like. Maybe that was why he was an ambulance driver instead.

"You know, Moe, you're pretty insightful about this kind of stuff. Science and human nature, you must watch Dr. Phil a lot."

"Shut up."

And that was that. Both men stood there for a few more minutes, watching the tugboat. When the small, sturdy ship reached the mouth of the harbour, more than a couple dozen people had already gathered along the pier and in the plaza. Shopkeepers, harbour workers and residents who had gotten wind of the incoming visitor. Odd news, like an unannounced Coast Guard ship, spread quickly in Peaks Bay.

The radio on Moe's belt crackled to life. It was Ryan Hutchison, the tugboat operator. "Moe, we got 'er on the binos. The ship's not got any signal flags up. Not seeing any movement on deck, either." There was a garbled discussion between Ryan and Tim, the younger of the Hutchisons. "It's sure coming fast, too. They don't seem to be slowing down for the harbour."

"Damn, those stiff-collared Coast Guard limeys. Another yahoo captain who thinks the world revolves around him. That boat's wake better not damage any of the fishing trolleys in the harbour."

Another voice came across the radio. "Moe? Hi, it's Tim. Something's wrong, Moe . . . some of the bridge windows look smashed up . . . plus, can't see anyone anywhere on her, you know."

"That doesn't make sense," Moe spoke gentler whenever he talked to the younger brother, mostly because he was a simpler kid, raised by his brother, and had not a bad bone in his body. "Get yar blow horn ready to signal them to slow down. Those government idiots aren't going to—"

"Moe! What the hell! You won't believe this; we can see the back of the ship. There's a big fat yellow chopper sticking out the stern. It's sticking straight up out of the stern deck. Do you hear me, Moe?"

"What? Say that again, Tim. Yar not making any sense," complained Moe.

Keefer heard the brothers argue on the other end, and Ryan's voice came back on the radio.

"Moe, you won't believe this. There's a helicopter crashed in the back of the ship! It's sticking straight out of—" Ryan yelled at his brother. "Tim, pull the tugboat back. That ship's gonna run us over. It's not slowing down."

The tugboat's blow horn blasted across the harbour multiple times, signalling the Henry Dawson to slow down.

"Moe, I don't know what is going on, but that ship is still chugging like a bat out of hell. There is no way they didn't see or hear us."

Moe started to swear but stopped suddenly. He looked between the Henry Dawson and the crowds of people lined up on the pier, made a croaking sound and dropped the radio on the wooden planks. He grabbed Keefer by the arm and ran toward the crowd, which had grown to at least a hundred people.

"We gat to get them off this pier! We gat to get them off!"

Keefer realized what had gotten into Moe, and his stomach knotted. If the icebreaker did not stop, it would plow straight into everything. It would crush the people watching. Keefer found it hard to breathe. Moe yelled and waved his arms at the crowd manically. People looked at him, puzzled. It took Keefer hollering at the crowd for them to catch on. The crowd panicked as they realized the danger, and a mini-stampede ensued as dozens of people ran toward the shore end of the pier.

In the commotion, an old man with a cane fell right in front of Keefer. Keefer instinctively bent down and shielded the man with his own body as the people rushed around them. He could see the fear in the old man's eyes. As the flow of people subsided, Keefer stood, grabbed the old man under the armpits, and ran as best he could toward the plaza. They were the last two people to make it to the end of the wooden structure.

The tugboat's blow horn split the crisp morning air again. Keefer turned in time to see the giant metal-reinforced bow of the Henry Dawson, meant to crush three-metre-thick ice, crash into the far end of the Pride of Labrador. The first few hundred feet of the pier split in a deafening crunch. The plaza shook angrily. Wood planks piled up in front of the ship's bow as it slammed upwards over the splintering wood, its momentum pushing it forward. Planks snapped like toothpicks, and the giant wooden poles holding the planks up exploded like grenades, sending wooden shrapnel everywhere. The underwater cement pylons anchoring the poles were ripped out of the ground, and the pier's metal railings twisted inland like screaming curly strings. The smell of freshly splintered wood and burning diesel fuel flooded the air. The giant ice-breaker came to an arduous halt when the underside of its massive belly scraped against the rocks of the shore in one last screeching metal gasp.

Keefer looked around. Sergeant Reilly was running about the plaza, yelling orders to his officers and the medical personnel. Miraculously, no one on shore was seriously injured. A few people had been hit by flying pieces of splintered wood, but they were quickly tended to.

Keefer stared up at the giant red and white metal hulk that lay on top of the smashed pier. The ice-crushing bow of the ship was propped on the edge of the rocks that protected the plaza from the ocean waves, while its stern was partially underwater. The middle of the ship's outdoor deck was almost even with the small portion of the pier that was still relatively standing.

Sergeant Reilly pointed at that portion of the pier and gave Keefer and the others the order to enter the ship. Then, the sergeant started yelling at civilians to move away from the edge of the plaza, where the ship could still tilt and potentially crush people.

***

Keefer led the three police officers and Elsie along the slanted ship's deck. The astringent scent of fuel overpowered that of the splintered wood. They reached the side door of the superstructure, and an officer stepped through the threshold ahead of Keefer. Keefer followed closely behind and walked right into the back of the officer, who had stopped dead in his tracks.

"What's wrong?"

The officer didn't answer.

Keefer stepped around him and came to a halt himself.

"What the hell?"

A dried liquid covered the passageway deck, and a metallic smell lingered in the air. The splatter was blood.

"No one loses that much blood and lives," the police officer muttered.

None of the other rescuers said anything. They stood in the doorway.

Keefer pointed at the red cross on the door of a nearby room. "That's the medical bay right there. There must have been an accident, and for whatever reason, it went south before they made it in." He stepped forward cautiously, making sure not to slip on the blood. "Let's keep moving."

Stale, flickering neon lights replaced the brightness of the day, making the blood look almost black . . . or was it black? Keefer couldn't tell for sure.

The medical bay was a mess. Everything was turned over, and there was no sign of life. That worried Keefer. With all that blood, he would have expected to find someone . . . anyone.

"Let's head to the bridge," he said.

The group followed him to the officer's quarters deck next. They quickly surveyed the rooms and established this deck was empty too. The stillness of the vessel made Keefer jumpy, and he hurried up one more deck, everyone else in tow. With all the blood they had seen in front of the medical bay, none of the five rescuers bothered to comment on the occasional bloody handprints on the bulkheads. Like cave paintings, these led them straight to their destination.

They stayed quiet as they made their way up the final stairs. The only sound was the low rumble emanating from deep inside the belly of the Henry Dawson. The engines were groaning, unsure if they should go to sleep or stay awake.

The bridge door was open, and they filed in one after the other. Sunlight coming through the large bridge windows washed out the gloominess of the passageway.

The first thing Keefer noted was the shattered window. "Something ugly happened here, too."

"The ship must have been boarded by pirates. That's the only explanation. They must have taken the crew and left the boat running," one police officer said.

Keefer mulled it over while looking around. "Maybe." But his instincts were telling him something else.

"Look over here. This would support your theory," another officer said, running his hand along the bullet holes in the back wall of the bridge.

"So much blood," Elsie said. It was the first time she'd spoken since they'd boarded. She stood by a puddle of dark, dried blood in front of a storage-room door.

"Careful, Elsie." Keefer eyed the battered door suspiciously. There were bloody handprints all over it and hundreds of dents in its metal façade. *Why would pirates be trying to break down a door with their hands?*

Elsie stepped carefully into the pool of blood, her hand reaching for the door handle. The blood was soft enough for her boots to sink in and make a slurping sound. Her hand gently rested on the door handle. She stopped. "I heard something!" Elsie gasped.

Keefer stopped what he was doing. Two of the officers moved and set up like bodyguards behind her. Elsie slowly turned the handle and gently opened the door.

Blood covered the floor of the storage room, and lying in the middle of the red canvas was a woman. She was passed out, but Keefer could tell right away she was alive—her chest was moving up and down.

"Bring the stretcher!" Keefer ordered as he moved to the woman and felt for a pulse. He was not surprised but still relieved to find one. He quickly assessed her for injuries; blood completely covered her face and chest, and one of her arms had a blood-soaked towel wrapped around it.

With the help of the officers, Keefer positioned the woman so they could lift her onto the stretcher. As they were about to lift, the woman opened her eyes and screamed, "No! Get off the ship!"

Everyone jumped back. One officer slipped in the blood and fell on his rear while another yelled a bunch of profanities. The woman grabbed Keefer by the shoulders and pleaded, "Please, help them!" Her eyes rolled back in her sockets as her speech slurred, and she passed back out.

"Bloody damn! She almost gave me a heart attack!"

"What the hell. Is she awake or not?"

"She's in shock. She's going in and out of consciousness. We need to get her to the hospital," Keefer answered.

They quickly loaded and fastened the woman on the stretcher and carried her outside. Once out in the open, the sea air cleared the stench of copper again. Reaching the pier, Keefer and Elsie took the stretcher from the officers and awkwardly made their way along the mangled planks.

"We'll meet you back on the ship in a few minutes. Start sweeping the lower decks!" shouted Keefer over his shoulder.

***

Joseph, the most senior of the three officers, led the other two back through the door of the Henry Dawson's superstructure. He started down the ladder near where they came in. He'd seen a lot of things as a cop and had even been in charge of a domestic murder scene once, but this was a whole other level. He didn't know what to say to the junior officers, so he said nothing.

When they reached the level below, he stopped and held his hand up for the two men to do the same. The deck, bulkheads and overhead were all covered in blood—again. At this point, he was worried making any kind of noise might wake something up, though he was unsure of what.

After a few seconds, Joseph gently stepped off the last stair onto the carpet of blood. He moved down the open corridor to his right, cautious not to slip on the gore. With a crisp chop of his hand, he signalled to the youngest officer to check out the crew quarters near the ladder landing; then, he pointed to a sign that read *Mess Deck* with an arrow indicating a location further down the passageway. The two officers nodded. He was relieved they also did not want to speak.

Joseph and the other officer walked slowly to the mess-deck hatch, where the door was ajar. He cocked his head as he got closer. *What's that noise?* He could barely hear it. *It sounds like someone snoring?* He stopped to listen more carefully. It was coming from the mess deck for sure, but it was too loud to be one person, more like a harmony of snores. He turned to the officer behind him. The man heard the same noise and appeared as bloodless as a corpse, his eyes round and unblinking. Joseph pointed to his ear with one hand, then did a finger-point chop toward the mess deck. The officer behind him barely managed a slight nod in response.

Joseph's curiosity overcame his fear, and he stepped through the hatch. Every part of his body stopped moving, including his jaw, which was semi-open. A large group of people were slouched on the floor: some on their knees, some on their rears, some on their sides. But all their heads were bent forward, chin to chest, and they all faced the galley away from the mess-deck door. Joseph still couldn't move. Every ounce of his experience as a cop froze his body in place, like when a deer hears the crack of a branch in the woods and goes completely still. The invisible scent of death hung in the air. There were multiple uniforms represented in the room: grey engineer suits, sailor outfits, a handful of ship officer uniforms and a bunch of orange jumpsuits. This was the Henry Dawson's crew, yet Joseph's sense of self-preservation knew not to alert them to his presence.

The stench of infected flesh hit him. His eyes watered, and he tried to pull his forearm to his nose and mouth to block the vile smell, but his brain still insisted he not move. Every fibre in his body, tuned by thirty-five years of service, told him to leave. His subconscious took over and forced his limbs to articulate. He stepped back through the mess-deck door with one leg . . . slowly.

That was when the younger officer stuck his head over Joseph's shoulder. The young man gasped. "What the mother and Jesus fuck?!"

The two dozen men and women on the floor of the mess deck snapped their heads up, pulled out of their trance. Then, in laborious yet fast movements, they all rose and lunged at Joseph and the other officer. For the first time, he noticed everyone's skin was rotten grey, and everyone's eyes were black.

Self-preservation had done all it could for him.

11

BEST SEAT IN THE HOUSE

K eefer and Elsie hurried toward the ambulance, doing their best not to shake the unconscious woman. Dirk, Sergeant Reilly and two other officers met them and relieved them of their burden.

"What do we got?" said Dirk, surprisingly professional.

"Unconscious woman, probably in her thirties, heart rate is faint, injury to her right forearm," Keefer answered. "All the blood on her *seems* to have come from a nosebleed, best I can tell. Could be from her arm . . . but could also be from someone else. There was blood everywhere in there." He still struggled with the puzzle pieces. So much blood everywhere, but no other bodies.

"Where's the rest of the crew? Where'd you find her?" Sergeant Reilly asked.

"On the bridge. She was the only one there." Keefer handed off his end of the stretcher to an officer.

"The only one? That doesn't make sense. Where's the rest of the bridge personnel?" Reilly asked.

Keefer wished he could answer. He couldn't make sense of what he had seen or not seen. There were no people on the bridge; it was the one place where there should have been people.

"I don't know." It pained him to say this, since Sergeant Reilly had trusted him to lead the rescuers onto the ship. "Your men are still looking."

"Sarge, she was hiding in a storage room," added Elsie uneasily.

"Why would she be hiding in a storage room?"

"There was blood everywhere. The three top floors were covered in it. One of your guys thought they'd been boarded by pirates," Keefer offered unconvincingly. Deep down, he didn't believe this, but it was the one theory that could make sense.

"Pirates?" Sergeant Reilly said doubtfully. "There has never been a pirate attack in the North Atlantic, son. Not since I've been around, anyway."

"Come on, Keefer, pirates? There must have been something else," Dirk added in a derisive tone. "I would have figured it out."

"That's the best explanation I got. Feel free to come up with your own theory," said Keefer. What could be worse than pirates?

Keefer watched as the blood-covered woman was transferred to a gurney and slid inside the ambulance cube. Elsie climbed in and started pulling out a saline IV kit.

Sergeant Reilly signalled to a couple of officers to join Keefer. "You two, go back in with him. Just in case. Check if—"

A shriek cut Reilly off. The whole plaza hushed as people turned toward the sound. Keefer spotted the person, a woman with a bright purple rain jacket, closest to the ship's bow. The woman had one hand on top of her head, and her other hand pointed at the tip of the ship. On the bow of the Henry Dawson, a man was clumsily climbing over the metal railing. The man wobbled there for a few seconds, and Keefer wondered if he was drunk. Then the man walked off the edge. He plummeted ten metres from the top of the bow to the plaza. The impact of his body on the stone-covered ground made most of the crowd turn away in disgust. Keefer didn't turn, but he gasped in surprise.

Another shriek came from someone else. This one sounded as horrified as the first. "There's another one!"

Another man climbed over the bow's railing, followed by two more, then three, then four.

Keefer broke from his stupor and jumped forward, hurrying through the crowd to help. The thick, transfixed crowd slowed his progress. He'd made it halfway when yet another shout came from the mass of townspeople in the harbour plaza.

"The crew! They're coming onto the pier from the side of the boat!"

Keefer stopped and looked toward the pier. A dozen people were flooding out of the Henry Dawson from the same spot he and Elsie had with the stretcher. The scene looked odd.

Why are they running?

Dirk and two police officers headed to the group on the pier, so Keefer kept moving toward the first man who'd fallen off the bow. Ahead of him, the woman with the purple rain jacket bent over the man. Keefer expected to find the jumper crumpled and unconscious, but he was starting to rise. He even opened his arms and embraced the woman when she offered him help.

The woman's screams were different from her earlier ones; those had been of surprise and warning, but now they were of pain and fear. Her guttural howl echoed off the stone buildings of the small plaza. Keefer was still a few metres away, and what he witnessed did not make any sense. It stopped him dead in his tracks. The man sank his teeth into the woman's face, sending blood pouring down her purple rain jacket and filling her rubber boots.

Keefer stood paralyzed by what he was seeing. Then total mayhem erupted.

The people from the front of the crowd started screaming. Those from the back who were rushing forward to help encountered a wave of panicked people trying to run the other way. In the chaos, he thought he caught a glimpse of the other sailors who'd fallen from the bow of the ship, starting to rise.

Keefer's attention was pulled in multiple directions, depending on who was screaming the loudest. He saw it again: a man in a Canadian Coast Guard uniform grabbed a man by the ears and bit his right eye out, just like that. It was the same as the woman with the purple jacket. The jumpers were getting up to bite people; he was sure of it now.

Gunshots echoed over the screams. Keefer looked for the source of the discharges. It took him a few seconds to see through the crowd. A police officer who'd run toward the pier was blindly shooting her sidearm into a pack of people who had tackled her fellow officer to the ground. The officer on the ground was being ripped to pieces by his assailants, and the gunshots were doing nothing to stop the carnage.

Nothing made sense. Keefer wasn't sure where to run or who to help. He walked aimlessly until his feet bumped up against a body on the ground. He looked down. It was the woman with the purple rain jacket. Her face was covered in blood, so much so that Keefer could not see exactly where her injury was. His medical training kicked in.

Check for pulse. His fingers darted to her neck. *She's alive. Got to get her to the ambulance.*

He picked the woman up. She almost slipped from his grip because of the blood-slicked jacket. He turned and ran back toward the ambulance, hearing screams and more gunshots but staying focused on the one life he could help. He crossed the wide plaza with people running haphazardly and bumping into him. Reaching the ambulance, he noticed Elsie still beside the unconscious woman from the ship. Elsie stared at the madness, her mouth wide open and her hands frozen in mid-motion, holding a saline pack.

"Make some room in there. We need to stabilize this woman!"

Elsie, given a purpose, jumped to action. She started to move things in the back of the cramped ambulance. Keefer bent to put the woman in the purple rain jacket down to get ready to take a stretcher from Elsie. As he did, he felt her grip tighten on his arms.

She's regaining consciousness.

Looking down at her blood-covered face, he was met with black eyes staring back at him. The woman's arms tightened even more, and she tried to pull him in toward her mouth. Shocked by the woman's actions, Keefer pushed her back and dropped her on the plaza's cobblestones.

"What's wrong?" Elsie shouted.

Keefer had no answer to give. The woman wrapped her hands around his ankle, and a deep gargle rose from inside her chest. She pulled with a strength that surprised Keefer, and he fell to the stones beside her. The woman quickly rolled over and wrapped her arms around him as she tried to bite his face. Keefer barely held her at bay.

"What are you doing?" he shouted.

A splintered wooden cane came shooting down and speared the woman right through the eye. Keefer felt her life leave her body instantly. He pushed the limp meat bag off and scrambled to his feet.

Leaning against the ambulance to get his balance was the old man Keefer had helped on the pier earlier. The elderly man looked down at the dead woman, his cane lodged in her head like a toothpick through an olive. The old man was shaky, yet his voice was surprisingly firm. "You alright, son?"

Keefer babbled, "Yes . . . I'm not sure what . . . why did she . . . you killed her?" Even if the woman had tried to bite Keefer, he struggled to process that this man had killed her.

"Son, look around. Now is not the time to ask why. Now is the time to move."

Keefer looked at what was happening. It was like standing on Lookout Point early in the morning when the fog lifted, and he could now see things. The crew from the Henry Dawson were viciously attacking the town folks—they were the ones trying to kill people. Some people ran toward the shops and alleys to get away from the slaughter. Others ran toward the abattoir, thinking they could help fend off the attackers. Finally, some were howling in pain as gory teeth ripped through their skin. Even worse, those who had been mauled were rising from the ground—rising from their pools of blood—and attacking others. Keefer looked down at the woman in the purple rain jacket with the cane still sticking out of her eye. *They're doing what she did.* Though it was hard to believe, people were getting infected. His brain concluded what logic could not believe: people were getting infected, and it was making them attack other people.

His thoughts were interrupted by the slurping of the old man pulling his splintered wooden cane from the woman's head.

Two infected rounded the ambulance, saw the old man, and tackled him to the ground. All right in front of Keefer.

Bang. Bang. Bang. The gunshots rang in Keefer's ears, and he winced as two bullets hit one of the infected in the shoulder, sending it spinning to the ground. Three more shots rang out. *Bang. Bang. Bang.* These hit the other infected in the side as it was biting the old man. The impact slammed it sideways to the stony ground.

"You alright, lad?" Sergeant Reilly asked breathlessly.

Keefer didn't answer, but looked down at the old man with his throat ripped out. Then he looked at Reilly, who had splatters of blood on his uniform. He was still wearing his Stetson.

Reilly put his hand on Keefer's shoulder and shook. "You all right?" he asked again.

"I'm fine. The blood?" Keefer pointed at the red and black blood on the sergeant's uniform.

"I'm fine. It's not mine. One of those maniacs from the ship came at me."

"What is wrong with these people?"

"I don't know, but they don't stay down for long."

Reilly pointed to six more infected running at them and pushed Keefer toward the open ambulance doors.

"Get in the ambulance! Elsie, get in the front and start her up."

Elsie, still crouched in the back of the ambulance, was staring at the nightmare in the plaza and shaking her head.

"Elsie, now!" shouted Reilly.

Elsie blinked hard, jumped to the driver's seat and turned on the engine of the big white and red vehicle. It roared to life.

Keefer jumped into the ambulance cube and extended a hand to Sergeant Reilly, who climbed in after him just as the two infected he'd shot started to rise.

"They're getting up. Bastards are getting up," Keefer said in disbelief.

"They all do," said Reilly as he slammed the doors. The six infected crashed into the backside of the ambulance.

"Drive, Elsie. Go! Go! Go!" Keefer shouted. The ambulance lurched forward. Keefer and Reilly were thrown against the back doors, their faces pressed against the windows.

Despite the engine noise, Keefer heard gunshots echoing through the plaza.

"There! On the pier!" Reilly pointed.

Dirk Danerson and an officer were stuck on the far end of the shattered pier, fighting off infected. The officer was firing her sidearm into the crowd, running at them.

"Turn around. We need to help them!" Reilly shouted to Elsie, but Keefer could tell she was not listening.

The officer was shooting the legs of the infected, trying to keep them at bay while Dirk stood behind her. When she ran out of bullets, she pulled out her police baton, and Dirk picked up a large plank of wood.

"They won't get out of there alive. Elsie, turn the ambulance around!" Reilly shouted again.

Elsie ignored him. She navigated a group of infected pounding on her door as she squeezed the ambulance onto a small side street.

Keefer moved to the front of the vehicle to get her attention. If he'd watched out the back window a little while longer, he'd have seen what Sergeant Reilly saw. He'd have seen Dirk lift his large wooden plank and smash it down, not on an infected, but on the officer's knees. He'd have seen Dirk hobble to the end of what remained of the pier as the infected piled on the squirming officer, giving him enough time to reach the water.

"Bastard!" Reilly's anger exploded.

Keefer barely registered it as the ambulance swung wildly from side to side, bouncing him off the walls of the cube and sending medical supplies raining down on him.

"Where am I going?" shouted Elsie from the front seat. "They're everywhere!"

The ambulance bounced up and down as it ran over the infected as if going over speed bumps.

"Head to the police station!" Keefer shouted, and Sergeant Reilly nodded approval, still scowling.

The ambulance swerved into another small street. The engine roared as the ambulance accelerated through the maze of old stone and brick buildings.

"We're clear! We're clear! There aren't any of them out here!" Elsie shouted.

"Still . . . be careful," Keefer said as he pulled himself into the front passenger seat.

Elsie turned to him with tears in her eyes. "You don't understand . . . We're clear . . . They're not here . . . I don't have to drive over them anymore . . . I ran over them like they were nothing."

"I know. It's okay." He wanted to comfort her, but she was still driving. "Keep your eyes on the road."

Exactly when he said this, an infected ran in front of the careening ambulance. Elsie jerked the steering wheel a split second too late. The vehicle hit the infected dead-on, and the body was sucked under the undercarriage. The ambulance jumped onto the sidewalk, snapped a stop sign like a toothpick and drove straight into the brick wall of an old building.

12

NO SUCH THING AS ZOMBIES

T he airbags deployed and took the brunt of the impact for Keefer
and Elsie. He was relieved to see Reilly had avoided injury as well.
Silence settled over the accident, and the smell of leaking gasoline and
brick dust floated in the air.

"There's a group of them coming down the street!" Elsie said, her
breathing coming in rapid, shallow puffs.

"Get in the back and lie low. If they don't see us, they might run by."

Keefer helped her out of her seat and into the cube as the hissing, gurgling infected ran by. One stopped to look at the ambulance, intrigued.
It stood at the back of the crashed vehicle, and for a second, Keefer was
convinced the door would fly open. Elsie had her hand on his forearm,
and her nails dug deep into his skin. Sergeant Reilly held his pistol aimed
at the doors. They waited.

The infected's moans became more agitated until a ruckus down the
road attracted its attention, and just like that, it moved on.

Keefer waited a few seconds, then peeked out the back window. "It's
clear."

Sergeant Reilly squeezed in beside Keefer and holstered his sidearm.

"We should move while the street is clear and make our way to the
police station." He grabbed the handle, and Keefer positioned Elsie and
himself behind Reilly.

"Don't!" a voice from behind them said.

Keefer jumped, hitting his head on the ceiling of the cube. Elsie shrieked. The blonde woman, still strapped to the gurney, raised her head from under the blankets and equipment that had covered her. Keefer had completely forgotten she was there, and, by Reilly and Elsie's reactions, they had too.

"I've seen them . . . the infected . . . set ambushes," the woman said in a raspy voice. "I don't know how they know to do it . . . but they do." She coughed.

Keefer moved to her side. "Let me untie you. What's your name?"

"Abelone—" She coughed again. "Abelone Jensen. Where am I? Is this Peaks Bay? We were on a course for Peaks Bay when . . ." Abelone trailed off. Her face contorted, and her eyes squeezed shut. He could tell she was reliving some horrible memory.

"They're all gone. They were all infected," Abelone stated, more to herself than the group. She asked again, "Is this Peaks Bay?"

"Yes." *All infected?* Keefer wondered. *Is that true?* Could the whole crew have been infected? It made sense. The blood was everywhere. The crew's absence. But how did she survive?

"So we made it. How did the infection get out? Why wasn't the ship quarantined?"

"We didn't know there was an infection *to* contain," said Keefer. "And to be honest, we didn't have a chance to even consider a quarantine." He brought her up to speed as Sergeant Reilly and Elsie kept watch at the ambulance windows.

Then it was Abelone's turn to recount her story and that of the Henry Dawson. She told them about their mission, the infection, and how she got barricaded in the bridge storage room. Keefer understood the words she was using, but couldn't reconcile the outcome of the tale. It felt like she was leaving out the part about her arm getting injured.

"That can't be," Keefer resisted Abelone's explanations. "You're talking about zombies? That's ridiculous."

"There's no such thing as zombies. They're people," Abelone replied. "They're infected . . . with something . . . They need our help."

Reilly shushed them as an infected ran by shrieking. It hardly paid attention to the ambulance.

"So your goal was to avoid having this virus make landfall?" Keefer asked.

"Yes."

"That didn't work out too well."

"No," Abelone answered, dismayed.

The pit in his stomach grew bigger. He was going to be sick. "What's to stop the virus from spreading across the country?" His question sucked the air out of the small square space they huddled in.

Abelone did not answer. Thin films of water appeared along her lower eyelids.

Keefer stared hard at the blonde woman covered in dry blood until she hesitantly offered an answer. "We need to make a vaccine for this virus. Those people . . . the infected . . . they can all be saved. We need to get in touch with the WHO."

Keefer realized Abelone had given the people with the virus a name: *the infected.*

He couldn't comprehend her answer to his question. "What I saw out there . . . those infected . . . they cannot be saved by a vaccine. Those people cannot be saved." He didn't know if they could, but he refused to believe it. His voice rose. Why had this been brought to shore? "This virus, these infected, they need to be . . . we need to neutralize the spread." He almost said the infected needed to be killed, and he hated himself for it, but he couldn't imagine letting this virus reach more populated areas.

Abelone dismissed his comments. "They can be saved." Keefer could see the determination on her face. She changed the subject. "Have you talked to them?"

"What? To whom?" Keefer asked.

"The WHO, the World Health Organization."

Sergeant Reilly and Keefer looked at each other. In all the life-and-death commotion, he hadn't thought to pick up a phone and call someone. Both he and Reilly scrambled to get their phones out.

"Thirty-six missed calls. Damn," Sergeant Reilly said to Keefer, who looked over his shoulder and saw the officer tap the redial button for the Coast Guard headquarters in Halifax.

Busy signal.

Reilly tried three more times without luck.

Keefer turned his phone on and opened his web browser. "Oh my God! It's all over the internet!"

Reilly, Elsie and Abelone squeezed in beside him. Every news site he brought up was covered with stories, pictures and videos: the Henry Dawson crashing into the Peaks Bay pier, the ship's crew jumping off the bow, and a handful showed townspeople being attacked by bloodied, grey-skinned individuals. Every video was a few seconds long and ended quickly. Only a few showed an infected biting a person.

"People don't believe this is real," he said, dismayed while scanning comments. "They think it's a hoax, a movie teaser event or something."

"Would you?" Abelone said flatly.

The phone in Sergeant Reilly's hand vibrated unexpectedly, startling them all. Reilly almost dropped it. "Reilly," he answered crisply, while putting his phone on speaker.

"Sergeant Reilly, thank God I've finally reached you. This is Director Frederick in Ottawa. We've been trying to reach you non-stop for the past twenty minutes."

Keefer wondered who this guy was and what he knew.

"Sir, we were a bit busy over here. With people trying to bite our faces off and all." Putting his other hand on the phone, he whispered to the others, "It's the director of B Division."

Keefer shrugged with his hands.

Reilly clarified, "RCMP big wig. The guy in charge of everything related to Labrador and Newfoundland."

The voice on the phone continued, "Sergeant, I am here with Canadian representatives of the Public Health Agency, the CDC and the World Health Organization. We need to know what is going on up there. The things we are seeing online, the phone calls that PHAC and the CDC have been getting, none of it makes sense."

"Sir, that's because *it* doesn't make *any* sense. When the Henry Dawson crashed, the ship members started attacking the civilians gathered in the harbour plaza . . . *It's* insane, that's what *it* is!"

Keefer could hear voices in the background, people behind Director Frederick, all speaking urgently.

"Sergeant, can you confirm the crew of the Henry Dawson is alive? Have they broken quarantine by leaving the ship?"

Keefer was dumbfounded; it was an obvious answer if they'd seen the videos.

Sergeant Reilly answered, his tone edgy. "Yes, they have. And whatever they are sick with, well, it looks to be spreading on contact. They—"

Abelone put a hand on Reilly's shoulder and her other hand on the phone. The sergeant let her speak.

"Hello, this is Abelone Jensen, Director for the Danish Institute of Rare Viral Diseases. No offence, Director Frederick, but I need to speak with the representative of the WHO in the room with you." Her voice was still hoarse, and she cleared her throat a few times.

There was a muffled conversation at the other end of the line, and a heavily accented voice came on.

"Ms. Jensen, is that you? This is Deider Birchmeier. We met last year at the Symposium on Viral Diseases of 2025 in Geneva. We had—"

Abelone cut him off and went straight to the point. Keefer was starting to like her.

"Deider, listen to me. You must call the Office of the Director General at the WHO in Geneva and declare a Code Q2-98."

Deider was quiet for a few seconds, ignoring the barrage of questions from faceless voices.

"Yes. I will call the Office of the Director General right away."

The RCMP director came back on the line and started asking rapid-fire questions: How did the infection start? What happened to the ship's communication capabilities? How many people had died in the town? Abelone stared at the phone. Keefer could tell she didn't know where to start. The questions kept coming.

Abelone looked lost. Keefer reached over, took the phone and handed it back to Sergeant Reilly.

"Let him handle the questions for now," Keefer said. Abelone nodded and took a drink of water. Keefer sat back on the paramedic stool bolted to the floor.

As Sergeant Reilly answered questions, he picked up his Stetson from the floor, dusted it off on his leg and placed it back on his thin, grey-haired head.

Elsie, who had stayed quiet, sat between the driver and passenger seats facing inside the cube, her elbows on her knees. The driver-side window suddenly shattered and showered her with glass. She screamed in surprise. An infected leapt through the broken window up to its stomach and grabbed her by the hair.

"Fuck!" shouted Keefer as he grabbed her by the legs. He and the infected engaged in a tug-of-war with Elsie's body. The hissing and shrieking of the infected echoed in the ambulance. Elsie screamed first in fear, then in pain as her hair ripped out of her scalp.

The passenger-side window shattered next, and two other infected tried to climb over each other to get in. One grabbed Elsie's flailing left arm and pulled the young woman in a third direction as if she were caught in a gruesome medieval torture apparatus.

Sergeant Reilly dropped his phone and pulled out his sidearm. He levelled his arm on Keefer's shoulder. "Block your ear!" he shouted at Keefer. Keefer put a hand on his right ear just in time.

Two quick shots rang out, straight into one of the passenger-side infected's head. It exploded into chunks of bone and brain; its body flopped down and stopped moving. The second infected in the passenger-side window, not flinching at its peer's demise, latched its second hand on Elsie's wrist.

Reilly lined up his sidearm again. An empty click resonated twice, then a third time, and the lawman swore. Without missing a beat, he turned the handgun and, leaning over Keefer's shoulder, used it to pound the other infected's arm until it let go. Elsie snapped sideways toward the infected on the driver's side still pulling on her hair. She screamed even louder as the infected sank its teeth into her forehead. Blood spurted across her face. A second bite pierced her right eyeball, and clear liquid poured down her cheek, mixing with the blood. She stopped flailing, and her legs went limp in Keefer's hands. Realizing he could not help her anymore, he let go.

Keefer turned to the back doors of the cube and hollered, "Go!"

He slid his arm under Abelone's and helped her up while Reilly swung the cube doors open. A half-dozen infected were trying to climb over each other to get into the ambulance through the broken windows. The trio took off running into a pedestrian alley across the street.

The alley was lined with art boutiques and cafes, which made up the first floors of quaint three-storey buildings. The area, usually packed with people enjoying coffee and pastries, was empty. As soon as they reached the edge of the alley, an infected spotted them and shrieked. Every infected stopped what it was doing and turned to look in their direction. They lost interest in the ambulance and took off after the fleeing prey.

"We won't outrun them like this!" Keefer shouted.

Abelone was moving as quickly as she could, but she was still groggy and stumbling along.

Keefer pushed her to a red wooden door beside a coffee shop. The door led to stairs, which led to apartments on the upper floors, so it was unlocked. They all stumbled in, and Reilly slammed the door behind them, blocking it in place with a snow shovel.

Keefer knew the door would not last long, so he urged the others up the stairs to a second and third floor, which housed an apartment each.

All the apartments were locked, but the stairs continued to the rooftop. The trio exited as the door on the ground floor broke open. Shrieks and hisses floated to the top floor, and a flurry of footsteps pattered up the tight cement staircase.

The rooftop was cluttered with junk, a few air vents, an old picnic table and a fire escape ladder at the opposite end.

Sergeant Reilly hurriedly grabbed a chain from a pile of scrap and fastened the door closed. Once he was done, he stepped back from his work, unimpressed.

Keefer was drawn to the side of the rooftop facing the harbour. The sky was cloudless and blue, and for a second, he felt warm and comfortable until his eyesight drifted to the harbour plaza, and he was chilled to the bone. "Fuck—"

Despite the distance, he could tell the harbour plaza was covered in blood. There were all kinds of things scattered over the cobblestone: clothes, bags, shoes, but one thing was glaringly missing—bodies.

The Henry Dawson was jacked up on the crumpled pier. Its bow pointed up at an angle, and the end of its stern deck was below water. The splintered logs and planks were piled all around the crushing weight of the icebreaker's hull, like snow in front of a plow.

"How many people were in the plaza when we arrived?" Abelone asked, walking up beside him.

"Probably over a hundred," he answered, the words barely escaping his throat.

"We need to tell Deider. They have to know how much the infection has spread," Abelone gasped out. She turned away from the plaza and spoke to Sergeant Reilly, who was making his way toward them. "Mr. Reilly, I need your phone."

Reilly swore. "I don't have it. I must have dropped it in the ambulance . . . when Elsie was being . . ."

Abelone looked at Keefer and didn't need to ask. He shook his head. "I dropped mine on the seat in the ambulance when those things attacked." He felt stupid. Both their lifelines to the outside world had been lost.

Abelone corrected him, "They're not things. They're people. They're just infected. If we can come up with a vaccine, we can still save them."

Keefer liked Abelone. He didn't understand why, but the second she had startled him in the ambulance, he had been drawn to her. It might have been her confidence or the life-and-death situation that caused the attraction. And now her unabashed hope people could be saved. He admired it, maybe because it wasn't something innate to him. He wanted that, but he was pragmatic.

"Save them? We can't even save ourselves right now. We need to eradicate this virus, or it eradicates us. We don't have time for a vaccine. The vectors need to be . . . neutralized," Keefer said with more of an edge than he wanted.

Sergeant Reilly stepped in. "Vaccine or not, it doesn't matter. Talking about it is all for nothing if we don't get in touch with Ottawa. We have a phone and radio at the police station. If we get there, we can figure things out."

"Before we go," Keefer said, looking at Abelone. "On the call earlier, you said to that Deider guy he had to get a hold of the WHO to declare this a Q2-98. What did that mean?"

Abelone hesitated to answer.

Reilly was not pleased. "Speak up, Ms. Jensen. The three of us are in this together. Tell us what that meant."

She nodded. "It's a quarantine designation. In 2007, the United Nations and one hundred and thirty-two countries signed the World Viral Pandemic Containment Protocol . . . the '07 Protocols. It's an agreement between governments and the United Nations on how to handle the worst of the worst viral outbreaks, the ones that could have . . . significant world-impacting repercussions." She paused to let her words sink in.

Keefer spoke up first. "I've been a military medic for fifteen years, and I have never heard of this World Viral Containment thing."

"Most people wouldn't have. It's classified legislation. Only high-ranking government officials like presidents, prime ministers, and a few key members of their governments and health agencies know about it."

Reilly jumped in, "And you know this because?"

"I'm the head epidemiologist of the Danish Institute of Rare Viral Diseases. It's my job to know. I report to the WHO as much as I do to my government."

"How bad is it? Where does Q2-98 sit in the worst of the worst outbreaks?"

Abelone looked at them without answering. Keefer realized it was bad by the look on her face.

"How bad?" he insisted.

The way she looked at him felt like she knew him. Like she trusted him. He asked again, "How bad?"

Abelone sighed. "It's bad. The community will be fully quarantined. No one will be let in or out until the viral outbreak is fully solved."

Keefer looked at the Henry Dawson disquietingly and was startled when the door to the rooftop rattled against its chain. Grey clutching fingers with black fingernails slipped between the door and the frame. Hissing and gargling emanated from the darkness of the stairwell.

"Time to go!" Keefer ordered as he put his hand on Abelone's elbow and directed her to the back emergency stairs.

As they reached the alley, they stopped at the sound of a foghorn going off in the distance.

"What is that?" Abelone asked.

"Sounds like the horn of the tug in the harbour," Sergeant Reilly said.

A body landed between them in a nauseating crunch. Keefer pulled Abelone across the alley before another body crashed down where she was standing.

"They're jumping off!" Keefer blurted, staring at the rooftop they had come down from. "We need to go." He took off jogging with Abelone and Sergeant Reilly in tow. The infected on the alley ground tried to get up to follow them, but their splintered legs only allowed them to crawl. The foghorn in the distance went off again—twice.

13

WHAT IF SHE BITES A FISH?

C old, salty water splashed Eric Martel's face and snapped him back to consciousness. He gasped for air as his eyes adjusted to the dim surroundings.

Why can't I move? He struggled as another splash of cold water went up his nose. *Where is this water coming from?* Turning his head straight up, away from the freezing water, he came nose to nose with the grey dead face of Roger Powers. The massive body was still draped on top of him. The memories of the engineering-room massacre came flooding back.

I must have passed out. I'm alive! he thought ecstatically, but when another splash of ocean water hit him in the ear, his excitement turned to panic. The water was rising.

Martel struggled under the heavy weight of the massive body, but he was too weak to free himself. The water was now covering his ear and touching his chin. He kept pushing and kicking, but his limbs felt like noodles.

The frigid water lapped over his mouth. Even worse, he was cheek-to-cheek with Powers' face. The grey pigment in the dead man's skin and his cold, dead black eyes chilled him more than the freezing ocean water.

Water reached over Martel's mouth without receding. Eyes wide open, he held the air in his lungs for what felt like an eternity as water covered his face. A sudden jarring of the ship tilted the room. Tables, tool chests and bodies slid to the backend of the big room. The water lubricated the movement of anything not bolted down. His lungs burning, he felt his and Powers' combined mass shift and slip in the same direction.

As they hit the far wall, Powers' large body rolled off him. After a few seconds, Doc Martel's head popped out of the water, and he heaved for air between coughs. He was free of his dead captor and scrambled up to his knees. Water gushed in from multiple fissures in the bulkheads. The saltiness irritated his throat, and the noise was deafening. The watermark reached his thighs when he stood.

He scrambled up the slippery slope to the previously barricaded door. The water level rose as quickly as he moved now. Flotsam and bodies splashed below him as he clambered to the gaping hatch.

On the other side, the water slid down the deck and pooled at the bottom. The trauma finally caught up with him, and he shivered violently from the icy coldness of the ocean water. He forced himself up and scaled the tilted deck toward the stairs leading to the decks above.

Where is everyone? What the hell did we hit?

When he reached the door to the weather deck, sunlight and fresh air came streaming in, helping clear his head. The water still bubbled from below the deck, but it had stopped rising.

Instead of stepping out into the waiting sunlight on the weather deck, he headed for the medical bay a few metres behind him. Opening the door to his workplace, he gaped over his medical bay, woefully taking in the scene. Papers, equipment, and books were scattered everywhere from the ship's titling. His attention was drawn to the bed where Jerry White had lain after the helicopter crash. The bed was covered end-to-end in blood. Martel shook not from the cold but from the memory of Tom Virtanen and Jerry White attacking him and the others.

He shook his head and grabbed a yellow sealable medical case from the floor. Martel rummaged through the clutter, looking for some very specific items. It took him a few minutes to find what he was looking for and carefully put it in the medical case, which he held on tightly to as he exited the medical bay and laboured up the slanted deck back to the hatch.

Outside, there was a massive crushed wooden pier. He could easily get off the ship there if he could get to the railing without slipping down the slope of the weather deck. Way down, he could see ocean waves hitting the partially submerged helicopter pad. The whole thing reminded him of a water slide, the kind he would have avoided at a water park.

The sound of laboured movement made Martel turn. Trudy Barns, his medical assistant, was making her way around the T-junction a few metres down from the medical bay. She was crawling more than walking as she struggled to stay upright on the uneven deck. When she saw Doc Martel, she hissed and shrieked in excitement.

"Trudy?" Doc Martel shouted reflexively, despite knowing she would not answer. He knew she wasn't . . . herself anymore. The infected accelerated her wobbly pace, and as she got closer, Martel saw the massive hole in her left cheek, which Tom Virtanen had bitten off. The flashback of Virtanen eating part of Trudy's visage spurred Doc Martel into action. He turned back, stretched his one free arm toward the weather-deck guardrail and jumped. His feet slipped on the wet, sharply angled deck, but he managed to grab hold of the railing.

Thank God!

He pulled himself up and secured his feet onto the railing.

Barns kept coming, half-running on all fours now. When she reached the hatch, she flung herself toward him. Both her hands clasped his waist, and her weight made Martel's feet slip off the railing, followed by his hand. In a blink, they both went sliding down the angled wet weather deck to the ocean below.

Martel hit the ice-cold water head-first, and the frigidness took his breath away. For a few seconds, his head bobbed up and under the waves splashing against him, but then he started to sink. He flailed his arms, trying to swim, but Barns was still holding on to him, pulling him down like an anchor. The thought of letting the sealed yellow medical case go crossed his mind. He could swim up better without it. But he didn't.

He stared at the small yellow case through the blurry, churning waters. The water distortion played tricks on his vision, and the case seemed to grow the further down he went. His eyes shifted from the yellow case to the sun penetrating the water above him. It looked like a light at the end of a tunnel; a light that was shrinking.

The water reverberated. Even four feet under, he heard a loud foghorn blare overhead. The light above him rippled, and something jabbed through the water and lassoed him; it caught him by the arm, and he felt an aggressive tug on his shoulder. Something had seized him and was pulling him up.

When he broke the waterline, he gasped for air. A long life hook, the kind used by lifeguards to save drowning victims had snared his arm. But instead of a lifeguard by a pool, it was a young man with a lumberjack vest and a black tuque reeling him in. Doc Martel panted fresh air into his lungs.

Only when he was pulled over the side of the boat did he realize, Barns had disappeared. *Will she drown? Can she swim? What if she bites a fish? Oh God, I am getting delirious.*

The young man wrapped a dry blanket over his shoulders and sat him down on a metal bench in the middle of the tugboat.

"Sir. You okay?"

He looked at his rescuer. The young man in the tuque and lumberjack vest was young, but sturdy. "Where am I?" Doc Martel asked through chattering teeth, not answering the young man's questions.

"Oh. You're on the harbour tugboat. It's me and my older brother's boat. Ryan's the captain."

Doc Martel smiled, realizing his interlocutor had no way of knowing he had been unconscious for a while. "Yes, and where is this tugboat located? Where are we and the boat?"

The young man looked at him quizzically but answered, "Oh. Well, we're in Peaks Bay harbour . . ." Then added hesitantly, " . . . Labrador."

Another man, older-looking and wearing the same tuque and jacket, gently moved the younger one aside.

"I'm Ryan Hutchison, the captain of this here tugboat. And like my little brother told ya, you're in Peaks Bay. Now tell us, who are you?" The tugboat captain crouched down with his arms on his thighs so his eyes were aligned with Martel's.

"Yes, well . . . I'm Eric Martel . . ."

"Well, Eric Martel, can you tell us what the *hell* is going on?"

***

Doc Martel quickly told the story of the Henry Dawson. He was sure they wouldn't believe him. But after Ryan recounted the arrival of the Henry Dawson to Peaks Bay, he realized his story wasn't the worst of it. Neither story seemed real. One was about a ship full of infected crew members infecting each other like zombies; the other was about a ship crashing into a town and unleashing a plague of unholy hell on the population.

"Why are you still here?" Doc Martel asked.

"What do you mean?"

"The Henry Dawson crashed an hour ago. Why are you still here?"

"Fair question, Doc. Truth is, we don't know where to go. Those crazies are crawling all over the shore. We've been circling the harbour for survivors in the water, but it's been slim pickings. We tried to reach the sheriff on his phone but haven't had any luck yet."

"We've tried everyone in town with a phone. No luck at all," Tim added nervously.

Ryan went back to the helm and set a course up the shoreline. Tim picked up his pole with the life hook on the end and watched the water for survivors again.

As the diesel engine came alive and chugged the small boat forward, Doc Martel sat back. The watertight yellow medical case was at his feet. He picked it up and hugged it to his chest.

He was surprised when he noticed another man in the boat with a thick grey wool blanket pulled over his head.

"Hi, I'm Eric. They picked you up too, I guess?" Doc Martel said and reached out his hand. A gesture that looked and felt absurd considering the situation, so he pulled it back after a second of reflection.

The man looked up. He analyzed Martel, then pulled down the blanket from over his head. He was in his thirties, and his blond hair was long and curly, though slicked back and still wet. He looked straight through Doc Martel and answered, "Does it matter who we are?"

Doc Martel didn't think the man wanted an answer.

"I guess it still does—for now. I'm Dirk. Dirk Danerson." He stretched out his hand but was unapologetic about it.

Doc Martel shook it hesitantly.

"So, you're the reason this all happened?" He didn't seem mad. "Thank you for changing things. Thank you for changing everything."

The man smiled at him, but nothing was reassuring about the show of emotion. Doc Martel's skin prickled.

14

TRAINED NOT TO KILL CHICKENS

The sun was slightly past the sky's mid-point, and the air was warm and muggy, making Keefer sweat as he, Abelone and Sergeant Reilly crept up to his bungalow. It was on the way to the police station, and he wanted to pick up his shotgun. The others had easily been convinced as there were more and more infected roaming the streets, like eighties-style street gangs loitering around the neighbourhoods looking for people to mug. He fumbled for his house keys while standing in front of his red weather-beaten door.

As he slid the key into the lock and cracked the door open, he felt vibrations in the porch planks before he heard the hissing. He spun around. A man and a woman, blood dripping from the fresh wounds on their faces and arms, came running at them. Keefer caught the first one. He held the man—the infected—by the shoulders. He recognized him right away—it was Mark, his neighbour.

They sprawled onto the porch and rolled off the front stairs into the yard. As he wrestled with his infected neighbour, he saw Abelone and the infected female—Mark's wife—crash through the unlocked door of his bungalow.

"Abelone!"

He shifted an arm and grabbed the infected by the throat. The infected's head caved in when Sergeant Reilly hit it with a crowbar. Mark—his friend—fell over, dead. Keefer bounced up on his porch and ran through the doorway of his house.

In the middle of the living-room floor lay Mark's wife; her skin was as grey as her dead husband's, her hair partially ripped out, and a huge chunk of skin and muscle bitten off her face. Keefer stopped in his tracks. He blinked hard a few times to confirm what he was seeing. The infected was pinned by Tigger, his German Shepherd. His black and brown fur shook violently every time a muffled shriek escaped the infected's throat.

"Ben!" Abelone called out. She knelt in a corner of the living room, holding the back of her head. Keefer crouched beside her.

"Are you . . . did she . . . ?"

"No, I'm fine," Abelone answered as he gently rested his hand on her shoulder. Abelone's hand found its way to his knee.

A muffled bark from Tigger brought their attention back to the infected in the centre of the room. Sergeant Reilly put his boot on the infected's neck, and with one swift blow of the crowbar, he pierced the infected's skull through the eye socket. Tigger let out a final growl and sniffed the corpse. Satisfied she didn't pose a threat anymore, Tigger ran to Keefer and barked a greeting, which Keefer welcomed with a strong pat down.

"Good boy. You did well."

Keefer was rubbing Tigger's sides when Abelone said worriedly, "He might have swallowed some of the infected blood." She got up and stepped away from the dog. "I've seen a man turn after swallowing blood," she clarified.

Keefer looked up at her, then back down at his dog. His heart sank deep in his chest as he realized the implications. He slowly put both his hands on Tigger's collar while watching his dog's eyes. Tigger tilted his head sideways, wondering why the petting had stopped.

"Can this virus transfer to animals?" He looked back at Abelone. "Things like this don't usually transfer from humans to animals . . . right?" He was wishing it more than asking.

"I don't know. We've never seen anything *like* this. Until yesterday, we didn't think a virus could cause people to act the way they are acting," Abelone reminded him.

As Keefer returned his attention to his dog, a thin film of water covered his eyes. Reilly walked to the front door and looked out at the street to see if any more infected were around before closing the door and locking the deadbolt. He reached over and picked up Keefer's old Benelli 12-gauge shotgun, which was resting in the corner by the door. He made sure it was loaded, pumped it once, flipped the safety off and slowly aimed it at Tigger.

"Hold on one second," Keefer insisted, keeping one hand on Tigger's collar and the other palm-up, facing Reilly.

Sergeant Reilly answered hesitantly, "Ben, I know he's your dog, but can we take the chance?" He circled Keefer and Tigger to get a better angle. "We need to get to the police station. We can't be worried about a zombie dog coming after us."

Keefer was unconvinced.

Abelone stepped in and placed herself between the sergeant and the dog, also with both her palms facing Reilly. "Hold on, we'll know in a few minutes if he is infected. Chances are this virus is not zoonotic."

"Zoonotic?"

"Yes, transferable to humans. I mean, between human and animal, or vice versa." Abelone paused and looked down at Tigger, still held by Keefer. "Most"—she emphasized the word—"viruses are not zoonotic. They don't jump species, so even if the dog swallowed blood or got bitten, he's probably not infected. In any case, we'll know soon."

Sergeant Reilly looked at her, then at Keefer, and last at Tigger, who looked at him confused. He slowly aimed the shotgun down.

"Well, let's at least put him somewhere safe. And zoonotic or not, he's not coming with us. He would give us away too easily, and we wouldn't hear those things coming." Reilly moved back hesitantly.

Keefer took that as his cue and guided his furry companion to the nearby bedroom. *He has to survive.* He got Tigger to lie down at the foot of the bed, closed the bedroom door behind him and let out a long, calming breath.

Sergeant Reilly flipped the safety of the shotgun back on and looked around the small house. "Where's your phone? I can try to call the RCMP from here."

"I don't have a landline," Keefer answered matter-of-factly.

"That makes no sense. How can you not have a phone in your house?"

"I *usually* do have a phone," Keefer corrected him. "My smartphone. Times have changed, Sarge. People don't have landlines anymore."

"That's the stupidest thing I've ever heard," Reilly said as he picked up two boxes of shotgun shells from a shelf on the entrance wall. "Who doesn't have a phone in their house?"

"For what it's worth, I don't have a landline at my house either," Abelone interjected, smiling at Keefer.

Sergeant Reilly paused and looked at both of them, realizing he was out-manned. "Shut up. Both of you."

Keefer smirked and went to the kitchen to get some water bottles. His thoughts lingered on Abelone, and his heart sped up. What was it about her? Maybe he wanted to feel what she felt. He wanted to believe people could be saved. But he couldn't convince himself. Weren't they too far gone? He shook away the conundrum and went back to the living room.

"He hasn't made a sound in there." Keefer pointed with his head toward the bedroom.

"We should check," said Reilly. "But before we do, how about Ms. Jensen finish her story?"

"Story?" Abelone asked as she stepped out of the washroom. She had cleaned most of the blood from her face and arms. Her shirt was still stained with dry blood, but at least Keefer could see her face properly now. Elsie must have re-wrapped her forearm in the ambulance because the bandage was clean.

"What happens to the people who try to break quarantine?" Sergeant Reilly urged her to continue from where she'd left off earlier.

She nodded, but still hesitated. "You need to understand, Q2 is extreme . . . These are impossible theoretical scenarios no one thought would happen." She stood up straighter and turned to face them. "Anyone caught trying to break a Q2 quarantine is shot on sight."

Keefer blinked hard as he processed what she'd said. Reilly sat back in his chair and let out a long, slow breath.

"A virus that warrants a Q2 essentially . . . theoretically, I mean . . . could wipe out all human life."

Sergeant Reilly got up, swearing under his breath. "You are telling me that any of my townsfolk who try to leave Peaks Bay to find safety . . . will get shot?"

Abelone nodded slowly.

"That's insane. There are thousands of people in this town. Are we in a fucking movie?" Reilly fumed. "What's the ninety-eight? Is that how many times they shoot you? Dumbass government."

"No. That's the infection rate," answered Keefer.

Both Reilly and Abelone turned to him. Abelone tilted her head.

"My virology classes are pretty far off, but nothing has ever warranted this type of drastic containment measures. Hence, it has to be a level of infection we've never seen. Ninety-eight is for ninety-eight percent, correct?" he asked Abelone.

She nodded.

He continued, "And for you to be able to label it a ninety-eight percent infection rate, you needed to have a large enough sample size to do the math, a controlled sample size . . . the isolated crew of a ship, for example."

Abelone nodded again as she touched her bandaged arm.

"And for it to be ninety-eight percent, that means a couple of people on the boat would have avoided getting infected when bitten." Keefer paused and shook his head. "Actually," he corrected himself, "on a ship the size of the Henry Dawson, it would only be . . . what . . . one person?"

One more nod from Abelone, who slid both her arms behind her back, effectively putting the bandage out of sight.

"But that one person had to do more than avoid getting infected. That person *had* to *be* infected, too. *She* had to be infected." Keefer looked down at the arm Abelone was holding out of sight. "You were bitten but didn't turn . . . How?"

Abelone held Keefer's stare and pulled her arm back in front of her. She rubbed the bandage again.

"I don't know." She hesitated, but Keefer stared more out of her. "I was bitten on the bridge right as I was thrown in the storage closet. I passed out with the infected trying to break through the door . . . the next thing I knew, I woke up in your ambulance." She was shaking, and her eyes glossed over as they stared into the distance. Keefer stepped closer, but hesitated.

"I saw everyone on the Henry Dawson get bitten and turn into . . . an infected." A tear rolled down Abelone's cheek. "The whole crew turned . . . my friends turned." She put her head down and sobbed quietly.

"Oh, shit." Reilly gasped and took his Stetson off. He rubbed his head with his other hand.

Not knowing what else to do, Keefer broke the hesitancy barrier and put his arm around her.

"And it's been what? A day or two since you were bitten? You could still turn into one of those, right?" Reilly blurted.

Abelone looked at him, worried, but still answered, "Yes."

Keefer scowled, but the affirmation filled him with determination. "We need to get to the police station . . . to contact the authorities again."

Keefer gave Reilly a watch-what-you-say look, then walked to the bedroom door. He put his ear to it and listened.

"What does a zombie dog sound like?" he asked. When no one answered, he slowly opened the door.

Tigger sat a few feet from the door; his head was tilted sideways, and his tail was wagging. He had a confused but happy look on his face. Keefer crouched in the doorway and stared at his dog for a few seconds. Tigger let out a low, quizzical whine. Keefer couldn't help but smile.

"Come here, boy!"

Tigger leapt into Keefer's arms and licked his face, which earned the dog some pats and scratches from Abelone and even Sergeant Reilly. Suddenly, Tigger stopped and looked toward the front door. He stepped forward cautiously, growling. The dog lay flat on his belly. Keefer recognized this as a signal Tigger had learned in hunting class. It was meant to indicate the presence of fowl in the brush, but somehow Keefer doubted Tigger was trying to tell him there were ducks outside. It could only be one thing.

"Get away from the windows!"

Abelone and Reilly crouched on the floor behind the furniture. Keefer bent down beside Tigger and put his hand gently on his muzzle to tell him not to bark. Four infected slammed into the windows, looking into the house haphazardly, as if drunk. After a few seconds, they lost interest and sprinted across the street toward another home.

Keefer held his breath until Tigger got up. Keefer looked at Abelone and Reilly in relief. "I trained him in fowl hunting, mostly so he wouldn't kill the local chickens. Maybe he's using that training to warn us?"

Sergeant Reilly spoke up. "That mutt is coming with us."

15

HELLO, OLD FRIEND

Abelone followed Reilly and Keefer as they made their way to the police station. They navigated side streets and stayed hidden as much as possible. Three times along the way, Tigger lay down flat and growled quietly, alerting them to the incoming infected. Initially, Tigger had spent some time sniffing Abelone's bandaged arm, but had decided she was not a threat and had taken it upon himself to watch over her. That had eased the others' minds.

The last few blocks to the police station turned out to be a surreal experience straight from a Salvador Dali nightmare. Abelone witnessed things her mind simply had no frame of reference for. Three old ladies in Sunday church wear had taken down a cow wandering the streets with an infected toddler chewing on its teats. Then came a pickup truck with four infected in the flatbed; two of them trying to smash the rear cab window while the others looked like they were hooting and hollering on their way to a bonfire party. The closest call they had, though, was when a dozen infected boys came jogging down the street aimlessly. Keefer had called them a troop of Boy Scouts, terminology she was not familiar with. The troop stopped barely ten feet from their hiding spot, but ran off in another direction after hearing a scream in the distance.

She still believed these were people, but what she was seeing shook her to her core. How could she save them? How could people—humans—become so . . . inhuman? She unconsciously kept rubbing her bandaged forearm every time a new nightmarish sequence played out in front of her.

Finally, she and the others stood in front of the Peaks Bay police station. It wasn't what she'd expected. The one-storey building was the size of four bungalows. Painted completely white with a big, blue wooden door, its large flat façade was a couple of feet removed from the sidewalk. It had two large windows covered with closed storm shutters with the lettering *Peaks Bay – Royal Canadian Mounted Police* glued on them. She'd expected some sort of modern-day building, but instead, she stood in front of an old Western-style sheriff's office.

"At least the polar-bear shutters are down," Sergeant Reilly said. He walked up to the blue door and used his keys to open it.

Abelone wondered if there actually were polar bears in Peaks Bay. Before she could ask, Reilly spoke up. "Let's go. We're in."

She and Keefer followed him into the shadowy interior. Reilly made his way straight to the front desk and picked up the landline phone receiver. He stared at the phone for a bit before putting the receiver back down with a cross look.

"What's wrong?" Keefer asked.

"I don't fucking know what number they were calling us from! They weren't in Halifax; they were somewhere in Ottawa." Reilly aggressively pawed his pockets. "Their number is on my phone back in the damn ambulance!"

Abelone understood. No one knew phone numbers anymore; everything was saved on their phones.

"Just call Halifax. Can't they patch us to Ottawa?" Keefer said.

Sergeant Reilly cocked his head, approving of the idea. He jabbed at the numbers. "It's ringing!" He placed the call on speakerphone.

As it rang, Abelone walked along the front windows, protected by the polar-bear shutters. Thin strands of light squeezed through the gaps between the shutters. After seven rings, a young man's voice answered. "RCMP emergency service."

"Hi . . . hello . . . I need to be patched to Ottawa, straight to Director Frederick of the B Division. Hurry!" Reilly said into the speakerphone.

"Sorry, sir. Please identify yourself. All phone communications are reserved for emergency personnel at this time," the young man responded with a twinge of panic.

"It's Sergeant Reilly, RCMP detachment, Peaks Bay. Now patch me into Director Frederick right away."

"Sorry, sir. Please provide your badge identification to confirm your identity," the voice on the phone answered, showing signs of excitement now.

Abelone thought Reilly would slap the young man if he stood in front of him.

Sergeant Reilly let out a loud sigh of frustration. "Badge number is 1114."

There was a sound of ruffling papers, and after thirty seconds, the voice came back on with renewed excitement, "Thank you. Please hold."

Abelone wondered why they were screening calls. There was a click on the line, and for a moment, she thought they had been disconnected. Then the line started to ring again. Each ring reminded Abelone how far they were from any major urban centre—a blessing to contain the virus but a pain to get a hold of anyone.

Someone answered. "Please hold."

The line rang again, and Abelone had to step back as Sergeant Reilly exploded into a tirade of expletives.

"Frederick speaking," someone answered, stopping Reilly mid-sentence, which relieved Abelone.

"Dom, it's Matt."

"Reilly!" Director Frederick exclaimed. "Where the hell have you been? When the line cut off last time, we thought you were dead."

"Well, I'm not. We're not. Not yet, anyway. Listen, Dom. It's bad over here."

Director Frederick cut him off. "I know, Matt. The whole world knows. You can't keep something like this contained in today's social media world. It was out minutes after the Henry Dawson crashed into the harbour. You've probably noticed all communications—radio, TV, cellular and landlines—have been cut off to and from Peaks Bay."

"I hadn't. But that explains why the kid on the phone wouldn't patch me through."

"Yeah, we're getting hundreds of calls from Peaks Bay residents. We have call centre agents screening every call out of town. The calls that get through now are from emergency personnel. We gave them a list of names from Peaks Bay police, fire department, hospital and municipal government officials; those are the people they let through after identification. You were second on our list of importance, but no one thought you were alive. Imagine the kid's surprise when you said your name . . . Fuck, Matt, imagine my surprise!"

Abelone wondered who was number one on the list. Maybe the mayor?

Reilly didn't have that same concern. "Dom, I am here with the scientist from the ship, Abelone Jensen. She knows what's going on."

Abelone took her cue. "Director Frederick. This is Abelone Jensen from the—"

The director cut her off. "I know who you are, Ms. Jensen. We've been fully briefed on you and your fellow scientists, along with the mission you were on with the Henry Dawson."

There were muffled voices in the background, and after a few seconds, he started again, "Is that what this is? Is this some form of Yers . . . Yersina . . . Yersinia pestis? Is the outbreak in Peaks Bay related to the Black Death outbreak found in Greenland?"

"I believe it is, Director. And that is what I was going to explain when we were attacked in the ambulance. Is Mr. Birchmeier still there?"

There was another pause on the line, and more muffled discussion followed.

"Sorry, Ms. Jensen, he is unavailable at this moment. I am the official liaison to Peaks Bay. Can you tell me if your assessment of the situation in Peaks Bay has changed from a Q2-98?"

"I can confirm that my assessment from a few hours ago stands. Can you confirm that full quarantine measures have been put in place for the town?"

There was another long pause, with the sound of muffled voices arguing. Finally, Director Frederick answered, "Ms. Jensen, due to your clearance and involvement with the WHO, I can tell you all Q2 quarantine measures are in place."

This brought angry stares from Keefer and Sergeant Reilly, but to their credit, they both kept quiet. The director took a deep breath and added, "Now, we have some questions for you."

While she answered questions and recounted her story, Sergeant Reilly pulled Keefer aside. She heard him say something about activating the emergency VHF broadcast system and getting guns from the gun locker in the back. Then he disappeared through a back door.

***

Keefer stood watch at the front door of the police station while he listened to Abelone tell her incredible story to the folks in Ottawa. It was late afternoon, a time when the streets should be bustling with cars and people, but today they were empty. Literally. Except, every so often, an infected would run down the street hissing and gurgling.

Are they dead, or are they alive? Lost in his thoughts, Keefer jumped when Abelone put her hand on his shoulder.

"You okay? I called out to you," Abelone said. "The director asked for a break to process what I was telling them."

"I can't believe what you went through on that ship." Keefer turned to her. "I can't believe what is going on out there. We killed Mark and Suzie . . . we killed my neighbours!"

He had killed his *friends*. He decided then and there that there was no way they were alive, no way they could be saved. Otherwise, he couldn't live with what he'd done.

Abelone gave him an emphatic look. "We can't go around killing these people. They are sick. You don't kill sick people!"

"With everything you've been through. With everything you've seen. How can you believe the infected out there can still be saved?" He wanted to believe her, but he couldn't.

"People can always be saved. I need to believe that in my line of work," Abelone said surer than anything else Keefer had heard her say up to now.

Tigger sprang up from where he lay near the door. His ears went flat, and the fur on his back stood at attention. From deep inside his throat came a low warning growl. Keefer tensed. He moved to the little window on the door to look outside.

Five men ran around a corner a block down the street. One of them was yelling to the others to keep running, that they were getting close, and was waving his arms toward the police station.

From around the same corner, an infected sprinted after them. It was a dozen strides behind them, and its spastic twitch was accentuated by the running. A few more strides behind came another infected, then another, and another. Within a few seconds, the end of the street was filled with hundreds of infected, all pursuing the runners.

"We need to help them," said Abelone, standing beside Keefer.

"There're . . . hundreds of them out there. And what if they're infected?" asked Keefer, weighing the risk of helping these people.

"Ben, people can still be saved."

There was that altruism again. He admired it and wanted to believe in it so badly.

Keefer unbolted the thick blue door and swung it open. He took the safety off his shotgun and stepped outside.

"Hurry!" Keefer shouted.

The street behind the running men was filled with infected. An angry wave of hissing and shrieking spilled down the asphalt road toward the police station.

The men ran straight past Keefer and into the station. He jumped inside behind them, and Abelone slammed the door shut and bolted it.

The infected hit the police station like a wave crashing on rocks. Everyone in the station stepped away from the front wall as it shook, looking like it would cave in. The polar-bear shutters rattled like thunder as arms and heads were repeatedly smashed against them. The big blue door shook in its frame, taking a pounding from angry hands.

The group was frozen, watching, until Keefer spoke up. "The awnings and doors are holding. We're safe for now."

He turned and went straight for the tallest and oldest. Moe, the harbour master, was keeled over with his hands on his knees, trying to catch his breath.

Keefer grabbed him by the shoulders and bear-hugged him. "Grumpy old bastard. You're still alive." Moe looked like he wanted to answer, but he was too out of breath.

Keefer let go of Moe and put his hands on the shoulders of Tim and Ryan Hutchison. They were in their usual red and black lumberjack outfits. Tim was shaking from head to toe.

"Tim. You're safe here, okay?"

"Hi, Benjamin . . . Ben . . . Sir," answered Tim as his shaking slowed.

Ryan stepped over and put his arm around his younger brother. "Thanks, Ben. It's good to see you. It's good to see anyone in this madness."

"Madness, my ass," said another man in a hood. "This is the bloody apocalypse straight out of the Old Testament."

Keefer knew who it was before the hood came down. He couldn't believe he was standing in front of Dirk Danerson.

"It's New, actually," said the fifth man, whom Ben did not recognize.

"What?" Dirk snorted.

"It's from the New Testament. Book of Revelations," the man said. "It has nothing to do with the Old Testament."

Dirk looked at him crossly. "Are you fucking kidding me? Who gives a damn? It could be from a Dr. Seuss book for all I care. It's the end of the fucking world. God is dead. We're on our own. Do you get that?"

"Dirk," Keefer said, partly to acknowledge him and partly to get him to stop.

Dirk looked at him coldly. "How long have you guys been here?"

"We just got here—" Keefer answered.

"Eric!" Abelone shouted. The short, bald, portly man Keefer did not know was caught in a hug from Abelone.

Do they know each other?

Abelone looked up with watery eyes. "Benjamin, this is Eric Martel. Doctor Eric Martel. He's the doctor from the Henry Dawson."

The revelation took Keefer by surprise. In the mad rush of things, it had never occurred to him that there could have been more survivors from the ship.

"Doctor? You survived too?" Keefer said.

"I'm as surprised as you are, young man," Doc Martel said, sniffing back his own waterworks. "I didn't even know we had made land until I woke up a few hours ago. These fine folks over there"—Doc Martel pointed to Tim and Ryan—"saved me from the water."

Keefer could tell the gratitude in the man's voice was genuine, and he liked him immediately.

Dirk stepped forward and looked at Abelone from top to bottom suspiciously. His eyes lingered over her body. Abelone crossed her arms and turned slightly away.

"Who the hell are you, bitch?" Dirk said.

Keefer stiffened at Dirk's aggressive tone.

"My name is Abelone Jensen. I'm with the WHO."

Keefer stepped sideways, partially blocking Dirk's path to Abelone as a precaution. Dirk noticed and smiled smugly.

"You the one who brought this plague here? You're responsible for what is happening?" He didn't wait for an answer and turned his attention to Keefer. "Protect her all you want. She is the cause of what is happening here. I don't know if I should thank her or hate her. In any case, God will make sure they get what's coming to them."

It was unlike Dirk to reference anything religious, let alone God, and it made Keefer uneasy.

"Listen, Dirk, we are in contact with Public Health and the WHO. They are working on figuring out how to help us. We need to stay calm." Keefer tried to placate Dirk.

Dirk walked to the front door to look out the small square window. "How did the two of you even survive this long? How did you get in here? I thought old man Reilly kept this place locked up pretty tight?" he asked without looking back.

That was when Keefer realized he'd forgotten about Sergeant Reilly in all the commotion. "He's with us."

Dirk spun back to face Keefer. "What?" he asked as his eyes narrowed and flitted about the room. "Where is he?"

"He's in the back activating the VHF emergency broadcast and getting the spare guns," Keefer said, nodding toward the door that led to the rear of the police station.

"That's the smartest thing anyone's done all day. I'm going to go help him." Dirk ran his hand over his chin a few times and scratched at his nose as he left via the same door Sergeant Reilly had used.

"Wow, that guy is something else. A good friend of yours?" asked Abelone as she moved in close to Keefer.

"Let's say I've had a complicated relationship with him since I moved here," Keefer said.

"Ha!" blurted Moe. "That's an understatement."

Tim, who'd been quiet to this point, pitched in, "Dirk the jerk. He's not nice to anyone."

Ryan gave his little brother a stare, and Tim refrained from further comments.

"A truer name has never been spoken," Moe grunted, smiling at Tim.

16

WIPE IT ALL OUT

I t took a few minutes for the onslaught on the door and awnings to subside. When the phone rang unexpectedly, it sent Abelone's heart racing. She jumped over to the desk and answered before the end of the first ring. It wasn't quick enough. The assault on the police station resumed.

"Abelone Jensen," she blurted as she eyed the shaking windows.

Keefer, Moe and Doc Martel crowded around her while Ryan stayed with his brother on the bench. She smelled Keefer's musk as he reached over her arm and pressed the speakerphone button. A voice came on mid-sentence.

" . . . and the quarantine is fully established. We believe we have full containment at this point."

Director Frederick, Abelone mouthed.

"Have you collected samples yet? Do you know what this thing is?" she asked.

Director Frederick paused and again seemed to be getting his answer from a group of people in the room with him.

"No reports on that."

A couple of seconds of dead air didn't sit right with Abelone. "What aren't you telling us, Director?" She couldn't help the edge in her tone.

"Ms. Jensen, you need to understand we are only talking with you because you are a member of the WHO rapid response team, and you might have more information concerning this virus. Mr. Birchmeier insisted we call you one last time. If it weren't for a phone call from the Director General of the WHO herself to the Canadian Prime Minister, we wouldn't be talking right now."

The statement took Abelone off guard. *One last time? Why would they be breaking off communications?*

"What is Mr. Birchmeier's message?" Abelone asked.

"Mr. Birchmeier wanted me to let you know the WHO teams sent to Greenland following your expedition have not found any trace of this virus at the site of the Nuovo Mondo, only the Yersinia pestis bacteria." Frederick took another aggravating pause. She almost slammed the phone receiver on the desk, waiting for him to continue.

"He also wants me to tell you, as per the protocols you helped write, for the safety of the people in Peaks Bay, all communications will be cut off until full containment is achieved."

"Why is he—" Abelone's thoughts congealed. They were being written off. Her old acquaintance, Deider Birchmeier, wanted her to know they were moving to Level Three. He must have known she would understand . . . or at least he must have hoped. Abelone's heart pounded against her rib cage, and she plopped down in the chair by the desk.

"Ms. Jensen, is there any more information you can provide us at this time?"

She steadied herself enough to mutter, "Does it matter?"

"Umm . . . pardon my interruption," Doc Martel said.

Abelone tried to focus her blurry vision on him.

"I have the samples . . . I mean, um . . . I picked them up . . . of the two original infected."

In one blink, Abelone's vision went from blurry to tunnel. For the first time, she noticed what he was holding.

Martel continued, "There was this young man who had rabies on the ship . . . and well, the other man was our helicopter pilot . . . he crashed his chopper right on the beach. That's where I think they got the Yersinia pestis . . . and it changed them . . . and well, when I woke up, I was in the ship's engineering room. Everyone was dead or gone . . . and after almost drowning, I made my way through the ship and happened across my medical bay . . ."

Abelone got up and grabbed Martel in a bear hug again, but this time for a different reason.

"Oh . . . wow . . ." was all Martel could say.

There was muffled arguing over the phone, and Deider Birchmeier's voice came onto the line. "Who is speaking?" he asked excitedly.

"It's Eric Martel, ship doctor for the Henry Dawson." Doc Martel moved closer to the phone, extricating himself from Abelone's hug.

There was a short pause on the line. This time, it was a different pause—not to collect opinions or instructions, but one of surprise.

"Doctor Martel, this is Deider Birchmeier from the WHO. We were unaware you had survived. Did—"

Abelone interjected. "Eric, show me the samples."

Doc Martel unlatched the clamps on the case and opened it. The seal made a small, clean, popping sound. Inside the case were six vials, each full of blood, each snuggly protected in grey foam. Abelone looked at the vials, dumbfounded. She had a surge of adrenaline, and her vision became crisp and alert again. She read the blue-inked hand-written labels on the vials:

06-29-2017 T. Virtanen Sample #1.a

06-29-2017 T. Virtanen Sample #1.b

06-29-2017 T. Virtanen Sample #1.c

06-29-2017 J. White Sample #2.a

06-29-2017 J. White Sample #2.b

06-29-2017 J. White Sample #2.c

"Oh my God!" she exclaimed.

"Ms. Jensen, what is going on? What vials are in your possession?" Birchmeier asked frantically.

"Deider!" Abelone dropped the Danish formality in her excitement. "We have the blood . . . we have the blood of Patient Zero!" She could hardly contain herself, knowing this would mean the Level Three quarantine wouldn't need to be enacted.

"What? How?" Birchmeier asked, clearly confused.

A cacophony of voices on the other end of the line all talked over each other. At first, she thought the uproar of exchanges was excitement, but Birchmeier's yelling in the fray was upset. Someone yelled out: "It's too late!"

To which Birchmeier responded, "It is not. They can be saved!" But he was drowned out by other responses, all similar to: "We need to protect the world!"

Her earlier excitement dissipated as fast as a teapot whistle taken off the burner.

The shouting grew more intense until a gunshot rang out over the line, and all voices stopped.

Everyone in the police station, thousands of miles away, stared at the speakerphone.

One last shout broke the silence on the line: "Officers! Arrest those three men and place them in holding."

Someone on the other end covered the phone, and all sounds were muffled again. The phone had not been hung up, as there was no dial tone. Abelone and the others waited nervously. After a gruelling minute of waiting, a voice came back onto the line. It was not Deider Birchmeier.

"Ms. Jensen—" It was Director Frederick.

"What is going on over there? Where is Deider? What was that gunshot?" Abelone interrupted.

"Ms. Jensen," Frederick insisted. "Mr. Birchmeier and his colleagues from Public Health have been removed from the room as they were being ... uncooperative."

"Uncooperative?" Abelone asked angrily.

"Yes. This is a time of great crisis, and we need everyone to make decisions in a coordinated fashion. Mr. Birchmeier explained the samples of blood you have *might* be helpful?"

Abelone didn't like the way the director emphasized the word *might*.

"Please stay where you are so we can reach you at this number. We will confer with further experts on our end and will call you back with instructions."

The line went dead, and the dial tone beeped obnoxiously from the speakerphone.

"Abelone, can these blood samples help?" asked Keefer, confused.

She hesitated. "Maybe . . . I mean, yes. If they hold the original virus, theoretically, we should be able to develop a vaccine."

Doc Martel piped in, "They do hold the original virus. This all started with Jerry and Tom, I'm sure of it. I saw them eat—" He changed his mind on the wording. "—attack my assistant Trudy Barns, for God's sake!"

This confirmed what Abelone had suspected. Tom was the only one without bites.

"Okay, so if these are the original samples, wouldn't the WHO and the Canadian Public Health want them ASAP?" Keefer interjected.

"They would," replied Abelone.

"But what were those gunshots? And why arrest the WHO officials?"

"They must be planning how to come and get us," Moe said, speaking up for the first time.

"Why would they cut off communication like that?"

"Aren't you worried about the gunshot?"

"Why was Birchmeier removed?"

Everyone was talking at once. Abelone couldn't concentrate. She put the palm of her hand on her forehead and pressed. Her thoughts congealed, and she blurted out, "They don't need the vials. They have already given the order to move to Level Three quarantine." Her voice was emotionless.

The group looked at her, heads tilting and hands scratching scalps.

Abelone added with finality, "They can't risk the virus spreading, so the plan is in motion. They will eradicate the virus. Wipe it out completely . . ." Abelone breathed deeply. "They've already decided to kill every living thing in Peaks Bay."

***

Dirk stomped down the long stuffy hallway connecting the front of the police station to the car park at the back of the building. The hallway was lined with three grey holding cells on one side and three closed office doors on the other. Dirk looked at the cells with contempt. He'd been here a couple of times. Reilly and his officers knew him well. In Peaks Bay, the holding cells were more to hold drunks than criminals. He paused to look at the holding cells and contemplated how he could have ended up behind those bars for more than just being drunk and disorderly, but never had. He was at peace with whom and what he was, but still he hacked up some phlegm and spat at a cell.

Things were changing. There was a light shining brighter and brighter in his mind. Society always had a way of interfering with his urges. No more, though. Peaks Bay had changed with the arrival of this virus. The rules of society were falling apart. He could see it, but he could also feel it in every fibre of his body. *Fuck that asshole, Reilly; that prick, Keefer.*

He slowly opened the thick metal door to the car park and looked around the dimly lit space. The smell of oil and grease enveloped him right away. The garage was large enough to hold three police vehicles but housed none at the moment. He figured they had been dispatched to the harbour plaza. He frowned, having hoped to get a car to drive out of this hellhole.

Well, look at that. Going through the door, he noticed a massive metal hatch on the ground in a corner, like those found on top of a submarine. He had never noticed it, probably because he was drunk and in handcuffs whenever he walked by here. *That must be the old World War II bomb shelter people always talk about.* He'd seen the hospital bomb shelter and had heard stories that the police station had one too.

A loud clanking at the other end of the garage attracted his attention. Sergeant Reilly had his back to him and was sliding a rifle into a black police-issue duffle bag. Dirk could tell the bag was full of other guns and ammo by the lumps and bumps in the canvas.

In the background, the static-filled VHF emergency broadcast played on the radio a few feet from the large gun locker in front of which Reilly squatted.

"BEEP—This is the Peaks Bay Emergency Broadcast System—BEEP—Take shelter immediately. This is not a drill—BEEP—There is a biological hazard across all of Peaks Bay—BEEP—Take shelter in your home, office or nearest building—BEEP—Await further instructions via the emergency broadcast system—BEEP—End of transmission."

Sergeant Reilly's recorded voice was on a loop and grated on Dirk the more he heard it. He knew it would be playing over the local AM radio signals, but he wondered who would actually hear it. *No one listens to the radio anymore. What an idiot.*

He walked casually up to Sergeant Reilly.

"Hey, old man. Thought I'd come and give you a hand," he said, pleased he would surprise the police officer. *Maybe I'll give him a heart attack.*

Sergeant Reilly spun, startled.

"Danerson! You survived the plaza?" Reilly blurted as his face scrunched up and his eyes squinted. That was when Dirk realized the old sergeant might have seen what he'd done on the pier.

Despite his age, Reilly sprang forward like a cobra and grabbed him by the throat. The sergeant was bigger and heavier than Dirk, and he spun him into the wall. The impact knocked over a tall shelving unit, and it crashed to the ground in a clamour. The noise immediately attracted a response from outside the car park, and a drumming of hands and arms started playing on the metal door right beside where Dirk was pinned. He could feel the vibrations of the assault all through his body.

"You son of a bitch! You killed Tricia!" Reilly growled.

Dirk was stunned by how quickly the old man had moved. He hadn't expected to be attacked like this; all he could muster was, "What?" *Need to buy time.*

"Don't play dumb, you weasel. I saw what you did on the pier. You are going to pay for it. I am going to make sure you spend the rest of your life in prison," Sergeant Reilly snarled, squeezing his grip on the smaller man's throat.

"I don't know what you are talking about. I was trying to help her on the pier when she was overrun by all those . . . things . . ." Dirk croaked, barely able to breathe.

Reilly shook his head. "I saw you with my own eyes. You hit her with a plank to buy yourself time to get away. I don't know what you are doing here, but I am throwing you in a holding cell."

"Sergeant, please! Let me go! Those things were attacking everyone. There was one already latched on to her. I tried to help! It was horrible. They were everywhere." Dirk's voice could not have sounded more scared. "I tried to help her! I did. But . . . but it was too late."

It worked. Sergeant Reilly hesitated, a look of doubt washing over his face. Dirk could tell Reilly was struggling to remember exactly what he'd seen in all the commotion. The sergeant scanned Dirk's scared and imploring face, and his grip loosened from his neck—just enough.

Dirk grabbed Reilly's arm with both hands and pulled it away. He moved quickly and violently, a vile look replacing the helplessness on his face. It was Reilly's turn to be caught off guard as Dirk stepped forward and kneed him in the groin. Reilly collapsed to his knees with a grunt.

"Stupid, old man. Don't you get it? Holding cells, murder charges, none of that matters anymore. Everything we know is coming to an end. The slate is being wiped clean!" Dirk grabbed a screwdriver off the ground. "Just like you're coming to an end." In one rapid strike, he stabbed the screwdriver into Sergeant Reilly's chest. He pulled it out and stabbed Reilly's chest two more times before stepping back to admire his work. Reilly gasped and heaved as his left hand pawed at the leaking wounds. Dirk breathed a long sigh as the tension left his body. His adrenaline pumping as he took in as much as possible.

"You . . . son . . . of . . . a—" Reilly stammered.

"The world doesn't belong to you anymore. Your laws, your morals, they're gone. The world belongs to people like me now. People like me are the ones who will survive this . . ." He wondered what to call it. "End-of-days."

"Maybe . . ." Reilly managed to say. "But not you . . . it won't belong to you . . ." Sergeant Reilly raised his sidearm from his holster and aimed it straight at Dirk's chest.

Dirk saw the gun come up and backed into the wall. His hand landed on the doorknob. He turned it and swung the door open as the shot went off. The blast echoed in the car park, and the bullet lodged itself into the metal door now protecting him.

Three infected crashed through the open doorway. They landed on the sergeant in a heap, their teeth sinking into him. Dirk stepped out from behind the door and watched. Sergeant Reilly didn't scream, and he didn't fight. He closed his eyes and went quietly. Dirk felt liberated. He looked around the parkade smiling, but his smile quickly faded when he spotted Tim standing at the open door leading to the front of the station. *Fuck, did he see?* He couldn't be sure. The kid was an idiot. Still . . . Dirk waved at Tim to wait for him there as he picked up the duffle bag without attracting the attention of the feasting infected.

Tim took off down the hallway. *Damn it, he saw.*

17

TRUE NATURE

Keefer turned from Abelone when he heard the gunshots. Her revelation that "the government was going to kill every living thing in Peaks Bay" would have to wait.

"What the hell was that?" Ryan heard it, too, and automatically looked for his brother. "Tim must have gone in back!" he said with alarm.

Keefer followed Ryan to the back door just as it swung open, and Tim ran straight into his brother's big chest.

"Tim! What the hell! You had me scared shitless. What was that gunshot?" Ryan barked.

Tim was shaking. "Dirk...Reilly..." Tim couldn't get a full sentence out.

Ryan squeezed his brother by the shoulders gently. "Calm down, Tim. Tell us what happened."

Tim focused on his brother's face, then looked at Keefer and back at his brother. His breathing slowed, and he calmed. He opened his mouth to speak, but a deafening bang resonated through the hallway.

Tim's mouth froze, still open, as if he would speak at any second, but his eyes squeezed shut. Life drained from his face. The young man smiled like he always did, and then he was gone, still held up by his brother.

Keefer looked down the hallway and confirmed what his gut already knew. Dirk stood holding a rifle with a thin film of smoke coming out of its muzzle. Dirk was smiling with both sets of teeth showing, like a child who'd won a carnival prize. Keefer raised his shotgun and fired down the hallway in anger. The slugs punched holes in the wall near Dirk, sending splinters flying. Dirk recoiled and scrambled for cover in the closest office before unloading a magazine of bullets in response. Keefer ducked to safety with Ryan and Tim as the open hallway door exploded into pieces.

Keefer rummaged through his pockets for other shotgun shells. His hands shook, and the smell of gunpowder almost made him sneeze. He dropped the first shell he tried to load. Concentrating to calm himself, he managed to get the three next shells loaded. *Why is Dirk doing this?* He took a deep breath, then peeked around the doorframe. Another wave of bullets rattled down the hallway. Several bullets rushed by his hair as he jerked back to safety. The bullets shattered the police-station windows and tore part of the storm shutters off. Grey bloody hands with broken fingers and ripped-out fingernails reached through the holes, trying to rip down the rest of the metal armour of the windows.

Dirk shouted, "Keefer, I've wanted to kill you since I met you! But, of course, that kind of thing was frowned upon! Not anymore! Guys like you don't have a place in this world. In this new world, it's all about me!"

Another shower of bullets burst down the corridor. *He's totally out of his mind.* Keefer checked to make sure Moe, Abelone and Doc Martel were behind something. They were.

As he peeked around the doorframe, he saw Dirk standing defiantly in the middle of the hallway, aiming his rifle toward the front room.

"No one will know how you died! No one will care! Tell those scientists they will reap what they sowed!"

Keefer peeked around the doorframe in time to see Dirk open the door leading to the car park, then duck back in the office and slam that door shut.

Why did he open that door?

The hissing and shrieking were unmistakable. He knew what it meant. Five infected came rushing through the open doorway. They bumped against each other and off the hallway walls as they scurried to get to Keefer. Keefer lifted the shotgun toward the oncoming group and squeezed the trigger—once, twice, three times. The infected absorbed the slugs without falling, but grey skin and black blood splattered across the walls—they kept coming. Keefer looked for a door to close, but it was on the ground, blasted to pieces by Dirk's bullets.

"We need to get out!" he shouted to the others.

As he looked back down the hallway, the first infected leapt at him. He flinched and closed his eyes. When nothing happened, he reopened them and saw Ryan standing in front of him. He blocked access to the front room and held the infected by the neck.

"Go! Up the ladder to the roof!" Ryan jerked his head toward a metal ladder bolted to the side wall of the office.

As another infected sidestepped the one held by Ryan, he grabbed it by the chest with his other hand and pinned it to the wall. The two infected and Ryan now clogged the doorframe, blocking the other infected from getting by.

"You need to come with us!" shouted Keefer.

"No, I can't. I'm staying with Timmy. Go!"

Keefer noticed for the first time Ryan was bleeding. The bullet that killed Tim had gone straight through and wounded Ryan as well. Blood poured down his chest and covered his pants.

"Go! You can't save me," Ryan said as two more infected jumped on top of the pileup and bit into Ryan's arms, one after the other. Ryan grimaced.

"Go!" Ryan pleaded.

Keefer took a step back and saw Moe hustling Abelone and Doc Martel to the metal ladder. Dirk came out from the office at the other end of the hallway, a repugnant smile on his face. He saluted Keefer before triumphantly spinning around and stepping through the car-park door.

To Keefer's surprise—and even more to Dirk's—Dirk ran straight into a tall grey infected. Chunks of flesh had been chewed off his face, and his chest was covered in blood, but Keefer recognized Sergeant Reilly right away. He stood as tall as ever, and even without his Stetson, he resembled the sheriff of Peaks Bay as much as before. The lawman bent down and sank his teeth into Dirk's neck. Dirk dropped his rifle and tried to bring a pistol from his belt up as he punched at Sergeant Reilly. As the two of them struggled, they stumbled into the car park and disappeared. Seconds later, gunshots echoed out of sight.

Ryan, still holding the infected, fell to a knee. He pleaded meekly to Keefer one last time, "Go!"

Keefer lunged for the metal ladder as the infected burst past Ryan. He scrambled up the ladder and grabbed the outstretched hands of Moe and Abelone at the top. A bark made his heart skip a beat. Tigger was still in the room below. The infected were pouring into the office from the back hallway as well as through the window where the shutter was now torn off. Tigger's fur was standing straight up, and his bark was deep and loud as he looked at his master for instructions.

"RUN!" Keefer yelled, tears welling in his eyes.

Tigger's ears perked at the command, and he darted off, zigzagging through the multiple shuffling legs and groping grey hands. He disappeared down the hallway leading to the garage.

Keefer listened for a few seconds. No bark. No whimper. He held the hatch door and watched the infected fill the room. Abelone, Moe and Doc Martel stood beside him quietly. Then they all heard it. Keefer locked eyes with Abelone in disbelief. He let go of the hatch door, and it slammed shut, cutting off all sounds from the inside—including the ringing telephone.

***

Abelone stared at the hatch. Had they changed their minds? Would they give them a chance to bring the blood of Patient Zero to a lab? It didn't matter. They didn't answer the phone; no one would know they were alive.

"How much time do we have?" Keefer asked, looking at Abelone.

There was no reason to withhold anything from them at this point. "They will attempt to eradicate the virus. All collateral damage is accepted..."

"What? How? How do you 'eradicate' something like this? Are they going to drop a nuke on top of our heads?" Moe asked, exasperated.

Abelone stared at him with a blank expression.

"Hold on one second. They're not going to do that, are they?"

"No," Abelone said. "But it will be as devastating. They need to make sure this virus doesn't spread beyond this town. Once Q3 is enacted, naphthenic and palmitic acids will be used to raze the area and burn off the infection completely."

"Naphthen-what?" Moe asked, clearly annoyed by the use of words he didn't understand.

Abelone looked at Keefer.

"Naphthenic acid," Keefer stepped in. "Napalm."

There was an awkward silence between the survivors as they pictured the scenario.

"How much time do we have?" Doc Martel asked.

"At best, an hour," she answered. "Once Q3 is enacted, it's considered a race against time. We either eradicate the virus, or *it* eradicates *us*."

Moe was beside himself. "How stupid are the people who wrote this protocol thing? I mean, no offence, as you were one of them, but seriously, you can't imagine any country would burn down a town with thousands of people in it."

Abelone didn't want to answer his question. The Geneva Protocols were clear. If a country did not act, it would be violating international law, and other countries would be allowed to take matters into their own hands and do it themselves. No one ever thought a Q3 would be mandated. It was for an extinction-level event.

***

Keefer drifted off from the group as he listened to Abelone answer more questions. Her voice grew fainter as he moved away. From where he stood, he could see Lookout Point, where his day had started. He couldn't believe that early this morning Peaks Bay looked so serene, and now it was overrun by . . . *what? Zombies? Are they actually zombies? Are they even alive?* The questions spun in his head, and the faces of the people who'd died floated across his vision: the lady in the purple rain jacket, his neighbours, Sergeant Reilly, Tim, Ryan . . . and even Dirk. There was a pain in his chest when he thought of what Dirk had done.

He walked to the front of the police station to overlook the street. The hissing and gurgling got louder the closer he got; it sounded like the low murmur of river rapids as you approached from the woods. When he looked over the edge, his breath stuck in his throat. In front of the building stretched a horde of grey-skinned infected as far as he could see down the street. Hundreds upon hundreds of bloodied, maimed bodies, twitching and shoving.

"Um, guys, we should get out of here," Keefer said.

A handful of infected on the sidewalk heard his plea and looked up. When they spotted him, they stretched their arms toward him and started wailing and shrieking. A frenzy spread from the police station down the street through the myriad of grey bodies. They renewed their push, and the closest ones were squished against the walls of the building. Wave after wave started to climb on top of each other.

"This is not good!" Keefer yelled out as he stepped back. The others stopped talking and looked at him.

The mound of gnarled grey bodies was getting higher as more infected climbed on top of the others. One especially tall infected got its hands on the edge of the roof and pulled itself up.

"Oh shit! Guys, we got to go!"

Keefer swung the shotgun off his shoulder and aimed it at the tall infected's chest. He squeezed the trigger. The slug hit it straight on and propelled it backwards. The body slowly dropped through the air and crashed on top of the layer of infected covering every inch of the street below.

More hands grasped at the roof edge. Keefer spun and ran toward the others. "Got to go! *Now!*"

Moe was the first to act. "Over here! I picked up the keys to the police panel van parked in back." He waved the keys as he ran to the back of the rooftop. The van was parked alongside the police station's rear wall.

Keefer scanned the alley. It was still empty. He wasted no time and jumped the gap to the top of the van. He landed with a thunk on the metal roof. Moe jumped next, followed by Abelone. She landed awkwardly and fell into Keefer's arms. He held her for a few seconds while she looked up at him.

"Thanks."

Moe groaned. "Save it for later, you two. We got to roll!" He lowered himself off the side of the panel van and unlocked the door.

Doc Martel was on the edge of the rooftop, hesitating. Keefer could see he was worried and probably not as nimble as the others.

"Come on, Eric. *Jump!*" Abelone whispered loudly.

Three infected were on the roof.

Martel jumped. Keefer caught him as he landed with a thud and caved the metal roof half a foot. They all looked down at the deep dent.

"Hush," Doc Martel said.

The three infected from the rooftop came hurtling over the edge. Two of them bounced off, but the third one landed face-down on the van's roof and managed not to roll off.

"Off the van! Hurry!" shouted Moe as he slid into the driver's seat and turned on the engine.

Keefer and the others slid off the vehicle's roof and jumped into the now-open side door. One of the infected that had hit the pavement was already up, its arm bent at a backward angle. It lunged at the open door. The shotgun in Keefer's hands exploded like thunder and caught it straight in the head, sending pieces of bone, flesh and brain spraying backwards. The body dropped to the ground.

The blast inside the confined metal walls was like a stun grenade. It disoriented Keefer. He put his hand on the wall to hold himself up. Abelone braced against the frame of the panel door just as the other infected grabbed her arm and jerked her out.

"Abelone!" Keefer shouted, one hand still on an ear. He stumbled forward, unsteady, to try to help as the infected stood over Abelone.

A deep growl preceded Tigger tackling the infected and seizing it by the neck. The German Shepherd shook the infected with small, violent jerks while pinning it to the ground. Abelone got up, still unsteady from the shotgun blast, but she was able to leap back in, grabbing Keefer's outstretched hand.

The van lurched forward as Moe slammed his foot on the gas pedal. The vehicle skidded across the parking lot as more infected poured around the corner of the police station at a full sprint.

Keefer leaned out the panel van door and whistled as loud as he could to signal Tigger to follow them. The dog immediately let go of the infected and bolted after the van. Hundreds of infected were sprinting behind the dog while he tried to catch up.

"Slow down!" shouted Keefer to Moe over the engine noise.

Moe looked back in the mirror and eased off the gas for a few seconds. Tigger caught up and leapt in. Keefer caught him. His dog was panting hard. Doc Martel slammed the panel van door shut as Moe hit the accelerator again.

18

DYING LIGHT

A belone clutched the seat as the van sped through the empty streets of Peaks Bay. Now and then, an infected would pop up, and Moe would swerve to avoid it, sending her sliding up and down the seat.

"Mr. Moe, do you know where we are going?" Doc Martel asked from the passenger seat while reaching for his seat belt.

"If what Ms. Jensen told us is true, we need to get out of town before this place gets levelled," Moe answered.

"We won't be able to outrun this. They're going to raze everything within eighty miles of the town. At best, we have thirty minutes to get somewhere. At worst—" A particularly big bump tossed Tigger aside, and Abelone quickly reached down and brought him back between her legs and squeezed him there. "At worst, naphthenic and palmitic acids could start falling on us any minute. Hard to tell exactly when they triggered the Q3 protocol."

"Can you just say napalm? Why do you have to say *napatonic palmo-live* acid? Just say *napalm!*" Moe shouted back over his shoulder.

"It's naphthenic and palmitic, and we don't call it napalm because it's an outdated term from the seventies," said Abelone, irritated.

Keefer leaned over and squeezed Abelone's shoulder. She looked at him, and his smile told her Moe was scared.

"Fine, call it napalm," she said. Their possible impending death meant it didn't matter what they called it. "The point is, we can't outrun what's coming. Plus, even if we were to get to the perimeter, the military would shoot us on sight. They've given up on saving anyone in Peaks Bay. They won't take the chance of the virus escaping into the rest of the world. Total eradication—at any cost."

"Can't we find a safe basement and hide out until they are done?" asked Doc Martel.

"It wouldn't be safe either . . . a basement would simply be a grave. The quantity of *napalm* they will use will incinerate the very air we are breathing all the way into the basement. We'd have to be really deep."

"How deep?" Moe asked as he swerved around two grey infected standing in the middle of the road, gawking at the onrushing van.

Abelone turned in her seat and looked back at the two infected as they whizzed by her window. *Were they holding hands?* She strained her neck to look backwards, but they were too far off to see now.

"How deep would this bomb shelter have to be?" asked Moe again.

Abelone had to think for a few seconds.

"We'd have to be at least fifteen or twenty feet underground for the napalm not to burn our oxygen and the chemicals and heat not to harm us."

Moe hit the brakes, and the van skidded to a stop, propelling the occupants forward. Keefer dropped the five remaining shotgun shells he was trying to reload in the shotgun. Tigger growled as he slid into the back of Doc Martel's seat, but was quickly corralled back by Abelone.

"What are you doing?" shouted Keefer as he picked up three of the dropped shotgun shells.

Moe turned the van around and headed up a side road that meandered south along a hillside.

"You heard the lady. We need to get underground!" shouted back Moe.

He continued toward a long two-floor building, probably five kilometres away. The building was lined with windows that reflected the late afternoon sun and overlooked Peaks Bay.

"The hospital?" asked Keefer, leaning on the middle seat in front of him to see up the hill.

"Not the hospital, *dumbass*. The old bomb shelter behind the hospital!" Moe growled while staring intently at the road and pressing the gas pedal as far as it would go. "It was built in the seventies during the Cold War when Peaks Bay was nothing but a military outpost for the Americans. I don't know how deep it is, but if it was deep enough to withstand a nuclear attack, I'm guessing it should be deep enough to withstand whatever's coming, right?" He looked at Abelone in the rear-view mirror.

She had to think, then nodded.

True to his nature, Doc Martel verbalized his vast knowledge of historical tidbits, "Mr. Moe, if it's truly a World War II nuclear shelter, it's probably twenty feet underground, at least." He was breathing rapidly. "It probably has built-in air pockets too. Those were built into the rock base to extend the life expectancy of occupants in case of nuclear war. You see, they couldn't recycle air back then like we do today. This bomb shelter—"

"Okay, we get it. It will probably do the trick," interrupted Moe. "And stop calling me Mr. Moe. Sounds stupid. Call me Moe."

Abelone looked back out the window. The small wooden houses on either side of the hill were flying by. The hospital, which looked like a toy model in the distance a few minutes ago, was becoming more life-sized as they approached.

She chewed her nails as she calculated over and over. They probably still had thirty minutes—maybe—if the government had enacted Q3 shortly after their last call. She also wrestled to understand the voraciousness of the virus and that a Q3 protocol had been ordered. She had seen some of the worst outbreaks around the globe and had helped defeat them all: the 2016 H7N9 Avian Flu outbreak in the Chinese province of Guangdong—over five hundred dead; the 2007 Middle East respiratory syndrome coronavirus in Saudi Arabia—over one thousand dead; the 2014 Ebola outbreak in West Africa—over eleven thousand dead. Then there was the big one, COVID-19, with over seven million dead around the world. This new virus, whatever it was, was going to surpass that if they didn't stop it in its tracks.

***

Keefer stared out the back window. Even though the van was approaching the hospital, he was mesmerized by the view behind him. The beauty of the seaside town and its majestic shoreline was marred by a dark wave, made up of thousands of infected, racing up the hill after them. From this far up, the pursuing infected looked like jelly squeezing through closing fingers as they streamed between buildings and undulated up the hill. He couldn't quite make out individual bodies, but it didn't matter. They were all dead. They had to be. That was the only way he could justify what he had done.

The amorphous mass kept growing, covering roads and fields as it ran. The town behind the rising darkness looked serene; it lay by the ocean peacefully. The harbour plaza was empty and would have looked like a postcard if it weren't for the massive red and white icebreaker sticking up out of the sea. The infected were ten or twenty minutes behind if they kept up their pace. *Will they even reach the hilltop before the bombing starts? Will we?*

***

Moe drove straight to the back of the hospital, climbing over curbs and grass and taking out a few garbage cans for good measure. He stopped near the hospital's empty helicopter pad and in front of a large mound of grass with a rusty metal door.

The four survivors stumbled out. The van engine, having been pushed beyond its limits, spewed thin plumes of smoke. Abelone was relieved not to see any infected. She knew they were coming up the hill, but the respite allowed her shoulders to loosen, and she breathed a bit deeper.

The group gathered at the back of the van, where Moe promptly opened the rear doors and rummaged through the back, looking for something. The sun was low on the horizon, and the van cast a long shadow along the helicopter-pad tarmac.

Abelone looked at her watch, then up at the sky nervously. "We probably have fifteen minutes. But the quicker we get in"—she nodded toward the metal door—"the safer we'll be."

Doc Martel walked to the metal door. "There is a massive lock on this thing. How are we going to find the key in time? If I had a blowtorch, I could cut through it in five minutes, or if I had some hairpins, I could try to pick the lock. It looks like an old tumbler lock. Alternatively, if we had liquid nitrogen, we could freeze the lock and snap it off, or even—"

"We don't have time for all that, Mr. Doctor," said Moe in his usual growl. "We're gonna pry it off." He stepped away from the back of the van, holding the tire iron and car jack. "We're going to stick the bar in the lock and snap the lock open with the jack."

"Brilliant, Mr. Moe," said Doc Martel as he hurried to help with the tools.

"While you two get that door open, Abelone and I will get food," Keefer said, pointing to the hospital cafeteria, which was thirty metres away, lining the back of the hospital's first floor.

Moe looked up at the sky with fear. "We can't waste time. We need to get to cover."

"No, he's right," chimed in Abelone. "We'll need to be in that bunker for at least a week before we can come back out. We'll never make it without food or water. What's the point of surviving the *napalm*"—she hated calling it napalm—"if we die of starvation, anyway?"

Moe let a long breath out and leaned his chin on his chest. "Fine, go. It will take me five minutes to crack that lock open, anyway. But take the shotgun with you."

Keefer picked up the shotgun and pumped it once to put a round in the chamber. He turned to Tigger and gave him a command to stay and guard Moe and Doc Martel. Tigger acknowledged with a groan of understanding and took up a post a few metres away, sniffing the air with his ears perked.

Abelone followed Keefer as he jogged across the helicopter pad. She felt uneasy, which then became more of a deep-rooted sense of fear that something was wrong. She slowed her pace. Looking at the giant white H on the helipad, she thought, *This is how it all started. If the Henry Dawson's helicopter didn't crash into the wreckage of the Nuovo Mondo, we wouldn't be here right now.* She remembered how the Bo 105 hit the icebreaker superstructure, then smashed into the resting place of the frozen Italian caravel. As she looked up at the dimming sky, she couldn't shake the sense of dread making the hair on her neck stand up.

"What's wrong?" Keefer asked as Abelone settled in beside him by the door to the hospital cafeteria.

"I don't know. Something doesn't feel right," she answered. "I can't help but think about how this all started. What if I missed something? What if there was a way I could have prevented this and stopped all these people from getting infected?"

"Let's first survive what's coming. We need to focus on getting food and getting into that bunker."

***

The cafeteria lights were off. The late afternoon sun filtered in, but the back of the room was still cast in shadows. *Where are the staff and patients?*

The cash register nook, serving counter, and shelves of drinks and pre-packaged food were also covered in gloom. On the wall opposite the windows, two doors led to a long hallway that went all the way to the front of the hospital. The hallway itself was dark, but the doors at the far end, where the admittance and waiting room were, were bright with light from outside. *Light at the end of the tunnel. How fitting*, Keefer thought.

When they reached the food sales area, Keefer grabbed a handful of grocery-style canvas bags and handed a couple to Abelone. He pointed to the shelves of drinks and sandwiches. She nodded, walked over and started filling her bags with loot.

Keefer jumped over the counter and headed into the kitchen. He made his way quietly to a row of metal shelves filled with cans and dry goods. The only light this deep in the room was the green glow from the emergency exit sign. The stillness made Keefer's skin crawl. He'd never seen this place so quiet. Even for a small hospital, it was usually bustling with people. He quickly started filling his bags.

As he worked, a hand slowly stretched out from under the shelving and wrapped around his ankle. Being wound up, Keefer jumped and swung the shotgun toward the origin of the hand. Its barrel was aimed straight at a pair of saucer-sized eyes hiding under the shelving unit.

A blonde orderly stared breathlessly into the shotgun barrel. She slowly brought her hand to her face, putting her index finger perpendicular to her lips, then pointed behind Keefer down a small side corridor. The spastic and choppy movements of three people in the hallway gave them away as infected. He breathed a sigh of relief as they turned down another hallway and disappeared out of sight.

He watched for a few seconds, then extended his free hand to help the woman from her hiding spot. She was young, probably in her mid-twenties. He'd been to the hospital so many times he must have crossed paths with her before. She was a lot shorter than him, and her hair was pulled back into a messy ponytail.

"We need to leave," he whispered.

She followed him without saying a word.

"No, wait," a voice came from the shadows behind them.

There was some ruffling behind a large laundry bin, and two dark-haired employees dressed in light brown clothing nervously stepped forward.

"We are Hector and Maria. Can we come with you?" The couple held on to each other as they stood still.

"Of course, but we have to go," Keefer insisted, waving them over frantically. The orderly scurried over the counter without his help.

"I'll go next so I can help Maria down on the other side," the man whispered and patted his partner's hand.

Hector pulled his short, heavy body onto the counter awkwardly. As he swung his legs over the countertop, his feet clipped an empty sandwich rack, tipping it over. It crashed into a pile of empty metal pans. Everything spilled on the floor in a loud, resonating clatter. The noise echoed throughout the kitchen and down the hallways. Keefer froze. Everyone froze.

Shrieks and hisses erupted from the darkness and quickly grew louder. The three infected from earlier sprinted around the hallway corner. They headed straight for Keefer and the others in the kitchen. Maria screamed, rooted to the floor in fear.

Keefer brought the shotgun up in time to fire once, barely aiming. To his surprise, the slug caught the first infected right under the chin, sending tissue, blood and bone spraying backwards. The partially decapitated body crashed into Keefer's legs, almost toppling him like a bowling ball on pins. He barely had time to steady himself when the next infected pounced and locked its hands on Keefer's head. Luckily, the shotgun was wedged between them, and it was enough to hold the snapping mouth inches from his face.

As Keefer struggled to break free, Maria screamed, followed by Hector shouting. Keefer was too entangled with his own menace to look at them. He stumbled until his back was against the counter, the infected biting furiously at the air. The counter gave Keefer leverage, and with a quick flip of his hip, he was able to throw the infected off him and send it crashing into a large metal fridge. Holding the shotgun by the barrel, he swung it like a baseball bat at the infected's head. The hard resin butt of the shotgun caught the grey infected squarely on the temple, and the crack of breaking bone resonated in the kitchen. The infected squirmed until Keefer smashed his foot down into its head—it stopped moving. Keefer's breathing was rapid, and his blood pumped hard in his ears. It took him a few seconds to realize there was another thumping behind him. He spun to see Hector standing over the grey body of the third infected, bashing its head in with a cast iron pan. Maria, in her bloodied brown uniform, was motionless on the floor.

Keefer approached Hector cautiously as the short, stout man swung the pan violently into the pulp of what used to be the grey body's head. Within reach, Keefer sprung, armlocked Hector, and took the pan from his hand. Hector didn't look up, then let go and started pummelling the fleshy pulp of the infected's head with his fists.

"Hector, we have to go," Keefer said. He slid his arms under the man's armpits and lifted him off the ground. To his relief, Hector let himself be lifted, and the fight drained out of him. Keefer pushed him onto and over the counter into the waiting arms of Abelone and the young orderly. He quickly followed and handed his bag of food to the orderly, then swung his arm around Hector to help Abelone.

"Benjamin, they're *here*!" Abelone said, staring over his shoulder toward the hallway that led to the front of the hospital.

The light at the end of the tunnel was dimming as body after body plastered violently against the large glass doors. The doors rattled and bulged inwards. Like a bubble, the doors burst, sending shards of shattered glass all over the lobby and infected bodies sprawling over the floor. A gale of shrieks and hisses blasted down the long hallway and filled the cafeteria.

"Run!" shouted Keefer.

The orderly took off right away out the back cafeteria door. Keefer and Abelone followed her, dragging Hector by the shoulders. The sun was low on the horizon, and dusk was creeping in. Once the cafeteria door closed behind them, a constant whir in the distance replaced the loud, chaotic clamour of the infected. Keefer looked up as he and Abelone ran awkwardly. A dozen CF-18 Hornets materialized over the Atlantic Ocean east of Peaks Bay.

As they ran across the empty helipad, Moe waved at them frantically from the open bunker door. The door's lock and chain were discarded in a pile to the side. Doc Martel pulled Tigger by the collar down the stairs into the safety of the bunker.

The orderly ran straight past Moe and hurried down into the bunker, clenching the three food bags to her chest as best she could.

"Take my side!" shouted Keefer. He handed Hector off to Moe, then doubled back to the open side of the panel van. He stretched his arm under the middle seat, searching for a few seconds before pulling out the remaining two shotgun shells that he'd dropped earlier. Keefer slid them into his pocket and ran back to the bunker where Moe and Abelone were helping Hector down the stairs into the darkness. Keefer grabbed the heavy metal door and turned around.

The infected frantically squeezed through the shattered door and windows of the cafeteria. Hundreds more spilled around the outside of the hospital. Pretty soon, the entire hospital yard was overrun with grey bodies.

The first explosion startled Keefer as he focused on the approaching wave of infected. From his vantage point on the hill, Keefer saw the long stretches of fire cover most of the harbour area. Flames stretched out in the direction the bombs were dropped, and the earth shook on impact. Even the hospital trembled, and a number of infected fell.

The noise of the incendiary bombs igniting drowned out the shrieks and hisses of the thousands of infected converging on the bunker. Some infected turned, their attention drawn to the thundering inferno, but most kept racing toward Keefer.

The Hornets flew over him and the bunker. A sonic boom thundered overhead, followed by an ear-splitting explosion when the napalm drop hit the front side of the hospital. A red-orange glow radiated around the two-floor building like a rising sun. The radiance—warm for less than a heartbeat—turned to hell on earth as it blew through the two-floor hospital, and all the windows shattered. The red-orange glow turned red and black as balls of fire engulfed the hospital, and the smell of gasoline and laundry detergent flooded the air.

Keefer shielded his eyes as the fire and chemicals spread through the yard, covering the endless horde of infected. The stench of burning flesh mixed with the chemicals and assaulted his nostrils. A powerful gust of hot air hit him straight in the chest, sending him flying backwards into the darkness of the stairwell. The last thing he saw was thousands of burning bodies, followed by the thick metal bunker door slamming shut, propelled by the percussion of the explosion. Keefer crashed down the dark stairwell, slammed his head on the concrete, and everything went black.

19

TRUE DARKNESS IS NOT THE ABSENCE OF LIGHT

Abelone opened her eyes slowly. A soft light barely pierced the darkness around her, and she could just make out the bunker ceiling. She lay on an old dusty couch in the main room. A flashlight propped up on a small table beside the couch spread a hazy light and long shadows everywhere. Not enough light to read a book, but it allowed them the luxury of walking around without running into things. As she sat up, she rubbed her face and rested her elbows on her knees.

The room trembled, and thunder echoed through the concrete walls. Dust drizzled down from minuscule cracks in the ceiling and floated about in the streams of light. *Not something you get used to*, she thought as she ran her fingers through her hair to shake the dust off. The bombing had been on and off since they'd found refuge in the bunker. Every thirty minutes or so, the hill shook as another load of napalm hit the hospital grounds.

Abelone stood, every joint in her body complaining. Looking at the bandage on her forearm, she noticed how dirty and frazzled it was. She would have to change it soon. She checked her watch; it was past seven in the morning. It was hard to believe it had been a day since the Henry Dawson had arrived in Peaks Bay. *Crashed into Peaks Bay*, she corrected herself.

She could make out the outline of someone sitting near the stairs leading to the bunker exit. The rotund shape, the head with no hair—Eric Martel. He was slumped in an old metal chair, holding the shotgun.

Abelone looked at the stairs nervously and reminded herself they had barricaded the lower blast doors. It would be impossible for anyone *or anything* to break in. Luckily, the bunker had two doors: the entry one, which opened to the outside, and a larger, thicker door halfway down the stairs, which acted as the real blast protection in the event of an atomic detonation.

She stood in the middle of the living quarters. There were a couple of old, musty couches, a few tables and a bunch of piled-up chairs with dilapidated leather backs. There were also some footlockers with various derelict knick-knacks inside. Attached to the living quarters was a smaller room—the sleeping quarters—with three bunk beds, a couple of sinks that didn't work and more footlockers. That was where she headed to check on Ben.

***

"I think he's coming to!"

The voice pulled Keefer out of a dream where he and Abelone were at Lookout Point, taking in Peaks Bay.

"Benjamin, how are you feeling?"

Keefer slowly opened his eyes. "I was dreaming about you," he said hoarsely. "We were together—" He tried to sit up, but a sharp pain in his ribs stopped him. Keefer slid his hand over the woman's hand on his shoulder.

"I'm glad you are safe," the woman said.

"Look, I don't know if we will make it out of here, but I wanted you to know . . . that I felt . . ." He stopped, embarrassed, when he realized it was nonsensical to tell someone he'd just met he liked her when the world was ending around them. So he held back. His head still pounded, and his vision was adjusting to the gloomy room.

The young face in front of him smiled and squeezed his hand back. With her free hand, she brushed a loose strand of blonde hair and adjusted her long ponytail.

That's not Abelone. Keefer focused on his caregiver's face: it was the orderly.

"I'm Karen, by the way. We've met. I mean . . . not in the cafeteria when you saved me . . . at the hospital, when you would come in for meetings with the doctors." She smiled shyly. "I've always . . . had a crush on you . . . you know. Not sure why I am telling you now. I guess it's like you said. Who knows if we will make it out of here?"

He quickly let go of Karen's hand and cleared his throat. He did somewhat remember Karen, but had never seen her in any other way than a helpful person at the hospital. His face flushed as he looked at her, wondering what to say, how to correct what he'd said.

A voice interceded, a voice he recognized right away. "All right, Karen, we need to let *Mr.* Keefer rest," Abelone said from behind the orderly. The way she'd stressed the title *Mister* emphasized how much older he was than Karen.

Keefer looked over Karen's shoulder. Abelone eyed him with a stare of fleeting displeasure.

Karen seemed annoyed but deferred to the Danish scientist.

"No problem. I'll go check on Hector." Karen squeezed Keefer's forearm and disappeared beyond the circle of light from another flashlight resting on its end on the table by his bed.

"I thought she was . . . I was sure it was . . ." Keefer babbled, unsure what to apologize for. He'd barely said anything.

Abelone bent over him and clumsily poked him in the rib as she adjusted his blanket. The sharp pain made him catch his breath and stop his explanation short.

"I'm sorry. Did that hurt?" Abelone said. "Don't worry, it's nothing too serious; it'll be sore for a few weeks. I'm more worried about the laceration on your head." She prodded at his bandaged head injury a little harder than he would have expected a nurse to.

"It isn't deep, but I'm worried it might get infected," Abelone said, her Danish accent coming through a bit.

He tried to lock eyes with her, but she refused to meet them while she adjusted the blanket again.

"You did a number on yourself falling down those stairs. You need to get more rest. Nowhere to go anyway." She pushed herself up clumsily, or maybe purposefully, using Keefer's side, sending another shot of pain through his rib.

Keefer's gaze followed her as she walked into another room where he could see another faint flashlight glowing.

"Dumbass," came a voice from the darkness on the far side of the room. Moe materialized from the shadows and walked over, dragging a chair to the bed.

"Sometimes I wonder how you even find your way out of your house in the mornings." Moe plopped down in the chair beside Keefer's bed and looked closely at the bandage on Keefer's head. "You might make it after all," he grunted.

"Glad to hear that," Keefer said, looking Moe over. His friend looked tired.

"The tall Danish lass has been asking all kinds of questions about you since we got here. The world is ending around us, and what is she most interested in? *You*. The schmuck who saved her a few times." Moe reconsidered his words. "Actually, from what she said, it wasn't even you who saved her today. It was that furry mutt of yours—twice!"

Keefer turned sideways and leaned down to rub Tigger, who rested beside the bed. A low growl of pleasure echoed from the pile of fur. Tigger got up and leaned over to lick his master's face a few times. That earned him a neck scratch.

"Oh God, that's disgusting. I saw him lick his arse two minutes ago," said Moe.

Keefer smirked as he pushed Tigger off. The dog obeyed and scurried after Abelone.

Another explosion shook the room, sending more dust meandering through the stale air. The aftershock shook the foundation of the bunker, rattling the bunk beds, tables and massive air vents at the back of the room. The shaking knocked the flashlight over, and Moe propped it back up.

Keefer almost jumped out of bed.

"Relax, that would be our government friends, making sure Peaks Bay is sterilized to the bone." He coughed and cleared his throat. "They've been bombing the place since we got in here twelve hours ago."

"I've been out for twelve hours?" Keefer gasped.

"Yep. You took a pretty nasty spill when the first volley hit. Luckily, the door shielded you from the heat, but the blast sent your arse backwards down the stairs." Moe leaned forward and rested his elbows on his knees. "Thought you were dead when I got to you, blood all over your face," he said gravely, before he flashed a rare smile of yellowish teeth. "But no such luck, just a small cut on your head." With that quip, Moe leaned back into his creaky metal chair.

"They've been hitting the area pretty steadily since. They must have all the Hoser Air Force out and about because it has not stopped."

Keefer looked around the room suspiciously. Moe sensed his friend's concern and reassured him, "Don't worry. Your Danish girlfriend says this place should be deep enough to protect us from the fire and chemicals."

"I'm more worried about the whole thing coming down on top of our heads," answered Keefer, still looking at the ceiling.

"Well, Mr. Doctor—he's a talker, that one—is convinced this place will hold. Plus, he says we should have plenty of air for days down here." Moe nodded toward the large rusty air vent at the back of the room. "He says shelters like this have air pockets built in the ground fed by those tunnel-looking air vents. The guy won't stop talking, I tell ya."

Stretching his head to see the other room again, Keefer asked, "How big is this place?"

"It's two rooms. Bunks here and the living area in the bigger room. Not very comfortable, but who are we to complain? We're alive. That's all that matters."

That statement reminded Keefer that everyone out in Peaks Bay would probably be dead by now. If Abelone was right and the whole place was being blanketed with napalm, thousands of lives would have been extinguished. Maybe more . . .

Another blast detonated right on top of the shelter. The bunker convulsed, releasing ever more dust from the ceiling. The massive vent at the back rattled in anger, and the rattling continued down the ventilation system as the shockwave made its way deep into the hill. The echo continued long after the shaking of the shelter stopped. Keefer and Moe stared at the large vent, but the far-away rattling kept going.

"Spooky," said Moe as he got up, grunting his joint's displeasure at the movement. "Awwright, I need to go relieve Mr. Doctor guarding the door. He's been there for the last two hours. Without anyone to talk to, he's probably going to explode." Moe rolled his eyes and added again, "Have I said he's a talker, that one?"

Keefer watched his old friend shuffle his way to the other room. Moe stopped in the doorway and looked back over his shoulder. "Kid. I know I give you a hard time, but I'm glad you're okay."

"Moe, are those feelings you're sharing?" Keefer asked, mocking seriousness.

"Dumbass," Moe muttered and disappeared into the darkness.

20

No, thank you. We're not hungry

Abelone walked back to the couch in the living quarters. She was upset with herself for the small pang of jealousy. It made no sense that she would be bothered by Keefer confusing Karen for her, considering all that was happening around them. Thousands of people were dead—the thought made her shudder. She dwelled on the role she played in bringing the virus to Peaks Bay. She sat in a stupor of blame and loathing. In the dim glow of the light, she stared at the barely visible wall ten feet in front of her. Her mind was a muddle of guilt, anger and fear.

It took an hour for her to settle down.

Abelone was exhausted. She needed to sleep, and this couch wouldn't cut it. She got up and shuffled to the sleeping quarters. Tigger groggily got up and walked over to Moe standing guard at the stairs and lay at his feet.

She was relieved to see Keefer asleep and watched him for a bit, wondering how they would have gotten along if it weren't for the blight she'd brought to Peaks Bay. She shook her head once to push the idea from her mind; there were more important things to think about.

She chose a cot on the opposite side of the room and sat down, taking a deep breath. Every muscle in her body was ready to collapse on the bed. Hector had also found a home on one of the upper bunks. She was glad he was getting some sleep. The man hadn't said a word to anyone since they'd found shelter in the bunker. Being responsible for his wife's death was weighing heavily on him.

Abelone's Spanish was not very strong, but it was enough for her to make out a few Catholic prayers from Hector's monologue. Sometimes, he spiralled into sobbing and requested forgiveness, though she wasn't certain what he was asking forgiveness for. Either for being the cause of his wife's death or for having killed the man that had killed her. She could understand that. Those people, the infected, could still be saved. Her heart sank deep in her stomach when she realized the error of her thought. There was no one to save anymore. Everyone who was infected was dead, burnt to a crisp.

With that troubling thought, she lay back on the bed and slowly exhaled. At least she hadn't killed *any* infected, despite everything she went through. Not on the Henry Dawson and not in Peaks Bay. It was a small solace considering all the deaths that had occurred, but it was something she held on to. It was what made her feel human. In the face of all the horror, she had not resorted to killing anyone. Her mind shut down, and she had one last thought. *There haven't been any bombings in a long time. Has it been over an hour?* Then sleep dragged her into the deep.

She was in a dreamless abyss when a loud clatter jolted her awake. In a daze, she looked toward the massive air vent, which was trumpeting clinks and clanks from deep within.

Another bombing, she assumed groggily before noticing Keefer was up too. In the gloom of the flashlight, she could see him standing by the table as he contemplated the small piles of food they had retrieved from the hospital cafeteria. She rose and subconsciously waved the dust away from her face, but no dust was falling from the ceiling. Had there been a bombing? She stretched her arms like a cat as she moved over to Keefer.

He turned to look at her with a smile on his face. "How'd you sleep?"

"*Ikke sove godt*," she replied without thinking.

"Huh?"

Abelone realized she'd used a Danish expression. "Sorry. Not sure I could call it sleep."

Keefer's stare lasted a few seconds more than it should. Abelone looked away, worried she might stare back.

"So this is all the food we've got?" Keefer motioned to the pile of sandwiches, yogurts, muffins and juices on the table.

"We figure there is enough for the six of us to last six days if needed. The bombings should be done on day three, so we should be okay to stay here for an extra day and let the chemicals dissipate from the air."

"Well, I don't know about three days of bombing. It seems to have stopped a while ago," Keefer said, picking up a granola bar.

Surprised by his claim, Abelone looked at her watch. *Ten a.m.—that can't be.* Was that why there was no dust earlier? What was the noise that woke her?

"The protocols are clear, seventy-two hours of cleansing. Why would they have stopped already? It's barely been . . . fifteen hours?" She pinched the bridge of her nose, trying to think if there were exceptions, but there were none.

"We were waiting for you to wake up so we could ask you that exact question."

"Once it starts, there is no stopping it. That was something all scientists agreed on. If it gets bad enough, this type of"—she hesitated—"*sterilization* is needed. They don't stop until they are certain the virus is eradicated." *Why would they stop?* She pinched her bridge harder.

"Well, I'm sorry to break it to you, but the bombings *have* stopped." Keefer looked at his watch. "It's been three hours with nothing. No bombing whatsoever."

"What woke me then?" Abelone asked, confused, looking at the large air vent at the back of the room.

"The air ducts have been acting up since the bombings ended. Maybe some of the air pockets have caved in, and the rattling we keep hearing is the strain on the rest of the system."

"What about that smell?"

Keefer sniffed deeply. "Yeah, the smell of charcoal has been getting worse. We assumed it was normal considering the amount of napalm dropped on this place." As he finished, the vent rattled again, even more loudly than when it woke Abelone.

"The thing is . . ." Abelone walked to the vent, sniffing deeper this time. " . . . Napalm does not smell like burnt charcoal." Her brain stumbled over itself, trying to remember what did.

The vent rattled again, even louder. Closer. The noise didn't stop, and it was rushing toward them.

"Skin!" Abelone yelled.

"What?" Keefer responded, startled by her shout.

"Skin! Burnt skin smells like charcoal. That's the smell!"

Something slammed into the large metal vent from inside the air duct. The impact dented it out of shape. Keefer and Abelone jumped back in surprise.

The second impact snapped the vent off its rusty screws and sent it flying outward. It hit Abelone in the face, splitting the skin on her forehead. Blood streamed over her temple and cheek. She stumbled back into Keefer, sending both of them to the ground.

The smell of charcoal—burnt skin—filled the dimly lit room. A grotesque figure appeared, spilling out of the large air duct. It fell to the ground in a heap. The infected was scorched from head to toe, ears singed to stubs, lips burned completely off. Its clothing and skin were melted together in a hot mess of an outer shell.

From behind the nightmarish ghoul, out of the blackness of the air vent, popped another disfigured head. This one had all facial features burnt off except for the teeth. Even its eyes were singed black. It couldn't see, but it was still moving, following the noise of the other infected. It fell into the room on top of the first invader who was trying to get up.

Abelone caught a glimpse of a third and a fourth scorched figure scrambling out of the hole from hell. They were like rats scrambling out of a sewer pipe filling with water.

Keefer picked her up as the first infected lunged at them. Its mouth was open, and it was straining to scream, but no sound came out of the lipless mouth. Its vocal cords were burnt out.

From above her did come a scream, though, one of unfiltered anger as Hector leapt down from his bunk. He landed on top of the infected, and his weight crushed it back to the ground.

"*Mataste a mi Maria!*" yelled Hector as he charged the other infected. His fist connected with the blind infected's head, sending it crashing into the wall. A kick caught another infected in the knee, buckling it backwards at an ungodly angle. For a few moments, Abelone thought Hector was getting the upper hand on the half-dozen burnt monstrosities. Until Hector slipped on blood—Abelone's blood—and lost his footing. He stayed standing by stretching his arms out for balance, but the blind infected latched on to one of his arms and sank its teeth deep into it. Hector howled in agony, and the others enveloped him, all sinking their charred teeth into his body while they dragged him to the ground.

Keefer stepped toward the mound of burned bodies to help, but before he could get there, it was his turn to be grabbed from behind, along with Abelone. Doc Martel and Moe pulled the two of them out of the room, and Karen slammed the massive bombproof door behind them.

"What was that?" shouted Moe as he slid a thick metal pipe through the door handle to lock it in place.

"Did you see those . . . things . . . They're totally . . ." Karen asked no one.

Doc Martel grabbed a medical kit and applied a compress to Abelone's bleeding head.

Keefer stepped up to the metal door and looked through the small, square glass window.

"They came out of the air vents. The fucking air vents!" he shouted. "If it wasn't for Hector, Abelone and I would be dead."

***

Abelone stood looking through the window. "They must have found the outside air vent and a way in."

"What about Hector? We need to do something for him," said Karen.

"What can we do?" Keefer answered, watching the infected still on top of the man.

Despite all the commotion, the flashlight was still standing on its end on the table, and it cast an eerie glow in the room.

"They're stopping," Abelone said.

The infected stopped biting Hector in unison. They looked around and stood up one by one as if triggered by the same signal to break it off.

Abelone and the others stared through the window—like tourists at a zoo.

"They must have felt Hector's blood get saturated with the virus," Abelone reasoned.

"You think they can register something like that in such rapid fashion?" asked Doc Martel.

"What the hell are you quacks talking about?" grunted Moe, turning to them.

Abelone stayed quiet, mesmerized by the infected standing in the locked room, as if assessing their surroundings. They hadn't spotted their spectators yet.

Doc Martel couldn't help his know-it-all instincts and answered Moe.

"These people . . . the infected . . . well, they seem to be more interested in, well, um . . . infecting people. I guess they could have eaten poor Hector, but they didn't. It seems after a few . . . what should we call it?" He struggled to find the right words. "A few bites, they somehow sense it is time to stop."

Moe looked at him, annoyed. "Couldn't they have been full?"

"What?"

"Full, like had enough to eat. Hector was pretty plump," Moe answered deadpan.

Abelone interjected. "No, that's the thing. They're not eating Hector. They're biting him. And more so, they all stopped at the same time."

An infected's gaze was drawn to the little glass window and locked eyes with Abelone, which made her shudder. The infected threw itself against the door, with no apparent strategy other than to run right through it to get to her. The other ghoulish-looking infected joined the frenzied ramming, mimicking their peer. They moved their mouths, or what remained of their jaws, trying to scream and hiss, but very little sound came out.

After a nerve-racking few seconds, Moe reassured the group, "Looks like we're safe. This antique door won't budge."

The others moved away from the door, leaving Abelone staring through the little window, which was partially covered in black blood from the infected. Abelone looked at her watch. She wondered how much time it would take for Hector to change. She'd seen people change. *Not people... friends*, she corrected herself. *He saved my life, and the best I can do is watch him change into one of those things.* The thought made her feel sick to her stomach.

The infected were still frantically trying to break down the door but had changed their approach and were now taking turns throwing themselves against it.

There. Was that movement? Abelone tried to see past the infected and through the shadows created by the flashlight on the table.

It was! He's getting up.

"Hector is getting up!" She directed her comment to Keefer unconsciously. She checked her watch. "Two minutes, fifty seconds. Faster than Alex," she said as Keefer moved in beside her.

Hector's head was the first part of his body to move. He lifted it off the ground, then slid both arms under his chest as if to do a push-up. He pushed himself up, and his right leg bent and slid under him to provide leverage and crouch on one knee.

"Something's not right. The way he's moving," Keefer said, verbalizing what Abelone had noticed.

"He's not moving like the others," she said.

Hector pushed all the weight of his body over his legs and stood up straight. His skin had turned grey, and she could see his eyes were pitch black, but his movements were off. He didn't move herky-jerky like the other infected.

Hector looked at his hands, palms up, and slowly rotated them.

"He's assessing himself," Keefer said.

A look of fear and confusion spread over Hector's face. He pawed at the bites on his arms and neck. He took a step backward and gaped at his bloodied hands, then raised them toward the ceiling and implored at the top of his lungs, "*Dios, por qué me has abandonado?*"

The forcefulness of his shout startled Abelone and Keefer, who took a half-step back. But more so, it surprised the infected, who all turned to face Hector. They stared at him for half a dozen seconds. Then, their decision was made. They pounced on the man, not looking to bite him this time. Instead, they tore him apart.

Hector was ripped to pieces in seconds. His innards were pulled from his stomach, and his head was bashed to a viscous pulp. Abelone's stomach turned, and she heard Keefer vomit.

The commotion attracted the other survivors to the door again.

"Why would they attack him?" asked Karen, disgusted and confused, her hand on her mouth, ready to hold back what might come up.

"He didn't turn like them," Abelone surprised herself with an answer. "He wasn't infected like they were." Abelone's thoughts were rushing through her memories of the last few days. *The grey sailor back on the ship who'd jumped overboard with the lifebuoy, the grey couple in the town, holding hands in the middle of the road.* Then, looking down at her bandaged arm, *Me!*

"How did I miss it?" she scolded herself. "Not everyone gets sick like they are," she said, nodding toward the pack of infected now moving away from Hector's carcass. Flesh, blood and innards were strewn all over the floor and walls of the sleeping quarters. Blood had splashed over the flashlight, bathing the room in a dark red gloom.

"He—Hector—showed signs of infection, but his faculties seemed intact," Keefer pointed out.

"Yes. And maybe that means some infected are not mindless." Something stirred inside her, and she dared to hope. They could save people. Her enthusiasm dwindled when she saw the stash of food and water was still neatly piled on the table not far from the flashlight, surrounded by infected and covered in guts.

21

RISING UP FROM ASH AND DUST

Abelone woke up with a gasp, dusty air stuck in her throat. She coughed. *I was asleep.* She sat up and rested her head in her hands with her elbows on her knees. She shook her head and opened her eyes, trying to shake the cobwebs off. The constant thumping on the door had diminished but not subsided. Its steady beat was counting down how long they could last without food. Tigger stirred at her feet, and she reached down to rub his head.

"We're going to go soon," she said. The group had made the decision—it was time to go. She still did not know why the bombings had stopped, but she did know that they would barely last a few more days with only a couple of bottles of water and no food.

Her watch showed six twenty-two in the morning. Her body felt like it had been thrown from a moving car, but her mind had some semblance of being rested. As she looked around, she saw Keefer and Doc Martel in the shadows near the stairs. They had ripped the leather off the chairs and were fastening it around their limbs. They also had thick cloth wrapped around their necks and heads—presumably to protect their ears from getting bitten. They looked ridiculous.

Moe was sleeping on the ground, and Karen was snoring away on the second couch, not far from Abelone. Abelone zipped up an old bomber-style leather jacket Keefer had found in a footlocker. The leather would be thick enough to protect her arms and torso from bites. She ripped leather strands from the back of a chair and wrapped them around her neck.

Not the head. That's stupid.

***

Half an hour later, the group clustered at the bottom of the stairs leading to the first blast door. Keefer looked back at them. They were ready. Keefer and the other four survivors were all decked out in haphazard body armour made from chair leather and old clothing. Their noses and mouths were covered with makeshift masks of cloth and gauze built by Doc Martel to help filter the dust and chemicals they would face outside.

Keefer hesitated. What would they find outside? Would there be infected waiting for them? Did the sterilization work? He readjusted his neck protection, more of a delay tactic than an actual need. He—then subsequently Martel—abandoned his head protection as it kept dipping over his eyes.

Moe approved of their decision. "Thank ya. Ya both looked stupid with those things."

This triggered an unexpected laugh from Abelone.

Keefer smirked. He turned up the stairs. It was time. He patted Tigger on the head and moved to the first door. As soon as he opened it, a hint of chemicals tickled his nose through the mask.

"You are sure the air will be safe?" asked Karen nervously.

"It's been over twenty-four hours since the last bombing. We should be okay. Just make sure your masks are tight," answered Abelone.

Even though he had triple-checked his mask, Keefer adjusted it again.

Doc Martel, with his need to regurgitate information all the time, added, "As long as we don't spend a week in the area, we'll be okay. Drawn-out exposure to carboxylic acids would definitely lead to some unwanted consequences. Our lungs would start to deteriorate, our nose and throat mucous membranes would dry out and start to bleed—"

Keefer frowned and cut him off. "The plan is to walk out of the quarantine zone quickly, so it won't ever become a problem. We'll reach the military checkpoints in forty-eight hours, seventy-two at most."

"We haven't discussed an obvious gap with our plan," said Moe.

Keefer felt another awful scenario coming up.

"Why wouldn't they shoot us?" Moe asked matter-of-factly. "That's what you said they do. Shoot people on sight. Didn't you?" Moe looked at Abelone.

"Well, Mr. Moe, this is why they won't shoot us." The bald, rotund doctor tapped on the yellow blood-sample case protruding from the emptied medical kit slung around his shoulder.

"That's all good and well, Mr. Doctor. You can be the one who walks up to show them the case. I'll wait some ways behind you to see if they give you enough time to explain what you've got there," Moe gruffly answered.

"Enough guys, we'll figure that part out when we get near the check-point. Let's focus on getting out of here. Let's focus on surviving what is out there." Keefer pointed up the stairs, and that was the end of it.

As they climbed the stairs, a beam of light shone through the top edge of the top door. It was odd no light came through at the bottom, but Ben thought nothing of it. The light eventually out-shone the flashlight Moe was holding.

"Remember, once we open the door, stay close and go for the head if there are any infected." Keefer couldn't help but reflect on how right zombie movies had been all this time. He guessed most were based on science, after all. He shook the thoughts out of his head. "Anything else will only slow them down." He held his shotgun loaded with its last three shells. The others held an array of steel pipes and planks as make-do weapons.

He crept to the door, the smell of chemicals getting stronger, but there was another odour filtering through—the rancid smell of burnt human remains. It filled the top of the stairwell and made him dizzy.

Keefer tried to push the door with one hand, but it resisted, and his bruised ribs reminded him he wasn't at his strongest. He put his shoulder to it and pushed as hard as he could, his ribs protesting. The door barely moved an inch. A larger stream of light flooded the darkness, blinding him and was quickly followed by a putrid, burnt odour that washed into the stairwell. Keefer gagged and heard two people behind him throw up.

"What the hell is that smell?" gasped Moe.

Keefer answered through his mask. "Burnt bodies decaying in the sun." He coughed. "If the bombings ended early, I'm thinking the bodies were not fully incinerated."

"Yeah, that's probably right," Abelone confirmed with her hand over her mask. "We should go. We need to get away from this place."

Keefer waved Moe over, and they put their shoulders to it and pushed in unison. The massive metal door moved a couple more inches. It felt like the door was blocked by wet sand. The early morning sun burned his eyes, and it took a good ten seconds for them to adjust.

The two men pushed again until there was enough room for him to wriggle through. Keefer went first. He had the shotgun ready at his shoulder. To get through the opening, he had to climb over a pile of dirt. He didn't look down and kept an eye out for the infected. The smell was overpowering; he took small, shallow breaths to avoid gagging. The ground was crackling under his feet, but he kept scanning the area for movement. A few feet out, he looked back toward the door; he regretted it immediately. His eyes pressed shut, and he turned his head, trying to wipe the image he'd just witnessed. There were dunes of melted and coalesced bodies three feet deep. Stubs of hands, feet and heads littered the mound. It was impossible to tell where one body started and another ended. The blast had propelled bodies against the bunker and piled them up like sand against a beach house.

He slowly opened his eyes and looked again. His breathing was fast now, not to avoid gagging but to avoid panicking.

Moe climbed out and made his way over the dunes of human remains, his face completely blanched. All tint of colour had left his body. As soon as he had cleared the remains, he keeled over and transparent bile vacated his empty stomach.

Keefer put a hand on his friend's shoulder. "Try not to look at it. Help the others through. I'll stand watch," he said, knowing they had to move fast and get out of this human goulash.

Moe acknowledged with a hesitant nod, then looked down at his feet, saw he was standing on someone's skull, and repositioned himself. He looked ready to throw up again.

Keefer took a few steps out, looked around, and listened. His weapon was ready.

There were no shrieks, no hisses, no planes, no bombs, but there weren't any signs of human life either.

Tigger, released by whoever held him, made his way out of the bunker. His ears pointed up, and his back fur stood straight on end. He trudged through the piled remains, smelling at every step hesitantly. Once clear, he shook his paws, gave a low whimper, then quickly made his way to Keefer's side and looked up at his master in bewilderment.

The panel van was completely burned to its metal frame. Anything on it that was flammable was gone: seats, tires, floor, all charred to ashes. Behind it, further off, were the remnants of the hospital. The structural outline could still be made out of the few brick chimneys or partially standing walls, but most of it was gone. Two floors' worth of metal junk, which hadn't burned, was piled under a deep layer of ash. A few strands of smoke drifted up from debris piles.

Keefer had trouble adjusting to what he was seeing, and it got worse. Despite it being morning, a haze hovered over the town. The warehouse district barely had a few metal structures left, the residential districts were completely wiped out with no signs of anything but cement foundations, and the harbour district was turned to ash with only a few stone walls still standing. The famous wooden pier was completely gone, burnt, its ashes flushed away by the sea.

The only distinguishable landmark left in Peaks Bay harbour was the Henry Dawson. It was still in the harbour, its bow pointing to the sky at a forty-five-degree angle. The paint of the portion of the ship not underwater had melted off the hull. The whole thing looked like a monument made of dark volcanic rock. It occurred to Keefer the tide must have been high when the first bombing raids happened because the middle parts of the giant icebreaker were not burnt. The scene was apocalyptic, and Keefer was frozen, feeling dizzy and wobbling on his feet.

The hand on his shoulder made him jump. He brought the shotgun up and almost squeezed the trigger.

"*Vente!*" Abelone yelled in Danish. "It's me."

"Abelone," Keefer gasped. "Sorry."

"Benjamin...Ben...we need to get out of here," Abelone said shakily.

"Yeah . . . we do."

Keefer looked at what used to be a field of green grass around the helicopter pad. Now, it was a desecrated hilltop covered in black ash and thousands of partially incinerated bodies. "We really do."

He looked back toward the bunker where the rest of the group huddled, stunned by the unimaginable landscape.

A deep sorrow overtook him as he realized there were most likely several people he knew in the cremated remains on the hospital grounds. People he worked with, friends, or people he was used to crossing paths with. His eyes welled up, and for the first time since this nightmare began, he cried.

***

Abelone stood in front of Keefer, staring at him. His sobs triggered her own eyes to fill with tears. She didn't have any attachment to this town or its people, yet she could feel the pain of the loss through Keefer. She looked over her shoulder and could see Doc Martel comforting Karen as she also cried. Moe stood beside them, head down and eyes closed. This town was their home. All their friends and family who lived here were gone. Without realizing it, she reached for Benjamin and wrapped her arms around him. He welcomed the embrace and cried into her shoulder.

She was sad and scared and angry, but she didn't cry. Instead, she looked around while holding him. What was left of the hospital was hardly distinguishable. The panel van that had ferried them to safety was a burnt-out husk. Even the helipad was buried in ash.

A feeling of uneasiness swept over her again, like when she and Keefer had raced to the cafeteria to get food a few days before. She stood holding on to Keefer, who had stopped crying but was still secure in her embrace.

Abelone stared at the helicopter pad, which seemed to be the root of her discomfort. A feeling of dread was growing inside her as the realization of some grim omen materialized in her consciousness. Her heart pounded, and her breath ran short.

"Where is the helicopter?" she whispered, not to Keefer, but to herself.

"What?"

"*Where* is the helicopter?" Abelone repeated, louder and firmer.

Keefer let Abelone go and looked at her.

She yelled at him and at nobody all at once. "*Where* is the helicopter?! There is a helipad here. But there is no helicopter! *Where is it?*"

Keefer turned to look at the helicopter pad. Abelone ran to the crying Karen and grabbed her by the shoulders. "Where is the helicopter?"

Karen's tears stopped mid-stream by the sudden verbal attack. She was paralyzed, and her eyes fixated on the towering Danish woman.

"There is a medical evacuation helicopter pad here, but no helicopter. Where is it? Where did it go?"

Moe and Doc Martel gaped at Abelone. Her realizations made her incapable of controlling her voice. Her panic controlled her actions. Her vision tunnelled in on Karen.

Keefer stepped in and took Karen from Abelone. He understood. "Karen, listen to me. You need to calm yourself and think back to before the bunker. When we got here, the Medevac helicopter was not there. Where is it?"

Karen calmed under Keefer's more tranquil gaze. "The heli? The hospital heli?"

"Yes, Karen. It was not on the helipad. Where did it go, and when did it leave?"

Karen was composing herself and was able to put some sentences together. "The mayor ... the mayor was the first person brought in when the ... when the ..."

Keefer finished the sentence for her, "When the people started getting attacked and infected. Yes, I know she was with us at the harbour plaza. What does she have to do with the helicopter?"

"The mayor ... Mayor Ryerson ... she was the first person brought in after she was ... after she was bitten." Getting more comfortable, Karen went on, "When the mayor came in, Doctor Pawalski couldn't figure out why her life signs were all falling. She was dying, and he didn't know why. He stabilized and evac'd her."

"Evacuated her?" Abelone jumped back in, which startled Karen, and she cringed away.

Keefer put a palm up to Abelone. She stopped.

"Karen, where did Dr. Pawalski evac the mayor to?" Keefer said gently, trying to coax her back to talking.

Karen hesitated, but answered, "They took the helicopter. They took the helicopter with Mayor Ryerson ... They took her to Quebec City, to the hospital there. She was dying. They had to ..."

Keefer let go of the small orderly, who was still confused.

Abelone had to accept what she had already deduced. The thought of it made every muscle in her body tremble. Every inch of her being now knew why the bombing of Peaks Bay had stopped after one day. She should have known all along—the infection had gotten out. The infection had spread beyond Peaks Bay.

PART III - THE ROAD

22

WHAT PATH TO TAKE?

Like a fresh coat of snow on a winter morning, a layer of ash covered everything, uniform and undisturbed. Benjamin Keefer led the group single-file through the lunar landscape. Even Tigger didn't stray from their trodden path. The layer of ash was thinner on the road, only reaching their ankles. The group stayed silent as if attending a church service, knowing that if the silence were to be broken, they could be admonished by something worse than a priest.

Keefer led the survivors through the occasional stone foundations, metal supports and vehicle skeletons that were all that remained of Peaks Bay. The smell of gasoline and laundry detergent gave Keefer a headache and made his throat burn despite his mask. A blurry haze floated casually above the ground, limiting his vision to a stone's throw.

The town was gone. All life was gone. It was in no way a relief that the infected were also gone. Whatever feeling of victory he might have experienced was buried deep in the mass grave of all the people he had known who were now ashes.

When they reached the airport on the outskirts of town, melted hangars covered in grey blankets looked like monstrous sentries watching them in the ashy haze and warning them not to enter. The survivors listened and kept walking.

It took them a few hours to exit Peaks Bay. Keefer was slowed not just by his aching ribs, but by his food and water deficit.

There were very few houses outside of town, to begin with, but even those were gone. The remaining barren tundra was covered in ash, disturbed only by the wind practising its dune-building skills. Keefer was mesmerized by the similarity of these dunes with the burnt remains of the infected piled up against the bunker door.

The group trudged along, their silence broken only by an occasional coughing fit caused by the caustic vapours lingering in the air.

As they got to Muddy Bay a few klicks after the airport, Keefer noticed a disturbance in the smooth layer of ash down the hill from them. The air here was barely sprinkled with floating particulate, and he could see the long, winding track of someone . . . or something.

"Other survivors?" Abelone asked, slightly louder than a whisper.

"Likely. Can't imagine an infected, or even a group of infected, could walk so straight," Keefer answered, followed by a cough to clear his throat.

"Should we go down there?" Doc Martel asked.

"It is thick ash down the hill. Plus, they are ahead of us. Best to stick to the road we're on. That side road meets up with ours after Muddy Bay."

Invigorated by the idea of other survivors, they sped up as fast as their energy levels allowed. Keefer's lungs burned, and he was hacking more and more, as were the others. He needed to get them out of the napalm zone; otherwise, the chemicals would do permanent damage to their lungs.

The sun, now at its peak, was a warm yellow ball in the hazy sky. The ash and brume were thinning as they left the town further behind. Keefer could taste the air getting cleaner. It was another few kilometres before the other footprints—and they were footprints, to his relief—converged with their road.

"Not a group," said Keefer, inspecting the footprints in the ash. "Only one person."

"How did they survive? With the heavy concentration of chemicals in the air, they would have had to be as well sheltered as we were .

. . Otherwise, their lungs would have been burned on the first day," Abelone said.

No one had an answer.

Keefer looked out in the direction they were heading. "About ten klicks. You'd mentioned they would try to burn about eighty kilometres out . . . That would put the limit of the bombing where this road"—he nodded to the road they were on—"meets the 510."

"The 510?"

"The Trans-Labrador Highway. It goes through Goose Bay to Labrador City on the border with Quebec."

"We need to get to a phone. Let the WHO know we have the blood of Patient Zero."

Keefer looked at Abelone, then at Doc Martel, who was still holding on tightly to the yellow case housing the blood samples.

"Goose Bay is five hours," he said hesitantly.

"That's not too bad. Let's go," Abelone said resolutely.

Keefer realized she didn't understand. "Five hours by car. That's two days of walking."

Abelone paused, but her enthusiasm remained. "Fine, we'll find a car as soon as we get out of the burn zone. Let's go."

"You don't understand, Abelone. This is Labrador; there's one road in and out. The few houses will likely be abandoned. People will have taken their cars to evacuate." He was raising his voice, and the whole group was looking at him. How were they not angry about all the people dead in Peaks Bay? He'd lost his friends, people he cared about.

Abelone looked at him and whispered so only he could hear, "Benjamin, you know this area better than Eric and I. Moe and Karen trust you. You need to lead us out of here. We can't do this without you."

Keefer looked back at the three other survivors; they were all still looking at him. He wanted to yell at them. He wanted to yell at Abelone for bringing this virus to his town. But instead, he took a long, deep breath and closed his eyes. "You're right." He tried to ignore the madness of the nightmare they were in. He called Tigger over and dusted the ash off the dog's black and brown fur. It was like dusting snow off after a December walk—but it was July.

The musk of his dog calmed him. He knew he had to come to terms with the situation. Everyone was struggling in the prison of their own minds. He had to help them through it. He rubbed Tigger and pushed thoughts of those who had died in the bombing from his head. There were living people he could still help.

Keefer stood back up. "Ted's Taxi and Delivery is about thirty klicks out. Hopefully, there will be some wheels there. If not, the quarantine blockade will be the next logical place to find a vehicle. I'm sure we're going to find something there if need be."

Moe straightened, and Abelone and Martel nodded. Karen sucked in her last weep and steadied herself. Keefer smiled confidently at them, then turned and started walking, following in the footsteps of whoever was ahead of them.

***

Keefer followed a once familiar road through the desolate, other-worldly landscape, the others trailing behind him like a tiny funeral procession. The occasional cough or grumble broke the oppressive silence. The further they walked, the higher the burnt tree stubs were getting, indicating they were nearing the outskirts of the bombing zone.

Keefer's stomach rumbled, adding a new sound to the coughs and a new pain to his growing collection. His bruised ribs complained with every step, and it took a lot of his very limited energy not to snap at the insanity of their situation. He knew the others had to be tired and hungry, too, so he kept all this to himself and kept following the road—and the path of their mysterious predecessor.

Abelone joined Keefer at the front for a while. The air was clear enough that they shed their masks without saying anything. She looked

the end of their line now led by Abelone. Everyone remained quiet as they walked up the hill.

***

They walked for close to ten more hours with nothing but small breaks to rest. Keefer was relieved when the burnt tundra morphed into shrubs, then sparse boreal forest. They'd made it out of the blast zone. He wished the memory of the burnt town would fade away like a nightmare when he woke up in the morning, but it didn't. Some things the mind can't forget.

Keefer kept his distance from Abelone and Doc Martel, but he encouraged the group when they needed a boost. He hoped his support would be seen as a bridge to cross the divide he'd created.

The sun was sinking when they reached Ted's Taxi and Delivery. The old two-floor house was still standing, and Keefer finally had something to say to the group other than an apology for his earlier behaviour. He explained to Abelone and Martel that this was the local package delivery depot and the only tow-truck operation for the region. They nodded at his explanation, and he added that this was the only commerce, or house for that matter, between Muddy Bay and the Trans-Labrador Highway.

"If we are going to find a car, it will be here," he said, offering an olive branch to Abelone.

"Let's hope so," she answered, half-smiling.

Keefer smiled at her reaction until Moe made a face of surprise at her interaction with him.

The group huddled behind a grove of fir trees overlooking the cluttered property. Keefer scanned the house and the pre-fabricated, round-roofed garages like an owl scanning for field mice.

"I'm not seeing any movement," he said, kneeling beside Moe.

"I'm not seeing any vehicles either," Moe answered in his old harbour drawl.

"Yeah, Ted and his guys must have been able to get out in time. Otherwise, his pickup would be there, and I don't see his tow truck either." Keefer changed position to get a better view.

Moe looked west up the road. "It was probably out on the highway when all this happened. Or it took off the same as Ted and his truck."

"How many people lived here?" Abelone asked, kneeling a few feet behind them.

Keefer was relieved she had spoken to him—correction, spoken in his direction. "Ted, his wife, their son and a couple of hired hands who handle the towing business."

"If the infection has indeed spread out of Peaks Bay, some of them might have been infected," Abelone said, more to him this time.

"Yeah, we should watch for a bit to make sure. If it's safe, we can head down and barricade ourselves in the house or a garage. Maybe get some food and water."

After half an hour of watching the property, Keefer waved the group closer together. "It looks safe to go down there. We haven't seen any movement, infected or otherwise."

"Otherwise?" Karen asked, confused.

"Well, our friend who is in front of us." Keefer was nervous about not having seen them yet. "We have to assume whoever they are, they are nervous about meeting us. They know we are here, so why not reveal themselves?" He knew from his experience in Afghanistan that someone in a traumatic state of shock could react unexpectedly.

After a bit more discussion, they made their way down the slope leading to Ted's Taxi and Delivery. They agreed the old two-floored wood panel house was where they should go. There'd be food and water there, and hopefully a working phone. By the time they were all lined up against the side of the house, the sun was touching the horizon. Keefer eyed the hazy red ball, relieved they would be holed up for nightfall. The thought of being caught outside had been eating away at him for the last few hours. Something he had preferred keeping to himself so as not to alarm the others.

"I'll go in first," said Keefer, taking the safety off his shotgun.

He went around the corner and up the porch steps. Moe followed first, then the others. The door was unlocked; Keefer wasn't sure if that was a good sign or a bad one. The air inside was stuffy and a few degrees warmer than outside. A rotten smell lingered, which made him uneasy, but he looked at Tigger, sniffing and intrigued, but not raising any alarms.

From the vestibule, Keefer could see the den to their right. It was empty of any threats, so he signalled the others to follow him in. He crept through the large room, making sure every corner was safe. As he moved into the dining room, the smell of rot intensified, and he heard someone behind him retch. Laid out on the table was a four-place setting for dinner—probably from a few nights back. A ham covered in green mould sat on a large porcelain plate in the middle of the wooden table. A variety of other foods in smaller plates, also covered in mould of varying colours, sat untouched around the centrepiece.

"Looks like they left in a hurry," Moe whispered.

Keefer was relieved the source of the rotten smell was the food and not something else, but he still felt uneasy. The refrigerator door was open, which struck him as odd. Cool air prickled his skin as it escaped from the old, rounded metal fridge. The door must have been opened recently.

"There's a pickup truck in the back!" Karen said. "We don't have to walk anymore!" She stood at the rear kitchen window, almost bouncing.

Moe grabbed her by the shoulders. "Shhhh . . ."

"What? There's no one here, and we have a car now!" Karen continued.

Moe whispered back to her exactly what Keefer was thinking. "Ted only had one pickup truck. Be quiet, for God's sake."

Keefer brought the shotgun up to his shoulder. If the truck was here, that meant the people hadn't left.

Something crashed in a room on the second floor. There was a furious patter of footsteps as someone—or something—ran down the hallway. Tigger growled, and the fur on his back stood straight up.

Ted, the owner of Ted's Taxi and Delivery, appeared at the top of the stairwell; his legs kept cycling in mid-air as the floor gave way to the stairs. He landed mid-way down the flight and, for half a second, looked like he had maintained his balance and was going to jump the rest of the stairs—but his legs gave out, and he hurtled down head between knees, landing on his back in a violent crash.

Keefer and Abelone moved at the same time. Keefer took three steps forward and was standing on top of the infected, shotgun aimed at its head. Abelone dropped Tigger's leash, grabbed a chair and lunged. She bumped Keefer out of the way, and the shotgun deflagration hit the wooden floor, sending splinters spraying over the infected's head. Abelone slammed the chair over the infected's chest with the legs' cross-bar, pinning it to the floor as it tried to get up.

"What are you doing?" shouted Keefer. "We need to kill it!"

"Quiet!" said Abelone, her head tilted sideways—listening.

No other sounds came from upstairs or anywhere. Everything was quiet except for the hissing emanating from the infected.

"I think it's clear," Moe said, stepping to the window to scout the outside for any movement.

The infected pushed up against the chair, so Abelone put her knee down on it with all her weight. Doc Martel also put his weight on it, and this stabilized the chair. The infected kept hissing and gargling, trying to bite at the air. Keefer pumped the shotgun and moved toward it, but Abelone's defiant stare stopped him.

"Why?" Keefer asked. "Why would you do that? If he bites any of us, we are as good as dead."

"He's still a person. We don't have to kill them all. We can help them. We have what it takes to make a vaccine."

"Abelone, once infected, it's too late. They need to die." He thought of the people of Peaks Bay. They had all died to stop the infection. "Look at him."

Abelone looked down at the infected. Keefer wondered what she saw. From where he stood, he saw black irises with grey vitreous, meandering black veins, grey skin and patchy hair. He saw a corpse.

"Yes, he's infected," she said. "Yes, he's dangerous, but it doesn't mean he can't be saved."

"This is insane! You can't save them, Abelone. Not once infected." Keefer took another step, resisting her stare.

"Mr. Keefer, don't. I'm not as sure as Ms. Jensen that everyone can be saved, but we have him well secured. Shooting him like this would be akin to murder," Doc Martel pleaded.

Now Martel was resisting. Was he alone in thinking the infected should die? Keefer turned to Moe. "Moe? This is crazy."

Moe looked down at the infected, then at Keefer. "I know what you mean, Ben. But I knew Ted. I knew his wife and kid. If there is a chance he can be saved . . ."

As he looked down at the thing that used to be Ted, Keefer knew there was no saving him, but he hesitated.

Abelone seized her chance. "Moe, grab that duct tape over there. Tie up his hands and arms while we hold him down."

Keefer looked where she was pointing. There was a roll of duct tape on the counter. He couldn't believe they were doing this.

Moe grabbed the tape and spun it around the infected's wrists and ankles. With the infected immobilized, Abelone took her weight off the chair. Doc Martel sat down, making sure to keep his legs well away from the snapping mouth.

"Mr. Moe, maybe we should tape his jaw shut to make sure it's safe," Martel said.

"I'm not going anywhere near his mouth, Mr. Doctor. You can do that if yar brave enough." Moe's thick accent was accentuated by his concern.

Doc Martel looked at the infected under his chair. "Maybe we wait a bit for him to calm down."

Keefer grabbed the tape from Moe and bent down by the infected.

"Hold his head," he ordered Moe, who hesitantly complied. Keefer wrapped the tape around the infected's head as if it was simply a box that needed taping. When he was done, he stood up and looked at Abelone, hoping she was satisfied he was playing along with her mad plan. She nodded, reached over to Doc Martel, took the yellow protective case from his satchel and walked to Keefer.

"Ben, I know you think eradicating the virus is the only way. That is also the premise under which the Geneva Protocol operates: eradicate by all means if there is no hope for a vaccine and the virus is loose."

"So why? Why aren't you following that rule? A rule you helped draft."

"This." Abelone held up the yellow case. "In here, we have the blood samples of Tom Virtanen—Patient Zero. As soon as we get this to the WHO, we will be able to make a vaccine. We will be able to save people."

"Even if we let him live, it will be days before we reach a populated area and maybe weeks before these samples reach anyone who can do anything good with them. What happens to him until then? We will be letting him die like that . . ." Keefer pointed to the infected.

"I don't know," Abelone admitted, "but we can't kill him in cold blood."

Keefer stepped back. The fact she had been bitten and survived was an invisible wall that had stopped him from putting a bullet in Ted's head. He had to try to believe. He nodded without saying a word.

"I'll make sure upstairs is clear. Let's get some food and rest. We can head out in the morning," Keefer said. "Moe, see if you can find the truck keys. They've got to be somewhere." He pointed at the squirming taped-up infected. "Maybe they're in his pockets." With a sense of satisfaction at giving Moe an unpleasant task for not supporting him, he turned and headed up the stairs, shotgun at the ready.

***

No sounds came from any of the rooms on the second floor. Three doors were open, and one at the end of the hallway was closed. As Keefer crept to the first door, he thought about Abelone's insistence that not all infected had to die. Nothing good could come from it. They had slaughtered his hometown and his friends, but what if . . .

He peeked into the first room on his right. Nothing. Keefer moved to the next door. How could Abelone stay so good despite everything she'd been through? Second room. A quick peek through the door with the shotgun ready. Nothing. He moved on to the third door. When it came to dealing with the infected, they failed to agree, and yet Keefer still felt something for her. What, he wasn't sure. Was it her, or was it what she represented? Third room. Quick look. Pause. *What's that on the floor?* One of those little foldable dinner tables, the kind used to eat dinner while watching TV, was lying on its side. That was what the infected must have tipped over when he—it—heard them. *What were you doing up here, Ted?*

Keefer looked at the last door. He inched toward it, listening as his heart thumped loudly, making it hard to hear. He wiped his palms against his pants and repositioned his hands on the shotgun, then reached for the doorknob. The hinges creaked, and the sound made him twitch. The smell assaulted him where he stood.

Rotten food?

It was more intense than what he had smelled downstairs. Like the mouldy food on the kitchen table, two bodies lay rotting on the bed. A woman and a boy. Keefer stopped and breathed in deeply as he processed what he was seeing. He choked on the putrid air and lost control of his esophagus; it constricted violently and would have expelled the contents of his stomach if it hadn't been empty. It took a few breaths to get control back.

They'd been infected. He could tell by the grey of their skin. The upper quarter of the woman's skull was missing where a bullet had cut through bone and tissue. The teen was better off. He had a hole in his left eye only.

A hunting rifle was leaning against the wall by the door. He looked from the rifle to the bed to down the hallway and the stairs that led to the kitchen where the infected—Ted—was hog-tied. *They must have gotten infected first.* Keefer closed his eyes at the thought that Ted had shot his wife and kid. He shook his head like an etch-a-sketch, trying to erase the image from his mind. These were people; they weren't simply infected. He let out a long, slow breath as he left the room, picking up the hunting rifle as he exited. He respectfully closed the door behind him.

23

ONE OF THEIR OWN TURNS

M oe had not located the keys to the pickup truck, and the phone lines were not working, but at least they had a secure place to sleep. They'd made sure the doors and windows were locked and had barricaded everything except the rear door, which was locked but accessible in case they needed an emergency exit. Doc Martel and Moe brought down mattresses from upstairs and laid them out in front of the lifeless stone fireplace. Although they didn't say it out loud, no one wanted to be alone. They silently agreed they would sleep together on the main floor.

Keefer took the first watch. Even though Ted's Taxi and Delivery was in the middle of the wilderness, it wasn't pitch black outside. A faint grey light enveloped the landscape around the house. Nighttime never fully fell in this part of Labrador during the summer; he called it Mother Nature's night light.

He made his way back and forth between the living room and kitchen windows like a medieval sentry on a castle wall. After an hour, he checked up on the infected, the man who once had a wife and a teenager. He looked for a sign of life, some sign of humanity in its black eyes. He would have taken anything, a distant star in a black sky, anything. But he only saw one thing—single-mindedness. The infected wanted to bite him. That was all there was. No anger, no fear, no pain, simply a desire to bite. Keefer shivered to his core.

He walked away, wrestling with what he saw in the infected's eyes and what Abelone wanted him to believe. He carefully walked between the mattresses in the living room to Karen. No one looked up, but he could tell they were all sleeping restlessly. Even Tigger was having bad dreams as he twitched spastically beside Abelone.

He woke Karen up gently. She'd calmed down a lot with an evening of rest. He had as well. From her mattress, she stared up at Keefer and smiled—the kind of smile that said more than hello. Keefer looked past it. "Come. I need to show you how to use the rifle again."

He stood with her in the kitchen and re-enacted how to take the safety off the old Winchester. "Remember to leave the safety on until you see something."

"If . . . I see something," Karen corrected him. "We haven't seen anything since we got here. Everything is quiet outside. We're finally safe."

"You never know, Karen. There might be more infected out there."

"If they do come, you'll keep me safe?" Karen put her hand on his arm.

Keefer pulled back and scratched his neck as he looked around the kitchen. He needed to address this and let Karen know he wasn't interested, but not now. Tomorrow, when they had all slept.

"I'll keep everyone safe," he replied, unsure of what else to say.

"You mean you'll keep her safe?" She scowled toward the living room.

It didn't matter that Abelone was hardly talking to him. Karen had picked up that he had a connection to the Danish scientist despite their obvious differences.

"Karen, we all need to focus on surviving and getting help." He ignored her comment. "Will you be okay for the next two hours?" He redirected the conversation, not having the energy to deal with her misplaced emotions.

Karen's forehead creased, and her jaw clenched as she nodded. She turned her back to Keefer and looked out the window.

Keefer sighed and headed to the living room to lie on the mattress, still warm from Karen's body.

With his eyes closed, he listened to Karen's movements back and forth between the front and back of the house, a slow-walking metronome. She'd shuffle through the living room, go quiet at the front door for a few minutes, then shuffle back through their makeshift dormitory and go quiet in the kitchen.

The shuffling became background noise. He squeezed his eyes tighter, trying to will away the gut-wrenching thought that Peaks Bay was gone—thousands of people gone. Abelone was right. They had all lost people they were close to. He wasn't close to Abelone; he hardly knew her, but he felt connected to her. Would he have killed her if he'd seen her get bitten? The infected had to be . . . put down. That was the only way to stop the plague from spreading. But what would he have done in that situation? He wanted to be as sure as she was people could be saved. He wondered how much difference it made that they had Patient Zero's blood. Abelone and Martel were sure they had the least mutated form of the virus and that, combined with Abelone's blood, it was the best possible scenario to develop a vaccine. Maybe she was right.

Tigger's low growl pulled him out of his reverie. He hadn't heard Karen shuffle around for a while. *Have I been sleeping?*

Keefer looked up. "Tigger?" No answer and no pattering of paws on the wood floors. He propped himself up on his elbows, turning toward the kitchen. "Karen? Everything okay?"

"I'm fine," the young orderly's voice answered. "Tigger wanted to say hi. Go back to sleep." Was her voice shaking? She was probably still mad at him. He lay back down.

The kitchen floor creaked. The sound meandered deep into his nervous system. There followed a rusty squeak of an old door hinge that hadn't been oiled in years. Keefer quickly got back up on his elbows. "Karen? Was that the door?"

No answer.

"Tigger?"

The response was a loud, erratic fumbling from the kitchen. He recognized the noise, and his neck hair stood on end. It could only be one thing. How easy it was to differentiate sounds from the living compared to sounds from the infected.

"Karen?" he shouted as he sprang up to his feet.

The infected—Ted—came rushing into the living room and crashed into Keefer. They tumbled to the ground. Keefer's hands automatically went to the infected's neck to hold the head away. But he was too slow. Ted's head was already on Keefer's neck.

Moe, who was up and holding the shotgun, rushed over and kicked the infected off Keefer. In the grey darkness of the living room, the ignition of the shell flashed like a mini explosion, and the blast hit Keefer's eardrums like a gong. The top of the infected's head disappeared in the shadows, and the body slumped to the ground.

Flashlights sprang to life.

"Were you bitten?" Abelone gasped, falling to Keefer's side.

"Yes!" he uttered as his hand went to his neck and pawed around. "No . . . I don't know!" He brought his hand to his eyes. "No blood."

It was Abelone's turn to paw his neck every which way, followed by his shoulders, face and arms, before she looked him in the eyes with relief. They looked at each other for a few seconds, and he had his answer—he would not have shot her dead.

"He'll be fine," Moe grunted, then coughed.

Keefer and Abelone looked at the infected where Moe's flashlight illuminated the half-blown-away head. The mouth still had duct tape wrapped around it.

"His hands are still tied," Abelone pointed out.

An engine roared to life in the yard, and the pickup truck's headlights rushed by the living-room window. The cabin was filled with shifting shadows as Keefer glimpsed the truck go down the driveway before turning west and disappearing in the distance, its red taillights bouncing like angry shooting stars in the night sky.

"Karen!" Keefer said as he jumped up and rushed to the kitchen.

There was blood all over the floor, but only one body. The black and brown fur was motionless. A kitchen knife stuck out from Tigger's side, and a large cut across his throat was slowly draining blood. Despair flooded Keefer as he slipped in the blood while kneeling beside his dog. He put his hands over Tigger's slashed throat but knew right away his friend was gone. There was no movement in the dog's chest. *Why?* He couldn't process why Karen would have done such a thing. The more seconds passed, the more his despair boiled into a raging fire.

"How could she?" someone asked.

"I don't think it was her," said another voice. "We never found the keys to the pickup."

"It had to be someone else. That stranger ahead of us. It had to be." He looked at Moe with tears tickling his eyelids.

"Why?" Keefer grunted. He got no response from Moe.

"But what about Karen?" asked Abelone. "Doesn't look like she put up a fight. She would have had to open the door. It was locked."

"They must have left together," Moe growled. "They also took the food." Moe pointed to the table where their supplies had been. There was nothing left.

Keefer's lucidity returned. He looked around the room. "Damn it, they have the rifle too." Ted's rifle and all the bullet boxes were gone. He stood up, not daring to look back down at Tigger. "Who is this person ahead of us? Why would Karen go with them?"

Moe and Abelone offered no answer.

"That's not all they took," came the trembling voice of Doc Martel. He was standing in front of an open fridge. "The blood samples . . . They're gone."

***

Keefer stood by the window in the kitchen, the same one Karen had stood watch at. He watched the tree they had laid Tigger under. They hadn't buried him, too worried to spend extended time outdoors. As the sun crept up and the cooler air turned to light fog, he was able to make out his dog's black and brown fur. It was time to go.

"Let's go." He didn't have to say it twice. Everyone else was ready. He took the small bag of food they had scrounged from what remained in the kitchen and headed out.

Keefer shivered. Was it due to what lay ahead or simply the fact that the air was still cool? The sky was turning from grey to blue. The dry dirt crunched under Keefer's boot as he stepped into the driveway. It reminded him of leaving for an early morning patrol in Afghanistan. He was on high alert for anything out of place. Anything that was there to kill him.

"They left some food!" Martel pointed to a wooden bench in the yard.

Water bottles and a few cans of beans stuck out of a white plastic bag. Keefer found that odd. In Afghanistan, when something was odd, you needed to be extra careful. *Why?* Keefer looked around nervously—the food was out of place. If something was out of place, chances are it was—flashbacks of IEDs flooded his mind as Martel reached for the bag.

"No!" Keefer tackled him to the ground as a police-issued stun grenade rolled out from under the bag. It was wrapped in some sort of plastic wrapper filled with nails.

The deflagration sucked all sound from the area and replaced it with a high-pitched ringing in his ears. As he lay disoriented on the ground, it took a few seconds to realize he had a half-dozen projectiles lodged in his back. The pain was numb at first but ramped up as the shock of the flashbang wore off and his senses returned.

Someone was talking to him, but he could barely make out the words. It was like he was underwater, and everything was muffled. Abelone grabbed him by the shoulders and looked straight into his face. Her mouth was moving, but her voice was a wave of echoes, not making sense. Keefer's ears still rang, and he had tunnel vision.

Abelone pointed to the others, who were all fine. He nodded. Abelone tended the wounds on his back. His brain started deciphering some words as the ringing subsided slowly. "Don't worry . . . far off . . .

not injured." She pulled something from his skin through his shirt and showed it to him. "Nail . . . most of the blast."

He nodded again.

"Doc?" Keefer managed to get out between deep breaths.

"He's fine. You protected him." Her words were getting clearer, which meant his eardrums weren't punctured. "They're small nails, but you got a handful in your back." He felt her pulling things out of his skin and clothes. "They're not very deep . . . but good thing you pushed Eric to the ground. If he'd taken that explosion in the face . . ."

It took ten minutes for Abelone to apply bandages to Keefer's back under his shirt; by then, his senses had mostly recovered. As he sat on the stairs, Doc Martel came up to him.

"Thank you, Benjamin."

Keefer nodded, not able to produce a comforting smile.

"I can't believe someone would do that. Why would they want to harm us?" Martel wondered.

Keefer had been focused on his pain, but now realized what the IED meant. It was a trap someone had left for them. *A fucking trap! But why?* It made no sense. He ignored the pain of the little holes in his back as well as his sore ribs. He squeezed both fists until his knuckles were white. "Whoever it was, we will catch up to them. We need those blood samples." What he wanted was to catch Karen and whoever she was with. Whoever had killed Tigger.

Everyone nodded. They collected their things and followed Keefer out of Ted's Taxi and Delivery's yard. They headed west, following the tire tracks of someone who wanted to kill them.

24

BARRICADE SHOOTING

Keefer watched from a small grove of fir trees. The Trans-Labrador Highway was devoid of traffic. It flowed north to south like an asphalt waterway as far as he could see, whereas the smaller road they had arrived on meandered around hills and trees and spilled into the main vehicular artery like a creek into a river. The creek, however, was blocked by a military barricade acting like a great dam holding back a dozen cars and pickup trucks. Two tall scaffolds were erected on both sides of the barricade, which acted as lookout towers over the road. Beyond the hastily constructed metal fences were a handful of large khaki canvas tents strewn about like fishing shacks on the creek banks.

"What do we do?" asked Martel.

"We watch," Keefer answered.

"For what?"

"Movement." Keefer's eyes were glued on the barricade. He could smell the seared asphalt after a day of baking in the hot sun. The sun was setting now, and grey shadows stretched out as dusk settled in.

"How long are we going to wait?" Martel followed up.

"Until morning. With the low light, it's impossible to be sure what's down there," Keefer said. Deep down, he wanted to run down there and keep moving to catch up to whoever had killed Tigger. But the long walk had given him time to think. He needed to ensure the others were safe. The cars and trucks at the barricade were haphazardly spread on the road.

It was impossible to see if they were empty, let alone know if there was anyone or anything inside the tents. They had to watch.

No puffins or chickadees were chirping away in the foliage of stunted trees, which would be common in this area. He figured they'd been scared away by either the bombing or something hiding in the encampment.

Short on shotgun shells, they'd armed themselves with a machete, an axe, a tire iron and a pitchfork from Ted's shed.

"There hasn't been any movement. We should go." It was Abelone's turn to chime in. "We need to find the blood samples."

Keefer looked at her. She had been more open with him since the house. The fact Ted had almost killed him seemed to make her less closed off. Maybe she felt guilty; maybe she had realized killing the infected might be better than keeping them alive. He smiled at her reassuringly.

"We'll keep looking, but for now, we need rest. If there are any infected or if our mysterious friend sets another trap, we might not see it until it's too late. We have to wait until daybreak."

Abelone acquiesced, and the others agreed. So Keefer sat facing the barricade, and the others huddled up beside him—Abelone right by his side.

Sitting in the gloom, Keefer thought about Tigger. He couldn't believe his dog was gone. No one other than Karen could have killed him. Sliced his throat. Otherwise, he would have fought or barked . . . *why?* A tear meandered down his cheek, and Abelone's warm hand closed on his.

"I'm sorry about Tigger," she said, as if reading his mind.

He smiled at her and clasped her hand. "I'm sorry you lost your friends on the ship."

"Oh brother . . ." Moe murmured behind them.

***

Abelone and the others made their way to the barricade once the sun was peeking over the horizon, washing the grey shadows away. She'd had a restless sleep sitting back to back with the others, but Keefer said he'd been up all night and had not seen any movement. She admired his leadership despite their differences in what should happen to the infected. She couldn't imagine losing so much, so fast. She'd lost friends on the Henry Dawson, but the scale of his loss was on a whole other level.

The road leading to the barricade reminded her of those American junkyards she'd seen on TV, with cars scattered everywhere. Some had run into the ones in front, and one had rolled to its side in the ditch beside the road. She could smell gasoline but couldn't pinpoint which car had sprung a leak. The group slowly walked between the abandoned cars.

"Bullet holes," Keefer said.

Abelone followed his arm pointing at a blue sedan near the front of the abandoned procession. The windshield and the hood were riddled with holes, presumably shot from the guard towers.

"They fired on them," she said. Her statement was obvious, but her mind was translating what she was seeing into the paperwork of the Geneva Protocol: burn the area to the ground and make sure no infection escapes the quarantine zone. At the time, she never thought those protocols would be enacted. Ever. She felt disgusted.

Abelone looked inside the car. She shook and took a step back. The bodies of a man and a woman were inside, covered in blood. They'd been killed by the bullets that had rained down on their vehicle. She tried to open the passenger door, but it was locked. Keefer tried the driver's door—it opened.

"They weren't infected," he said.

Abelone walked to his side of the car. "They didn't need to be for the military to shoot them," she said, wrapping her arms around herself and crinkling her nose as the smell of death reached her. "If they approached the barricade, the soldiers would have had orders to shoot to kill." Her disgust grew. How could she have supported such a protocol? It was so theoretical. Living it now, she had to make up for this.

"Is it safe?" Moe asked, looking up at the guard towers nervously.

"Don't worry, it looks abandoned," Keefer answered.

"Sure . . ." said Moe as he made room for Doc Martel behind the protection of the car.

Abelone ignored them and walked to another car to find more dead bodies. As she did, Keefer pushed the dead driver aside from the steering wheel and turned the key to see if the car would start. Nothing. Not even a whirl of the engine.

"Bullets must have done a number on its engine. Try that one," he said to Moe as he pointed to an orange Chevy. No luck. All the cars were dead, like their passengers. But they did find some food and water in a few of them, so there was that.

As they cautiously approached the barricade, they kept an eye on the guard towers. No one materialized to mow them down with bullet fire. Keefer pointed to the tracks in the mud that went around the barriers. He didn't have to state they were probably from Ted's pickup truck. Abelone took it as another sign there weren't any soldiers left. Still, her adrenaline was pumping hard. With so many people shot dead behind her, it was hard not to worry.

Abelone stopped in her tracks. A half-dozen bodies were piled up in the ditch beside the main barricade. All had grey skin and bite marks, but more importantly, all had parts of their heads blown off. She didn't say anything. Neither did anyone else.

The group made it through the steel barricades without receiving any new holes in their bodies. Abelone paused beside Keefer as he took in the encampment. Moe and Doc stood behind them, rocking from foot to foot as they looked around.

"That looks like the command centre," Keefer said, pointing to a large green tarp tent with a bunch of tables, chairs and radio equipment inside. "And that one, some sort of medical tent."

Abelone gave instructions before Keefer could. "You go to the command one. Eric and I will see if there are medical supplies we could use."

Keefer hesitated. He'd been getting more and more protective of the group.

"Okay, be careful. There might not be soldiers here, but there might be infected."

Abelone entered the medical tent with Martel in tow. There were a few cots and tables placed along the tent walls, with a couple of metal rolling cabinets to hold medicine and supplies. She knew right away someone had beaten them to the spoils: first-aid kits and cabinets were open, and their contents were strewn everywhere.

"Whoever was here knew what was worth taking," she told Martel as she rummaged through a cabinet. "Penicillin and painkillers all gone."

"It had to be Karen," concluded Martel. "She was an orderly . . . but I can still pull together a half-decent first-aid kit with the gauzes, bandages and scissors that are left."

Abelone nodded. "Go ahead. I'll keep an eye out at the front of the tent." She walked to the tent opening and stood partially behind the rolled-up door flap. The camp was pretty straightforward, with the medical and command tents on opposite sides of the road and a third tent a few hundred metres away at the intersection of the highway.

There were no military vehicles anywhere, but crates, pallets and rubbish were strewn all over the ground, where tire marks sank into the soft earth by the road. *They took off in a hurry*, Abelone thought, looking back into the medical tent at all the stuff that had been left behind. As she looked the camp area over again, she noticed the bright yellow rear of a school bus, barely sticking out from the other side of the far tent. Martel popped up beside her, a freshly pulled-together medical kit over his shoulder. He nodded, and they made their way back to Keefer and Moe.

The command tent was stuffy. Electrical equipment and wires were laid out over four folding tables. No laptops, radios or phones—everything that was easy to take had been evacuated—quickly, too, as there were chairs knocked over and a tall stack of computer equipment lying flat on its front.

"No luck. Most radios are gone, and the few that are left are broken," Keefer half-whispered, anticipating what she and Martel would ask. He was looking over Moe's shoulder as he sat at one of the broken radios, grunting and fiddling with the wires.

"There's a bus—one of those small yellow buses for children," Abelone informed them.

That got both Keefer and Moe's attention.

"It's down the road, parked behind the far tent," Martel said louder.

"Shhh, there might still be infected around," Keefer said with his hand raised. Martel paled.

Abelone walked to the tent flaps and peeked out. The road was still clear. "We should go. We need to find a way to communicate with . . . others. Let them know to look for Karen and the blood samples. There must be a village nearby she is going to."

Moe looked at her. "You probably don't realize this, young lady, but Labrador's big. It's probably ten times the size of your country. And there are very few people. The closest town is Goose Bay, well Port Hope, but that's a tiny little shat hole in the middle of nowhere." He pushed the receiver back, giving up on the dead equipment.

"Yeah, we're better off heading to Goose Bay. Karen knows heading to Port Hope would be a dead end." Keefer walked to Abelone as he adjusted his makeshift leather and cloth armour. "Let's head for that bus. Hopefully, it still runs."

Weapons at the ready, they exited and quickly covered the distance to the third tent. Abelone was tense, expecting the infected to run out from behind every crate or bush. Nothing.

This tent was bigger than the others. In between the light crunching of dirt under their cautious footsteps, she heard a faint gargle that made her breathing stop. *I know that sound.* She quickly grabbed Keefer by the back of his jacket.

He stopped immediately and looked at her, alarmed. "What is it?" he whispered.

She put her fingers to her lips, indicating to everyone to be quiet. She tapped her ear while looking at Keefer.

Light snorts were coming from . . . behind the bus? No, behind the tent . . . No . . . it was inside the tent. She looked at Doc Martel as she expected he knew what it was. He did. He was pale as milk and gripping his tire iron. She looked back at Keefer and signalled back to her ear, pointed to the tent and mouthed the word *infected*.

Both Keefer and Moe stiffened and adjusted their grips on their weapons.

Keefer waved them away from the tent flap. In the slit of the opening, Abelone saw shadows moving and was acutely aware of the laboured wheezing coming from the infected inside. Abelone tried to make out how many, definitely more than one. Two, maybe three, she wasn't sure.

Crack! Abelone flinched at the sound, and the dust, barely a foot in front of Keefer, exploded up in a puff. *A rifle shot?*

Abelone looked up the highway where she believed the sound originated and wondered why the people in the pickup were shooting at them. *Is that Karen?*

She spun again as a burst of shrieks from inside the tent was followed by three infected stumbling over each other to chase the noise.

She lifted her machete to defend herself from the first infected, but it was crushed to the ground by the heavy firefighter axe Keefer wielded. As the infected crumpled, it pulled the axe from Keefer's hands. The body squirmed for a second before it started to get back up.

The second infected was also intercepted and impaled by the pitchfork wielded by Moe. He grunted as he partially lifted the grey body off the ground. It landed on its knees, tines sticking out its back. Moe held it in place, its arms still reaching for him. Doc Martel's tire iron crushed its head. The infected fell backwards from its kneeling position, slowly sliding off the tines of Moe's pitchfork, tire iron lodged between its frontal lobes.

The third infected leapt for Abelone, but Keefer intercepted it and, using its momentum, judo flipped it over his hips. The infected rolled onto the pavement in a ball of dust and hisses. When it looked up, its black eyes barely had time to focus on Abelone before they were skewered by the rusty metal pitchfork, like olives on the prongs of a dinner fork.

With Keefer's axe in its shoulder, the last infected regained its feet, tackled Keefer to the ground, and straddled him.

"Benjamin!" Abelone lifted the machete. She paused. That was a person—she couldn't kill a person.

Moe bumped her aside, grabbing the machete from her hands. Relief flooded over her. He swung the machete sideways, catching the infected above the ear and slicing through skin and bone until it lodged in the brain. The infected fell to its side—dead.

Moe glared at her. Blood rushed to her cheeks.

"Thanks . . ." Keefer said to Abelone.

She stayed quiet, looking at him. He could have died because of her—again. She was embarrassed, but she couldn't swing the machete. She couldn't take a life.

"That wasn't her," grunted Moe as he put his boot on the dead infected's head and pulled the machete out with a slurp. He handed the bloody tool back to her. "She doesn't believe in killing infected, remember?" Frowning, he walked away to help Doc Martel, who was still trying to pull his tire iron from the other infected's head.

"I . . ." Abelone hesitated. "I couldn't do it. I couldn't kill him." She was shaking for not defending Benjamin, but that was a person attacking him.

Keefer bent down to pick up his axe. "It's not a *him*." His eyes settled on her. "Not anymore. He's an *it* now. You need to see that, Abelone. We can't save these people. They are gone. We can't save anyone if we are dead."

Yet she refused to accept his premise. "No, they are still people. They don't all have to die." She was surprised when the angry retort did not come from Keefer, but from Moe.

"Listen, Missy. I like you most of the time." He moved close to Abelone, saliva spraying her face. "But you are going to get us killed. You need to fight. Otherwise, how da you expect to help anyone?"

Crack! The shot resonated across the landscape. A bus window exploded like candy glass. Everyone dove for cover.

"They're shooting from too far away," Keefer shouted from behind a metal drum. "They can't hit a target from that far out."

"Thank God for that," grumbled Moe.

"Looks like they are driving away," Martel pointed up the highway, his voice relieved.

The pickup truck disappeared over the horizon on the highway.

"Why are they doing this?" Abelone asked angrily. She couldn't believe Karen was behind these attacks. Why would people be turning on people? She had never seen this in her line of work.

A loud shriek from the green canvas tent startled her, and she brought her machete up. A tinge of guilt ran through her as she realized she wouldn't use it.

Keefer and Moe moved to the tent and looked in cautiously. The surprise was clear on their faces. Abelone was taken aback when they walked inside without saying a word. Martel looked at her, shrugged, and the two of them followed.

The tent flap swayed gently in the light breeze, but it wasn't enough to air out the putrid smell. Through the gloom, she could make out four metal jail cells lined along the fabric wall.

Keefer and Moe stood in front of one of the cells where an infected in army fatigues was shrieking and throwing itself against the bars. Every time it did, all the linked cells rattled.

"Why did they lock this one up after shooting everyone at the barricade?" Abelone asked, scrutinizing the person in the cell.

"Who knows?" said Keefer, taking the pitchfork from Moe's hands. "Maybe he was bitten, and they locked him in here because he was one of their own." Before she could react, he thrust the pitchfork through the bar openings and impaled the infected in the head. The body fell to the ground, sliding off the tines. The tent was suddenly silent.

Abelone glared at him. "He was no threat to anyone!"

"They all have to die if we are to survive," Keefer said calmly as he walked by her, picked up a set of keys from the table and showed it to the others. The key had a large white tag that said *BUS*.

He walked out the tent door into the morning sunlight.

25

DIE WITH YOUR BOOTS OFF

Abelone sat by herself in the middle of the small yellow bus. She bounced around the barely padded seat, deep in thought, as Moe hurtled the vehicle down the packed gravel road.

Keefer was asleep on the seat across from hers. He'd driven for a while before handing the duties over to Moe. She wondered what they would find in Goose Bay, but what was eating away at her more was that Karen and her escort seemed hell-bent on hurting them. The one gas station they'd passed had been void of people—or infected—but the gas pumps had been smashed to pieces. Luckily, the underground tanks were still accessible, and Moe was able to syphon plenty of gas—enough to refill their tank as well as a half-dozen red jerry cans they'd found inside the gas station.

She wondered when the owners had evacuated. It had been three days since they had left the bunker. Had the inhabitants outside the quarantine zone left the area before or after the military abandoned the Peaks Bay barricade? Nonetheless, the station had been emptied of any other useful supplies. Also concerning was that the phones were down. It was unclear if it was sabotage or if all communications into Labrador were down. They had no way of knowing.

She looked at Keefer and shivered at the thought of how close the first bullet had come to hitting him at the barricade. He'd been lucky. She wrapped her arms around herself, despite the heat of the day, thinking about how, once again, she had faced the dilemma of killing or not killing an infected. *A person*, she reminded herself. Her indecision had almost cost Keefer his life. Her head spun with questions: *What if Moe hadn't stepped in fast enough? Can the infected be saved once the virus takes hold of them? What if we don't get the blood samples back?* She shifted her gaze out the window. The gravel-packed road streamed by the side of the bus, too fast for her to make out the rocks.

It took another couple hundred kilometres, three driver changes, and one jerry can to reach the outskirts of Goose Bay. Abelone was at the wheel now, and she slowed the dusty bus at a bridge. She'd never seen a bridge like this—a low metal structure at least a half kilometre in length, it spanned a wide white-water river.

As the bus stopped, it took a few seconds for Moe to rise from between the vinyl seats. With a sleepy grunt, he said, "That's the Churchill River. A sight to behold, eh?"

Abelone heard every joint in his body creak as he stood.

Keefer and Doc Martel looked up from between their own bus seats, both grunting their aches and pains and shaking the cobwebs off.

Abelone gave up her seat to Moe. There was an Air Force military base in Goose Bay, and Moe knew how to get there. She took a seat behind him as Keefer and Martel joined them, rubbing their arms and shoulders.

Moe cleared the phlegm from his throat. "Here we go." The bus rolled slowly over the bridge and into the intersection where the highway continued east, and a smaller road went west to Goose Bay.

"Wait!" said Keefer, alarmed.

Fir trees obstructed the view on both sides of the road, but he pointed a kilometre ahead.

"Is that a military tent?"

"It is," confirmed Martel.

As the bus approached, a military encampment came into view. Abelone kept an eye on the trees and tents—scanning for anyone or anything. The camp was twice as large as the previous one, and it was easy for the bus to roll right up to the tents as the actual barricade and the scaffold towers were set up on the road going east to intercept anyone coming out of Goose Bay. *Not a good sign*, she thought. There was no ash here, no burnt buildings, and no smell of napalm in the air. Also not a good sign.

Moe stopped the bus right in the middle of the camp. Off the side of the road was a large green highway sign with the name Goose Bay and the distance to the town, which was overwritten with black spray paint.

DO NOT ENTER
TOWN QUARANTINED
CFB GOOSE BAY EVACUATED
MILITARY REGROUP AT CFB VALCARTIER
- MJR HOLLISTER, 5 WING

Abelone's heart sank. There would be no help here. She looked at the others. Their shoulders were sagging.

They discussed what to do as a grey dusk blanketed the landscape. Should they do as the sign said, or should they enter Goose Bay? In the end, the chance of getting help here trumped the message on the sign, Keefer argued. They were too close to possible help to simply drive away.

Abelone wasn't so sure. It was unlikely Karen and whoever she was with would have gone into Goose Bay. She reminded the group, "Without the vaccine, what good would it do to have the military around us? The virus will keep spreading. We need those blood samples to save people, and we need to get them to a secure production facility!"

They argued more. Keefer finally paused the debate, suggesting they check the encampment for supplies and a radio. Abelone thought to object but decided against it. Getting a radio would help to get them help. Keefer breathed a sigh of relief when she stayed quiet.

"Doc, stay with the bus and keep the engine running. If there is any sign of trouble, we need to get out of here quickly," Keefer said.

Abelone realized he wanted some time with Moe—hopefully, to talk about going after the blood samples. She looked him in the eyes as she squeezed past him.

"Let's stay together out there. We don't know if there are any infected in this camp," Keefer said as she stepped into the rapidly cooling evening air.

She pointed to the closest tent. They pulled up their makeshift weapons—pitchfork, machete and tire iron—and walked to the square, green canvas tent. The flaps were open, and from their distance, Abelone could tell it was empty of any bodies—live or infected. There were a lot more things left behind in this tent than in the ones outside Peaks Bay. Abelone set herself up at the tent entrance and signalled to Keefer and Moe by aiming her index and middle finger at her eyes, then at the road past the barricade, indicating she would stand guard. The two men nodded and entered the tent.

The sun touched the horizon, and evening twilight settled in. Nothing was fully light or dark. She strained to see down the road, assessing every shadow. She couldn't see to town, only to a bend around a rolling hill. Everything was quiet except for the purring engine of the bus resting after its marathon. Doc Martel had moved the bus back at an angle, which allowed it to be ready for any escape route if the need arose.

How many days had it been since she'd left St. John's? Or even gotten to Peaks Bay? She counted in her head, trying to piece together the missing day or so from when she was unconscious. The purring grew louder. She looked at the bus and could smell the exhaust in the cooling air. Martel had his arms perched on the steering wheel, looking around nervously. The purring was getting louder, but it wasn't the bus.

She looked up the road, past the barricade, and stepped out from behind her hiding spot, her head cocked to the side with her ear up. The sound was coming from the far end of the road, out of sight. In the dying light, it was hard to see the bend, but it sounded like a low-revving train. Whatever it was, it was big.

Abelone walked up to the barricade covered in barbed wire, straining to see.

"Ben, Eric, I think something is coming."

She stepped past the barricade into the middle of the road to get a better look. The sound was getting closer. It had to be a train. What else could it be? *But where are the train tracks?* She looked on both sides of the road to make sure she hadn't missed them. Nothing. She walked a few metres further down the road, staring at the asphalt horizon meandering around a grassy hill with no trees. Still, she couldn't see the source of the reverberation. All her senses were alert. *Is the ground shaking?* She looked at her feet to help discern the ground movement. A vibration made its way through the soles of her feet and made the hairs on the back of her neck stand on end. A giant black mass came around the bend and took shape in the low twilight. It spanned the whole road, and it was fast. *What is that?*

The ground trembled.

"Abelone?" Keefer's voice came from the entrance of the tent. She looked back at him with no answer to give.

She thought she'd heard a siren—it drew her attention back to the black mass. *Another siren? That's not a siren ... those are shrieks!*

Realizing what it was, she turned and ran. "Back to the bus! Back to the bus!"

Keefer and Moe did not hesitate. They sprinted back to the waiting vehicle. Doc Martel was standing behind the steering wheel.

The black mass broke into smaller individual parts, infected—possibly thousands of them—running down the road toward the sound of the bus.

Abelone sprinted around the barricade, looking over her shoulder as she did. An avalanche of grey bodies spilled down the road. Fear gripped her, but disappointment at seeing so many infected made tears squeeze from her eyes. The quarantine of Peaks Bay had failed.

Abelone's boot caught in a hanging barbed wire beside the barricade. The razor blades dug deep into the leather of her boot, and she crashed to the ground. She pulled at her leg to free it, but the more she tried to wrench her foot loose, the more the blades sank into the leather.

The avalanche was getting closer.

She tried to pull the barbed wire off, but the small razor-sharp blades cut into her hands. Keefer was yelling at her to get up. She looked for something to help pry herself loose—nothing. Dust bounced on the ground around her as the infected got closer.

One infected was ahead of all the others, barely metres from her. He was athletically built and covered in blood and dirt. Most of his hair was gone, and half his teeth were missing. His arms were spiralling in large circles as if swimming through the air.

Abelone got up and pulled hard to free her leg, this time twisting it at the same time. The barbed wire sank deeper into her boot even more.

She felt a rush of air by her shoulder, and the infected hurtled backwards, stopped in his tracks by the long pitchfork impaled in his chest.

Keefer and Moe grabbed her and sat her down roughly. They furiously clawed at her bootlaces.

"Hurry!" shouted Martel from the bus.

"Got it!" Keefer tugged her boot. It plopped off, and he dropped it to the ground. The coil of the wire sprang back to the barricade, with the boot, like a spider pulling in a fly.

Both men jolted Abelone up by the armpits, and they sprinted to the bus's open rear emergency door.

Abelone ran as fast as she could without a boot. Rocks pierced her foot through her sock, but she ignored the pain and kept running. The shrieks were right behind her, and Moe was huffing hard by her side, trying to keep up.

Keefer reached the bus first and scrambled in. "Go, Doc! Go!" he shouted as he turned and stretched his hand out for her and Moe.

She and the old harbour master both grabbed it and were pulled off their feet by the sudden lurch of the bus. Abelone got her bootless foot inside the bus, and Keefer pulled her the rest of the way in. Beside her, Moe stumbled. He was still holding Keefer, but the bus was dragging him along the road. Both his feet had lost their footing. She quickly grabbed Moe's hand to help Keefer pull him in up to his stomach. They bounced as the bus hit a pothole, still accelerating.

The infected could almost touch the bumper, like a pack of dogs chasing a mail truck. Abelone was shocked at how many there were. She pulled as hard as she could on Moe's arm. Keefer did the same, just as an infected grabbed Moe. Grey fingers latched onto the old man's leather-wrapped legs. The infected was yanked off its feet and dragged along the asphalt road.

"Kick it off!" shouted Keefer.

Moe shook his legs. Abelone's muscles screamed as she hauled on Moe's arm while trying to keep her balance. The grey head caved in by the tire iron Keefer had in his opposite hand, but it held on, glued to Moe's limbs. She thought it would drag Moe away from them, but it fell off when his boot ripped off. The infected, along with the footwear, rolled off behind the bus in a flurry of dust. Abelone breathed a sigh of relief as she and Keefer pulled Moe in and slammed the door shut.

"We're all in! Go, go, go!" shouted Keefer.

Once clear of the camp, Martel floored the accelerator. The engine revved, and Abelone latched on to a seat, expecting to lurch forward again. Nothing happened. The bus was slowing.

"Why are we slowing? What's going on back there?" Martel shouted.

Abelone looked through the rear window as a grey, bloodied hand smashed through it, sending glass shards everywhere.

A long carpet of infected was attached to the bus's bumper. At least five infected had their hands clenched on the bumper, and several dozen more were draped over those trying to crawl over each other to reach the bus. The weight of the long train of infected was slowing the bus, and even more infected were jumping on the pile to try to crawl their way up.

"We need to get them off!" Keefer shouted. He tried to reopen the door, but one infected's head was in the way. He kicked the door violently, and it flew open, knocking the infected off and taking two others with it. Moe, still sitting on the floor, kicked at the infected with both his feet.

Keefer held on to a seat with one arm and, with the other, swung his tire iron at the hands of the anchored infected. Abelone held on to Moe tightly as he kicked left and right. Two infected lost their grips and fell off. They were the linchpins. The remaining wedding-gown train of infected broke up as more and more lost their grip. The remainder crashed in a rolling pile of dust on the road. The bus swerved a few times before it sped off, heading west on the Trans-Labrador Highway.

The throng of infected grew smaller as Abelone pulled herself up onto a seat and put her bootless foot on her knee. Her sock was soaked with blood, and she gently pulled it off. Keefer bent down on one knee in front of her, gently taking her foot and placing it on his other knee.

"I'll take care of it," he said, as he reached back and grabbed one of their first-aid kits.

Abelone looked at him, vulnerable. Searing pain raced up her foot, and her heart beat faster.

Keefer pulled out a couple of rocks lodged in the thick skin of her sole and poured disinfectant into the wounds. She winced but felt better when his hand tightened on her calf muscle, holding her foot still.

"That whole town must have been infected," said Doc Martel. "How did the infection spread all the way out here?"

"Someone must have gotten out before the bombing in Peaks Bay—probably by car," reasoned Keefer, wrapping a gauze around Abelone's foot. "Someone must have been bitten and not realized they were infected and changed once they got to Goose Bay."

"Unlikely," said Abelone. "They must have brought someone who was already infected because the distance is too far. They must have turned once there. I saw my friend Alex turn..." She broke off to swallow the unexpected lump that formed in her throat at the memory of Alex and held back the tears threatening to spill before she continued, "Turn in under four minutes."

"Ahh, damn it," grumbled Moe from behind them. "Is that all I've got?"

Time on the bus stopped. Abelone looked over at him. Keefer put Abelone's bandaged foot down and turned around.

"What do you mean?" Keefer stood in the aisle.

"Don't get all mushy on me," growled Moe.

He pulled up his pant leg, the one now bootless. There was a deep gouge clearly showing where teeth had ripped skin above the ankle.

Keefer jumped to his side. "You should have said something!"

Abelone grabbed the medical bag and rummaged through it.

"What difference would it have made?"

There. She pulled out a roll of duct tape.

"I could have . . ." Keefer stared at the bite mark. "I could have . . ."

She squeezed past Keefer.

"Exactly." Moe coughed.

"Sit back," Abelone said, pushing Moe deeper on the seat and taping his calves to the legs of the bench.

Moe's breathing was already laboured, and he started coughing worse than usual.

She taped his hands and secured them to the seat in front of him.

"Don't worry. If we secure you tightly, you'll be safe."

"I think what you mean is you'll be safe, young lady," Moe chuckled, which caused him to cough even more.

Moe's skin was starting to pale as blood stopped flowing to its surface. His head drooped, and his cough subsided. The blood on his ankle, still trickling to the floor, was getting darker and darker. She was astounded by how fast the virus took over its host body.

"This does not feel good," Moe whispered his last complaint.

Keefer sat beside Moe across the aisle. "How you feeling?"

Moe didn't answer. His chin was on his chest, his skin had changed from pale to light grey and his breathing was more of a gargle. He shivered every few seconds, as if fighting off a cold breeze. Abelone watched closely, sad but intrigued. *Is he actually dying?*

Moe's head popped up a few times, then settled back down, eyes closed. His mouth opened, and his tongue—already black and thick with dark mucus—stretched out, tasting the air.

Moe's eyes opened slowly, revealing black irises and grey eyeballs marred by little black veins meandering around.

As soon as Moe spotted Keefer, he shrieked and tried to lunge at him. Keefer, surprised, pounced back to the end of his bench. Luckily, Moe's duct tape held.

"How can it be so goddamn fast?" Keefer swore as he jumped over the bench to join Abelone in the aisle a few seats ahead.

"Once the virus reaches the bloodstream, it takes a few minutes for it to be pumped to the brain. From there, it seems to hijack all bodily functions even quicker," she answered.

Moe thrashed against his bindings, but they held. His shrieks changed to gargles as he came to terms with his immobility. He stopped thrashing but stared at them, tasting the air with his black tongue.

"I can't leave him like this," Keefer whispered. Abelone watched his body sag as he looked his friend over. "He's my friend. He doesn't deserve this."

Abelone put her hands on his shoulders. "We can save him, Ben. He's safe. He won't hurt himself . . . or us. We can save him; we just need to get the blood samples, get to a lab, and make a vaccine."

Keefer looked at her, expressionless. "What if we don't find the samples? They might be gone; Karen might not even have kept them. Plus, even if we did get them, how long before we find a lab? How long before a vaccine gets created? It won't work, Abelone. There is only one way to stop this thing from spreading. There is only one thing Moe would have wanted me to do."

Keefer reached for the machete. Moe, who was drooling thick saliva, snapped his teeth in their direction.

"Ben, don't." She kept her hands on Keefer's shoulders and looked him in the eyes. She wasn't willing to kill to stop the infection, but she hadn't stopped anyone else from extinguishing lives. Maybe because, deep down, she knew it needed to be done, or maybe it was simply her drive to survive. "We can't keep killing people. We have to find a cure." She wasn't sure if she was trying to convince him or herself.

"Abelone, you'll have to come to terms with this. The only way to save humankind is to make sure every carrier of this godforsaken virus gets eradicated."

Keefer raised the machete and paused for a second—barely a second. The long rusty blade fell heavily onto his old friend's head. Moe didn't shriek or fight his bonds. He took the blow like a grown man takes the needle of a flu shot.

The long blade cracked the skull and lodged itself deep in the brain. Abelone flinched and turned away. Keefer breathed a long, shuddering sigh. When she looked back, Keefer tried to pull out the machete, but the suction of the brain cavity was stronger than his pull. After a few tries, he simply let it go. The machete and Moe's head hung forward, unmoving.

Keefer turned and walked past Abelone with tears in his eyes. "We need to kill the infected if the world is to survive," he whispered. He sat on the front bench behind Martel and put his head in his hands.

Abelone stood in silence, staring at Moe's body. Black blood oozed out of his cracked-open head. Her body shook from the inside. *Not everyone has to die.* She sat in the seat beside Moe, put her head against the window and cried because Moe was dead or because she didn't stop it from happening; it didn't matter which. The small yellow bus rolled down the lightless highway, the landscape grey and bleak with no lights anywhere except for the two small headlights at the front of the bus as they barrelled down the gravel-packed road.

26

CHANGE OF SKIN

They laid Moe's body on the dew-covered grass of an anonymous rest stop along the highway. Keefer stood overlooking his friend under the stars, tears slowly rolling from the corner of his eyes. It wasn't the sea, which Moe would have preferred, but it would have to do. The machete was still lodged deep in Moe's cranium, and every attempt at pulling it out had failed so far.

"I can't leave him like that," Keefer repeated a few times. Abelone and Martel had retreated to the bus, its headlights casting eerie grey shadows around Keefer.

He looked at the machete with disdain and put his hand on the hilt again. He pulled, softly at first, but the weapon would not move. He grabbed it with both hands and pulled harder. The dead body shifted with his efforts.

"I will not leave you like this!"

His blood was boiling, and he jammed Moe's head down onto the ground with his boot and pulled with all his strength onto the machete. It budged, barely at first, and then it sprang out with a loud plop, and Keefer stumbled backwards and fell on his ass. There was a gaping crevice left in Moe's head, with black blood and bits of brain oozing out.

"Fuuuckkkkk!" He tossed the machete into the woods as far as he could, then sat there crying.

He wasn't sure for how long.

"Ben, I'm sorry, but we have to go," Abelone said.

And that was that. His blood had tempered. He wiped his sleeve across his face, got up and took one last look at Moe.

"Goodbye, old friend." He turned and walked back to the bus.

It took five hours for them to get to the next town, Churchill Falls. Keefer didn't talk much along the way. The small town had a welcome sign that said *Population 706*, but this was no longer true. It was deserted. No people, no infected.

Keefer existed in a daze until they stopped for supplies at the town's gas station. The pumps were sabotaged. Abelone was relieved since it meant they were still on Karen's trail, but Keefer didn't much care.

He syphoned gas from the above-ground tanks like Moe had shown them. A few tears tracked down his cheeks, and he tried not to think about the machete he'd driven into Moe's head.

The town had limited supplies, and the phones were down here also, so they trooped back onto the bus and continued their journey west.

As they exited Churchill Falls, a large green sign dominated the roadside:

Labrador City 250KM
Quebec City 985KM

Over the white letters and green background of the sign, once again, was painted a message in black:

EAST OF QUEBEC CITY EVACUATED
MILITARY REGROUP AT CFB VALCARTIER
- MJR HOLLISTER, 5 WING

"We should be able to resupply in Labrador City," Keefer said. He was in the seat opposite Abelone's while Doc Martel drove the bus. The sun was rising, and the grey dawn was lifting.

"Yeah, we need more food," said Martel.

"And armour," added Abelone, pulling a loose leather wrap off her right leg. It was barely hanging on with torn duct tape. Keefer thought of Moe's leg armour, which had fallen off and allowed an infected to bite him. That could not happen again.

"There should be plenty of food and clothing to wrap us in once we get to Labrador City. It's an actual city with plenty of stores." Keefer was resolute. The better equipped they were, the more chance they would have to make it to Valcartier. "We'll need better weapons too."

As the bus bounced along the highway, Keefer stared at the Danish scientist as she removed her loose, beaten-up armour. How could they have committed their lives to saving people, yet have such different points of view on how to do that now? Like her, he wanted to believe everyone could be saved, but he couldn't get over his mental block that the infected weren't anyone anymore. They weren't living anymore. He wanted to believe, but couldn't. She looked up and caught him staring. It struck him at that moment how ridiculous she looked in her get-up. The bomber jacket with the leather duct taped on the forearms. He looked at himself, at the ripped-up leather from the bunker chairs hanging in tatters off his legs and arms. He looked just as ridiculous.

Abelone watched him, looking himself over. They both smiled. Anyone uninfected who saw them would think they were a bunch of homeless crazies all wrapped up in whatever they could find.

"I'm missing a boot," Abelone said seriously.

Keefer stared at her foot and was surprised when she broke out laughing. The stress of everything he had been through came rushing out of his own body. Both of them guffawed as the little yellow bus drove down the highway.

Doc Martel stared at them through the rear-view mirror quizzically at first, but after watching them laugh for a few beats, tears coming down their faces, he started laughing too.

It was a few minutes before the tension was released by their hysterics. Keefer, overcome with fatigue, stopped laughing as abruptly as he had started. So did Abelone and Martel. Abelone got up and sat beside him.

She leaned into him and put her head on his shoulder. He hesitated, but wrapped his arm around her. Keefer wondered what things would have been like if they had met under different circumstances, not having to debate who lived and died.

He gently rested his chin on the top of her head and took a deep breath of her messy blonde hair.

Abelone looked up. "Did you smell me?"

"No."

"Don't smell me. I haven't showered in over a week."

"I didn't smell you," Keefer insisted unconvincingly.

"Good." Abelone rested her head back on his shoulder.

"I don't care how you smell anyway," Keefer added nonchalantly.

They stayed like that for a while. The scenery rushed past the side of the bus. The morning coolness changed to warmth as the sun bathed the tree-lined highway.

Keefer kept thinking back to Moe. Was Abelone right? Could he have been saved? Was he wrong in killing the infected? Could they be saved?

As if reading his mind, Abelone blurted without looking up, "I haven't killed anyone yet. I do think they can be saved. In the darkest hour of any outbreak, we need to keep hope."

"What if they can't?"

"I have to believe they can. That's why I became a field epidemiologist."

"We've never seen an outbreak like this." Keefer shifted Abelone off his shoulder to be able to look into her tired blue eyes. "This is not Ebola or COVID. What if the infected can't be saved?"

"Yes, it is. A virus is a virus. With my blood and the blood samples from the first patient—his name was Tom . . . Tom Virtanen—we can quickly come up with a vaccine and find a cure," Abelone insisted.

They still had one part of the possible cure. Abelone's blood. Keefer realized even if he felt the infected had to be killed to stop the spread, Abelone had to be kept alive no matter the cost. Her blood might be the only hope for those not infected yet.

"Even with both your blood and the original blood samples, the infected are spreading this thing too fast. We need to cut it off. Otherwise, there will be nothing left to save."

He looked into her eyes, trying to find something that would make him change his mind. They had nothing else to say. Keefer wrapped his arm around Abelone tighter, and she leaned her head back onto his shoulder.

***

The small bus idled at the top of a hill overlooking the bridge into Labrador City. The sun had passed its zenith seven days since the infection had arrived in Peaks Bay. Keefer watched the city like a hawk on a branch looking for something to eat, except he was looking for something that could eat them. From their vantage point, they could see most of the city and the two-lane road that meandered through it like a river. They didn't lack food or gas; those were easy to pick up anywhere now. Best they could tell, everything was abandoned and like an untouched orchard in mid-season, ripe for the picking. Except for cars and weapons. People tended to evacuate their homes with those, so that was what they needed to find.

With no sign of life—or infected—Keefer drove the bus down the hill, over the bridge and into the city. He drove straight to the closest car dealership. Once in the parking lot, he let the bus idle for a good ten minutes, and the trio observed—again. Keefer never stopped expecting to have infected come running out at any moment, and every time they didn't, he was surprised as much as relieved. He opened the bus doors, and they exited. Keefer and Martel walked through the front lot looking at the slim pickings—a handful of sedans and three small pickup trucks.

"This is the one," Keefer said, stopping in front of a truck. He tried to open the doors. "Locked."

Martel did not look convinced. "The bus might still be a better choice. Our supplies will be exposed to the elements, and the open bed means infected can climb on easily."

Keefer looked back at the bus and, for a second, thought he saw Moe sitting inside. He squeezed his eyes to reset his brain, and Moe was gone.

Keefer looked at Martel. "We need something nimbler. We're changing vehicles. Get the supplies from the bus. Abelone and I will get the keys inside and see if the phones work."

Keefer was relieved that Martel didn't argue.

Keefer had to smash the glass front door to get inside the dealership. He listened and watched for any unwelcome guests following the act. When satisfied no surprises would materialize, they went in. The warm, stuffy air inside the glass building reminded him of his gramps' greenhouse, but instead of dirt and plant smells, it was linoleum and new car smells. Keefer rummaged through the service area for the pickup truck key while Abelone looked around.

He knew Martel was right. The pickup, although nimbler, would be an easy grab-on target for the infected, but he couldn't keep riding the bus. Moe's spirit lived in that yellow coffin. Right when he found the key, Abelone called him over. She was standing at the far end of the showroom, looking outside.

"I found a better vehicle," she half-shouted to Keefer.

"What kind?" he answered and headed her way. The stillness of the dealership was disconcerting, and he wanted to get moving again.

Abelone was looking into the front area of the dealership with a smile on her face.

"Oh hell no," Keefer said.

"This is what we need."

"I'm not riding in that."

"Ben, it's not about appearances. It's about what will get us where we need to go."

Keefer stood silent for a few seconds. She was right. This vehicle was made to roll over things. It had shatterproof windows, reinforced doors and, most importantly, no open-air flatbed where the infected could climb in. He felt an embarrassing chill go through his spine.

"Fine," he said, turning away abruptly to go find the keys, leaving Abelone alone to admire the bright pink, four-door, soccer-mom Hummer H2.

It took ten minutes to transfer their ample supplies. Keefer threw the last box into the back of the Hummer before climbing into the driver's seat. He fired up the engine, and it roared to life, trying to make up for its ridiculous colour.

"Moe would never have ridden in this thing," Keefer mumbled to himself.

"What's that?" Abelone asked from the passenger seat.

"Nothing."

He put the vehicle into drive, and the soccer-mom battle tank lunged forward. He had to admit that it was a lot more maneuverable than the school bus, and a lot safer. He navigated the roads of Labrador City, going off memory from his handful of visits. The city had become a ghost town. The empty streets and buildings around the main road made it feel like it was the middle of the night and everyone was at home sleeping, except the sun was out and shining brightly. Finally, he found what he was looking for and pulled into the Walmart parking lot. He parked in the nearest stall to the front doors, avoiding a handicap spot out of habit.

It took them a while to get in. Once again, Keefer had to break in by smashing the glass, and once again, nothing was attracted to the sound. The trio quickly made their way through the aisles of the lightless store. They moved quietly, still cautious. Keefer headed to the back, where he knew they would find the hunting section with an array of guns and ammo. They walked by a display with a dirt bike straddled by a dummy, getting ready to jump over a make-believe creek. Keefer stopped and observed it. Abelone and Martel paused behind him.

"I thought we had settled the Hummer question?" said Martel.

"We have. I'm not looking at the dirt bike."

"What are you looking at?"

Abelone smiled. "He's looking at that." She pointed to the full-body leather gear of the dirt-bike rider.

It took less than twenty minutes for them to shed their ramshackle armour and replace it with reinforced, thick black leather motorcycle gear. They were now armoured from neck to toe with no exposed skin other than their heads. Keefer had chosen a full black leather suit with a blue stripe down the arms. His jacket and pants had thick plastic plates in the arms, legs and back. Abelone went with a full race leather two-piece bodysuit with similar protection plates built into the cat-woman-like attire. Doc Martel, with his shorter and rounder body, found some hog-style thick leather overalls and a tight-fitting, greaser Harley Davidson jacket. All three had on knee-high black leather motorcycle boots.

"You have two boots again," said Keefer to Abelone, smiling. She smiled back.

Satisfied they were well armoured, they turned and made their way to the large *Hunting* sign on the back wall of the store.

It was another thirty minutes before they exited the Walmart. Their transformation was complete. They carried an array of hunting rifles, short-barrelled shotguns and Glock handguns.

Keefer threw duffle bags of ammunition, more food and three black motorcycle helmets with chin protectors into the back of the Hummer. For the first time since the Henry Dawson plowed into Peaks Bay, he felt ready for what lay ahead.

27

BLURRY BOUNDARIES

A belone was standing in a mess deck, definitely a ship's mess deck. It had to be the Henry Dawson's. She jumped back when an onslaught of banging rattled the closed hatch door. Her heart pounded. The hits echoed through the compartment, and the door bulged in with every blow. She took another step back. *They're breaking in*, she thought, her breath getting shallower.

"Abelone?" someone called. She looked around but didn't see anyone. The door kept bulging inwards like a bubble. She took another step back toward the galley. The door was about to burst.

"Abelone!" Her name and the abrupt halt of the Hummer snatched her from her dream.

"There's someone there." It was Doc Martel. He was riding shotgun and pointing out his window.

Things were blurry, so she shook her head and opened her eyes. The Hummer was stopped in the middle of the two-lane road that followed the St. Lawrence River. A large green sign said, "Forestville, Pop. 3,237." This sign had no spray-painted message on it. She wasn't surprised. The directions from Major Hollister had gotten fewer and farther apart, and it'd been a while since they'd seen one.

"Are you sure you saw someone?" Keefer asked Martel.

"Yes. The way the person moved. It was definitely not an infected."

They'd seen a few random infected when they drove through deserted towns on their nine-hour journey, but no uninfected people.

"He ran into the gas station," Martel added.

They watched the gas station for a few minutes. Abelone was sure they should try to save the person, but she wasn't sure Keefer would agree.

"We need to save him," Keefer said, surprising her. "If he's alone, we need to get him."

"What about the blood samples?" Martel asked, conflicted.

"We'll catch up to them." His voice showed no uncertainty. "We need to save him." Keefer's statement was final, and he opened his door and stepped out, taking his shotgun with him.

He looked back inside the car. "We'll be fast," he added, softer this time. "Abelone, can you jump in the driver's seat in case we need to take off in a hurry?"

Abelone nodded, relieved by his decision. Maybe they weren't so far apart, after all.

Martel slid out of the Hummer, and she watched them put on their helmets to complete their anti-infected armour set.

She climbed into the driver's seat and immediately felt the V8 engine rumbling through the steering wheel. The smell of gasoline from the trunk mixed with the thick, warm air made her nauseous. She watched from her pink fortress as Keefer and Martel quickly approached the gas station and entered it cautiously.

The longer they were out of sight, the tenser she got. She reached for her own helmet, thinking of checking up on them, when a fast-moving figure caught the corner of her eye. A man moved confidently along the side of a wooden church a few lots over from the gas station. He scampered up the front steps and slid into the sanctuary via the big wooden doors spanning the front of the building. There was something off about the man. He didn't move like an infected, but his movements were . . . different.

With Keefer or Martel out of sight, she decided to go after him. If this was the man Martel had seen, it would be faster for her to get him than wait for the guys. She stopped the Hummer's engine and slid her black full-face helmet on while exiting. The heat was worse in direct sunlight. Right away, her back and forehead started to sweat. She steadied her rifle, made sure the safety was off exactly how Keefer had shown her and walked determined to the church.

The doors were thick, heavy wood, and she pushed one of them wide enough to slip in. It was a lot cooler inside. The stained glass windows filtered most of the sunlight and gave the narthex an eerie feeling. Abelone listened, but the only sound was the whistling of the wind through the open door.

She took a chance. "I saw you come into the church," she said louder than one would normally speak in a place of worship. Her voice echoed across the nave while she walked down the middle aisle a few pews in.

"You don't need to be afraid. We won't hurt you." She paused and listened. A rustling sound came from beyond the altar at the far end of the room.

"We can help you. We aren't infected. You don't need to be afraid." Abelone removed her helmet and held it in one hand with the rifle in the other.

The room was filled with darkened corners, and the sunlight coming through the stained glass windows accentuated the shadows where someone could be standing unnoticed. Abelone was getting uneasy. She walked a few more pews but froze when a voice answered her.

"Maybe you're the one who should be afraid." A deep, low voice came from a shadowed corner beyond the altar. This was the first voice she'd heard in over a week.

"We can help," she said. "We have supplies and weapons." She wanted to help, but there was something about the voice that made her wonder if they should.

"Others have tried to help."

"Who?" Abelone decided not to walk further up the aisle. She looked back at the slightly opened church door.

The voice laughed melancholically. "Everyone."

Abelone waited for more.

"The cops. The army."

"Did they evacuate this town like the others up north?" she asked, wondering why this person was still here.

"They tried. But it was too late." The voice had shifted to the other side of the transept.

Did he mean the town had been evacuated already, or was it already infected?

"The disease . . . the infection . . . that's what they called it on the news." The voice had changed location again.

There was a shout outside, followed by a shotgun blast. Her adrenaline pumped harder. "We need to go!" She ran back to the door and swung it open, squinting at the sudden brightness.

A third shotgun blast echoed from the gas station, and she heard Keefer shouting at Martel. The heat and the stress made her brow perspire into her eyes. She wiped the sweat with the back of her hand holding the helmet.

"We need to go. Come!" she shouted over her shoulder. It triggered a shriek from around the church corner, sending her stomach into convulsions. Two infected ran around the corner of the building. She brought up her rifle with one hand and shot at the legs of the first one. It rolled to the ground, shrieking. She had her answer—the town was infected.

She moved back into the church. The second infected bound up the handful of stairs.

She pushed the heavy church door, but it moved slowly. It was almost shut when the infected thrust its arm in the gap between the door and frame. The infected shrieked and gargled angrily, its hand trying to clutch Abelone.

"Help me close this door!" she shouted over her shoulder.

Her feet were slipping on the stone floor, and the door inched open slowly as the infected pounded their shoulders into the large wood planks. One particular push was too much. She stumbled backwards and fell to the ground, her rifle and helmet sliding away on the slate floor. Both infected tumbled into the church.

Abelone scrambled sideways until she hit the first pew of the nave. One of the infected, this one missing both ears, lunged at her from its own fallen position. Abelone put up her legs in time to catch it. She tried to stretch out to throw it off, but it was too heavy, so she rolled sideways. It fell beside her and grabbed her ankles. It bit her calf—the leather resisted. She rolled again, trying to get loose; the infected moved up and bit her thigh—the leather resisted. She rolled one more time and pulled her knees in. The infected lost its grip. Abelone quickly got to her feet, but the earless infected snatched her arm and bit—the leather protected her again.

She tried to punch her aggressor off, but it was holding too tightly. She lost her balance and fell back to the ground, allowing the infected to scurry up on top of her. Its weight squeezed the air from her chest, and its mouth opened, ready to bite her face.

Get off me! She couldn't breathe, and her blood pounded in her ears so loudly she thought her ears might explode. A blackened tongue hissed in her face, and the putrid smell of the infected's innards made her gag.

Get off me! Abelone cocked one arm back as the infected was about to bite and punched straight into its gaping mouth. A shower of blood-stained teeth rained on her face. Her fist was completely in the infected's mouth. It bit down with gums and whatever remaining teeth it had. She tried to pull her hand out and panicked when she couldn't. With every pull, she almost threw up. Luckily, her leather glove stopped her from being bitten.

The second infected appeared and bit her shoulder. She felt the pressure, but her leather gear held up. *Fuck!*

Get off! She felt a rush of angry emotion as a large man appeared in her limited vision. He grabbed the shoulder-biting infected and tossed it away like a pillow, then pulled the one on top of Abelone off. Her fist popped out of its mouth, sending a few last teeth trickling out. Air rushed into her lungs like a crowd rushing into a store on Black Friday.

The man tossed the infected viciously at the wall, impaling it on an iron candle sconce. The infected flailed and shrieked, unable to move, stuck a few feet off the ground.

"Get up!" the man said as he stepped to the nearest pew. Something was definitely off with his voice.

Abelone scrambled up.

An irate shriek rose from the pews, and the tossed infected jumped up. Abelone's saviour stepped in front of her, wrapped his hands around the top and bottom of the nearest pew and lifted it.

What the hell! Abelone stepped back at the show of strength. Nothing about this person was registering as normal.

Another flood of angry emotion rushed over her as the infected ran toward them. It confused her because she wasn't feeling angry. What was she feeling? *Stay away!* The man heaved the massive bench. It slammed into the infected's head and crushed it against one of the nave's stone pillars. Black gore, bone and brain exploded from the pew's end. The long wooden bench fell to the ground in a rattle.

How? Abelone looked at the man. She saw him closely for the first time, and she stepped back further. His skin was pale grey, his hair thick and dark. Was he one of them? Her mind did somersaults, trying to comprehend what she was seeing. It didn't add up.

"How?" she said.

The man noticed her unease. "I won't harm you."

It hadn't crossed Abelone's mind, but she unconsciously took another step back. "You're infected?" she said, more than asked. Scrutinizing his face, she saw his irises were deep black.

"Yes . . . well . . . I don't know," the man said, unsure. His voice was a bit deeper than he probably normally would have had.

He's not dangerous, is he? Abelone took a step forward this time, curiosity getting the better of her.

The man picked up her helmet and tapped on the chin guard, then looked at her leather outfit. "Motorcycle gear. Smart," he grumbled. He held the helmet out to her. She took it from him but didn't slide it on.

"How?" she asked again, more to her scientific mind than the man in front of her.

He didn't answer. She wondered if he even had an answer to give.

Trained to see patterns, and with decades of experience, she pieced clues together. In the bunker—Hector—he had turned differently, and the other infected had ripped him apart. *He was . . . like this man.* The sailor on the Henry Dawson, who had run from her and jumped in the water. *He was trying to get away.* Pieces fell into place, like a puzzle. The infected couple she'd seen holding hands in Peaks Bay when they were driving to the hospital. They hadn't been running after them but trying to get away from . . . other infected. *They weren't mindless infected!* She looked at her arm, at the bandage she couldn't see under her leather sleeve. *I was bitten but never turned.*

"You're not like them," she stated the obvious. How had she missed this all along? "I've seen other infected like you—" That didn't feel like the right description. "Others who changed, like you." Her fear was forgotten, and she took another step closer. The man's skin was flawlessly grey. She couldn't tell how old he was. "Are you alone?"

"No."

"There are others like you?" The thought was shocking. She looked at his hands; they seemed a bit larger than a normal man's hands, and veins protruded slightly from the back of them.

"No . . . no others like me . . . but I am not alone." The man tilted his head, uneasy about how Abelone was observing him. "Are you with the military?" There was caution in his deep voice, maybe even distrust.

"No, I'm a scientist."

The infected impaled on the sconce shrieked and kicked, surprising both. Abelone's fight response kicked in, and she lunged for her rifle. The man stepped back, his fists clenching. She was acutely aware of his concern, almost as if she'd *felt* it.

"I won't hurt you," she said. "You don't need to be scared." She aimed the rifle at the ground. The infected on the wall was still thrashing and hissing but could not free itself.

"Others have shot at me already." The man took a few more steps back to stand in the aisle a few feet away from the crushed infected's body. "Cops at first, then neighbours, then military coming through town."

"We are here to help. Come with us." Abelone nodded to the door.

"Abelone?" Keefer shouted out her name outside.

"I can't." The man took a step back. "There are people who rely on me here. Like I said, I am not alone. There are others . . . not like me . . . uninfected. Families."

"Abelone?" Keefer was outside the church. The man took a few more steps back as Keefer and Doc Martel came careening through the doors of the church, helmets on and shotguns ready.

"Abelone!" Keefer shouted as he saw her. His shotgun quickly targeted the man in front of her.

"Don't!"

He pulled the trigger.

She smacked the rifle upward as the slug exploded out of the barrel. The pellets ripped wood off the foyer's ceiling, sending splinters everywhere.

"He's not infected!" That wasn't fully accurate, but how could she tell Keefer and Martel quickly before they tried to kill the man again? "He won't hurt us!"

Keefer and Martel looked at her, confused. Both kept their shotguns in the man's direction. Keefer pumped his weapon, spitting out the used shell and making a new one enter the firing chamber.

Abelone realized he was ready to shoot again. "Don't! Listen to me, don't!"

Martel moved toward Abelone but jumped away, startled when the impaled infected shrieked and tried to grab him. Martel aimed his shotgun at it but didn't shoot.

"What about him!" Martel shouted at Abelone, confused. "Abelone, what is going on?"

"He's infected," she referred to the one on the wall. "The other is . . . different."

"Are you hurt?" Keefer asked, stepping close to her. He looked her over, concern in his eyes. She could tell he was looking for signs of a bite.

"I'm fine. I'm not hurt. The leather . . . my outfit . . . it protected me."

"I know. Both Doc and I got bitten, but the leather held up. There are infected in this town. We need to go," he said.

"Wait." Abelone turned to face the man—the Grey. The aisle was empty. He was gone.

Keefer and Martel, also noticing the man gone, swung their shotguns around, panicked that he might jump at them from a corner.

"We need to go!" Keefer said again. Shrieks could be heard in the distance.

Keefer grabbed Abelone by the arm and dragged her through the church doors. She looked back toward the altar—in the far shadows, a grey silhouette watched them.

"Who was that . . . What . . . was that?" Doc Martel asked as they ran to the pink Hummer.

Abelone didn't answer.

As they got to the Hummer, a dozen infected ran down a side road from the gas station. All three survivors jumped in, Keefer in the driver's seat.

"Abelone, what was that?" Martel asked again.

Abelone looked down at her arm, the one that had been bitten on the Henry Dawson, then she looked at her friend.

"That . . . was . . . Not. An. Infected."

28

NOT LIKE IN THE MOVIES

*T**his is not like in the movies,* Keefer thought as he navigated the Hummer down the two-lane road that was completely clear of any cars; most roads in end-of-the-world movies were clogged with vehicles trapped bumper-to-bumper, like frozen rush-hour traffic jams. Contrary to that, they had the highway to themselves. *People must have evacuated before the infected started running around . . . or people are locked up in their homes to ride things out.*

They were making good time, clear roads and all. And small towns were slowly giving way to sprawling neighbourhoods in the suburbs of Quebec City.

Another large green sign came into view. It indicated the distance to the downtown core. To his relief, it had large, black-painted writing on it.

MILITARY REGROUP AT CFB VALCARTIER
AVOID THE CITY!

Major Hollister from the 5th Wing had not signed this one. Had something happened to him? Had the city fallen? In any case, Keefer wasn't planning to head into the core; Valcartier was north of the urban area. He blocked thoughts of the millions of inhabitants in the city possibly being infected and guided the pink SUV down the road, the air conditioner struggling to keep up with the hot summer afternoon.

Keefer's eyes drifted from the road ahead to the passenger seat, where Abelone was curled up like a cat.

A parade of thoughts kept rattling in his head: the stolen blood samples, Abelone's immunity, the Grey from Forestville, and what they would find in Valcartier. The trees and the houses morphed into his home in Peaks Bay, the burnt hospital, his departed friend Moe, and then Tigger. Peaks Bay was gone. His friends were gone. Tigger and Moe . . . were gone. He had to take a long, deep breath to stop tears from escaping. He struggled to understand everything that had happened since the Henry Dawson had arrived in Peaks Bay seven days ago . . . or was it eight? Everything was a blur.

In Afghanistan, he had saved more people than he could count. He remembered how many amputations he had done—six, and in each case, the patient had survived. This was what he saw now; the infection was growing too fast to take the slow route. They had to amputate. Kill the infected. Stop the infection from killing the body. If you hesitate, you lose. He was sure of it.

Taking blood samples, testing them, finding a vaccine, and finding a cure was Abelone's world. In her world, you tried to save everyone; the arm or leg could be saved. In his world, you didn't have that luxury.

Abelone stirred, so he looked the opposite way. The enormous St. Lawrence River stretched as far as he could see. He opened the window a crack, wanting to smell the salt water rushing into the gaping mouth of the river. The rush of humid July air tasted salty in the back of his nose. The brine coming in from the gulf clashed with the freshwater coming the opposite way. Both needed a place to go, and both were destined to become one. He always wondered why this was the place where brine and freshwater merged.

Abelone shifted in the passenger seat to look at him, her attention attracted by his opening of the window. Their eyes met and stayed locked for a few seconds. He pinched and stretched his lips, not in a smile but in acknowledgement of her. His lips felt dry and cracked, and when he tried to swallow, his gullet struggled.

What about her? She'd been bitten. It was a question he kept coming back to. As if she knew what he was thinking, Abelone turned in her seat and looked away.

What about the Grey we saw?

Is it too late for both of them? How do you make exceptions when the fate of humanity is at stake?

He looked back at the river. The salty smell was gone; they were now in freshwater territory. Could brine and freshwater co-exist other than in that junction of the two waters? Could he and Abelone both be right? He didn't know the answer. He closed his window and focused on the road.

***

Abelone wrestled with the pull of unconscious darkness, knowing it'd be filled with the horrors of the last week. The whoosh and rush of warm air from Keefer's window dragged her back to the land of the living. She locked eyes with him. Despite the warm air coming in, a shiver ran down her spine, and her focus became acute. She momentarily forgot about the infection and noticed him struggle to swallow as he looked at her. The electricity between them merged, and for a split second, it flowed both ways. Then it snapped and became unbound; confusion flashed across his eyes. Something—a thought—had broken their tether. It unnerved Abelone, and she turned back in her seat. Keefer was hell-bent on stopping the infection in its tracks by exterminating it. She couldn't reconcile that approach with her own beliefs. She hadn't killed anyone. Extermination never worked. Vaccination was the way to make sure people were safe in the long term. The rushing air cut off as Keefer closed his window.

The steady purr of the Hummer's engine slid Abelone back into her trance. The faint vibrations and the warm leather seats made her sink into a state of deep thought. Reality came creeping back, pushing out thoughts of Benjamin. She did what she always did when faced with a spreading virus—she became analytical.

This was the first time in the last week when she could properly and safely assess the facts. This virus was beyond anything the world had faced before. It was definitely more virus than bacteria, but it was no different from other viruses: it was transmitted via human-to-human exchange of blood or saliva and wasn't airborne like a lot of viruses in the world. It had a very short incubation period compared to other viruses. It had a transmission ratio like any virus, but again, this one was off the chart, almost perfect, but not quite. Some hosts were immune, like herself or the . . . the Grey she'd encountered in the church in Forestville.

The Grey was different. Other viruses did not *change* people like that. How was he stronger? This was the anomaly that didn't fit a regular virus profile. Did it alter the genetic code? A classmate of hers had done a paper on the Hunger Winter of 1944. Famine, caused by the Nazis' blockade of food supplies to the Netherlands, led to a genetic quieting of babies born during that period. Those babies had been changed permanently with higher obesity, schizophrenia, and smaller physical statures. More and more studies showed that exposure to a virus under specific conditions could cause cells to quiet a gene or boost its activity, sometimes permanently. Was this what she saw in the man in the church? Since everything else about this virus was hundreds of times faster than regular viruses, it could make sense.

She stared at the road ahead, but her brain was not processing the sensory input; it was completely focused on her cognitive peeling of the viral onion she faced. The significantly quicker factor of every aspect of this virus meant the same would need to be done for the vaccine. Whatever vaccine they came up with would need to be done quickly, with no red tape—straight to the population. No trials. The trials would need to be live. It either protected from this virus or it didn't. She knew there was a significant risk. But what was the alternative? People needed an active, acquired immunity to a virus like this one, and they needed it yesterday.

She instinctively looked at her bandaged arm. She wondered how many hosts the virus had gone through before it had reached her. Getting the original virus before the multiple dilutions of moving from host to host was critical. There must have been two or three, maybe even four, hosts before she was bitten. Alex had bitten her. Her mentor. Her friend. A painful tingle shot from her heart to her brain, and it triggered her stomach to twist into a knot. Analytical thought went out the window. She remembered Jon Brown, who was also gone. Captain Vanderfeld. The helicopter pilot, Jerry White. Rebecca Fields. Hector and his wife. Sergeant Reilly. The crew from the Cormorant who came to save them. The young cook from the mess deck. The young engineer with the rabies bite. She sank further down the rabbit hole, her vision turned to shadows, and she found herself in the Henry Dawson mess deck again, with the door about to burst open.

A bump in the road woke her. *How long did I doze for?* The sun was low on the horizon. Her right hand was covering the bandaged bite on her left forearm. *Why me?* The thought rose from the pits of her consciousness. Why hadn't she been infected? She unpinned the end of the bandage and unrolled the dressing.

She felt Eric watch her with one eye from the driver's seat, but he remained quiet. She'd slept long enough for a driver change. The end of the dressing was partially fused with the crusty scab over the circular bite mark. She tugged at it gently to break it loose. There was a slight tingle as the last of it peeled off. No smell wafted from the uncovered wound, which was a good sign. She could still see where the teeth had broken skin, even though the incisions were crusted over with dry blood.

Why me? That question again. Maybe she'd received a vaccine meant for another disease that protected her, maybe the virus didn't transfer when the bite happened, maybe . . . It dawned on her. "Maybe it was genetic."

"What?" Martel said, his attention still split between the road and her arm.

"Maybe it was genetic . . . the reason I didn't get infected." She sat up in her seat. "I doubt it was a vaccine; Alex and Jon had all the same vaccines as I did. It comes with our line of work. The WHO doesn't ship you anywhere without you getting every vaccine known to exist." She brought the bite mark closer to her eyes. "Also, I saw people with smaller bites than mine turn."

"You might still be infected." Martel winced, realizing what he'd said.

"Maybe . . . Probably." She was still caught in her racing thoughts.

Abelone could tell her genetics statement got Martel's gears working, and he was sifting through the myriad facts he was so fond of collecting. His face contorted as he strained for information buried deep inside his head. Finally, his face relaxed, and an uncorking sound popped out of his throat.

"Yes! Little known fact, the plague"—he sounded like a computer—"in the Dark Ages petered out in Scandinavia. Once it ravaged most of Asia, the Mediterranean and Europe, it met people who were genetically predisposed to resist it. The populations of the northern countries were hardly ravaged by the bacteria." The doctor was excited. Martel was in his element, and he was filling in the gaps in her understanding of Yersinia pestis.

"The people from what is now Finland, Sweden . . . Denmark . . . any northern people at the time had a gene . . . or was it an allele? Anyway, it made them resistant to the bacteria."

Could that be why she didn't get infected? If it was, her blood was even more important than she'd thought. They needed to protect it. She looked out the window, and an answer materialized on the road up ahead.

"Stop!"

Doc Martel slammed on the brakes. The Hummer fishtailed for a few metres, tires screeching on hot asphalt. Keefer, who had been sleeping, rolled off the back seat and slammed into the front seats.

"What the fuck!"

The smell of burnt rubber seeped through the vehicle's undercarriage as it ground to a halt. The road was completely clear except for a few remaining hot air eddies undulating off the asphalt.

"What?!" said Martel, scanning the road.

Keefer bounced up off the floor and crouched between the two front seats. "What's going on? What happened?"

Abelone pointed to the side of the road ahead of them. "There. Pull into that parking lot." She indicated a row of one-level buildings spanning the non-river side of the road.

"What? We have all the supplies we need," Keefer said.

Abelone looked at Martel. "Go."

Doc Martel looked at Keefer, then back at Abelone. He shrugged and complied.

As the Hummer pulled into the empty lot, it slowed to a crawl, and they surveyed the area attentively.

"These stores serve a few farming communities. We won't find supplies we don't already have. Why are we stopping?" Keefer said, shifting his attention to Abelone.

She pointed to the last structure in the small rural strip mall. A white sign spanned the front with large black letters: *Hôpital Vétérinaire.*

"We've got first-aid supplies, meds, water . . ."

Abelone grabbed the spare gauze and wrapped her bite with a clean dressing while she looked at both Martel and Keefer. "Yes, but we don't have my blood." She searched their faces for understanding. "My blood might not be Patient Zero's blood, but it still holds part of the key to creating a vaccine. Why didn't I turn? There is something in my blood that will help."

"But we've got you," insisted Keefer. "As long as we get you to the government, we can use your blood."

"We need to get her to them first," Martel interjected. Abelone saw he understood. "If something happens to Abelone . . . we lose her blood."

Keefer didn't accept the idea. "We're not going to lose her."

Abelone focused on Keefer and touched his hand. "Ben, what if we do? What if something happens? You and Eric need samples of my blood. All we need is a blood-sample kit from the vet hospital. We'll be quick."

Keefer's jaw tightened. "Fine. But we stick together."

Abelone nodded. Martel pulled the Hummer up to the door of the animal hospital and stopped the engine. The minute that they waited lasted forever in the quietness of the vehicle now that the loud engine was off. Nothing moved outside.

They climbed out of the pink military vehicle, all leathered up, helmets on and guns ready. The hospital doors were locked, and the lights were off inside. Summertime dusk was setting in, and it filled the inside of the hospital with shadows. A quick blow of a rock shattered part of the glass, enough for them to unlock the door from outside.

They stepped inside a gloomy waiting room. Its walls were lined with metal and fabric chairs two decades late from being contemporary. The shadows made it hard to see through her closed visor, so she opened it but immediately regretted it. A pungent smell filled her helmet and attacked her nostrils.

"What is that smell?" Martel asked.

"Something died in here," Keefer said, heaving lightly as he moved to the single corridor leading to the back rooms. Abelone stepped in front of him into the corridor.

"I know where to go. I've been in these vet hospitals more than I can count with . . . Tigger," he objected.

"So have I—I've got two dogs at home. Two German Shepherds, actually." She kept walking, but she could feel Keefer watching her and likely realizing why she and Tigger had bonded so easily. Her heartbeat sped up.

This hospital was a bit different from the ones back in Denmark, but the principle was the same: reception and waiting room, a corridor lined with a few four-legged patient rooms, surgery rooms would be at the back . . . along with the kennels. She walked down the corridor, straight to the surgery room, where they would find syringes and blood vials.

The smell got worse as she neared the end of the corridor. She'd smelled death in her line of work before. It was common. She often found herself in small villages in underdeveloped countries where Ebola, smallpox or another deadly virus was separating people from life. It always smelled the same: pungent, like rotting hamburger meat splashed with a cocktail of exotic fruit sweetness. This was not the smell of the infected, whose scent had no sweetness, just the sickly smell of an infected wound. On her left was the surgery room, and on her right was the source of the stench. The kennel room door was open, and on the back wall, eight animal cages contained the furry remains of abandoned pets in different states of decomposition. The grief she felt stabbed her in a different part of her heart.

She turned her back on the pet cemetery and pushed the vision out of her mind so she didn't start crying. She hurried to the surgery room cupboards and rummaged around, knowing exactly what she needed.

Keefer stood at the door of the kennel. "People must have evacuated quickly to leave their pets behind."

She ignored him to avoid her emotions spilling out. "Found it." Abelone pulled out a syringe and a couple of test tube-like vials to store blood.

"Here, we'll need this too." Martel lifted a carrying case similar to the one he'd carried from the Henry Dawson before it had been stolen. This one was . . . grey.

"Great. Let's go." Keefer moved quickly to the corridor. "We can draw the blood in the car." A noise filtered to them from outside—they all froze. Abelone strained to listen through her helmet. It took a second, but she heard it too. A piercing shriek shrilled through the evening air from somewhere in the dusk-filled outdoors.

"Hurry," Keefer whispered. Abelone followed him this time, well aware her unwillingness to kill an infected put them in danger.

Keefer navigated the way back outside. "Fuck!" he blurted when he saw the three infected stalking around the Hummer.

They turned to the survivors and pounced as blasts fired from Keefer and Martel's shotguns, making Abelone jump. One shot missed, and the other hit one of the infected straight in the chest, staggering it. The other two infected landed on the two men.

"No!" Abelone kicked the infected wrestling with Martel. It fell sideways and let go of the doctor, who swung his shotgun up and aimed for the head. The detonation made her wince. The pellets missed but got it in the throat, almost completely severing the head from the shoulders. The body spun like a ballerina and toppled to the ground.

"Get this off me!" Keefer shouted.

The infected had its jaw locked on Keefer's leather-protected forearm. Martel swung the shotgun like a club, catching the infected in the temple. It let go and swaggered sideways, dazed, its grey temple oozing black blood. Keefer's shotgun was up. He fired, and the back of the infected's head disintegrated, and it fell to the ground.

The third infected regained its balance and shrieked, its grey gullet straining and its arms waving in some sort of simulated anger.

Keefer and Martel's shotguns came up and fired at the same time. Two dozen shotgun pellets made the infected's head disappear in a spray of confetti that splashed on the pink siding of the Hummer like a bloody Rorschach.

"In the car!" Keefer shouted.

Another shriek came from behind them. Abelone spun. A lone infected thrashed behind a chain-link fence on the side of the animal hospital. She let out a long sigh of relief. They were safe. It was safe. The infected was trying to squeeze its arms through the links to get to them. It was shirtless, and its grey skin made it look like a shadow dancing wildly. No other infected were around. She looked at the others, relieved they could leave and let it be, but Keefer quickly traversed a couple of metres to the fence and pumped his shotgun. The infected's hands were mangled and stuck inside the fence's links, grey skin scraped off the wrists. Keefer aimed the tip of the barrel through one of the links, inches from the infected's head.

"No!" Abelone blurted.

He paused.

"Ben . . ." Abelone said from behind him. "Don't . . . please."

She could see his finger twitching on the trigger.

"It's of no threat to us. It . . . he . . . can't get to us." She put her hand on Keefer's shoulder. "Let's go. We have what we need."

The breeze picked up. The warm, stuffy air was being swept up, and cooler air from over the St. Lawrence River was replacing it. Abelone steadied her breathing, her hand still on Keefer's shoulder. "Please. You don't need to kill him."

The infected still shrieked and thrashed, but try as it might, it couldn't reach them. Keefer's finger lingered on the trigger. Abelone squeezed his shoulder. The shotgun came down. Keefer turned and blinked at her, his eyes glistening.

"Come." Abelone led him back to the Hummer. Doc Martel was already in the driver's seat. The engine roared to life, and the headlights sliced through the evening twilight.

***

Keefer sat in the back seat with Abelone while Martel drove them down Highway 138 along the long, straight St. Lawrence River. Nighttime had settled in, and the Hummer travelled alone in the darkness.

"Lights are all off. Hadn't noticed," Martel said. "Can you see those stars? With no lights around, it's incredible. It's like we can see the whole galaxy."

Keefer looked out his window. The world outside was indeed devoid of human light: no street lights, no car headlights, no house lights; the world was closed for business.

"It's time," Abelone said, taking off her bodysuit jacket, revealing a white tank top she had donned at Walmart. The top revealed the white, untanned skin of her arms and the round curves of her chest. Her neck was red from the chaffing of the leather jacket's collar.

Keefer's fingers brushed against the red marks. "Does it hurt?" Her skin felt warm.

"Not any worse than the rest of my body." Abelone smiled at him.

He smirked back, understanding as he adjusted to face her and felt sore in every one of his joints. His hand glided over the bump of her shoulder and slid down her arm into the crook of her elbow. He'd collected thousands of blood samples in his line of work, but this one was different. He was nervous. Was it her, or was it what her blood meant? His fingers caressed the vein at the top of her forearm.

"Thank you for not shooting that man."

"I wanted to. What does that person have to look forward to? Even if we get a vaccine, it won't help him. Not by the time we get it done."

"We don't know that."

He decided not to argue and instead focused on the flecks of grey in her blue eyes. He took a slow breath and looked at her arm. His hands moved quickly, experienced at what they were doing. He tied the rubber tourniquet at her elbow and clasped her forearm while his thumb massaged the vein so it would bulge. He brought up the needle and holder system, and the needle penetrated her vein effortlessly. His hands trembled slightly. Abelone put her other hand on his knee, which calmed him. He quickly filled three vacutainers of blood, and it was done. He slipped the needle out. Abelone bit her lip. His hand slid back up her arm slowly, feeling the hardness of her triceps. He leaned in, looking for the grey specs in her eyes again. He could feel her warm breath on his lips.

Abelone trembled as their lips touched lightly. He paused. She leaned into him, and her mouth pressed harder against his. He moved his hand to her cheek and bit her lip lightly. She responded with a barely audible groan. He felt the dampness of her tongue on his, followed by . . . the cold, hard steel of a barrel at his temple.

Keefer opened his eyes. The Hummer had stopped, and Doc Martel was holding a pistol to his head.

"The saliva . . . her saliva!" Martel's voice was trembling as he spoke.

Abelone jerked back as if waking up abruptly.

"What have I done?" She pushed Keefer away hard.

"What?" Keefer looked between them, the pistol still held to his head.

"My saliva . . . the virus . . ." Abelone's eyes filled with tears.

His understanding congealed quickly. The virus might be in her saliva; she might have passed it to him. *How could I have been so stupid?*

"Abelone, move away," Martel said.

"I'm okay," Keefer gulped. "I don't feel anything." He tried to sound reassuring, but he couldn't be sure. His heart was beating so fast that if indeed the virus was in his body, it was sure to be spreading already. His thoughts flashed back to Moe and how quickly he had turned, the lady with the purple raincoat in the harbour, Sergeant Reilly.

"Abelone, please . . . move away," Martel pleaded.

Abelone hesitated.

"It's okay. Move back. It's my fault. I'm sorry." Keefer urged her back. It was his fault. He shouldn't put her in danger. If he turned, he could still hurt her, which was the last thing he wanted.

She listened to him and moved to the opposite end of the back seat.

Keefer coughed. *Is it the virus, or am I having a panic attack?* His temples pounded, and he couldn't focus. He wasn't sure what he was feeling. He coughed again and felt Martel stiffen and push the pistol harder to his temple. The gun was trembling.

Keefer coughed loudly. It startled Martel, whose arm jerked and hand clenched.

"Eric, no!"

Abelone lunged for the gun. Keefer's head was spinning. The deflagration went off. The smell of burnt gunpowder filled the cab of the Hummer.

PART IV - HAVEN

29

Safe Havens Are for the Strong

The binoculars scanned the gas station. There were at least a hundred infected around it. The plywood-fortified building harboured something that was attracting them. Keefer put the binoculars down, and his right hand gently felt the bandage on his slightly mutilated ear. If it hadn't been for Abelone, he'd be dead. If she didn't believe an infected could be saved, he'd be dead. *I wasn't infected, though.* But the truth was, at the time, he thought he had been. For a few seconds, he believed he was indeed turning, and at that moment, he realized he didn't want to die; he wanted to be saved. Abelone had knocked Martel's gun away in time. Even if he'd been infected, she had wanted to save him. Maybe he'd been wrong; maybe those who were infected deserved to have a hope of being saved, no matter how slim it was.

"We should go around," Keefer said, taking one last look with the binoculars. "No, wait. Something's going on. The infected are moving. They are going to the back of the gas station—something is attracting them."

Doc Martel and Abelone leaned forward in their seats, trying to see without the help of field glasses.

Keefer watched as the majority of infected ran to the back of the building, and as soon as the front was somewhat clear, the door opened and a man in military fatigues with two teens and a woman behind him ran out. They sprinted to a small military vehicle parked across the lot.

"We need to help them!" Abelone said, grasping her rifle tightly.

"They're heading for that military patrol vehicle." He started the Hummer but hesitated, still unsure if they should try to help. Maybe those people would make it; they were close to the vehicle, but then the woman running behind stumbled and fell. Keefer flung the binoculars aside and stomped on the accelerator, launching the Hummer forward.

Abelone picked up the binoculars and provided a play-by-play while he concentrated on driving.

"The soldier is helping the woman," she commented. "No, he didn't make it in time."

Keefer pressed harder on the accelerator, but had to relent when the road turned, and he almost sent them into the side of a house.

"He's dragging the kids, tossing them in the car."

"They'll be safe in there. That's a reinforced vehicle. What about the woman?" Keefer asked, not looking up from the road ahead.

Abelone took a few heartbeats to respond. "I can't see her."

Keefer didn't ask for clarification; he knew it meant she was under a pile of infected.

"The vehicle is moving. It's driving off," Abelone said, her voice rising in excitement.

Keefer slowed the Hummer. "What direction are they going?"

"I don't know . . . wait . . . it stopped. What are they doing?"

Keefer stopped the Hummer, and Abelone gave him the binoculars. The patrol vehicle was indeed stopped. He swung the binoculars to the gas station and understood.

The door to the gas station was ajar. The infected were trying to pull it open, but someone inside was trying to fight them off.

"There are still people inside!" gasped Keefer. That was how they had attracted the infected to the back of the gas station. The people inside must have been making noise from the back to clear the lot so the others could make it to the patrol vehicle.

These were the first uninfected people they'd seen since Peaks Bay, and a dark hole opened up in his stomach when the gas-station door was breached. An older woman was pulled out and bitten limb from limb as more infected stormed inside. If there were other survivors, they would not stand a chance.

He swung his view to the patrol vehicle in time to see it turn and head straight for the gas station. Swinging the view back, he saw why: two people were on the gas-station rooftop.

He didn't hesitate this time. He gave Abelone the binoculars and floored the gas pedal again. They had to help.

Keefer concentrated as he sped down the residential hill toward the small commercial area. A few infected ran into the streets when they heard the roaring engine, but they were too late and faded in his rear-view mirror.

Abelone provided a cryptic play-by-play of the gas-station events as she bounced on her seat, held down by her seat belt. "Patrol vehicle crashed into the gas station—one person on the roof jumped down—other person attacked by infected—everyone out of patrol vehicle—they climbed on some sort of small structure."

Keefer couldn't follow what she was saying, and he didn't want to look up because, at their speed, they would crash into a building if he missed a turn.

Finally, he angled the Hummer down the road leading into the gas-station lot. For a few seconds, he slowed down. Two soldiers stood atop a dumpster shelter, fighting off the infected who were trying to climb on. The two teens were behind the men, trying to stay out of reach of their clutching fingers.

Keefer sped up again and crashed into the pile of infected who were making a slope up the dumpster shelter. Bodies flew up and sideways and the Hummer skidded to a stop, leaving long, black, bloody marks on the asphalt.

"Take the wheel!" Keefer shouted at Abelone. She would be of no help outside if she wasn't willing to shoot the infected, and he wanted to spare her from having to make the choice.

"Helmet on," he ordered Martel, and they both jumped out. Their shotguns mowed down any infected still standing. They moved in unison, shoulder to shoulder.

One infected got up from under the pile of run-over bodies and leapt onto Keefer's back, trying to sink its teeth into his shoulder. Keefer held his breath, waiting for the searing pain of ripping skin. It didn't materialize; the infected's teeth could not pierce the leather. Keefer grabbed the infected by its black, greasy hair and pulled it over his shoulder to the ground in front of him. The infected bit his hand, but the teeth, again, did no damage through the thick leather. He pinned it with his metal-reinforced biker boot, slid his knife from its scabbard and, in one quick motion, penetrated the orbital cavity of the squirming infected. The blade sliced through the grey and black eye all the way to the knife guard, and the infected stopped moving instantly.

He looked for more infected. None were standing, but plenty were squirming, trying to get up on broken legs. Keefer looked up at the people on the dumpster shelter.

"Are any of you bitten?" he shouted.

They all stared at him.

"Are you bitten?" Keefer yelled again.

Martel's shotgun made Keefer jump as he blasted the head off an infected who managed to get up.

The taller of the two soldiers wiped his hand over his glistening brown forehead. He looked his party over. "No."

"Then come on already, get in the Hummer," Keefer ordered, but the man hesitated, staring at the car.

Keefer looked at it, too, and imagined what the man was thinking: a pink Hummer with a couple of leather-clad, helmet-wearing men. Not your usual rescue party. Nonetheless, each soldier grabbed a teen, jumped down and squeezed into the Hummer.

***

The air conditioning aggressively pumped cold air into the Hummer, but Abelone barely noticed. She continued to sweat, and her blood drummed through her temples. The rescued soldiers were on either side of Eric in the backseat, and the teen boys were crammed in the open back trunk area over the supplies. The soldiers were a contrast to each other. The one with two gold bars on his shoulder was tall and athletic with light brown skin; the other was short and muscular and looked like he'd never been in the sun.

"Wait." Keefer put his hand on her shoulder. He opened the moon roof and stood on his seat with half his body out of the vehicle as she slowed and stopped.

"Flare gun," he said to Martel, who dug through a duffle bag at his feet, pulled out an orange toy-looking pistol and handed it to him.

The man with the gold bars turned to see what Keefer was looking at.

What's he doing? Abelone wondered.

Keefer aimed the flare gun at the building.

"No, wait!" the man with the gold bars tried to get Keefer's attention, but it was too late.

A flare rocketed out of the gun in a loud, burning hiss. It landed at the feet of one of the broken gas pumps spewing gasoline. The gas ignited with a loud whoosh. The ground shook under the Hummer, and the shockwave rattled the vehicle's thick windows. A giant red and yellow sphere burst into the sky, engulfing the gas station and the four dozen infected in and around the building. Their shrieks were extinguished by the explosion.

Keefer dropped into his seat before the heat wave hit the Hummer. He closed the moon roof and waved at Abelone to go. She drove away from where a giant hole now sat instead of a gas station.

"You didn't have to do that!" the man with the gold bars shouted. "Those were people. Even if they were infected, they were people!"

Keefer didn't respond. He slowly removed his helmet and wiped some black blood off the face shield. He put it between his feet, then pulled off his leather gloves before grabbing a bottle of water from the cup holder and taking a long gulp.

Abelone was torn. This was the same argument she'd had multiple times with Keefer.

"There's water and food in the back underneath the boys," Keefer said, as if he hadn't heard the complaint. "You folks are lucky we happened to drive by when we did."

"You didn't have to kill all those people," the man said again, calmer this time.

Keefer turned and eyed the man for a few seconds. Abelone wasn't sure how he would react.

"Captain . . ."

She noticed Keefer look at the man's lapels and his name tag on his fatigues.

"Captain Jennings. I'm Captain Keefer from the 51st Ambulance."

Abelone looked at Jennings in the rear-view mirror. His eyes were light brown and stood out against his brown skin. They were filled with sorrow.

"Those things were not people anymore." Keefer caressed his bandaged ear and continued as if he didn't believe himself, "If we are to stop the infection, we need to stop the spread—"

"They were people, not things," the man cut him off. "You didn't have to—"

"They were trying to kill you!"

"Most were stuck in the building; we would have been gone when they got out."

Abelone did not want to take the side of a stranger, but the sorrow in his eyes resonated with her. "Ben, he's right. You didn't *need* to kill them." She pulled the Hummer to the side of the road. She turned in her seat and smiled. A friendly smile, but full of sorrow.

"I'm Abelone. This is Benjamin. The man between you and your friend is Eric Martel or Doc."

"I'm sorry about the people in the gas station," Abelone continued. She scowled at Keefer. "Things are complicated."

The shorter, muscular soldier spoke up, revealing a thick French accent. "I'm Sergeant St-Pierre, and he"—he thumbed toward Jennings—"is Captain Jennings. We're both with the 12th RBC. He used to fly choppers but came to his senses and joined the best-armoured regiment in Canada a few years ago."

"12th RBC?" Abelone asked.

"It's the armoured regiment out of Valcartier," answered Keefer, still eyeing his slightly larger officer counterpart.

Abelone looked back and forth between Jennings and Keefer. "You're both captains?" she said. "So . . . then . . . who is in charge?"

Keefer smirked and turned, facing the road. "Let's go. Best we not stay here. The explosion will attract every infected in the neighbourhood."

They drove away from the crater filled with burning debris and bodies, sending black smoke into the sky.

***

Abelone was surprised and relieved their new passengers left the gas-station incident behind them. She gathered they had their own complicated relationship with the infected. She definitely could relate to their anger with Keefer, but she knew it was better they stuck together. The pink Hummer, now driven by Sergeant St-Pierre, navigated the streets leading back to Valcartier, since he knew the streets better.

Abelone and Martel told the story of the Nuovo Mondo and the Henry Dawson, while Keefer described the infection and destruction of Peaks Bay. Abelone felt uneasy the whole time she recounted her story, wondering if the newcomers would blame them for bringing the virus to the mainland. Jennings and St-Pierre listened attentively, not saying a word. Both stayed quiet for a while, probably piecing together everything they had heard with everything they had experienced.

Abelone and the others remained quiet for a while. She counted five turns before Jennings spoke.

"The city was overwhelmed within days before anyone knew what was going on," Jennings started tentatively, picking up from what he had just heard. "What you've been telling us about Peaks Bay . . ." Jennings paused for a second. "That was . . . internet rumours. Most thought it was a hoax, a flu breakout dressed up as a zombie apocalypse by internet trolls. And that ship . . . your ship . . . the Henry Dawson?" He looked at Abelone. "No one had heard of it, let alone some fucking secret mission to Greenland."

He paused and shook his head. "Once people started getting infected in the city, no one cared what was happening in Peaks Bay. And if what you are telling me is accurate—time-wise—then Quebec City got infected shortly after you arrived in Peaks Bay. I'd heard military personnel had been dispatched to look into Peaks Bay, but they were from Goose Bay, so we didn't get any details. Orders were on a need-to-know basis, so anyone not involved knew fuck all."

"It was the mayor," said Keefer. "They evacuated her when the town was . . . fuck, I don't even know what to call it . . . attacked."

Abelone didn't like that perspective. It was an infection, not a war.

Keefer continued, oblivious to her objection, "The mayor was there when the ship crashed into the pier. Best we can tell, she was bitten and rushed to the local hospital before being air evac'd to Quebec City. Fuck."

"Well, it doesn't matter now," Jennings replied. "However, the virus got here, and once it did, nobody cared about anything else. Most news channels or radio stations never even made sense of what was happening before they went off air. The few who made it—I mean, they were still transmitting—by day three, they got government warnings out, but those were vague: stay indoors, don't let anyone in and wait for further instructions. Even the government couldn't make sense of the reports they were getting. Can you blame them?"

Abelone nodded, but was thinking about the breakdown of the Geneva Protocol. The government should have been ready. If they'd set up a barricade, they should have reacted quicker. She conceded that people biting people had never been one of the scenarios they had pre-planned communications strategy for, though.

"By day four, every local TV and radio station was off air. Anything broadcasted from outside the area was amateur videos taken off the internet. That's when Valcartier lost contact with Ottawa."

The Hummer swerved around an infected standing in the middle of the road, and everyone tilted the opposite way. Abelone was pressed against Jennings; she steadied herself on his large shoulder. He smiled at her.

"How many people are infected? Did some sort of resistance get set up?" Keefer asked.

"I've never seen an infection report or a casualty report—like I said, nothing was operating anymore by day four—no cops, no hospitals, no nothing."

The speed with which the virus spread didn't surprise Abelone, but the fact these were humans becoming infected was grinding her insides into pulp.

"The military in Valcartier, even though cut off . . . they . . . we were able to hold out for a few more days, but that was it. The base fell like everything else. All that was left was the fortified camp around the helicopter landing pads on the far end of the base."

Jennings looked at St-Pierre with sadness. "That's where we were. We were the lucky ones. Survivors trickled in for a couple of days, usually by car. We had to shoot any of the infected people chasing them. But we hadn't seen anyone in twelve hours when we got this distress call . . . We had two choppers fuelled up and ready to fly." He paused and looked at the boys huddled in the back. "We got a distress call from their parents. There were a handful of survivors at that gas station. It was still our duty to save people." Jennings said this last part with confidence.

Jennings leaned forward to St-Pierre and instructed him to take a different side street.

"There were two other survivors who showed up as we were leaving base camp for this last rescue mission. We let them into the camp and took off to get the people at the gas station."

St-Pierre interrupted the storytelling and brought them all back to the present. "Captain, what will we do when we get there? LeBlanc and those guys might be back."

"Who's that?" Keefer asked.

Jennings tensed. "Those are the bastards who deserted us at the gas station. A few guys weren't thrilled about risking their lives for one last group of survivors. As soon as the infected people started showing up, LeBlanc and a couple of others took off. Left us to deal with the civilians."

"They deserted. That's what they did," St-Pierre added, his French accent coming out with his anger.

"That's a bridge we'll cross when we get there," responded Jennings with a pinched mouth.

Abelone wondered what justice looked like in his mind, considering everything else happening.

30

FANCY MEETING YOU HERE

A s the Hummer sped down the road, Abelone looked back at the dozens of infected in pursuit. More and more joined the procession as the vehicle made its way through the small neighbourhood near the military installation.

"Where did all *dese* bastards come from?" asked St-Pierre to nobody.

They'd seen groups of infected on their long journey from Peaks Bay, but from what Jennings had told them, the somewhat isolated base had been fairly clear since the base had initially been overrun.

"When we left, the neighbourhood was quiet. Something must have happened," Jennings confirmed her concerns.

"Any chance the camp was overrun?" asked Abelone. "Or more survivors showed up with infected following them?" These infected looked . . . *fresh*, for lack of a better way to describe it.

"The camp was solid. It would take hundreds to break through. The engineering corps did a heck of a job with nine feet of concrete barricades and fences. Plus, none of these are dressed in military garb," Jennings pointed out. "As for survivors, other than the last two who showed up yesterday, they had no infected people in tow, and we hadn't seen anyone for twenty-four hours before that. Unlikely more showed up. And if they did, they usually only had a handful of infected people after them."

"Well, wherever they are from, it doesn't matter. We're home." St-Pierre pointed up the road to the fortified structure.

Abelone gawked. The nine-foot concrete walls stretched out in an oval around what she assumed were the helicopter pads. A chain-link fence covered in barbed wire acted as a gate and blocked the way ahead. The gate was surrounded by a scaffold stretched over the top, with a large circular spotlight attached to its railing. It wasn't pretty, but she could see how this place had kept the soldiers and the survivors safe.

As the Hummer drove closer and slowed, Abelone could see two soldiers standing on the scaffold, attentive but unmoving, perhaps confused by the arrival of a pink Hummer with a cortege of angry infected behind it.

The vehicle came to a stop in front of the gate, and Jennings jumped out. "Open the gate!" he shouted at the two men.

They looked at each other, then back to Jennings, but didn't move. Perhaps it wasn't confusion. They looked at Jennings with recognition, yet still, neither moved.

St-Pierre slammed on the horn a bunch of times to get them moving. Finally, one brought up a handheld radio and seemed to be asking for instructions. It was obvious something was off, but Abelone couldn't understand what. She stretched her neck to get a better view past the gate, but couldn't see anyone else.

"Private, open the gate. That's an order!" shouted Jennings again with enough conviction to induce one of them to move to the ladder leading to the gate, but the other told him to stop.

"What's going on?" asked Abelone from the back seat. These soldiers were not under Jennings' command.

"I don't know. Those aren't my men. They were from another unit that joined us a few days in."

St-Pierre honked the horn again, holding his hand on it. Abelone's gut reaction was that this would attract any and every infected in the area, but what did it matter? They already had a crowd of them about to crash down on them.

The man holding the radio was a barrel-chested behemoth who reminded Abelone of Roger Powers from the Henry Dawson. He was taller than Jennings, but instead of being quarterback fit like Jennings, he looked more like a lumberjack, thick and hefty, with his belly protruding. His hair was shaved to the skull, and his eyes never left Jennings. If she'd seen him while out on an evening stroll, she would have crossed the street.

"The infected . . . they are almost here," Keefer said to Jennings.

Jennings' hands moved down on his rifle as if he was about to bring it up, but before he did, another voice shouted from beyond the gate.

"Open the gate! Sergeant Braggs, Private Pickett, open that gate!" The voice was stern and came from someone out of sight. The smaller man, presumably Pickett, looked up to the larger first, but then jumped to the ladder and scampered down. The gate was unlocked and rolled open.

Barely four car lengths behind them, the infected were swelling like a wave about to crash on a rocky shore. When the gate was wide enough, St-Pierre slammed on the accelerator, and the Hummer almost hopped into the camp. Jennings jogged through the opening, still staring at the barrel-chested man on the scaffold.

The gate closed behind them, and the infected crashed into it instead of the Hummer.

As the Hummer skidded to a stop, Abelone saw the soldier who'd ordered the door to be opened. He had a black beret, a big golden badge with twelve on it and a rifle casually swung over his shoulder.

"Captain," said the man to Jennings.

Abelone noticed the sergeant's bars on his arms instead of his shoulders when Jennings addressed him as "sergeant" in a cold, unfriendly voice.

They stood apart from the group and talked. Jennings was agitated and half-shouting his questions: Where are the survivors? Were the deserters back in camp? Where is some lieutenant or other?

The other man stood quietly through the barrage of questions. When Jennings paused, the stern-faced sergeant pointed to a tent near the middle of the camp.

Jennings turned to St-Pierre and the others. "Sarge, take them to the mess tent." He pointed to Abelone, Doc Martel and the two boys as they exited the Hummer. "Watch over them." Jennings' face said a lot of things only two brothers-in-arms could understand. The muscular sergeant tensed, understanding way more than she did. Abelone sensed there was danger at hand and leaned back into the Hummer and slid the grey case with her blood-samples under the front seat.

"Captain Keefer, come with us," said Jennings. There was no doubt which captain was in charge here. This was the first time Jennings addressed Keefer by his rank.

Keefer nodded. "Stay close to him," Keefer whispered to Abelone and pointed to St-Pierre, giving him his own meaningful look. St-Pierre nodded. Keefer followed Jennings and the black-bereted sergeant toward the command tent.

Abelone tried to give Martel a look, the way Jennings and Keefer had communicated without saying a word. She tried to convey her concern, how she wondered if any of these soldiers could be trusted, including St-Pierre. She tried to have her face say, *Stay close and keep the boys even closer.*

"What's wrong?" Martel asked her. "You look dizzy."

She shook her head, opened her eyes wider and looked at the soldiers, then at the teens.

"Abelone, you okay?" Doc Martel asked.

Damn it, she wasn't coming across. "I'm fine," she gasped. "Just keep the boys close to you."

Martel nodded, waved them over and gave them a look that they seemed to understand. They nodded at the doctor.

Abelone sighed. Maybe it was her; maybe her face couldn't speak. She looked around for the first time, really taking in the camp. It was nothing more than four large green military tents. The command tent was nearest the helicopter pads, with two army green helicopters basking in the sunlight behind it. They were similar to the one that had crashed on the Henry Dawson, but these had gas tanks jury-rigged to their sides, making them look like train tanker rail cars with a rotor on top.

Braggs, who'd made his way down from the scaffold, faced the infected and kicked at the fence in amusement. The power of his kick sent a few stumbling backwards.

"Stay here and watch the deadlies," he told the other soldier called Pickett.

They call them deadlies. It must make them easier to kill. Calling them infected meant they were sick and possibly savable.

"Let's go," Braggs said to her and the others. He pointed to the mess tent.

St-Pierre didn't move. Abelone and the others did the same.

"Braggs, where are de people . . . the survivors who were here when we left?" St-Pierre asked suspiciously.

"Relax, I'll explain everything in the mess tent. Let's get you some food."

Braggs' hands slowly moved down his rifle, which caused St-Pierre to do the same. Abelone held her breath.

"Braggs . . . everything okay?" Three men from the tent had walked up behind them with their rifles held tight.

St-Pierre sized them up, then slowly lowered his rifle. "*Okay, pas d'probleme,*" he said and put his free hand on one teen's shoulders and gently guided him past the soldiers. The other teen walked behind his brother, and Abelone stayed close behind him. Braggs was last. None of the other soldiers lowered their guns.

The inside of the tent was cooler, but Abelone barely noticed. Guns pointing at you did that. A handful of tables were set up down one side of the tent. A few men were sitting, a couple in army fatigues and one in a t-shirt and jeans. She barely noticed them. All her senses were on alert as she watched the soldiers walk into the tent behind them. The smell of cheap coffee floated in the stuffy tent, tickling her nose. On the periphery of her attention, which simply couldn't alter her focus from the rifles pointed at them, was a small woman with a blonde ponytail standing by a ration-covered table.

"Okay, that's far enough," Braggs said in a low, heavy tone like a street brawler about to start punching.

St-Pierre spun while bringing up his rifle, but he wasn't fast enough. The butt of Braggs' rifle caught him on the cheek, splitting it open and spraying blood on the two boys still close to him. The muscular sergeant stumbled backwards, and Abelone and Martel each pulled a teen back for safety.

A melee ensued, with shouts erupting from all the soldiers. It was St-Pierre against a handful of men. One versus many.

The violence between grown men was jarring. She tried to take a step forward reflexively, but a rifle barrel was jabbed in her chest.

"Get back!" the soldier ordered. He was young, barely an adult, and sported a shaved head like Braggs.

Considering the odds, St-Pierre fought like a cornered animal and caused incredible damage. One soldier had his ear partially torn off. Another's knee was completely snapped sideways. He got as much as he gave, though; his left eye was mangled shut, and his split-open cheek was a crevice filled with dirt. Blood trickled from his mouth, and when he wiped his chin, a finger on his left hand was at an angle not meant for a digit.

Abelone, Martel and the boys were manhandled to the back of the tent by the young soldier when Abelone noticed the graffiti over the Canadian flag on the arm of his uniform. She'd recognize that symbol of hatred anywhere—a swastika had been drawn with a black marker over the maple leaf. Her stomach clenched, worse than when she faced the infected.

"Fucking St-Pierre. You couldn't stay calm, could you?" Braggs said to the sergeant, who was kneeling and hunched over in the middle of the tent. "I've always despised you, you know. You always acted like you were too good to hang out with us. Big muscle man who likes to hang out with fucking monkeys." Braggs' leg snapped forward, and the thick-soled boot caught St-Pierre on the side of the jaw with a crunch. Multiple teeth erupted from the sergeant's mouth as he spun and crumpled to the ground.

The teens yelped, and Abelone stepped forward again but was stopped by the young soldier.

"Shut the fuck up! Or you'll get the same thing," the young man shouted.

Braggs stayed focused on the battered sergeant. He crouched down to look at him eye-to-eye. "I never understood why you fucking looked up to that nigger. He didn't deserve to lead us."

"Why are you doing this?" shouted Abelone, her voice shaking. For all the horrors she had seen over the last week, there was something about these men that shook her to her core.

"Why?" Braggs looked up at her. "Why?" He laughed.

Looking straight at Abelone, he smiled, revealing blood-stained teeth. His hand slid into Sergeant St-Pierre's hair.

"Why?" he repeated. "Because I can." He slammed St-Pierre's head against a table and motioned to a soldier. "Hold his hand."

St-Pierre grunted.

Braggs pulled out a long military-issued knife, still looking at Abelone. She stared at him with as much anger and fear as she'd ever felt.

"You see, lady, the world has changed. Guys like us"—he motioned to the other soldiers—"we always had to hide. The world didn't like the fact we knew we were superior. We had to live amongst inferiors." He smiled again. "Not anymore."

"You fucking racist pig," St-Pierre muttered loud enough for everyone to hear, despite his broken teeth.

"Racist pig?" Braggs snarled. "Look around you. We are the last people standing. Who cares what we are?"

"You killed the civilians, didn't you?" St-Pierre struggled against the two men holding him down, but barely nudged them.

Abelone's heart sank. They'd walked right into a nest of monsters far worse than the infected.

Braggs laughed. "The fucking Frenchman didn't even notice."

The soldiers smiled, and Braggs moved closer to St-Pierre. "They were trying to fucking eat you, man. Those useless dipshits you saved, they were trying to eat you!" He laughed as if it had been the best joke ever uttered. "To be clear, though, no, I didn't kill them . . . They killed themselves. It was some demented game of tag. I can tell you that much." Braggs laughed again.

St-Pierre shook furiously and tried to free himself.

"Stop moving!" Braggs shouted. He cocked his giant knife back and slammed it into St-Pierre's hand. The blade sliced through skin and muscle, pinning St-Pierre's thick hand to the wooden table.

St-Pierre winced but did not scream.

"No!" Abelone shouted. She didn't understand. St-Pierre and Jennings were sure this place was safe. She couldn't comprehend how people could become so evil, so dangerous.

Unexpectedly, Doc Martel sprang forward and knocked the young soldier over. She hadn't been paying attention to him, but he must have been as angry as she was. The crack of a gun firing stopped her from moving herself.

"Sit down!" Braggs shouted, holding a large, obnoxious golden pistol he'd pulled from his belt, a light plume of smoke whiffing up from the barrel.

Abelone moved back. *Has St-Pierre been shot?* "Eric, is he . . ." She turned to Martel for reassurance, but her words caught in her throat. Martel was holding up a blood-covered hand. Burgundy liquid dripped out from under the bottom of his leather jacket.

"Eric!" Abelone pushed him down on his chair and pressed her hand on the fresh hole in his jacket. Memories of Alex and John flashed in her mind.

"Abelone?" was all the doctor could muster.

She squeezed down on his belly, but blood still seeped through her fingers as if she was squeezing down a jelly donut. She couldn't lose her last connection to the Henry Dawson. She frantically felt around the doctor's back. When she pulled her hand back, it was covered in blood. "The bullet went completely through. We need to stop the bleeding."

"I was shot?" Martel asked, confused.

"Yes." She looked frantically around. "Give me those hand towels." She pointed to the table beside the two boys.

The bigger boy blinked hard and turned toward where she had pointed. He looked back at her. His mouth closed, and he swallowed. His hands opened up. He shifted. He grabbed the towels and handed them to Abelone.

She folded them and put the towels over the leaks in Martel's body. *I don't want to lose anyone else. How will we remember?* Her whole body shook.

"You see what you made me do?" Braggs walked over to them. "At least you now know what Mr. Goldfinger can do." He waved his vulgar golden gun as if in a trance, not caring about what he had done.

"You're a monster. You sent those survivors out to be infected," Abelone snarled at him.

"A monster?" Braggs feigned insult. "I'm not a monster. They're the monsters out there." His voice got louder. "This world never accepted my point of view!" He looked at his accomplices. "Our point of view!"

He bent in front of Abelone, still shouting, so his breath still washed over her even though he wasn't close. "Those monsters"—he pointed at the gate again—"they allowed us to rise. And with this man's help, they freed us!" He nodded at the civilian now standing beside the blonde woman.

The violence of the last minute had garnered Abelone's whole attention, but she looked at the man and woman now. The woman and her blonde ponytail drew her attention first. She was holding a red apple, her face frozen, unmoving, as if fearing being recognized. Her height. Her young face. The realization hit Abelone like a punch in the stomach.

"Karen?" she gasped. She blinked hard to make sure. "How?" Abelone wanted to scream and jump on her, but her body stopped working. None of her muscles moved as her gaze settled on the man beside her.

"Well, hello, Ms. Jensen—I think that was your name, right?" the man in jeans said as he smiled from ear to ear. There was nothing warm or friendly about his smile.

"You? But the police station—" She barely got the words out. How could he be here? Her mind was spinning so fast that she had to put her hand on a chair to keep from falling.

"Saved by the grace of God," Dirk Danerson answered and looked to the heavens. His smile changed to a look of feigned gratitude.

For a few seconds, Abelone thought her eyes were playing tricks. This wasn't Dirk, just someone who looked like him, but that smile . . . it was him.

"Braggs, believe it or not, this is the person I was telling you about. This is the scientist who is responsible"—he pointed at Abelone with his open palms, then outstretched his arms, indicating everywhere—"for the apocalypse, the end of times, the new world order."

Braggs looked from Abelone to Dirk, confused. "Her?"

"I told you the government planned all this. They sent some scientists to spread the plague in Peaks Bay as a test."

Everyone in the tent listened to Dirk attentively, wanting to hear what he would say next.

"*She* was the rider of death. *She* is to blame for the world ending." He spun in a circle, his arms outstretched and his palms pointing to the sky.

What was he doing? Abelone struggled to grasp the theatre she was seeing.

Dirk stopped spinning and pointed one finger at her disapprovingly. "She admitted—to me—she was responsible for this. She admitted—to the Chosen One—she had brought the plague to Peaks Bay."

"I what?" Abelone frowned, unable to follow this madman's logic. So much had happened since the police station she couldn't remember what she'd said to him. It didn't matter. This man was a murderer. "You killed people."

"I didn't kill people, Ms. Jensen. I liberated them. I freed those who were forced to help you end the world."

He's lost his mind. She looked at the soldiers for any shred of sanity, but none was to be found. They all looked at Dirk in admiration.

"Why? Why would you listen to him?" Abelone pleaded with the group.

Dirk answered for them, "Because, Ms. Jensen, God sent them the Chosen One. The one person who can help them rise from the ashes of a sick world. The one person God has chosen to lead these righteous men." He opened his arms, palms up again. "The only person who can save them from this deadly plague: the only person who is *immune.*"

Abelone blinked. He'd been bitten. She looked at her arm, the bandage that covered her bite, and understood. *He got bitten and survived.* He was immune to the virus—like her. But the bombing? The town was burnt to the ground. *How?*

"I can tell you are wondering how I survived the bombing of Peaks Bay. The hellfire cleansed the town. It's simple, Ms. Jensen—God protected me."

A few soldiers nodded. Her brow furrowed, and her thoughts swirled. *Where did you hide?* She stated an obvious fact: "You were the person walking in front of us."

Karen moved closer to Dirk, looking scared.

Abelone wondered why Karen betrayed them for Dirk, but as they stood side by side, Abelone saw a resemblance in the shape of their faces and the set of their eyes. Then, her attention shifted to the yellow case in Karen's hand.

31

DON'T WORRY ABOUT WHERE THE OTHERS ARE

K eefer stayed a step behind Jennings. The heat of the day was making his leather outfit tight and sticky.

"Head on in," the sergeant said, pulling open the door flap to the
command tent.

It took a second for his eyes to adjust to the dim light. The silhouette
of a smallish man bent over some maps took shape in the middle of the
tent. His fatigues bore a large and small bar on the shoulder instead of
bars on his arm.

"Lieutenant Stewart, what is going on here? Where are Phillips and
the others? Where are the civilians? The only people I saw were Braggs
and his cronies." Jennings wasted no time.

Keefer stood still, acutely aware of the lack of welcome from Lieutenant Stewart. He also didn't like that their escort was still standing
behind them.

"I'd left Lieutenant Phillips in charge—where is he?"

"It doesn't matter who you left in charge. It only matters who is in
charge now." Stewart's voice was resolute. He looked up at them.

He was not an imposing man. His musculature was wiry and tense,
like a trap ready to spring. The skin on his face was pulled tight by a
pointy nose, highlighting his clear blue eyes. He looked like a weasel that
had gone weeks without eating.

Jennings went quiet, processing his surroundings. His posture was slowly shifting, almost imperceptibly, to a boxer's stance or a shooter's if you happened to be holding a rifle.

"Put down your rifle, Captain," the wiry lieutenant said, picking up on Jennings' subtle shift, "or my men will shoot you."

The shadows behind the lieutenant moved, and two men stepped forward, both with their rifles aimed at them.

"You traitors . . ." Jennings uttered, but he contemplated the request. Without uttering another word, he put his rifle on the ground and nodded at Keefer. Keefer wasn't sure what to make of the situation, but one thing he knew, if Jennings was worried about these guys, so should he. He put his rifle down.

Stewart eyed Keefer. "Who are you?"

Telling him he was from Peaks Bay might make things worse. What if he found out Abelone was immune to the virus? What would happen to her?

"He's no one," answered Jennings. "A survivor we picked up on the way back." Jennings took a step closer to the table.

The men behind Stewart tensed, rifles squarely aimed at him. He stopped.

"Stewart, why are you doing this? Where are the others?" Jennings adopted a looser posture and used his hands to speak.

"Don't worry about where the others are. Worry about who is here."

Lieutenant Stewart walked over to an old stained coffeemaker and poured himself a cup.

"To be honest, I wasn't expecting you back." He drank from his cup without blowing on the hot liquid. "Not after the guys told me you were stranded at that gas station." He nodded at the two men behind him, which confirmed they were some of the men who'd deserted Jennings.

"Don't get me wrong. I'm really glad you are here. We all are." Stewart moved to a chair on his side of the map table. Sitting down, he motioned Jennings and Keefer toward the two chairs in front of them.

"You see, Captain, after you left, we received word from the government. Turns out the rest of Quebec isn't doing so hot either. So it's not just us who are in a pickle."

"What did they say?" Jennings asked abruptly.

"Well, they said"—Stewart eyed Jennings suspiciously—"plenty." He paused for a few seconds, then decided to answer. "Montreal was overwhelmed within days of Quebec City." Keefer gulped air as if punched in the gut.

"The Prime Minister has written off the province," Stewart said matter-of-factly and drank his coffee.

Keefer wobbled in place. All this time they were travelling from Peaks Bay, the province was . . . getting infected.

Stewart noticed Keefer's unease. "What's your name?"

Keefer shifted back. "Ben. Benjamin Keefer." Usually, he'd be more honest with fellow military personnel, but a few too many things weren't adding up.

"And where are you from, Benjamin Keefer?"

Stewart's gaze bore into him, but Keefer didn't let it get to him. "Upriver. Just outside the city."

Stewart lost interest, and his attention shifted back to Jennings.

"Like I was saying, the PM has quarantined the province at the Ottawa River, and the Americans have fortified the Appalachians into an unpassable death trap. A person gets within a few klicks of them, and said person gets blown to pieces—monster or not."

"Halifax, Saint John?" Jennings asked.

Stewart laughed. "You see, Jennings, that's your problem. You are sitting here, rifles in your face, your life on the line, death all around, and you still care what happens to others."

The man put his coffee cup on the maps spread out over the table between them. Keefer watched a stray droplet meander down the side of the cup and fall like a bomb onto the creased map. The droplet landed beside a large circle around Quebec City.

"I have no idea what is happening in the Atlantic Provinces, nor do I care." Stewart picked up the cup and took another sip.

"If Lt. Phillips and the civilians are *gone*, why aren't we?" Jennings asked, changing the direction of the conversation.

Stewart looked at him, amused. "Are you asking me why we haven't left yet? Or are you asking me why you aren't *dead* yet?"

"He needs you," Keefer answered. "They need you." He looked at Jennings. "When we met, St-Pierre said you used to fly choppers, right?"

They only need Jennings. Keefer hadn't realized it was possible to get more tense, but everyone from their group except Jennings was expendable to these people.

Jennings looked at Keefer, then back at Stewart. "Why even fly out of here? Last we heard, if we flew to Ottawa, we'd get shot down. Has that changed?"

Keefer looked at the maps again, trying to make sense of the circles and lines and the growing stain from the drop of coffee seeping into the map paper. "They don't know where to fly to yet."

Stewart was impressed.

"In that case, why fly anywhere?" Jennings asked Keefer since Stewart had not answered.

Knowing what the world was willing to do to Peaks Bay to neutralize the spread of infection, Keefer had a different perspective on the circles and flight paths on the map. The coffee stain was still spreading between the fibres of the paper.

"Nukes," Keefer said, barely audible. "They're going to nuke the cities." His voice trembled slightly.

Stewart looked at Keefer with renewed interest. "Mr. Keefer, was it? You seem to be more than you let on." Then, turning to Jennings, he continued, "Your friend is right. Phillips was the only person who could fly the Cormorant, and he's not with us anymore." Stewart drummed his fingers on top of the map. "He didn't like that we had to cull our group down to . . . let's call it . . . the essential personnel."

Jennings sprang up, slamming his fists on the table. Stewart flinched back. The two soldiers with the rifles also jerked up, their guns again aimed at Jennings.

Keefer stayed still in his chair, his muscles tight and ready to spring into action, as the room balanced on the tip of a sharp knife.

"You slaughtered civilians?!" Jennings' voice was low and rumbling. Before he could do or say anything else, he was kicked behind the knees and crumpled to the ground. The sergeant with the black beret peppered him with more kicks to his ribs.

"Okay, okay, stop!" Stewart shouted, coming around the table. "Remember, we need him."

"Nuking cities, killing civilians," Jennings coughed out, along with blood.

"I'm not the one nuking cities. But I'm not against it. There are no more people in those cities, only deadlies."

Jennings spat out a huge gob of blood and pulled himself to his knees.

"The UN even supports it. Last we heard, it was a major debate in Geneva. Something about Russia wanting to nuke the entire East Coast—opportunistic bastards—but the Americans warned them that doing so would start World War Three, and they would respond with their own nukes on Russia. The last info I got was they were nearing a compromise to nuke only Quebec's major centres."

Stewart paused to let the information sink in.

"Why kill the civilians?" Jennings growled, his fists tight as tree knots.

Stewart stood in front of the coffeemaker again, but turned back to Jennings without pouring a fresh cup. "We had two other survivors show up from a shithole Labrador town where this virus came from. They got everyone all riled up about being immune and having a cure. I'm a realist. We couldn't save everyone, and keeping the whole group here would have led to trouble. But technically, we didn't kill anyone. We simply sent them back out in the wild. It's not our fault they couldn't protect themselves."

The words meandered through Keefer's mind, slowed by the focus-altering guns pointed at him and the idea that nuclear bombs were scheduled to rain down on them. But the words started to take hold: *Labrador. Shithole town. Virus. Immune. Cure.*

"Wait, what? Did you say someone from Labrador showed up here?"

"Yeah, some town called . . . what was it again?"

"Peaks Bay." The name escaped Keefer's mouth.

"That's it. That's the place." Stewart looked at Keefer, annoyed. "You are sharp, buddy; I'll give you that. Unfortunately for you, you are useless to me—kill him."

A soldier stepped forward, aiming his rifle at Keefer.

"Wait! He's also from Peaks Bay," shouted Jennings. The soldier paused when Stewart held up his hand.

"Is he now?"

"He is. He was there when the virus arrived in Peaks Bay."

His life was on the line. Show value or die. "I . . ." Keefer swallowed. "I was there." He couldn't go as far as telling them about Abelone and her immunity, but he knew enough to show value. "I was there when the virus arrived. And I spoke to people from the ship it arrived on."

Stewart walked around the table, showing intrigue at this new revelation.

A gunshot echoed through the camp. Keefer winced and looked down at his body. No pain. No holes. He looked around. Everyone in the command tent was looking around too.

"What the fuck was that?" Stewart shouted.

Faint yelling came from the other end of the camp.

"It came from the mess tent. Something is happening over there." The soldier behind them said, looking out the tent flaps.

"Braggs. That stupid gorilla better not be wasting ammunition on deadlies again," Stewart said as he hurried from the command tent, the sergeant in tow. "Bring those two. Make sure they don't do anything stupid."

32

GOODBYE, KEEFER

A belone's throat was dry. The thick, warm air of the late afternoon made it hard to swallow. Shadows from the window tent flaps were getting longer as she sat in a chair, staring at Dirk and Karen. They were huddled with Braggs and his men talking near the passed-out St-Pierre, his hand still pinned to the table by the giant knife. She raced through her memories of Peaks Bay, trying to figure out how Dirk had survived. He seemed immune like her. He had scared her when they'd met at the police station, but now she was beyond scared. The way he positioned himself as a saviour to these men—if one could call them that—shook her to her core.

She glanced at Martel lying on the floor. His eyes were closed, and his breathing laboured, but the thick towels had stopped the bleeding. The teens sat on each side of the leather-clad doctor, tending to him.

A shout from outside got everyone's attention. The shout came again a few seconds later. Someone was calling Braggs' name angrily. The gunshot must have attracted the others. She wasn't sure if that was a good thing, but she was relieved Keefer might be on his way to help.

"Here we go," growled Braggs. "I now need to explain to the lieutenant that you can't handle sitting still." There was a tone in Braggs' voice. Not so much that he was sorry for having shot Martel, but that he disliked having to explain himself.

"Bring her." He pointed to Abelone. A soldier jumped at his command and grabbed her by the arm, pulling her up. He ordered a soldier to watch the kids, Martel, and St-Pierre. Everyone else followed him.

"Don't do anything unless I tell you to." She heard Braggs whisper to the group as they exited the tent.

The sun wasn't overhead anymore, but it still felt like walking into an oven. A group of six men was heading their way. They converged near the pink Hummer. Keefer and Jennings were part of the group, in a way. Her heart sank when she realized, like her, they were being escorted rather than being part of the group.

The infected milled outside the camp, and when one of them spotted them inside the compound, it let out a shriek, reanimating the whole infected mob. They rushed to the gate.

For a moment, everyone stared at the gate to make sure it would hold—it did.

The group's attention was brought back to the uninfected when Keefer shouted, "Piece of shit!" He exploded forward and was on Dirk Danerson before any of the soldiers could stop him.

He knocked Dirk to the ground with a punch to the cheek. Abelone felt a rush of satisfaction at the sight of Dirk's cheek splitting open and spilling blood. Keefer's momentum had him land on Dirk, straddling his body. His arms flailed up and down, raining punches on him. "You killed them!" Punch. "Reilly!" Punch. "Ryan!" Punch. "Timmy!" The violent attack did not make Abelone look away.

The onslaught stopped when Braggs kicked Keefer in the face. His thick military boot bent Keefer's nose sideways. Keefer fell backwards, blood gushing out.

"No!" Abelone screamed. She jumped to Keefer's side and cupped his nose, applying pressure to stop the bleeding.

"Kill him!" Dirk shouted, his face reddening under the dark bruises already forming on his face.

"Hold on!" Stewart stepped in. "I decide who lives and dies here." He looked at the group, asserting his authority. By the way he spoke, it was clear he'd had their loyalty up to this point. "Mr. Danerson, I know you are valuable to us. But don't presume to think you control us."

Dirk spat out a tooth. "My blood is your salvation. I am the Chosen One. I was sent here to save you." He opened up his arms with dirt and blood-stained palms facing the sky. "Kill *him*." His voice was low. "To be part of my flock. You must kill *him*."

Abelone put her arm over Keefer, but there was something in the way Dirk said *him*. He wasn't referring to Keefer anymore.

Braggs looked at Dirk, then at Lieutenant Stewart. The lieutenant took a step back, also realizing the conversation had shifted. "Wait a minute . . . Braggs . . . I'm your commanding officer. I'm the one who had the idea to jury-rig the helicopter with extra gas tanks so we can get to safety." Stewart eyed Braggs and Danerson fearfully.

"You're also the one who shot Captain Phillips. The only pilot we had," Braggs said. "You wanted to be in charge, so you killed him."

"You what?" Jennings blurted.

Braggs looked at Jennings with disinterest. "We don't need you either . . . sir." He raised his rifle to shoot Jennings, a hint of satisfaction pulling at his lips.

"Don't!" shouted Stewart. "Jennings can pilot the chopper." Abelone wondered if Stewart thought revealing that would somehow spare him.

Braggs' finger rested on the trigger as he stared at Jennings. He nodded a few times before shifting his body and aiming the rifle at Lieutenant Stewart instead. "Thanks for the reminder."

Lieutenant Stewart's head exploded as three bullets impacted his face a fraction of a second apart. Abelone stymied a yelp and wrapped her arms tighter around Keefer.

Dirk was smiling. As were the soldiers, except for the sergeant with the black beret. He was clearly in the Stewart fan club. He kept his rifle down. It didn't matter. At least six bullets hit him all at once. His body spun and fell face-first on the gravel, a few feet from Stewart.

Braggs and two of his men aimed their guns at Keefer and Abelone next. Abelone tightened her grip on Keefer and held her breath.

"Stop!" It was Jennings this time. "You kill them, I don't fly the chopper."

Braggs looked at him suspiciously.

"You're going to fly the chopper if you want to get out of the nuke's blast radius."

Despite her life being a mere trigger-pull away from ending, Abelone registered the word *nuke*.

"I won't. You'll probably kill me as soon as we land somewhere, anyway."

Braggs shrugged, indicating Jennings might be right. They stared at each other, neither seeming sure where to go from here.

Dirk walked up to the hulking Braggs and whispered something. Dirk's face was swollen like a purple balloon from Keefer's beating.

Braggs nodded. He gave hushed orders to two of his men, and they darted to the mess tent. Abelone looked around nervously. Things were bad, but a feeling that things were going to get worse crept up her spine. Within moments, the soldiers came back, dragging one of the teens screaming. Braggs pointed to the stairs leading up to the scaffold over the camp entrance. The men dragged the boy to the top. The infected stopped clawing at the gate and started clawing at the air toward the men and teenager.

That feeling was burrowing into her brain, making her muscles twitch.

"Now . . . let's negotiate again." Braggs walked away from Jennings without looking at him. "You fly the chopper, or these people die."

"Like I said, you're going to kill me anyway once we get to wherever we get to."

"Maybe." He signalled his men.

The feeling inside Abelone found the central core controlling her panic. She stood up, screaming, "No!" But it made no difference.

The soldiers pushed the teen over the edge. The boy flailed his arms as he fell. He landed on three infected who didn't have the coordination to catch him. Shrieks and hisses reached a feverish pitch as dozens of hands and teeth tore at the boy. His hair was pulled out, his eyes were gouged, and chunks of flesh and muscle splashed in the air. It was so quick, there was nothing left of the boy to be reanimated a minute later when the infected all stood back up and returned to assaulting the gate.

"Monster!" Abelone screamed.

Jennings leapt toward Braggs, who was ten feet away. He never reached him. The gauntlet of soldiers separating them knocked him down with the butts of their rifles and followed up with kicks.

"Stop, stop, stop," Braggs said coolly. "We need him alive if we are going to fly out of here." The big man walked back to Jennings. He pointed to Keefer next, and the two soldiers on the scaffold rushed down to get him.

They grabbed him by the armpits and dragged him up. Abelone punched one of them in the plexus, bending him over in pain. The other let go of Keefer and hit her with his rifle, crumpling her to the ground. She didn't notice the pain, muted as it was by her fear of what was coming. From her fetal position in the dirt, all she could do was watch, water pooling in her eyes, fireworks of angry neurons erupting in her brain.

***

Keefer's vision was blurry, and the crushed cartilage in his nose forced him to breathe through his mouth. His upper lip was bleeding, and the copper of blood mixed with dirt made the air taste like refuse. He tried to resist the two men dragging him, but all he managed to do was kick up dust from the dry gravel.

Dirk took over when they reached the scaffolding. He struck Keefer on the forehead with his pistol grip, opening up another gash that spilled red blood. There was a flash of pain, and for a second, all the other pain disappeared, but it all came washing back, and his knees wobbled. Dirk dragged him up the stairs.

He's going to throw me over!

At the top of the scaffold, Dirk pressed the pistol barrel to Keefer's bloody forehead and leaned into him. "You are probably wondering how I survived." He smiled haughtily. "By the grace of God, that's how." His eyes burned with madness. "And He has rewarded me with the glorious opportunity to rid the world of you."

The moment he spotted Dirk walking toward them in the camp yard, the pieces had come together. The tracks in the ash, the pickup truck at the farm, the sniper shot at the military gate. Every trap and sabotage they'd faced along the way was Dirk. Somehow, he'd survived Sergeant Riley's bite—like Abelone had survived her own. As for surviving the napalm, he knew it had to be the police-station bomb shelter. It was the same as the hospital shelter. He'd seen the hatch and heard the stories. That was how Dirk had survived.

"The bomb shelter . . ." Keefer barely managed to say aloud. He was unsteady. His breathing was shallow, and blood got into his eyes from the gash on his head. He tried to look for Abelone in the group below. *It can't end this way.*

"Bingo!" said Dirk, a look of glee on his face. "And now I get to finish what I started."

It can't end this way!

Keefer grabbed Dirk's pistol, but he was slow and weak. All he did was pull Dirk's arm toward his chest.

The gun went off.

The bullet tore through his leather jacket, penetrated skin and muscle and barely missed a lung before exiting his back in a jet of blood.

Keefer remembered playing with his mother and father in their backyard as a kid. Tigger as a puppy. Abelone's face after she scared him silly in the ambulance. He remembered the punch she gave him, which knocked him to his ass. Sadness hit as he saw Tigger lying in a pool of blood at Ted's Taxi and Delivery and grumpy old Moe staring up at him with an axe lodged in his head, his eyes rolled back.

A scream from far away snapped his mind back to the present, but his body was floating away. The blue sky hovered above him, with no clouds in sight. He'd never felt this light.

A silhouette of a man looked down at him. *Who is that?* The man had long, slicked-back, dirty blond hair and held a pistol. Keefer felt like he was flying away from that man, but then the dark realization hit him. *I'm not flying away—I'm falling!*

Keefer fell backwards in slow motion, but picked up speed. He landed flat on top of an infected, breaking her neck on impact. She cushioned his fall, but it didn't change anything. A dozen other infected were on him instantaneously. They piled on, teeth gnashing at every part of his body, grey scabby hands grabbing onto whatever leather garment they could.

Keefer tried to roll away but was blocked by the multitude of legs. He screamed, and his broken nose spurted a fountain of blood. He tried to push the infected off, but the pile was too heavy, and a piercing pain rushed to his brain from his chest. He'd been shot.

He felt bites on his legs and arms, but no ripping of skin. The leather was protecting him. A cocoon of safety. The light of hope was snuffed out as soon as he felt the first bite on his neck. Teeth piercing skin and ripping deep into muscle. A second one followed on his exposed right wrist and another on his left hand where his leather glove had been ripped off. He barely managed to bring up his hands to cover his face and head with his arms. The most painful bite happened on the back of his head, below the hairline. The teeth went as deep as bone; he was sure his head profile would now look like a half-eaten slice of pizza.

His heart was pounding, circulating blood at a frantic pace. All he could think about was the virus—the words *Grey Virus* flashed across his inner movie theatre screen. *The Grey Virus—has a nice ring to it.* His blood moved at eight kilometres per hour. That fact from med school materialized randomly. It meant the Grey Virus would reach his brain in less than a minute. Adrenaline kicked in and masked some of his pain, like paint over rotten wood. He was grateful, but he knew it didn't matter at this point.

His bullet wound was the first thing to stop hurting. The pain numbed and disappeared, yet he was still acutely aware of the hole in his chest. The bites on his hands were next. The pain simply stopped. In a matter of seconds, all the pain was gone. The afflictions remained, but their torture had disappeared. At that realization, his nerves caught fire, and every millimetre of his body exploded. He felt like his brain was frying from the inside. The burning sensation intensified as the virus burrowed deeper into his encephalon and came into contact with more and more brain matter. Neurons, axons and dendrites were fighting a losing battle as the virus crawled into his body's central computer.

His vision started going black. Was it the virus taking over his optical nerve, or was it simply shutting down once the brain was taken over? His ears rang until all sound stopped being transmitted to his brain. Keefer knew it was over when the infected stopped biting him. A split second later, his consciousness stopped. There was nothing. He was dead.

33

RISE OF THE GREY

Thirty seconds went by; it could have been thirty minutes or thirty days. Benjamin Keefer had no way of knowing. His mind was unplugged, his heart perfectly still, dead by any measure.

The stillness in his heart was broken, unexpectedly, like a shooting star appearing in the night sky. Then another, and another, until it became a full-on meteor shower. The spasms rippled throughout his cardiac muscles, erratic at first, but evening out into regular heartbeats. His central pump pushed thicker, darker blood through his intricate network of veins, arteries and capillaries.

Benjamin Keefer opened his eyes. He gasped and drew in a long breath of air, filling his lungs to the edge of bursting. The air felt thicker and not as refreshing. The darkness that covered his vision faded quickly, pushed away by the flow of blood to his head and the air in his lungs. Sensory input bombarded his brain, and it immediately started to hurt. The sun was too bright, and the noise too deafening.

He squinted to limit the sunlight attacking his retinas and made out the overexposed sky. He squinted harder, and the light became somewhat bearable. Keefer focused on the chaotic hubbub: shrieks and hisses, bodies slamming against metal, feet dragging on gravel, multiple teeth gnashing at empty air. He could even hear his heartbeat—he was alive.

Through all the noise, further out beyond it, he heard shouts, followed by gunfire. Voices screaming about finding an escaped teen. Something about St-Pierre being awake and fighting. The name was familiar. There was a crescendo of gunfire before the scene ended when a woman's voice pleaded for people not to kill the boy.

Abelone... that is Abelone's voice.

Memories rushed back to him. Dirk Danerson had a gun to his head. He fought back. Got shot and fell backwards, outside the compound, right in the arms of... the infected.

How am I alive? Keefer remembered the infected tearing at his body, biting him. His hands quickly slid up his pelvis, stomach and torso, looking for injuries. His leather gear had protected him from most bites. When his hands reached his neck, his heart sank. His fingers and palms traced at least three deep crevices where skin and muscle used to be.

How am I alive?

His hands continued exploring. His face had been spared. He remembered covering it with his arms, but one of his ears was missing its tip. Keefer stretched out his hands in front of his squinting eyes. The silhouette of his hands took shape, and details slowly materialized. He had a half-dozen bites, and his left hand was missing a pinky finger, severed at the joint with the palm. He squinted harder to see them better, but no matter how hard he squinted, their colour remained the same—they were grey. He was Grey.

An infected tripped over Keefer's outstretched legs and fell face-first on the road beside him. Even in the blinding light, Keefer saw the infected's reaction when it looked at him. Its black eyes recognized him as not one of them. Its shriek of arousal and alarm made Keefer hiccup in surprise.

Keefer bound up into a crouch, surprising both himself and the infected with his speed. His fist landed on the infected's jaw, crushing it to pieces, changing the shriek to a low gargle. He grabbed the infected—previously an average-sized man—and, in one spin, launched the body off the road into the ditch ten feet away. He looked at his hands, surprised by his strength.

The commotion attracted another infected, which ran toward him. Keefer didn't wait. He closed the distance in the blink of an eye and grabbed it by the throat, trapping its shriek in its larynx. In response, the infected grabbed Keefer by his own throat and squeezed. Keefer felt his cartilage crack, but did not feel any pain. The thick air continued in and out of his lungs. The infected squeezed harder. *Stop!* he thought, but the infected continued. His larynx creaked.

"Stop . . ." he whispered, his vision narrowing on the infected. But the infected did not listen and pulled at his throat in an attempt to steal his voice box.

"Stop!" he said louder, and the words escaped his shrinking voice passageway. Keefer squeezed his own hand and its larynx and esophagus crumpled as easily as a sheet of paper into a ball. He let go of the mangled throat, grabbed the infected by the shoulders, and threw the body aside like he had the other. Keefer regretted it right away. Unused to his new strength, the infected flew further than intended and landed on the windshield of a car. A spiderweb of cracks spread across the windshield, and the car alarm came alive like a barking dog when a doorbell rang. The two dozen infected at the gate turned, looking for the source of the noise. Their black eyes locked onto him instead. He stood still, and for two heartbeats, they assessed him. Maybe they would think he was one of them—they did not.

Their shrieks echoed in unity and they ran toward Keefer. Newfound strength or not, he knew they would tear him apart like they did to . . . *I turned like Hector!* The revelation stunned him.

He leapt to avoid the first infected that reached him. To his surprise, he landed almost ten feet back. He looked at the compound, thinking of Abelone as another infected lunged for him. He grabbed it by the shoulder and deflected it head-first into the asphalt. The larger group was almost upon him. He leapt again, this time over the car with the screeching alarm. He ran. Unsure where to go, he headed down a field toward a small residential neighbourhood built along a road bordering the military base.

***

Benjamin Keefer, Grey and alive, crouched motionless on the second-floor balcony of a two-storey duplex, watching the street. The paved road spanned the little neighbourhood of military housing; it was quiet and showed no signs of life. He'd easily outrun the infected chasing him. Testing his new jumping abilities, he'd bound up one floor to his current hiding spot. By the time the infected reached the neighbourhood, he was already well hidden behind a BBQ, watching from his perch. The infected rummaged along the street for ten minutes, but finding nothing, they'd dispersed between the houses.

He waited as the sun set and thought back to how easy it had been to crush the infected's throat or to jump to this balcony.

What is happening to me?

He inspected his hands, counting the bites and assessing how deep each was. None of the wounds hurt, and all had scabbed over already. More incredibly, he barely felt the gunshot wound. It was still there, but the entry and exit points were already crusting over. He wasn't feeling any pain.

Keefer felt his face, then his nose. It was out of place but didn't hurt. He turned to the balcony door to look at the angle of his nose in the glass and came face to face with an infected—grey-faced and black-eyed—staring right at him. He fell backward, ready to pounce off the balcony. The infected recoiled as he did. He watched the grey creature in the reflection. He shifted his position; it shifted the same way.

That's me.

Keefer moved closer to the glass. He was one of them, not quite the shrieking monsters he'd been killing since they arrived in Peaks Bay, but close. His skin was ash grey, and his hair had turned charcoal. He wondered how that was possible. How could the virus be altering his genetic makeup so quickly?

Observing himself in the glass, he thought of Hector in the bunker and the person who had saved Abelone in the church in Forestville. He'd thought they were infected, but maybe they were different. They must have been like him. His breathing accelerated, and the short, shallow breaths made his head spin. *Is this a step before I turn completely?*

His thoughts were spinning when he heard a woman screaming. *Abelone?!* He turned and looked up the street. It wasn't Abelone. A young woman was running, holding a bag of what looked like food. A few car lengths behind her were three infected, hissing and shrieking their excitement. Whether or not he was turning himself, he had to help her.

He leapt over the balcony railing, not considering the height until he was falling. Panic overtook him, and he flailed his arms and legs in a useless attempt to slow his descent. He crashed on the sidewalk, rolling on his shoulder and ending in a crouch.

Two of the infected spotted him, broke off their pursuit of the woman, and ran in his direction instead. They collided with Keefer at breakneck speed. Keefer tried to slam his fist into one of the infected, but he and the infected were moving too fast. He missed and went spinning. They all went down like bowling pins. The two infected grabbed at him, grey, bloodied fingers trying to rip his leather gear off.

Keefer rolled onto one of them and hammer-fisted the grey forehead. He heard the skull crack and felt it soften. He hammer-fisted two more times until it caved in, and the infected stopped moving.

The other infected wrapped its arms around his waist and bit down on his lower back. Keefer's leather jacket protected him. The infected tried again, this time finding skin between the bottom of the jacket and the top of the pants. The teeth sank in, and his skin ripped open, but no pain came rushing forth.

Keefer pushed himself up, overpowering the infected and knocking himself loose. As he spun, he kicked it in its chest, laying it flat on its back and with a short hop, he crashed his boot into the centre of its face, squishing it as easily as a watermelon. He turned his head away from the disconnected eyeballs and brain matter squeezing out from beneath his boot.

Checking the bite mark, his hand came back partially covered in darkish blood. Still, he felt nothing.

The woman!

He turned in time to see the third infected enter a boarded-up bungalow, presumably where the woman sought shelter. He ran toward it.

To his surprise, as he reached the house, the infected came crashing back out through the boarded window, landing right in front of him. It looked up at him, hissing in anger. Without hesitation, he took a few steps for momentum and kicked the grey head like a soccer ball. The blow almost decapitated it and spun the infected over itself. It did not move again.

Keefer ran through the door. Inside was dark, with most of the windows boarded. Slivers of dusk light came through the door and smashed window. His eyes adjusted quickly. Shadows disappeared, and he could see every detail. His vision became sharp, sharper than he'd ever had. It was the opposite of disorienting. His vision had been suboptimal even in the low evening light.

He took stock of where he was: living room with couch, hallway in the back leading to a kitchen and other rooms, open door with stairs to a basement. The hair on his arms and neck stood on end, followed by a tingling in the back of his mind as he felt words that were not his: *Get out!*

A green shape moved in the corner of his eye. He turned to intercept it, but the man was too fast. He slammed into Keefer below the ribs. *I won't let you hurt them!* There was that feeling again, not really words but feelings expressing words that flashed through his mind. Keefer shook his head, trying to shake off the thoughts that weren't his own as he slammed into the wall. He fell to one knee, leaving an imprint of his body in the drywall. He looked up and tried to speak. His voice came out hoarse and deep, "Wait, I'm here to—"

The man swung a tall ceramic lamp and shattered it across Keefer's shoulder, knocking him down.

"Stop!" Keefer hardly recognized his voice. "I'm not—"

He rolled away as the man tried to spear him with the remaining lamp pole.

"Enough!" Keefer pounced up and grabbed the man by the shoulders. His momentum carried them both into a shelf. He was still shocked by his strength and let go, hoping he hadn't hurt the man. He hadn't. The man spun, stepped one leg across Keefer's, pulled him over his hips and judo-tossed him. Keefer crashed into the frame of the basement doorway and tumbled head over foot down the rough wooden stairs into the darkness below.

"No!" the man shouted. Keefer realized the voice sounded like his. *What have I done?* There it was again, thoughts flashing through his mind that weren't his. He didn't have time to dwell on it as he hit the cement wall at the bottom of the stairs with a thud. No pain—still. There was no light in the unfinished basement, but he could see every detail of the room clearly: storage shelves with boxes, a hot water tank in a corner, a few old bicycles stacked along a wall, a knick-knack-filled workbench, a bunch of sleeping cots, and in the middle of the room, huddled together, stood a group of people surrounding the woman Keefer had tried to save outside.

Survivors! He stared at them, unblinking.

No! A rush of fear burst into his mind. "Stay away from them!" The hoarse scream came from up the stairs. The man in the green sweater bound down the stairs, landing on all fours like a wild animal. With his back to the wall, Keefer looked at the man closely. He was wearing a green high school football sweatshirt and had . . . ash-coloured skin. His hair was charcoal, and his eyes were as dark and piercing as those Keefer had seen in the window glass when looking at himself.

Keefer stood with his palms out to show he meant no harm. "It's okay, I'm not dangerous. I won't bite." It seemed like the right thing to say, but he realized that under other circumstances, it might have been ironic.

The man took a step back, unsure of what to make of things.

Keefer was at least a foot taller than the man and also wider. It dawned on him that the person in front of him wasn't a man at all. He was a boy—a teenage boy—fifteen or sixteen at most. And he was . . . like him, they were . . . Grey.

Don't hurt them. Don't hurt my sisters.

Keefer shook his head; those weren't his thoughts. They seemed to be the boy's thoughts. Could it be? He thought to himself in response. *I'm not going to hurt them. I'm not going to hurt anyone.* He was about to vocalize those thoughts, but the boy's posture relaxed.

Keefer moved slowly. "I'm Benjamin. I won't hurt anyone," he said to the group this time.

34

NEED TO HELP THEM

The survivors sat in a semi-circle with Keefer facing them. They spent ten minutes explaining who they were and how they got holed up in the basement of this small house. The whole time, he kept thinking about Abelone and the others in the compound. But he was also astounded these people weren't fazed by his appearance.

The house belonged to Joe and Fran, an elderly couple. They'd started taking in survivors by the third day of the event, which they called the start of the infection. Two young women were a couple from down the street, Alicia was a business lady from out of town, and a man with an injured foot was from the duplex Keefer had hidden in. Lastly, there were twin girls, Maddie and Ellie Buckner, along with their older brother, Eduard. Their mother had been bitten on the second day of the event. They weren't sure where their father was. Eduard had had the good judgement to lock his sisters in the washroom when he saw his mother turn. He had tried to help his mom but was bitten. Fran's voice cracked as she told this part of the story. Keefer looked at Eduard. He was standing a few feet behind his sisters, watching over them, trying to stay stone-faced, but Keefer could see the quivering in his lip.

I couldn't save my mom. There it was again, thoughts that weren't his own. Keefer looked at Eduard. They had to be his thoughts. But how? Keefer tried answering.

It wasn't your fault. Your mom, that is . . . at least you saved your sisters.

The boy flinched and shook his head as if trying to tap out water from his ear. He took a step back, scared, and his mind went blank.

Fran continued, oblivious to the exchange. The girls survived because of Eduard. He'd woken up Grey right when his mother was trying to break into the washroom. Not realizing his strength, he'd crushed her skull with a lamp.

Keefer looked up at Eduard. "I'm sorry about your mother."

Eduard didn't respond.

"Our brother doesn't talk much anymore," said one of the twins. Keefer wasn't sure if it was Maddie or Ellie. Both twins looked at their brother and reached for his hands. The boy accepted them warmly.

"Imagine our surprise when, a few days ago, these two little blonde girls came dawdling down the road with this infected-looking boy holding their hands," Fran said, smiling warmly at the twins.

"There was no way we could leave them out there," Alicia jumped in as she gave the man with the injured ankle a chastising look.

Keefer looked at Eduard again. He was still holding his sisters' hands. "Have you met any others like . . . us?"

The boy didn't respond.

"We haven't seen anyone else like Eduard," one twin answered.

"Until now," the other twin added.

"Well, I have." Keefer's admission got through Eduard's wall.

His black eyes opened bigger and focused on Keefer. *You have?* He hadn't spoken, so how did Keefer hear him?

"I didn't as much meet them as I saw them," Keefer continued. "I've seen a few, in fact. A handful. One helped me and my friend—" Keefer thought of Abelone in the church in Forestville. He had to leave. "He helped protect us."

"My brother protects us," one twin added.

"Yeah, he's almost a black belt in judo," the other blonde girl added.

"Ah, that explains how you threw me around up there," Keefer said, trying to smile to make Eduard comfortable but stopped, realizing his broken nose and ash-coloured skin were probably not that comforting.

"And what about you? What's your story?" a woman asked.

"I'm from Labrador." He debated how much to tell them. Did they even know the virus made landfall there? He didn't have time to tell stories. He needed to go help Abelone.

Not having felt any physical sensation over the last hour or so, Keefer was surprised when his stomach clenched in a pang of hunger. The pain came and went, but it surprised him nonetheless, and he grimaced.

"What's wrong?" asked the man with the injured ankle. "Are you turning?"

"Turning?"

"Into the mindless version of those... things." The man was genuinely scared.

Keefer thought for a second. He didn't feel like he was losing control of his mind. He had this feeling in his stomach. "I don't think so."

A vise squeezed his intestines again and made him groan. It subsided as quickly as it had appeared.

The man got up, hobbled over to the wall and picked up a pitchfork leaning on a chair.

"Whoa!" Keefer's hoarse voice came out louder than he'd wanted. Everyone backed up nervously. "Don't do anything stupid, buddy." Keefer was keenly aware everyone was eyeing him suspiciously. "I feel fine. My stomach is bothering me, that's all."

The man pointed the pitchfork at Keefer, shaking it. "How do we know... how do we know you aren't changing?"

"*Simon, calme-toi,*" Alicia said.

He looked at her. "You've protected Eduard since he showed up, and now you're protecting this guy?" The man pointed the fork at Alicia, then back to Keefer.

"Those things killed my wife! They killed everyone I knew. Everyone you knew!"

Keefer couldn't help but sympathize. That was how he'd felt up to now. Infected needed to be killed if people were going to survive. He remembered how he felt when he saw the Grey in the Forestville church. Would he trust Eduard and himself if roles were reversed?

But Keefer was not going to hurt them, no matter what. He was not dangerous. The thought slapped him in the face like cold water on a sleepy mind. Was Abelone right all along? Maybe not every infected had to die.

His thoughts were interrupted when Eduard snatched the pitchfork from Simon's hands. He splintered the pitchfork shaft over his knee and threw it to the ground.

"He's not turning into those monsters," Eduard's voice was hoarse, but higher pitched than Keefer's. "He's hungry. Like I was after turning Grey."

The group stared at Eduard, stunned that he'd talked.

"Yeah, Eduard ate everything in our kitchen after he stopped Momma from hurting us," one twin said.

"He was really hungry," the other girl added.

The group looked at Keefer, hoping for an answer.

"I do feel hungry. That must be it." The vise squeezed again, and this time, he was sure his intestines would burst.

"He needs lots of food," Eduard clarified. "After I ate, I was fine and could eat normally afterwards."

"Well, you can't eat our food," Fran said. "We barely have enough to feed the group for a few more days."

"There are tons of houses up the street we haven't scavenged yet," Joe said to Keefer and the group.

"That should do. I need to go." He stumbled up the stairs. "Stay here until I get back." *Am I really coming back?*

"Wait." Eduard's hoarse voice made him stop on the first stair. "You're not coming back."

"I have to help my friends." Keefer realized the boy had heard—or felt—his thoughts.

"But we need you too," Fran interjected, realizing what the exchange was about.

"Are you sure your friends are still alive?" someone else asked.

"Please stay. We need you to stay with us," one twin said in a soft, pleading voice.

Keefer crouched down in front of her. "Your brother will protect you. I wish I could stay, but I have people who need me. They are in danger, too."

The group went quiet, listening to Keefer and the little girl. Their hopes rested on her innocent plea for help.

"If you stay together as a group, you can protect each other, and like I said, you have Eduard to watch over you."

"I know that—" The girl paused. "We lost our mommy and daddy, and my big brother will protect us." She smiled at her big brother, who smiled back, lips clenched. "But he lost his mommy and daddy, too. Who's going to protect him?" Her question sank deep into Keefer.

Her twin, on cue, kept the pressure on. "You're like Eduard."

"Grey," the other chimed in.

"Yes, you're Grey. Like Eduard."

"You need each other."

Keefer looked between the twins, with tears pooling in their eyes. *I can't stay. I have to save Abelone.*

"Maddie, Ellie, leave him be," Eduard stepped in, acting grown up, but Keefer could see the tears lining his grey lower eyelid too. "He has people he loves who need him."

The girls surprised Keefer by jumping in his arms and hugging him. "Please come back and help us after—we need you too."

To his dismay, he didn't feel the warmth of their little bodies in his arms. He consoled himself with the thought that he could feel the pressure of their hug. He had trouble letting go, but he did and addressed the group. "If I can come back, I will. But you have to leave here when the sun rises. Pack up all your food and head north or west, if possible, all the way to Ottawa."

"Why? Aren't we safer here?" one lady inquired.

"Before I left the military compound, I heard the area will be . . . bombed." Somehow, it made it more palatable if he didn't say what kind of bomb.

"But why, aren't we safer—"

"Just listen to me!" Keefer said louder than he wanted. His guttural voice echoed through the basement. The girls let go, ran to their brother, and hid behind his legs.

"We've heard from other people who were heading west that it's safe in La Tuque. Our neighbours had family up there and took off the day before last," Fran said.

"Yes, start there. Leave as soon as possible," Keefer agreed. "Move at daylight. Please." His voice was calm again, more under control. "Wherever you go, avoid Quebec City. Avoid Montreal."

He moved to the stairs and paused. "Take care of the group. You'll be fine," he said, looking at Eduard. Then he left. The group erupted in debate about whether to listen to him. The one voice he could not hear was Eduard's; he had gone quiet again. Keefer pushed it all out of his mind. He needed to get to Abelone and the others, but her voice kept rattling in his head. She kept saying they had to try to save everyone.

***

Food packaging and tin cans littered the kitchen floor around Keefer, who sat on a wooden chair. He had never felt so famished. He ate everything from cookies and dry cereal to canned foods. Nothing heated. Within twenty minutes, he'd eaten everything he could find that didn't have mould on it—well, not too much mould, anyway.

He sat at the table, leaning on his elbows, deep in thought in the dark. His metabolism had to be accelerated, which explained his strength and speed. What he didn't understand was why he didn't feel pain and why he and Eduard hadn't gone fully infected. And he'd given up trying to understand how the hell they could hear each other's thoughts. He knew one thing for sure: he was infected, Eduard was infected, Hector had been infected and the man in Forestville, too. But they weren't *like* the infected, they were . . . Grey. He didn't know how else to refer to it.

He had no answers. It was all too crazy. He stuffed the last processed cake in his mouth and stood up. Now that the hunger had been fed, he was thinking clearly again—he had to go back to the compound. He'd been gone for hours and was worried about Abelone and the others. Were they still alive? Had Braggs and his men finished fixing the helicopter to take off? He couldn't help thinking about the survivors down the street. He hoped they would listen. He wanted to help them, wanted to help Eduard. The twins were right. Who would take care of him?

35

I THINK, THEREFORE, YOU ARE

Abelone sat on a metal chair surrounded by shadows. Her hands and ankles zip-tied to her chair. Martel lay on the ground, unmoving, covered by her leather jacket, while the now brotherless teen was passed out and tied to his own chair. The coolness of the night made Abelone's bare arms prickle as she danced in and out of consciousness. Holding on to one of those moments of wakefulness, questions floated in her mind: *What time is it? Is Martel alive? Did Benjamin suffer?* This last thought roused her, and her vision crystalized. The animated voices of two soldiers pulled Abelone from her contemplation, and when they walked through the flap, she saw a faint orange glow. *Dawn.*

Abelone half-listened to their conversation as they loaded food from the table into boxes. She was more focused on the image of Keefer disappearing over the edge of the wall and Martel slowly dying beside her, but out of reach.

"If I'm going to get nuked, I want it to be on a full stomach."

Nuked? Abelone's focus was now solely on the men. Her thoughts swirled. The Geneva Protocols never considered a nuclear option to eradicate a pandemic. Then again, no one ever considered a pandemic like this. She corrected herself; the Centers for Disease Control and Prevention in the US did. It was always tongue-in-cheek, though. They called it a Zombie Preparedness and Response Plan. It was a public relations campaign to get people thinking about what an actual world-impacting pandemic response would look like. That scenario always came down to the nuclear cleansing of large infected areas.

"When are they bombing?" Abelone croaked, her voice catching in her dry throat. She had to repeat herself to be heard. "When are they bombing?" she tried again.

The soldiers turned her way.

"Look at you, eavesdropping on us."

"Don't you worry your pretty blonde head. You'll probably be dead by the time it happens," one of the soldiers eating a ration pack of banana bread said, crumbs spilling out of his mouth. He walked over and crouched in front of her. He was young, in his early twenties maybe, and smelled of sweat and dirt. His hair, shaved short weeks ago, was now a prickly mess. He chewed with his mouth open as he looked Abelone over, his eyes lingering on the curves in her tank top.

"We probably have time to have some fun with you," the soldier said while putting a hand on her inner thigh.

A wave of repugnance washed over her, quickly followed by a tremble acknowledging her helplessness.

"Yeah, that would be nice," said the other soldier, "but Braggs was clear. Don't hurt her, and bring her to the command tent."

"Maybe later," the soldier said, stuffing the last piece of banana bread in his mouth. He took the knife from his belt, cut her restraints and stood back, aiming his rifle at her.

"Get up. You heard my friend here. The boss wants to see you."

A growing sliver of orange peeked over the horizon. Cool air tingled against her skin, but she wasn't cold. The sky was cloudless, and it was lining up to be another scorcher. The soldiers bustling about the helicopter were kicking up dry dust everywhere. She could feel the tension in the air; the idea of nuclear bombs dropping on their heads made everyone move with urgency.

"I don't care what he says. Handcuff Jennings to that fucking chopper until he fixes it." Braggs' voice boomed from the shadows inside the tent. Two soldiers hustled out, looking resigned.

"We should throw Jennings to the deadlies; he's too much trouble," the one holding the food box said.

"Zombies don't fly helicopters," the other stated, not joking.

"Zombies? You think they're zombies?" The other soldier laughed.

"Deadlies, whatever. Call them what you want. They aren't human anymore."

Despite every inch of her body hurting and having lost Keefer and probably losing Martel, Abelone couldn't help herself. Her epidemiological background was too strong to resist. "There's no such thing as zombies. These are people who are sick."

"People who are sick? Those people who are sick want to eat us, stupid bitch."

Abelone recognized the hostility in the man's voice but continued, "Those people are not eating other people; they're trying to infect others. That's how a virus spreads, from host to host."

The soldier behind her grabbed her by the shoulder and spun her around. "You should open your fucking eyes, blondie. Those people are not people. And they're not a virus. They are fucking monsters, and they are trying to kill us by eating us."

"When they want to kill, they tear people apart," she mumbled, realizing she was triggering the man.

"What? Speak up, bitch!" The soldier was in her face.

She cleared her throat. "When they want to kill, they don't try to eat you. They tear you apart. I've seen it—"

The pain was swift as the rifle butt hit her abdomen, and air whooshed from her lungs. Abelone fell to the ground, and pebbles dug into her leather-covered knees as she gasped.

"You are going to fucking stand there and argue the details about how those fucking things kill people? How they killed my friends, how they killed my family . . . how they killed my kids?"

The soldier had the barrel of the gun aimed at her head, his finger shaking near the trigger.

"Nelson, stop!" Braggs walked out of the command tent with Dirk and Karen in tow. "Put your rifle down."

The soldier did not move.

"Put your rifle down!"

The rifle went down, and Nelson took a step back, but Abelone could still see his hands shaking. He could snap at any moment.

"Ms. Jensen, seems like there was more to your little crew than you let on." Braggs extended his hand to help her up. She refused it and stood by herself. Her stomach muscles screamed from the blow, and she could feel a bruise forming.

Braggs smiled at her refusal of help. His massive frame towered over her despite her own height.

"Mr. Danerson here has filled me in on who you are."

"And who might that be?" Abelone said, eyeing Dirk distrustfully.

"Well, to put it in his words, you are the four horsemen of the apocalypse all rolled into one; you are the holder of the handbasket taking us to hell; you are death incarnate." He smiled a big, greasy smile.

Abelone didn't answer.

"You see? She doesn't deny it." Dirk pointed his finger at Abelone. "Cleanse us of her. Kill her, so we are done with her evil presence."

Braggs contemplated the instructions.

"Remember our deal, Braggs." It was Jennings. "You kill her or the doctor, and I don't fly you out of here." He was being escorted by the two soldiers from earlier.

"The Cormorant is ready to go. Those jury-rigged gas tanks will add seven hundred kilometres of flight capacity, so close to two thousand klicks in all. More than enough to get us to Thunder Bay, way past Ottawa. But if you break our deal, it doesn't matter how far the bird can fly because you won't have a pilot."

Braggs looked at his former captain dubiously.

Jennings looked exhausted, but his admonition was stern enough that Braggs let go of any intent to follow through with Dirk's request. "Don't worry. I'm living up to my side of the deal. You live up to yours."

Abelone looked from Braggs to Jennings. She was grateful he'd saved them, but wondered if the deal would be enough. Would Martel survive his injuries? Would they be able to get away from the nuclear blast?

"You made a deal to spare the witch?!" Dirk was livid. His stare was a spotlight of venom, which he swivelled from Braggs to Abelone. He took two stomping steps and slapped her, sending lightning to her brain. "She doesn't deserve to live."

Dirk turned his spotlight to Jennings. "You believe this man will hold his part of the deal? He'll probably crash us into the ground the first chance he gets."

"Not Jennings. He's too good for that. If we spare his little friends, he'll fly the eleven of us where we want." Braggs looked at Jennings.

Jennings nodded but gave Braggs a look of you-have-a-bigger-problem. Abelone felt Braggs tense. "There is one problem, though. With the extra fuel tanks, the chopper can only take nine people. And that will be tight."

Abelone had counted eleven people and looked at the ones near her to see if they realized not all of them could fly out of here.

"What?!" Nelson rushed up to Jennings. "You are not leaving any of us behind!"

She instinctively took a step back, knowing this soldier was already volatile.

"Calm down, Nelson." Braggs did the opposite and took a step closer.

"Calm down? You're going to let this asshole tell us who gets to survive or not?" His finger was on the rifle trigger.

"Don't worry, he's not telling us anything. I'm the one who decides who lives or not." Braggs' voice was eerily quiet yet satisfied.

Nelson turned back to Braggs and found himself staring down the barrel of the big man's golden gun. Abelone heard the firing pin click before the gunpowder exploded. The bullet penetrated Nelson's eye socket and erupted from the back of his head. His body fell backwards. Dead.

"That's ten." Braggs smiled at Jennings before looking at the others. "Nelson was cracking. He was becoming unstable, and we can't have that."

The other soldiers nodded but looked uneasy, knowing they were still one over the limit for the Cormorant.

Dirk walked up to Braggs. "We must do what we must do." His earlier tirade was forgotten. He was up to something; he had an air about him that said he would not be outdone. Dirk turned to Karen, who was still holding the yellow blood vial case. Abelone wondered if she had ever let it go since Ted's Taxi and Delivery. She seemed in a constant state of shock.

Dirk carefully reached out for the case. Their likeness was unmistakable when they stood face to face.

"I'll take that." He had to tug the box for Karen to let go. Her eyes were wide and unblinking, with dark circles under them.

"Dirk?" Karen was confused.

Abelone wanted to tell her to step away, but she tightened her jaw, fearing what was coming.

"Sometimes journeys have to come to an end, *cuz*." He smiled.

That was why she went with him. Abelone saw it clear as day: why Karen had left with Dirk, why she trusted him—they were cousins.

"Whose journey is coming to an end?" Karen still did not blink.

Dirk brought his pistol up to her chest.

"I love you, cuz." Nothing in his voice hinted he meant it. "Thanks for helping me get this far. You played a part in an important change for mankind."

"Dirk, I was happy to help. You know you've always been my favourite cousin." Karen smiled, still clueless.

The two gunshots echoed across the compound. The smell of burnt gunpowder filled the crisp morning air, and the deflagrations excited the infected at the gate from their walking slumbers. A handful of them got back to assaulting the gate.

Karen's body fell to the ground. She lay face up at Dirk's feet. He wiped a drop of blood from his cheek and looked at Braggs. "Nine."

Braggs smiled. It dawned on Abelone that Braggs and Dirk kept trying to out-smile each other. *Are they both insane?*

"Jennings, you better have that chopper ready to fly as soon as we are done loading the supplies." Braggs pointed one of his huge fingers at Jennings and ordered the soldiers guarding him to bring him to the chopper.

"As for you"—he turned to Abelone—"I want to know everything you know about the virus." He grabbed her by the shoulder. "And you'd better talk; I don't plan on being here once the nukes start falling in a few hours."

The big man shoved her into the arms of the soldiers standing beside her. "Make her talk. I want to know what she knows." An older soldier with an Iron Cross tattoo poking out of his collar nodded.

Despite the soldiers, Abelone was still most worried about Dirk. Being near him made all her senses alert and her neck hairs stand on end. The man was a complete psychopath. She looked at Karen lying in a pool of her own blood. Dirk had not given killing her a second thought. He hadn't even looked at his cousin's body since shooting her. He was staring at Abelone. If he wanted to kill her, he would kill her, no matter what Braggs' instructions were.

The sun was above the horizon and peeking over the treeline beyond the compound's nine-foot-tall cement walls. The heat was rising, and she was sweating as her heart pumped hard.

"Let's go, blondie." The soldier with the Iron Cross tattoo shoved her toward the mess tent.

Dirk walked beside her for a bit, then put his hand on her shoulder to redirect her to the compound's gate.

"Go get the doctor and the boy." He motioned to two of the soldiers trailing them. The men complied with no hesitation.

The smell of putrid flesh filled the air as they got closer to the gate. The infected had been in the oven-like heat for days, and their grey, sickly skin was rotting off their bodies.

Dirk took a deep breath. "Smell that? That's the smell of change. That's the smell of cleansing."

He let go of Abelone a few feet from the rattling gate where the infected were hissing and shrieking, trying to squeeze their hands through the fence. The soldiers stayed quiet.

"This creature right here"—Dirk pointed a preaching finger at Abelone—"she is the reason this plague is upon us. She admitted to me she brought the plague to Peaks Bay. She admitted to me she created the plague. She is the reason the apocalypse is upon us."

Abelone thought back to her exchange with Dirk at the police station. Her memory was uncertain, shaken by fatigue, pain and fear, but still. "I never told you anything like that. I told you I was—"

Dirk's hand struck out like a snake from under a rock. The open-hand blow caught her already split cheek, and blood trickled from the open wound. Water filled her eye on the side of the blow.

"Don't lie! You were on the ship that created this plague and released it into the world. There is no denying that!" Dirk's voice rose up and down like an evangelical preacher on Sunday morning TV. Abelone noticed the soldiers nodding, enthralled by his story.

Except one. A young man with slightly longer hair than the others. The young man cleared his throat. "Braggs told us not to hurt her."

Dirk smiled at the young soldier as a mother would at a child who'd asked a silly question. "Braggs told us not to *kill* her." He highlighted this as if teaching the young soldier a biblical lesson. "Death is too easy for sinners like her. We won't kill her. She will tell us the truth, or she will suffer."

"But—" the young soldier protested until a fellow soldier put his hand on his arm, shaking his head. The young soldier took a step back and looked at the ground.

A shout echoed from the mess tent as two soldiers came out, one holding Martel and one fighting to hold the teen.

Abelone's heart sank.

"Let me go!" The teen fought against the soldier, but the man laughed as he shoved him forward. When they were close to Dirk and Abelone, he pushed the red-haired boy into Abelone's arms.

Abelone hugged him tight.

The kid was trembling, and the infected beyond the gate were shrieking. Along with the rapidly rising heat, Abelone's thoughts were having trouble coalescing. Everything around her was insane.

Dirk smiled through it all. Abelone wondered if Braggs was also smiling in the command tent.

Martel, propped up by a soldier, was reunited with Abelone. He was awake but had trouble walking. His bandaged side was still showing spots of red, but no blood was seeping through the bandage. It was a good sign; it meant he wasn't bleeding anymore.

"Good." Dirk looked upon his small flock. His voice was sweet and low. "We were brought together for a reason. We were spared for a reason."

It was clear by "we," Dirk meant more than just the small group. He meant people who had similar beliefs to him. People who thought they were superior.

She had never thought a person could have such a demented look in their eyes while sermonizing to a group.

"These people brought a plague onto the world." Dirk pointed directly at Abelone. "This agent of the apocalypse brought the virus meant to wipe out humankind." Dirk pulled the red-headed teen away from Abelone. She fought to hold on to the boy. She knew she would not be able to save him if she didn't, but the teen was pulled from her grasp.

"She corrupted others." He squeezed his hands on the kid's shoulders, making him wince. "But know this. I was put here, and I was brought to you so our kind"—he looked at each soldier—"could survive and rebuild humanity in our image."

Abelone knew he meant the white Aryan supremacy beliefs held by these soldiers. He was religiously feeding their inner hunger, and they were eating it up.

"I am your salvation. My blood is your salvation. There is no other path to saving the world."

His blood? No other path? The opportunity presented itself. She seized it. "He's lying."

Dirk raised an eyebrow at her interruption. "Am I? I was bitten many times by the infected, the deadlies, the walking dead."

He pulled down his crew neck and revealed a scabbed-over bite—the one left by Sergeant Reilly—then he lifted his shirt to reveal two more scabbed-over bites on his flank.

"I survived bite after bite, and through God's will, I did not die. I did not change. I was guided here to save you"—he pointed at the soldiers—"the future of the human race." He paused, looking satisfied he had refuted her claim.

Abelone smiled for the first time since getting to the compound. He had said what she hoped he would.

"He lies!" She pulled at the bandage on her arm, slipped it off and revealed her own scabbed-over bite mark. "I was bitten too."

A barely perceptible look of panic flashed across Dirk's face as he realized what she was up to.

Abelone continued, "I was bitten by the infected back on the ship." She lifted her arm for the soldiers to see. "I'm not an agent of the apocalypse. I didn't release this virus onto the world. I was sent to investigate it by the WHO."

Some of the soldiers hesitated, and some looked unconvinced. However, the young man who had spoken up earlier was uneasy. He looked at the others. "Guys?"

All she needed was one to question their devotion. It might cause a domino effect.

Dirk realized this too. He let go of the teen and slapped Abelone again, this time so hard she spun and fell to one knee.

"Guys?" the young soldier asked the others again, louder this time.

A few of the others looked at him, doubt creeping into their expressions.

Dirk pulled his pistol and aimed it at Abelone's head. His voice quivered. "You are the one who is lying, bitch. You are the one who brought this plague to the world." He put his finger on the trigger. "And you are the one who must die."

Abelone held her breath.

"Don't." It was the young soldier. He was aiming his rifle at Dirk. "I don't know if she is telling the truth, but if her blood is also immune, we need to tell Braggs. Her blood might also be useful."

Dirk looked at the soldier and slowly aimed his pistol upwards, taking his finger off the trigger.

Abelone exhaled. It worked. She'd gotten through to some of them. She needed to keep the momentum in her favour, but before she could, Dirk spoke again.

"Son, it's normal to have doubts. Especially when the bitch is as beautiful as she is."

Well, that's new. Abelone wondered where Dirk was going with this.

The young soldier's rifle was shaking slightly, and his eyes were round and uncertain.

"Her blood is not a cure. This bitch will say and do anything to stay alive." Dirk put his pistol away and walked to the young soldier. "You want to know something else? She hasn't even killed one deadly since the plague started." He looked at Abelone disapprovingly. "Not one."

He must have heard me tell Keefer, but when?

The young soldier looked at her. He was slipping away. How could she explain? "People can still be saved. With a vaccine, we can save people." Her confidence was not what it had been a few days ago. She'd seen so many people die, and now Keefer was gone. She wasn't even sure if she cared about saving people anymore. But Dirk was right. She had not killed anyone . . . or anything.

Dirk seized on her indecision. "You see? Why would she kill the monsters she created? She wants them to live and multiply." He walked to the boy who was now with Martel, grabbed him by the arm and pulled him toward the gate.

"You will tell us where the virus was created and what government conspired with you. Was it the Canadian government? The US government?"

The soldier who'd had doubts was pointing his rifle at the ground; he'd gone quiet again. Abelone had lost him. She understood why Dirk grabbed the teen instead of her. Why push his luck with the soldiers by threatening her again?

He shoved the teen against the wired gate. The boy bounced off the fencing. Infected fingers tried to grasp at him through the chain links. Dirk pinned him against the fence until the infected's fingers latched on and held him there.

"If you don't tell us everything you know, those who follow you will suffer."

"You're crazy! The virus was not created by a government." Her heart was pumping hard, and her hands were clenched white.

The boy's pants had a growing wet stain down the legs, and the smell of urine mingled with the rotten smell of the infected's skin and the warming summer air.

"Stop, please . . . the government did not do this." Abelone stretched out her arms to the young man.

"Fine. You had your chance." Dirk smiled with his typical uncaring grin. "You might not have killed anyone yet, but know you are responsible for this."

Abelone tried to step forward to help the boy, but two soldiers held her back. Her adrenaline was revving her beyond what she thought she could do. She punched a soldier in the nose, sending him backwards, but he was quickly replaced by two more. It took three soldiers to hold her back from Dirk.

Dirk laughed, watching her fight. He grabbed the boy's hand and shoved his fingers through the fence. Two infected chomped down on the fingers sticking through. The teen howled. After a few seconds, Dirk let go and stepped back, pulling his pistol out of his holster. The boy pulled his hand from the fencing and went quiet as he stared at his blood-covered hand missing four fingers.

"Monster!" Abelone hollered, fully restrained by the soldiers.

Dirk grabbed Martel and shoved him to the ground in front of the teen.

No! Abelone seethed.

Doc Martel writhed in pain, holding his bandaged side. Fresh blood started seeping through the bandage. Martel tried to get up, but his legs weren't able to lift him, and he fell back to his knees.

The teen's eyes closed. His breathing got heavier. After thirty seconds, he let go of his hand and his arm fell limp at his side. His breathing was laborious, and he was turning a sickly pale.

"One more chance, bitch. Who created the virus?"

Abelone realized what he was doing. "Don't," she pleaded.

Dirk laughed. His eyes danced with glee. She was sure he knew there was no government involved. She was sure he knew she had not created this virus. He was pandering to the soldiers and their new enmity to the government, to her.

"I'll tell you what. Since you have not killed anyone—or anything—yet, I'll do you a favour." Dirk slipped a hunting knife out of the sheath on his belt. He flipped it and caught it by the blade.

"Let the bitch go to her friend," he told the soldiers. The men shoved her to the ground beside Martel. Dirk threw his knife in front of Abelone before moving back a safe distance. "If you protect your doctor friend, you can live, and we will believe you didn't create this plague. If not, he dies. Either way, you will be responsible for someone's death." He nodded as if genuinely thinking he was doing Abelone a favour.

Abelone looked at the soldiers. They looked between her and the teen. Even the young soldier who had resisted Dirk earlier was mesmerized by the spectacle. She was sickened by what he wanted her to do.

The teen slouched back on the fence, the infected's fingers still holding him up through the chain links. His skin had darkened from pale to grey, and his breathing had stopped. The boy grunted as if trying to clear his lungs. After a few grunts, the sound changed to a sharper low growl. That was the cue for the infected to let him go.

He's turned. Abelone grabbed the knife and stood between the infected teen and Martel, who was still squirming in pain on the ground.

Dirk was preaching about her killing her first infected, but she wasn't paying attention to him. The boy—the infected—opened his eyes, black in a pool of grey with meandering veins. His stare locked on her, and from deep inside his throat, a low, faint shriek materialized and rose quickly in pitch. She knew she would have to kill the infected for her and Martel to live. *He's just a boy.*

Dirk was cackling.

Abelone was frozen in place by fear until a powerful rush of anger flooded over her. She shook her head as it almost overcame all her senses. The anger was not her own. It seemed to be coming from outside of her mind, but she could feel it, nonetheless.

36

DRY, THIRSTY DIRT

A visceral howl echoed overhead, causing the teen infected to look up. So did Abelone and everyone else. A leather-clad man jumped down from beside the large circular spotlight on the scaffold above the gate. He landed on the infected teen, crushing him to the ground. The infected's shriek turned to a croak as the air was squished out of its lungs. The attacker's hands wrapped around the teen's head and twisted it in one swift motion. Abelone heard the cracking of his spine.

The leather-clad man stood back up, straight over the teen's body. His grey face and black hair absorbed the light from the sun, and his leather outfit was stained with dry blood. His black eyes scanned everyone until they paused on Abelone.

She tried to process what she was seeing. The Grey from the church in Forestville flashed in her mind. Hector, grey and confused in the bunker, was next. The Grey standing in front of her was familiar—very familiar. She felt a huge wave of relief wash over her, again from beyond herself.

The Grey moved with lightning speed. His hands took hers, and they were cold like a trout straight from the lake. The Grey took the knife from her and pivoted around.

He's so fast.

By the time Abelone turned, the knife was deep in the nearest soldier's throat. The limp body of the young soldier fell to the ground, the knife point sticking out the back of his neck.

A shot rang out from Dirk's pistol. It missed.

Abelone recognized the movements even though they were sped up. The Grey was on top of the next soldier, grabbing him by the throat. Another shot rang out, this one grazing the Grey's shoulder, but he did not slow down. He punched the soldier so hard it propelled him a car's length away.

Abelone tried to follow the Grey's movements, but the man was too fast. She tried to focus on his face, unsure if she had seen it correctly.

The Grey moved toward Dirk, who adjusted his pistol aim to lock on the assailant. A third shot went off, catching the quickly moving form in the shoulder. Abelone winced at the impact as skin and bones exploded out of the exit hole.

The Grey stumbled but still swatted the pistol out of Dirk's hand. His momentum carried him into Dirk, and they locked in an embrace and bounced onto the gate before falling to the ground.

One of the soldiers jumped on the Grey's back. He locked his arm around the Grey long enough for Dirk to wriggle free.

The soldier who had been punched came scurrying back and furiously kicked the Grey. After four kicks, the Grey caught his boot, and Abelone heard the snap of bone as the ankle was twisted in a complete circle. The soldier howled and fell to the ground, writhing in agony.

The Grey was still held from the back by the other soldier as they scuffled on the ground. Dirk scrambled on all fours to one of the rifles lying nearby.

No! Abelone jumped up and went for the same rifle. Both put their hands on it at the same time. Dirk punched her in the chest, and her vision turned black for a few seconds. He pulled the rifle away and stood up, aiming its barrel at her.

The Grey slammed into him, sending him bouncing off the pink Hummer and to the ground. The Grey limped quickly past her and picked Dirk up by the throat with one hand. The Grey was favouring the arm he'd been shot in. He didn't seem to be in pain, though.

Abelone looked up. She recognized his mouth, his jaw and finally his ear, with the top of it partially missing. It was him. "Ben?"

"Abelone," the Grey answered in a low growl.

A rush of euphoria erupted from her gut and filled her with energy. She stood and walked to him. "You're alive? You're . . ."

Dirk squirmed, trying to break Keefer's hold on his throat. "How the fuck? I saw them ripping you apart."

"You didn't watch long enough, I guess." Keefer smiled dangerously, squeezing Dirk's throat. Dirk's eyes bulged.

Abelone put her hand on Keefer's arm.

"Wait."

She saw the pressure released from Dirk's throat.

"There's been enough killing," she said.

"He's dangerous." Keefer looked at Dirk. "He's psychotic."

"I know, but his blood. He's immune like me."

Keefer thought about it for a few seconds. Abelone wasn't sure if he would listen. In one swift move, Keefer threw Dirk against the side of the pink Hummer, denting the passenger-side door.

Abelone half-smiled. It was really him. He could have killed Dirk. She would have understood. But he didn't.

A series of pops rang out from behind them. Keefer reacted instantaneously and moved in front of Abelone. Skin and gummy black blood splattered over her as at least two bullets caught him in the back. Keefer stiffened, took a step forward, and fell to one knee. His eyes locked on hers. His hands went to the ground, and he stayed on all fours, breathing heavily as black blood oozed out of the holes in his leather jacket.

Braggs and his two escorts ran from the command tent, rifles at the ready.

"How did he get in here? Are there others?"

They thought he was an infected. She fell beside Keefer and frantically examined his back. Her hands were quickly covered in the dark ichor that was Keefer's blood. He was still breathing.

How is he still alive?

Braggs and the two soldiers aimed their rifles at the grey body on all fours.

"No, wait, he is not an infected!" she pleaded, knowing there was no reason for them to listen. Their fellow soldiers lay dead around them. They weren't going to leave him alive.

Salvation came from an unexpected place. "Wait!" Dirk's voice was barely loud enough to be heard. Holding his chest, he walked painfully over to the group surrounding Keefer and Abelone.

She knew this couldn't be good.

The soldiers and Braggs looked at Dirk, confused.

"What the hell happened here?" Braggs asked.

"What happened here," Dirk said as he walked past them to Keefer, "is this guy won't die!" He kicked Keefer in the ribs, making blood ooze from the bullet holes.

"That's the Keefer guy?" Braggs said incredulously. "How?" Braggs looked at the sky, then at his watch. "It doesn't matter. We don't have time to waste. The helicopter is ready to go. Time to get out of here before nukes start landing on our heads." There was a sense of real urgency in Braggs' voice. He took his pistol out.

Abelone tried to protect Keefer, but Dirk punched her in the stomach, threw her to the ground and turned to Braggs. "Hold on, let me do it. It's not often you get to kill someone twice."

Braggs shrugged. "Fine. Make it quick. I want us out of here ASAP."

Dirk walked over to the young soldier with the knife in his throat and pulled the deadly tool out with a slurp.

Abelone coughed, trying to get her breath back. Anger swirled through her whole body, not like before, but not hers either. The infected outside the compound gate grew agitated.

Keefer put a hand to his head. "What? NO . . . go away!" Keefer half-shouted, half-coughed.

"Who are you talking to? What the fuck are you—" Dirk was cut off by the loud groaning of breaking metal.

He turned in time to duck the circular spotlight from the gate scaffold. The spotlight bounced off the gravel a few feet from him and crashed into one of the soldiers who'd been following Braggs. He was dead by the time the light stopped rolling.

A green blur flew through the air from the top of the scaffold. A guttural cry emanated from the assailant. He landed on the back of the soldier closest to Abelone. His fingers dug deep into the man's eyes, popping them. Abelone stepped back from the gruesome attack.

"Eduard!" The shout was from Keefer.

Braggs dove away from the attack, dropping his beloved golden pistol while he rolled. He grabbed the rifle from a dead soldier as he got back up, aimed and fired with full disregard for the eyeless soldier's life. The bullets riddled the man's chest but also caught the attacker's leg. The soldier died instantly, but the attacker limped quickly toward Braggs. The big man stepped backwards as an empty clicking echoed from the rifle.

Abelone realized the form was grey but smaller than Keefer.

It's a boy. He's like Ben . . . He's Grey.

The teen slammed into Braggs, clawing for the big man's throat, but before he could latch on, Braggs' massive leg lashed out in a violent kick, sending the teen rolling in the dirt.

More shots were fired, this time from the soldier with the broken ankle. Most projectiles peppered the ground, but one bullet tore through the Grey teen's calf. He didn't scream; instead, he scrambled around the pink Hummer for protection.

Abelone lunged forward and kicked the rifle out of the soldier's hands. He grabbed her leg and tried to pull her to the ground. She looked for something to help fight him off. Nothing. She didn't need anything, though, as Keefer rose from his hands and knees and let himself fall on the soldier. He grabbed the soldier's head. The man barely had time to scream before two grey, bite-ridden hands crushed his skull.

"There're two of them!" shouted one of the two remaining soldiers while he aimed his rifle at the Hummer.

"Give me that!" Braggs said, grabbing the weapon and unloading the clip into the vehicle's windows and side. When the empty clicking happened again, a guttural scream rose from the other side of the vehicle. The teen clambered quickly over the Hummer and flew at the soldier beside Braggs. He landed on the man, and they crashed in a flurry of dirt and punches.

Braggs swung the rifle club-like at the teen, who ducked and rolled away, leaving the soldier motionless and his face turned to a pulp. Not far enough, though. The rifle caught the Grey on the knee, felling him. Abelone jumped on Braggs, her arms barely fitting around the man's waist. She strained to move him, but he simply swatted her down with one hand.

He looked at her, hate sizzling in his eyes. "Jennings won't be happy, but I've had enough of you." He brought the rifle up, aiming its butt at her head. Abelone gawked as if caught in the middle of a road at night with headlights descending on her.

A grey hand caught the rifle a foot from Abelone's head. Keefer locked eyes with Braggs. The big man snarled and punched Keefer with his giant fist, knocking him back. Keefer bounced back up like a spring and grabbed Braggs the same way Abelone had. She could tell his muscles weren't responding properly with all the bullet holes in his back. Despite that, Braggs slowly lifted off the ground. Keefer spun his body and threw Braggs into the gate. The infected on the other side exploded in a frenzy, like fans after a touchdown. Keefer collapsed from his efforts, and Abelone heard his breath grating through a damaged chest.

Keefer looked up at her. His jaw muscles were clenched as he sucked in air. He got up slowly and staggered toward Braggs, who was on one knee by the gate. Keefer was going in for the kill.

It was Braggs' turn to be saved in extremis. Someone grabbed her from behind.

"Stop!" Dirk's elbow snaked around her neck, restricting her breathing. She could smell Dirk's sweat on his arm. With her airway getting smaller, she panicked and shook her head, but that made Dirk tighten more. She was barely getting a trickle of air when she felt the cold steel of a pistol press on her temple. Keefer spun, and his eyes locked with hers.

"You move, she dies!" Dirk snarled.

Abelone's eyes watered from the pressure on her neck arteries.

"I can't get rid of you, can I?" Dirk said to Keefer, then spat blood on the ground.

Keefer stood still, partially bent over, like a cat ready to spring. Braggs got back to his feet, grunting, and walked to a rifle on the ground.

"Don't hurt her," growled Keefer.

"If you stay right where you are, this bitch won't get hurt."

Keefer nodded. Abelone felt it, too. The nod was not for Dirk but to some other unseen, unheard cue.

Abelone heard the movement behind them before she felt Dirk react. Eduard jumped at them, going for the gun, but the teen stumbled on his first step, grabbing his wounded leg. Dirk reoriented his pistol, aiming at the boy, and shot two bullets. The first hit the Hummer in the passenger door; the second caught Eduard in the gut, spraying black blood onto the pink paint. The boy went down, one hand still on his leg and the other on his stomach.

Keefer closed the distance during the distraction, and the pistol went off in his hand right by her head. The deflagration sent an ice pick through her ear, and her eyes almost popped out of her head. Her ear was ringing so loud it made her head spin.

Dirk let go of her neck, and the first thing Abelone saw was the hole in Keefer's hand, still holding the pistol. She turned off balance and kneed Dirk in the groin. He sucked in air as he crumpled.

"You bitch," Dirk muttered before Keefer pulled the pistol from Dirk and punched him on the forehead with his uninjured hand. Dirk swayed once and fell backwards, semi-conscious.

"All of you have been a royal pain in the ass since you got here," Braggs' heavy voice broke through the cacophony of infected outside the gate. He held the automatic rifle aimed at them from his hip. "Be dead already!"

Keefer stepped in front of Abelone and put his arms around her. She felt his body on hers, but more than that, she felt his mind—she was sure it was his mind—wanting to protect her. She closed her eyes, ready for the shower of bullets.

Two shots—not automatic. She opened her eyes and looked past Keefer's shoulder. Braggs stared down at two expanding red circles in his fatigues and let go of the rifle.

Martel was on his knees holding Braggs' massive golden pistol, a faint trickle of smoke rising from its muzzle.

Eric!

Both Abelone and Keefer jumped to his side as he put down the golden monstrosity.

"I'll be fine. I need to rest and catch my breath. Finally, something that gets me to stop talking, right?" He smiled at Abelone as she helped him lie back down.

"He'll be okay," Keefer said in a low, growly voice while checking the bandage on Martel.

Abelone, reassured, turned to Keefer and hugged him. "I thought you were dead." She couldn't believe he was there with them, with her.

"So did I." He squeezed her back.

She admired his skin from up close. The scientist in her wondered how the melanin had been altered so quickly. She shifted her attention. "Your eyes . . ." His black irises were distinct from the grey eyeball, which had faint black veins meandering across the surface, but nothing like what she'd seen on the infected. "Does it hurt?"

Keefer's cheeks lifted, but his mouth didn't reach a full smile. "That's the funny thing. Nothing hurts." He pulled up his arm, exposing a few bites on his wrist before poking at some of the bullet holes on his side where the blood had already stopped flowing. Something stirred in Abelone. It took her a second to recognize what it was. Hope was peeking around the corner to see if it was safe to come out.

A low, maniacal laugh followed by a cough made both of them spin. Dirk was still sitting with his back to the Hummer. His bloody face was surrounded by bullet holes in the pink background. He was no threat.

"You two are *the couple* of the year, or maybe I should say, *the couple of the apocalypse.*" He coughed again. "This guy kills everything he gets his hands on . . ." Dirk stared at Keefer with hatred in his eyes. "And you, bitch, bring this plague to the world and don't kill anything with your own hands, no infected, no person, *nada.*" He moved something across his lap. "You fucking deserve each other."

Dirk raised his hand and crushed whatever was in it. The slim amount of hope she had left Abelone's body as the red liquid seeped between Dirk's fingers and trickled down his forearm. On his lap lay the now empty yellow case. There were little piles of glass around Dirk, each shaped like a cairn where a mini-body was buried. The blood from Tom Virtanen and Jerry White disappeared in the dry, thirsty dirt.

"No!" They'd spent so much time chasing those blood samples. Despair quickly filled the vacuum left by her waning hope.

Dirk laughed again, followed by multiple coughs.

"NO!" she screamed even louder, letting go of Ben. Deep inside her, she felt another rush of emotion, not her own. She knew it was Ben's. He was angry, but there was something else. She felt . . . restraint. He wasn't going to hurt Dirk because she had told him not to. They needed his blood; he was as immune as she was.

"I'm not going to kill him," Keefer's raspy voice whispered as he walked to Dirk and stood over him.

"I know." Abelone picked up the golden pistol and looked at Eric Martel, whose head sagged as tears filled his eyes. Even though Dirk should not live, Keefer would not kill him. Something had changed in him. He did not think everyone should die anymore.

She walked up to Dirk. He looked at her with a challenging smirk. "What are you going to do? Are you gonna kill me? You know you need my blood, plus you've never even killed anyone or anything." His smirk changed to a smile. "I'm the salvation of this world . . . bitch."

Abelone thought about her arguments with Keefer. He'd listened to her and come around to her way of thinking—not everyone had to die. He'd changed. As she looked down at Dirk, she thought of the people he'd killed, the vision of the world he had, her vision of what the world now was. She'd changed, too.

"There is a first time for everything . . . bitch."

Dirk's smile melted off his face as Abelone raised the golden gun and squeezed the trigger. The bullet created a tunnel right between his eyes and the back of his head exploded.

37

I CAN'T BELIEVE THEY'RE GONE

A belone needed to sit down. She couldn't remember the last time she'd slept. She trudged to the back of the command tent and sat on a metal chair while the others discussed possible destinations. She watched Keefer, Martel and Jennings argue about where they should fly to.

Luckily, they had found Jennings handcuffed to the helicopter, uninjured. His wrists were raw from trying to free himself from his restraints, and he had a few broken ribs, but he was alright. He'd said not being able to help had been one of the worst moments of the whole goddamned apocalypse. It took him a few minutes to absorb Keefer's new reality, but eventually, he accepted it and moved on. Abelone knew not everyone would be as accepting.

Abelone shifted on the uncomfortable chair. Her head drooped a few times, and her eyes became heavy. She was back in the Henry Dawson mess deck. The closed hatch leading to the passageway was going to burst like an overblown balloon. Each blow to the door made her take a step backward until her back rested against the cold, hard steel of the freezer. She knew the next blow would make the door explode. But it never came. She breathed a sigh of relief, but the escaping air stuck in her throat when two arms stretched through the metal behind her and dragged her into the shadows of the freezer.

She woke with a jolt, gasping for air. It was another dream. She looked about the command tent. Keefer and Jennings were still around the map table. Martel sat quietly beside them, doing his best not to fall asleep.

Abelone walked to the table. She mustn't have been out long, as the men were still arguing between Ottawa or New Brunswick as their destination. She squeezed between Jennings and Keefer, and both men went quiet. They watched as she pulled her hair back and readjusted her ponytail.

"There is one place we *have* to go," she said. Her tone made it clear not to argue. They stayed quiet as she oriented herself on the map. She picked up a red felt marker and circled a town.

"Here." She hoped the others wouldn't resist.

Everyone leaned in, even Eduard, who had been watching quietly.

"Oh, hell no!" Keefer said the moment he saw the circle.

"We have to," Abelone insisted. "Eric, you know why we have to go."

"How do you know he's there?" Doc Martel asked, holding his bandaged side.

She knew she was right. They had to see that.

Keefer resisted. "Abelone, that's insane. There is no one left there. The whole place was burned to the ground."

"We need his blood. My blood isn't enough."

"Why the fuck would we fly to . . ." Jennings looked closely at the map to read the name. "Peaks Bay, Labrador?"

Despite his grey skin, Keefer's face was expressive, and he made an "exactly" face to Abelone while waiting for her answer.

Abelone took a deep breath in. "We need to go to Peaks Bay. My blood might not be enough for a vaccine." Looking at Keefer, she corrected his earlier statement. "Not everything is burnt down there." She leaned into the map and placed an X where land met ocean within her big red circle. "The Henry Dawson is still there. *He* is still there."

"Who the hell is *he*?" Jennings sounded frustrated.

Abelone looked at Martel as she knew he understood. "Tom Virtanen, Patient Zero," he answered for her.

Jennings stared at them for a few seconds. Martel nodded reluctantly. Keefer shook his head.

"How do you know he's still there?" asked Jennings.

She knew. They had to leave.

"Because, when we left Peaks Bay, we could see the Henry Dawson in the harbour. The bow was charred black, but the ship itself was still intact, especially the midsection and aft. The tides were high when the bombing occurred, so those parts of the ship were underwater."

"That doesn't mean this Tom guy—Patient Zero—survived." Jennings was not convinced.

"He would have had to be buried deep inside the ship not to get burned by the napalm. The aft was flooded, and if he was anything like the other infected, he would not have known to lock himself in an airtight closed room," Keefer made his case. He had it wrong. She had never told him what happened. They had to go before the bombs fell.

"He was, though," Abelone said, staring at her red circle.

"How can you even know that?" Jennings asked.

"Because . . . I locked him in the galley freezer myself."

"Why him?" Jennings asked. "There are tons of infected around. Why not just grab their blood?" He thumbed toward Keefer and Eduard. "We even have these two."

"Of course we're going to grab a sample of their blood, but no, they won't do. We need the original blood, the original virus. We need blood from Patient Zero."

Jennings nodded slowly as he grasped what she was saying. He walked around the table to get a better look at the flight path to Peaks Bay. Using a ruler, he measured the distance to a few points between where they were and Abelone's circle over Peaks Bay.

Keefer remained quiet the whole time. The air was warm and heavy. Abelone sensed there was more bothering him than her suggestion of flying to Peaks Bay. She could feel it, but she couldn't interpret what it was. He kept looking at Eduard standing by the tent flaps, also watching and listening.

"Okay, so . . . let's say we do fly there. Our bird will only have enough fuel to get there. My best guess is that the added fuel tanks give us up to twenty-one hundred klicks of air time. Peaks Bay is—" He did the math based on his measurement. "Peaks Bay is just shy of . . . nineteen hundred kilometres."

"We'd need to refuel there." Abelone eyed the map, looking for options.

Martel chimed in, "What about the military airport at Goose Bay?"

"It was overrun last time we were there," Keefer said, sounding resigned that the momentum was shifting in favour of Abelone's suggestion. "It would be too dangerous."

"Maybe the infected have moved on. Or started dying off. How long can they live without eating? They must have some sort of limit," Jennings said.

"Where would you even go after?" Keefer pleaded, looking at Abelone. She could sense he was afraid for her, but there was something else.

"Iceland," Jennings said as he measured the distance between Peaks Bay and Reykjavik. "If we hold the cure to this thing, flying anywhere on the East Coast would put the cure at risk. We need to fly it to Geneva. Reykjavik is twenty-two hundred kilometres from Peaks Bay." He adjusted his ruler on the map. "Twenty-one hundred, actually. Then they can take it to Switzerland easily."

Keefer walked away from the table. Abelone could feel his sadness. She followed and took his hand in hers. It felt cold, and his grey skin stood out against her white skin. She ran her other hand on top of his. His skin felt no different from hers, except for the bite marks that pocked his hand.

"What's wrong?" She looked into his black eyes.

She felt it before he said it, and her heart broke. "I can't go with you."

She stopped breathing, and her hands froze on his.

"I have to help Eduard get those survivors to safety."

"But we're going to need your help. What if Tom is too strong?" Abelone pleaded, tears welling in her eyes.

Keefer rested his hands gently on Abelone's shoulders and pulled her against his chest.

"Go get the survivors. We'll fly them off with us." She knew it wasn't a good option, but she had yet to find another way.

"You know as much as I do that there is no time. The nukes will fall soon. Eduard's already said they left for La Tuque. By the time Eduard and I catch up to them, you and the others need to be long gone from here."

He put his forehead against hers. "You were right all along—not everyone has to die. We need to do what we can to save those who can be saved."

He was right. She squeezed him harder.

"The world is counting on you. I'm counting on you: get Tom Virtanen, get a vaccine, save people. I'll be waiting. I'll keep as many people alive as I can until a cure is brought back."

The last time they kissed—the only time—Keefer had almost gotten his head blown off. It was unclear if he had been lucky not to get infected by her saliva or if it was something else. Now, things were different; he was Grey. She leaned into him and did not pause to see if he leaned in too. She kissed him without hesitation. He kissed back.

When he let go, he didn't say a word, but looked into her eyes for a few more seconds. He turned to Eduard, and they walked out of the tent, disappearing in the morning light as the tent flaps closed behind him.

"Where's he going?" Jennings said, alarmed and oblivious to the discussion they'd had. "We're flying in a few minutes."

"He's not coming with us." Abelone breathed deeply. "He's going to stay here and save people." She was torn up inside and felt like staying, too, but she knew he was right. "If we're going to save people too, we need to get that blood and get a vaccine created."

Jennings still looked unsure about their destination. "You're sure this Virtanen guy is there? How do you even know he's still alive?"

"We'll just need to take a leap of faith," Abelone answered resolutely.

**

The compound shrank as the helicopter rose into the late morning sky. The thumping of the engine and the smell of fuel filled the cockpit. The military base beyond the compound was a lot larger than Abelone had imagined; it sprawled out for a few kilometres to the north and east. She searched the roads east of the base for the pink Hummer driven by Keefer. She turned and looked back at Eric Martel sitting in the helicopter's cockpit. He half-smiled at her. She looked at the deep scar on her forearm. Her blood was needed; that was how she could help the most. She needed to get to the outside world to help develop a vaccine. But first, they needed Tom Virtanen's blood.

There was a crackle of static in her helmet comms, and Jennings' voice materialized. "Should take us nine hours to get there."

Abelone nodded. She thought of Tom Virtanen locked in the galley freezer of the Henry Dawson. Would he still be alive? Would it be as easy as she thought to get him out of the freezer? How would they refuel? She was lost in thought and didn't notice how much time had passed before her helmet comms crackled again.

"There," Jennings' voice said with mixed excitement and fear. He pointed south through Abelone's window.

She followed his finger. Across the blue sky were two white streaks of exhaust left by jets over the skyline of Quebec City. She couldn't spot the jets—it didn't matter.

"Turn away!" shouted Jennings.

Abelone did, just in time. A yellow and red ball of fiery hell appeared in the centre of the city. In a fraction of a second, it grew to the size of the sun engulfing the horizon. Even though she was looking the other way, the flash of light illuminated everything around and ahead of them.

"The bomb!" Abelone stated the obvious.

"Brace for the shockwave," Jennings shouted, his face contorted. "We're about . . ." More face contortions. "Sixty klicks, so we have about

...twenty...forty seconds." At that, he pushed the cyclic stick forward, and his feet tap danced on the anti-torque pedals. The helicopter dove behind the backside of the hills below them.

"Hopefully, the hills can protect us," Jennings said.

The shockwave flowed over the hills like water over rocks, and despite the cover, it hit the Cormorant hard, propelling it forward. Abelone grabbed the sides of her seat, forgetting about Peaks Bay, the infected and her blood. The helicopter tail lifted, and Jennings fought to keep the aircraft from spinning out of control. He struggled against the erratic stick, and his feet pushed the pedals up and down angrily. She thought about all the people who died in that flash of burning light. A beeping alarm sounded, but Abelone couldn't identify its source from the large panels in front of them. Every light was blinking angrily. Her hands shifted to her seat harness, and she squeezed it tight as the aircraft was shaken in every direction. They had to live.

Miraculously, Jennings kept the helicopter pointed in the direction they were going, and after a few seconds, the shockwave passed. The searing light outside faded, although slower than it had appeared. It took over a minute for it to dissipate.

Jennings breathed deeply. "It's passed. We should be okay; we were far enough." He pulled the helicopter up to its original altitude. "I can't believe they did this. The mother fuckers nuked Quebec City."

Abelone looked through her side window. The skyline of the major city was gone, replaced by a giant grey and black mushroom cloud with an amber core near ground level. Around the cloud, the sky was pink, reminding Abelone of an early sunrise.

38

NOT EVERYONE CAN BE SAVED

The Cormorant hovered over the Canadian Air Force base in Goose Bay. It was dawn the day after they departed from Valcartier. The mushroom cloud was still etched in Abelone's mind. She wondered if it might be forever. All those lives lost. She kept reminding herself it had been necessary; it was for the greater good, but she wondered if it had been too late.

"We fly nine hours to find this—damn it!" Jennings' static-filled voice brought her back to the small, stuffy helicopter cockpit.

Below them, the Goose Bay military base was crawling with infected. They walked around slowly and aimlessly, heads down, until they heard the helicopter, which woke them up like a concert crowd anticipating their favourite band about to arrive on stage. There was no way to land and refuel. Without fuel, the helicopter would barely last a couple more hours. Peaks Bay was an hour away, and unfortunately, this far north in Labrador, there was nothing but tundra or ocean in any direction after that.

"We'll figure it out. Head to Peaks Bay." Abelone was resolute. "We've come too far; we need to get Patient Zero's blood. There's no going back."

Jennings' face showed how exhausted he was after flying the helicopter for nine hours straight, but he still looked at her with a piercing stare. She stared back, unwavering. He relented and tilted the helicopter in the direction of Peaks Bay. He stayed quiet, but she knew he was thinking through their options, and she could tell by the look on his face he didn't think they were good.

Abelone picked at her nails and glanced between the horizon, Peaks Bay and the fuel gauge. The faces of all the people who had died on the Henry Dawson swam across her vision. She wondered if Tom Virtanen would still be there, let alone still be alive. She leaned back in her seat and tried to rest, but the faces haunted her.

***

The ash in the harbour plaza swirled around the Cormorant as it touched down where the napalm hit around two weeks ago. The mid-morning sun was absorbed by the blanket of grey ash covering everything. All that remained of the town were building skeletons of stone and metal that hadn't fully burned, metal vehicle carcasses, and overlooking everything, the massive blackened bow of the Henry Dawson sticking out of the sea at an angle.

"We need to move fast," Jennings stated what Abelone already knew. They'd flown over a few hundred infected on the outskirts of Peaks Bay, all heading toward the harbour.

"They must all be from Goose Bay. But how did they know we were coming here?" Doc Martel said. Abelone was glad he was up, as he'd slept almost the whole flight. He was gaining strength.

"They couldn't have known. Something must be attracting them. They are too focused to be randomly coming here," Abelone said. Deep in her mind, she couldn't help but think they were all here for the same reason—Patient Zero.

"That trek would have taken days on foot," Jennings said as he shut down the helicopter rotors.

"We know," Abelone said, remembering their escape from Peaks Bay.

Jennings and Abelone exited the helicopter after a short argument with Martel. He might be gaining strength, but he was still in no shape to be scrambling around the slanted carcass of a half-burnt Canadian Coast Guard vessel. He'd accepted his fate, but not until he gave them the idea to bring the helicopter's reach-and-rescue pole. Great for saving drowning people, but also great for controlling and keeping a biting infected at bay. It could act as a livestock pole for capturing Virtanen. Satisfied he'd contributed, he agreed to watch the helicopter until they returned. He'd signal them with a handheld radio if there was any trouble.

The ash disturbed by the helicopter was still playfully floating in the air, caught on the ocean breeze. Jennings and Abelone covered their mouths and noses as best they could as they walked to the hulking bow of the Henry Dawson. It had settled on the large breakwater rocks. With the tide out, only the lower parts of the aft were underwater. The Henry Dawson looked like an ominous mausoleum, which made Abelone slouch and look around nervously as she approached.

They reached the main outside deck by climbing the breakwater rocks below the blackened portion of the bow. Abelone felt uneasy. She wasn't sure if it was due to being back at the Henry Dawson, with all the ghosts of the people she knew floating around or if it was from her exhaustion. The last few weeks had been a blur, but there was something else gnawing at her. Almost literally. A small nagging pain of starvation nestled in the back of her mind. She wasn't hungry, though. She'd eaten rations before they landed, and her stomach was full. But the hunger was there, faint and persistent.

"Abelone?" Jennings pulled her from her thoughts.

"What?"

"You okay? I asked you how far the mess hall is."

"Should be right down the stairs . . . errr . . . ladder, when we go through that door." She pointed to the main structure door.

Jennings looked from the door to her and nodded. "Are you okay? You seem . . . distracted?"

"I have this weird feeling . . . like I am feeling someone else's hunger."
It was the first time she admitted to anyone that she thought she was
feeling emotions that were not her own. She wondered how Jennings
would react, but he only looked confused.

The handheld radio Jennings had strapped to his belt crackled. "Abby,
Jennings, you making progress?"

"We're almost in," Jennings answered.

"Okay, hurry up. This place will be squirming with infected soon,"
Martel's concerned voice crackled through.

"Going in now." Abelone was relieved Jennings did not question what
she'd said. They had a job to do. The tall captain squatted down and let
himself slide on the floor to the door they had to go through.

He looked through the already open door. After a pause, he signalled
it was clear. Abelone slid to where he was. Jennings took his shotgun
off his shoulder, which was Abelone's cue to take her pistol out and the
safety off.

"Remember, we can't shoot him. We need him alive. He should be in
a fairly weak state—"

"If he's alive at all," Jennings interrupted, with a tinge of doubt in his
voice.

They proceeded into the shadows of the Henry Dawson's passageway,
leaving the morning sun behind. Abelone was surprised at how fresh
the air was. She'd expected the rotten, coppery smell of the infected and
blood, but instead, the air was salty and cool. The door to the mess deck
was a few metres from the bottom of the ladder near the entry point, and
her heart pounded harder with every step they took toward it.

As they paused again to scope the inside, Abelone remembered Alex
pulling her and Captain Vanderfeld into that very same mess deck. No
one would be pulling them in this time. To her relief, the room was
deserted.

"Over here." Abelone led the way through the bolted metal tables.
She had a flashback of her confrontation with Tom Virtanen, and she

instinctively looked around the floor. *There.* She spotted the frying pan she had used to defend herself.

She readied her pistol as she inched up to the freezer door. Jennings positioned himself beside her with his shotgun ready.

"We can't use that," she said, indicating his shotgun. "Like I said, we need him alive if we want any chance of a cure."

"With all due respect. If it comes down to him or you . . . I'm choosing you." There was real emotion behind his statement. "If I understand things correctly, your blood is as important as his."

Abelone locked eyes with him. There was something about him she liked. He was resolute in his convictions. She could relate. "Yes, my blood is important." She gave him that. "But his blood has the original virus. The unaltered version."

"Is that more important than your blood, which is immune to the virus?"

"Well . . . it's just as important."

"So if they are equally important, I will choose you—every time," Jennings said with finality. It made no sense debating it further. She smiled and nodded. It felt comforting to know he was watching over her. Like Keefer had.

She leaned into the door to look inside via the small window. The last time she did this, she came face to face with Tom's deformed grey visage. This time, she only saw her reflection.

"Are you even sure he's in there?"

Abelone didn't have to think to answer. "Yes, I can feel him." She couldn't explain it, but Tom Virtanen was alive—barely—and he was hungry.

"You wouldn't happen to have the keys by any chance?" Jennings half joked as he tugged at the lock on the freezer door.

"Wait." Abelone moved around him to the galley and reached into the sink. She rummaged through a few dirty dishes. It took her a few seconds to find what she was looking for in the lightless gloom of the mess deck.

She pulled the keys out and held them face high, rattling them to show Jennings.

Jennings took the keys and removed the lock. "Okay, let's do this."

Abelone stood ready with the reach-and-rescue pole. Jennings held his shotgun with one hand and reached for the door handle with the other. He flipped the door open. They stood ready to grab whatever came running out—nothing did.

The nagging feeling of hunger got more intense once the door was open. The fresh, salty air was quickly overtaken by the rotting smell of meat. Or was it Tom? Abelone wasn't sure. There was a series of clanking noises inside as something moved. Something was knocked over and fell to the ground. Laboured steps echoed in the small metal space. Abelone and Jennings took a step back.

From the darkness stepped the grey form of what used to be Tom Virtanen. He was hunched over, hairless, his clothes dyed dark by other people's blood. He moved slowly. His black eyes scanned the room. Immediately, he turned his head sideways and shielded them from even the low light of the mess deck. He let out a dry, visceral hiss. He looked devoid of all moisture, like an Egyptian mummy unwrapped after being taken out of its tomb. Tom took another step forward, but stumbled and almost fell.

Abelone felt sad for him. He probably never realized what was happening to him. He probably didn't even remember getting rabies and crashing into the Nuovo Mondo.

Tom Virtanen's eyes adjusted, and he looked straight at Abelone. She felt a flash of recognition—not her own—followed by anger.

"Now, Abelone!" Jennings shouted.

Tom moved slowly, lifting his arms. He was not a threat. She took a step back and cinched the loop of the reach-and-rescue pole around his neck. At his speed, he was unable to avoid it. The pole held him in place, easily countering his weak efforts to get to her. He could barely raise his arms to grab the metal rod. She could herd him in any direction she wanted.

"Well . . . that was anticlimactic," said Jennings. "I was expecting more . . . trouble." He looked Patient Zero over, and Abelone could tell he was trying to see the man who used to be Tom Virtanen.

"Did you know him?"

"I didn't. I only heard about him when Eric brought him to the infirmary." Abelone tested moving Tom with her, careful not to slide down on the slanted floor.

Jennings' handheld radio crackled. "Abelone, Jennings?"

Jennings pulled the radio off his belt and answered, "Doc, we have him. We have Virtanen. We're about to head out."

"Okay, hurry," Martel whispered. "I see ash rising close by. I think they are almost here!"

"Copy that. We're on our way."

Jennings looked at Abelone. "I guess it's not going to be easy after all." He took the safety off his shotgun. "You guide him out." He nodded toward Virtanen. "I'll provide cover."

Tom still had his arms outstretched toward her, looking like he wanted help. A dry hissing came from his parched throat as if whispering a secret.

"Okay, let's go."

She followed Jennings out, carefully navigating the tables and the slanted floor.

Despite the short distance, it took them a few minutes to get to the outside deck as their captive kept slipping on the angled floor. From there, Jennings helped Abelone onto the breakwater rocks.

The rocks were jagged and covered in a thin, slippery layer of algae, which made their progress, especially Tom's, excruciatingly slow. They were about to set foot on the ash-covered plaza when the radio crackled again.

"You need to run!" Martel's voice echoed from Jennings' belt. "They're here . . . Oh, God!"

Streams of infected poured into what used to be the town gathering place, and their frantic footsteps lifted a thick cloud of ash. They flooded in via remnant streets and pedestrian alleys. The noise of their arrival started like the trickle of a stream but quickly accelerated to the rush of river rapids. Through the ash, Abelone could see the silhouettes of men and women.

"You need to run!" Martel repeated.

Abelone trembled, and her breathing became shallow and rapid. She could see Martel in the helicopter in the plaza's centre, but it was framed by hundreds of infected running toward it. She tried to reassure herself the infected were twice as far away, and the swarm couldn't see them yet as they were on the opposite side of the Cormorant.

"Let's go!" ordered Jennings, moving even quicker.

Abelone pulled hard on Tom to make him move, but his weakened state made him stumble and fall to his knees. "He can't move that fast!" It couldn't end like this. She had to get him to the helicopter.

"Hurry!" Martel kept insisting on the crackling radio, making her breathing accelerate even more.

The far side of the plaza was obscured by a cloud of ash with a growing number of grey silhouettes at its core moving in their direction.

"Okay, pull back his head with the reach-and-rescue pole. I'll pick him up." Jennings bent and picked Virtanen up over his shoulder. The infected hissed and shrieked, but the sounds caught in his withered throat. Abelone pulled hard to keep his head away from Jennings. It was working. But the best they could do was an awkward jog.

Shots rang out from the helicopter, along with some cheers or swearing from Martel, depending on whether he hit or missed his target. There was more swearing than cheers.

The shooting stopped, and Martel's voice crackled on the radio again. "It doesn't matter if you make it. By the time you get the chopper going, they will have us pinned down."

Jennings was breathing hard from the exertion of his awkward carry. Abelone adjusted her hold of the pole to keep Tom from biting him.

"We need to get Abelone and Tom's blood to safety. That's the most important." Martel was stating facts.

His use of Tom's name reminded Abelone that, unlike her, Martel knew the crewman.

"Abelone, I know you'll develop a cure and find a way to help people."

There was something in Martel's voice that alarmed her. "Eric?" she called out, confused, though Jennings was not pressing the talk button of his handheld.

As they got within twenty metres of the Cormorant, still out of sight of the infected throng, she saw Eric gingerly step out of the helicopter. He looked at them and waved once. The motion had a finality to it; no coming back from what he was about to do. He ran from the helicopter in the opposite direction from them and also away from the incoming infected.

"What is he doing?" Abelone slowed. "No!" She wanted him to get back in the helicopter.

"He's giving us time," Jennings answered somberly. "He's drawing the infected away from the chopper. Keep moving!"

The swarm of infected saw Doc Martel stumbling toward the far end of the plaza, and like a murmuring of starlings, they adjusted their course as a group. The whole flood of bodies entering the plaza forgot about the helicopter and headed after the one warm, uninfected body they could see.

"No, he can't. He won't be able to get away from them."

"I think he knows that, Abelone." Jennings slowed as they reached the Cormorant. He opened the side door and dropped Virtanen inside. Abelone hesitated, watching Eric painfully stumble at the edge of the plaza.

"Get in!" Jennings urged her.

She climbed in, still holding Tom's head with the reach-and-rescue pole. The Cormorant's large metal sliding door slammed shut behind her. Jennings climbed through the passenger-side door to the cockpit and scrambled over to the pilot's seat. Abelone barely registered him madly flipping switches and pressing buttons. A purr emanated from the Cormorant engine and quickly changed to a groan. Within seconds, it vibrated to a roar, drowning out the infected. The massive propellers started to spin, slowly at first, but increasing in speed.

That was when the first infected spotted them. Some adjusted their trajectory back toward the large aircraft. Abelone knew their adjustments were too late. Eric had bought them enough time.

As the helicopter propellers blurred, the wheels rose right before the first infected reached it and slammed its fists on the side window. It was too late. The helicopter rose steadily. Safe.

As they gained altitude, Abelone pressed her face to the window, searching for Eric. She couldn't spot him, but knew where he was. He hadn't reached the ruins at the far end of the plaza. A large mound of infected piled on top of each other right at the plaza limits. She knew her friend, the Henry Dawson's doctor, the man who always had something to say about pretty much anything, was under them. She looked down at Tom Virtanen with tears in her eyes. Eric Martel had sacrificed himself to save his last patient. He'd sacrificed himself to save her. He'd given up his life to save the world.

"You'd better be worth it," she whispered angrily, unsure if she was speaking to Tom or herself.

***

The Cormorant hovered over the Peaks Bay harbour. Its long blades spun with a steady, loud thump. After securing Tom Virtanen with duct tape, Abelone climbed into the co-pilot seat beside Jennings. As she was strapping into her harness, a bright red light at eye level started to blink and beep angrily.

"Well, we knew this was coming," Jennings said as he tapped on the Cormorant's fuel gauge.

Abelone looked around the harbour plaza for a safe place to land. There was none. "There are hundreds of them down there." Goose Bay had not been razed by bombs, but she was still shocked such a large portion of the infected had been drawn to Peaks Bay.

"One thing's for sure, we aren't going back down there." Jennings aimed the nose of the helicopter down the coast.

"How long do we have?" Abelone eyed the fuel gauge nervously. The hand indicating the fuel level was entering the ominous red section.

"We can probably do forty, fifty klicks." He flipped a few switches and eased the Cormorant down the coast. "Problem is, where do we go? Grab the maps." He pointed to a plastic bag held to the ceiling by a net.

After a few minutes of opening and unfolding maps, Abelone looked up. "There's nothing. No towns, no villages, no roads except for the one leading into Peaks Bay." That wasn't an option, with the infected from Goose Bay squirming over every mile of that road.

"Damn it."

Abelone sat quietly while the helicopter glided between land and sea for five minutes. She watched the rocky coastline of Labrador flow underneath them and marvelled at how beautiful it was. It made it difficult to realize how much trouble they were in. She consoled herself that since there weren't any trees along the coast, they could probably land almost anywhere. At some point, they might be able to contact a ship or an airplane. But how long could they last?

The Cormorant's fuel alarm was still trying to get its occupants' attention, but Abelone barely noticed it. She turned to look at Tom. He didn't move, but he was still breathing. For how long? There was that question again. *How long . . .* Time was now their biggest threat. She had another how-long question. How long could the world go without a vaccine?

Another alarm pulled her out of her thoughts. This one had a different pitch and was less aggressive. It came from the radio between the seats, where a green light was flashing.

"What the fuck?" Jennings reached down and flipped a switch.

There was some crackling static, but it faded in a few seconds, and a voice with a thick English accent materialized over their helmet speakers.

"Cormorant, this is the HMS Albion of the Royal Navy. Please identify yourself."

"Fucking what?" Jennings excitedly fumbled with the radio's buttons to turn on his and Abelone's headset.

"Albion . . . hello? This is Captain Jefferson Jennings of the 12th RBC." He was shouting. "Are we ever glad to hear from you! We have critical cargo and are almost out of gas."

There was a pause. Abelone moved to the edge of her seat, listening. She forced herself to breathe when she realized she was holding her breath.

Jennings' excitement would not be contained. "Albion, isn't that . . . aren't you an LPD? We need to land."

The lack of answer continued.

"What's an LPD?" asked Abelone, filling the dead air.

"It's a landing platform dock ship. They have a landing pad on their ship!"

The radio crackled again. Abelone's hope hit the high point at the top of a roller coaster. Then it came rushing down.

"That's a negative, Captain Jennings. You are not authorized to land on our ship. I repeat, you are not authorized to land on our ship."

Jennings' excitement changed to anger. "Albion, let me say again. We have critical cargo on board. Plus, our chopper is running on fumes. We need to land!"

He reoriented the nose of the Cormorant out to sea. The Albion was now in view a few kilometres off the coast.

More radio crackling. "Captain, if you approach the ship, you will be shot down. This is the only warning you get." The radio crackled some more and went quiet.

Jennings let a grunt of exasperated thunder out of his chest. "Let me spell it out for you: I have Patient Zero of this goddamn plague, AND we have a person who is immune to the infection. Not only that, this person is a representative of the WHO initially sent to investigate some ship." He turned to Abelone with inquiring eyes.

"The Nuovo Mondo," she said. "It was on the Greenland coast." She nodded. "And tell them my name and to look up my credentials."

Jennings shared the additional details, but the Albion stayed silent.

Jennings raised his voice on the radio. "I have the cure to this whole shit show sitting right here, and you are telling me I can't land? You're going to have to shoot us down then."

"Jennings?" Abelone asked, worried.

He looked at her. "We'll just need to take a leap of faith, right?" His cheekiness in light of possibly being blown out of the sky made her smile. But her insides twisted as she watched the Albion get bigger, expecting to see plumes of smoke indicating missiles had been fired.

As they approached, Abelone could see a large landing pad on the back of the ship, large enough for at least three Cormorants. There were also two other ships a bit further out at sea. Slightly smaller than the Albion, but sleek and covered in cannons.

"Destroyers," said Jennings. "Probably an escort for—"

The radio crackled back to life. "Captain Jennings, this is Captain Thompson of the HMS Albion." The voice paused for effect. The only effect it had on Abelone was to make her want to slap the man. "We've looked into the name of the WHO representative you claim to be escorting." Another pause for effect. She was sure she would slap him if she ever met this man. "We are granting you clearance to land on the Albion. You will need to follow our instructions to the letter to avoid any spread of the infection." She changed her mind; she would hug him instead!

Jennings breathed a long sigh of relief and smiled at her. As the Albion explained quarantine instructions to Jennings, Abelone thought back to the crew of the CGS Henry Dawson and to the Nuovo Mondo. She looked at Tom Virtanen on the floor behind her, thought of Martel and Keefer, and thought of Dirk Danerson. She understood now . . . not everyone could be saved, but she would do everything she could to save as many people as possible.

39

Anyone Can Be Saved

T he mid-July temperature made the empty asphalt road feel like a frying pan. The sky was still cloudless, like it had been over Valcartier when they'd left Abelone, Jennings and Doc Martel. Keefer's attention oscillated between the dark mushroom cloud in his rear-view mirror and the road ahead. They were on the fabled and beautiful Route 155. The only road into La Tuque from the south was flanked by the St. Maurice River on one side and steep rocky slopes covered with trees on the other. The pink Hummer led a convoy of three cars along the winding road. Eduard sat quietly beside Keefer, and his sisters slept in the backseat. The ominous cloud was getting smaller and would disappear behind mountains as they made their way north.

Keefer had been relieved they'd caught up with the other survivors on the back roads north of Valcartier. They'd been far enough and low enough in the countryside to avoid the nuclear blast's shockwave. Catching up to the others had not been difficult. Eduard knew which roads they were taking, and in a world with no traffic or driving re-strictions, the Hummer had closed the distance easily. Now, they were a convoy. Joe and Fran, the elderly couple who had taken all the survivors into their basement in Valcartier, drove an old 1962 red Oldsmobile Jetfire. The old man was adamant he would not leave his automotive jewel behind. The convoy had to stop a few extra times for gas, but fuel was not an issue with so many cars and gas stations being abandoned along the way. The third car was a massive jacked-up four-door Ford 150. It turned out that one of the young women had a penchant for big machines that could run over anything in its path.

After his journey from Peaks Bay and this trek up north, Keefer had realized that as long as there weren't infected around, things like food, fuel and even shelter would never be an issue. These were in endless supply in a province that had been evacuated. They'd stuck to small unpopulated roads since Valcartier, and even then, they'd found everything they needed. There were unlimited resources out there. Any infected they encountered, they were able to outrun with their vehicles. Not once did they have to take the life of one of them, either. A few times, the Hummer could have run some over, but Keefer understood—not everyone had to die. He adjusted his rear-view mirror as the sun was lower in the southwest and pressed the accelerator. They were getting close.

It took another hour for the small convoy to reach its final destination. Keefer instinctively pulled the Hummer to the side of the road. Ahead of them was a ten-foot wall made of logs that stretched from the massive river on one side, all the way across to steep rocky cliffs on the other. The gate, which was one lane wide, was blocked by a fortified school bus. There was a long flagpole overlooking the fortifications near the gate. The pole stood naked in the sunlight.

"Stay here," Keefer said to Eduard and the girls, who were awake and craning their necks to see up front. He repeated the order via his handheld radio to the other vehicles, then stepped out of the Hummer and stood in the middle of the road watching the fortifications. There was no sign of life. Car doors opened and closed behind him, and the others joined him in the middle of the road. Even the twins tumbled out of the Hummer and huddled behind Keefer, holding his leather jacket. So much for orders. Keefer smiled.

"Logs," said Joe as he reached Keefer. "Makes sense. La Tuque is a forestry town. They probably had all the wood they needed to fortify the town once people realized what was happening."

"Should we walk up and knock?" Fran asked.

"I wonder how many people are in there."

"Maybe they know how the rest of the world is doing?"

Keefer nodded, but his thoughts were elsewhere. After their last experience with the compound in Valcartier, he was wary of any place that harboured survivors. Just a few days ago, he felt all infected had to die, but now he had Eduard to look out for . . . and the twins.

Will they accept us? Keefer looked at Eduard.

I don't know.

He had no idea how, but he could hear Eduard's thoughts, and Eduard could hear his. But it wasn't hearing; it was more like feeling. They could feel each other's thoughts. They'd talked about it on the journey up; they'd even experimented. It wasn't a perfect science, and it wasn't like talking. Thinking something didn't mean the other heard it; it was more emotion-based. And if they concentrated, they could block the other from hearing them.

Are they dangerous? Can you see them? What's up with the weird-looking cars?

That last thought made Keefer look back at Eduard again.

"That was not me," said the teen, using his actual voice.

Keefer looked at his convoy instinctively. The pink Hummer, the red vintage Jetfire and the monster truck—weird-looking convoy indeed.

"Stop talking, everyone," Keefer said, putting his hands up to shush them.

He took a few steps forward and concentrated.

Can you hear me? He wasn't sure what else to say . . . or think.

Are we welcome here? Nothing. It had been obvious when he experimented with Eduard that if you thought like you were talking, nothing reached the other person. They'd heard each other when they felt what they thought. Keefer tried again. *Who are you?*

Nothing.

He got mad and stepped closer to the yellow bus blocking the entrance to the fortifications. He needed to know. *Are we safe? Will you hurt them?* He looked back at the survivors huddled up behind him. *Can we trust you?* he thought to himself.

Who was that? ~ Is that them? ~ Look at the one who stepped forward. ~ Quiet!

The thoughts washed over Keefer. He looked back at Eduard, who seemed as surprised as he was.

Time slowly ticked by with nothing happening. An eagle flew high overhead and circled them before disappearing beyond the city.

Keefer was about to turn back when a loud squeaking echoed from the top of the fortification. A flag rose on the pole overlooking the road. It was white, with two hands embraced in a handshake. One hand had peach skin, and the other was . . . grey. The flag rose slowly, and as it reached the top of its pole, the bus engine roared to life. Diesel fumes reached Keefer before it started moving. The yellow bus crept forward. Beyond it was a crowd of at least a hundred strong, all gathered on the road, watching in anticipation. When the bus stopped, a dozen people broke from the crowd and walked toward Keefer and his fellow survivors. Most of them were normal-looking, but a few of them were Grey.

THE END

deb